THE DAMAGERS

Also by **Donald Hamilton** *and available from Titan Books*

Death of a Citizen
The Wrecking Crew
The Removers
The Silencers
Murderers' Row
The Ambushers
The Shadowers
The Ravagers
The Devastators
The Betrayers
The Menacers
The Interlopers
The Poisoners
The Intriguers
The Intimidators
The Terminators
The Retaliators
The Terrorizers
The Revengers
The Annihilators
The Infiltrators
The Detonators
The Vanishers
The Demolishers
The Frighteners
The Threateners

DONALD HAMILTON

A MATT HELM NOVEL

THE DAMAGERS

TITAN BOOKS

The Damagers
Print edition ISBN: 9781785654886
E-book edition ISBN: 9781785654893

Published by Titan Books
A division of Titan Publishing Group Ltd
144 Southwark Street, London SE1 0UP

First edition: February 2017
1 2 3 4 5 6 7 8 9 10

A CIP catalogue record for this title is available from the British Library.

Printed and bound in the United States.

THE ***DAMAGERS***

1

My crew reported for duty early in October, a strapping Viking of a girl with long blond hair. Well, I'd figured they'd send me a girl when the time came, if it came. I was supposed to be doing my best to look harmless—a tempting target for sabotage and assassination—and a man and a girl cruising together on a boat look much more vulnerable than two men, even if the girl is a tanned Brunhilde almost six feet tall.

Standing on the dock with a seabag over her shoulder and a bundle of foul-weather gear under her arm, the impressive lady requested permission to come aboard, in good nautical fashion. Permission granted, she threw her belongings onto the side deck, about three feet higher than the floating dock, and swung herself up after it, disregarding the ladder I'd hung at the gate in the railing to make boarding easier.

"Nice sunny weather we're having," I said. "Unusual for Connecticut so late in the summer, if you still want to call this summer."

"Connecticut is not so bad," she said. "Maine, that is much different, just fog, fog, fog all the time."

Okay. There was certainly no doubt that she was the right sex, the sex I'd expected, and she'd answered my Connecticut sunshine with Maine fog, so we had the official identification nonsense all taken care of.

"I live up forward, ja?" she said, after an appraising glance up the masts and around the deck. "You will show?"

"Let me take some of that stuff."

"I carry it okay."

My parents came from Sweden and I've spent some time in that country; but I couldn't tell if the accent was real, and it didn't matter. What the hell, nothing was real on this ship, particularly the skipper; as a sailor I make a great cowboy. Well, that was what the girl was for, to compensate for my nautical deficiencies.

I led her into the big, light deckhouse with its all-around windows giving a full view of the marina, the winding river that led to Long Island Sound, and the open salt marsh beyond. She followed me down two steps forward into the main cabin, considerably darker since it was illuminated by considerably less glass. The galley was to port facing a big table three-quarters surrounded by a U-shaped settee to starboard. The whole boat was paneled in teak and the upholstery was dark-red velour or something similar; kind of a bordello decor, but after living with it for a couple of months I'd grown to like it.

The boat was a husky thirty-eight-foot motor sailer built in Finland, of all places; and she was the most luxurious private vessel I'd ever inhabited, with wall-to-wall carpeting, refrigeration, hot and cold running water, and central heating, not to mention an intimidating array of navigational instruments, some of which I still hadn't really mastered, even after studying the manuals hard. Well, my worries were over; my blonde shipmate was undoubtedly familiar with all the modern electronic miracles.

"Go on forward; there isn't room for both of us," I said, moving aside to let her squeeze past. "Watch your head. For anybody over five-eight, this boat ought to be a hard-hat area. I still brain myself twice a week forgetting to duck."

"I know. They are all like that."

She unloaded her gear on the cabin table and made her way through the brief passageway to the wedge-shaped stateroom in the bow that had tapering twin berths obviously designed for a special race of people with very wide shoulders and very small feet. She surveyed her quarters with experienced eyes. She studied the overhead hatch for a moment to figure out the latch system and opened it, setting the braces to keep it from flopping back down. Having solved the ventilation problem, she tested the plushy red mattresses with her fingertips, checked for access, and decided that the port berth would be the easiest for her to operate out of; the starboard one would do for her gear. She hauled her seabag and oilskins forward and checked the doors along the brief passageway, returning to me.

"This is much fine," she said. "Much locker space, and I even have for myself a *klo*... what you call a head, yes?"

It's Swedish slang: *klo,* pronounced *kloo,* short for *klosett,* like in water closet. People can think of the damndest circumlocutions when they simply want to say crapper. The fact that she knew this one made me think her accent might actually be genuine.

I said, "Yes, there's more plumbing aft so this one's all yours. What do I call you?"

"My name is Siegelinda, Siegelinda Kronquist, but everybody calls me Ziggy."

I said, "Seems a pity. Siegelinda is a mouthful, but it's a pretty name."

"Ziggy is okay. I will not be called Linda. Every stupid little American girl who wants to be a movie star is called Linda. Ziggy is fine."

"Okay, Ziggy. I'm Matt."

We shook hands on it. Her hand was sizeable and her grip was firm.

"Now you will show me the rest of this boat."

I showed her the significant stuff in the galley: the groceries, the dishes, the drawer for the silverware (okay, stainless), the knife rack, the refrigerator, the sink, and the garbage can under the sink. I explained the three-burner propane stove and showed her the big butane lighter, the kind used to fire up charcoal grills, that I used to light it. I demonstrated the safety switch that, by remote control, cut off the gas at the propane tank in its vented locker aft. I explained to her how, any time you were through with the stove, you were supposed to turn off, not only the burners, but the main gas supply as well, and make sure the red warning light was out. Propane is heavier than air, and you don't want to run any risk of having it leak out and collect in the bilge waiting for a spark to set it off...

The trouble with the girl was that she'd obviously been on so many boats that she knew practically everything I was telling her about this one. I sensed her attention wandering.

"You drink," she said.

I saw that she was looking at the bottles. Behind the main cabin settee, along the side of the ship, were some small lockers flanking a couple of long shelves. There were seven bottle-sized holes in the bottom shelf for liquor storage—you don't want any glass containers bouncing around loose on a boat when things get rough. I'd filled the rack with two fifths of Scotch, two of vodka, and three of wine, a California Chardonnay if it matters. I saw no need to apologize for them.

"I drink," I said.

"That is good. I never trust a man who can not trust himself with *sprit.*" That was Swedish for spirits, meaning alcohol. "Now we will see the engine room, ja?"

The engine hid under the deckhouse floor. The instruction manual that came with the boat said that it should be checked daily when you were under way. That was obviously some kind of funny Finnish joke, since getting at the mill was a lengthy and laborious process that involved disassembling and removing the little pedestal table for the comer breakfast/cocktail nook, moving out the helmsman's stool and everything else in the deckhouse, hauling up the carpet, lifting up two enormous hatches that were lead lined for soundproofing, and then dismantling the lead-lined box that surrounded, for further soundproofing, the big four-cylinder mill itself. There wasn't a piece weighing much less than twenty pounds. The girl wanted to do the work so she would know how. I didn't fight her.

When she had it all open, I pointed out the eighty-gallon fuel tanks port and starboard, the valves that controlled them, the water separator and fuel filters, the three batteries strapped into their boxes—two house batteries and one reserved for starting the engine—the pressure pump for the fresh-water system, and the pressure pump for the saltwater system that was used for hosing down the decks—also for cleaning off the anchor and chain when they came up muddy. Siegelinda Kronquist studied the engine for a moment.

"Ford?"

I said, "Yes. Eighty horsepower. It's a Swedish conversion of a Ford block. Should make you feel right at home."

"I understand not." Then she laughed. "Oh, because it is Swedish? But I am American now. You know this boat pretty good, ja?"

"I've had since August to get acquainted with her."

"I will put it all back now. I must learn how."

"Be my guest."

She made it look easy, swinging the awkward slabs of lead-lined plywood back into place without much apparent effort. She was wearing short, but not excessively short or tight, blue denim cutoffs, well faded and fashionably frayed; her legs were brown and magnificent, and she had long feet tucked into ancient brown moccasin-style boat shoes. I had a hunch we wouldn't see much of those shoes; they were made to come off easily, and she looked like barefoot-nature-girl to me. As far as I'm concerned, broken toes hurt like hell, and cuts and splinters aren't much fun, either; besides, when you kick somebody with suitable shoes it's more effective than when you kick them without.

Above the waist, Miss Kronquist wore a thin T-shirt with a cartoon face on it. Even thought there was no TV on board and I don't watch it much even when I have it, I recognized a character that had recently taken the country by storm. What was under the idiot face was unfettered and spectacular. I helped her put the carpets back into place and replace the deckhouse furniture.

"Carpets on a boat are stupid," she said. "Where is the bilge pump?"

"It's the middle switch in the panel right behind you. It's marked. There's a manual pump for backup, in that locker to port. And the wash-down pump can be rigged to suck bilge water instead of seawater in an emergency. I should have shown you when we had the engine room open."

"You can show me later; let us hope we do not sink today." She looked ahead through the windshield at the machinery mounted in the bow. "An electric windlass? What if the electricity fails?"

"It can be worked manually. The emergency handle

is clipped to the bulkhead right over there by the port deckhouse door." I pointed to it, a one-inch stainless steel pipe about eighteen inches long, with a plastic grip.

"And what is aft?"

"My stateroom, down two steps. Plumbing to starboard. Double berth, well, you can see it from up here. The rudder head, emergency tiller, and hydraulic steering machinery are under it."

"A double berth is convenient, ja?" she said, looking down into the aft cabin without expression.

"If you can find somebody to occupy the other half," I said. I hesitated, but it was a lot of girl on a boat that seemed to have got a lot smaller since she came aboard. As a normal male, I had to be thinking along certain lines—well, I was—and it had better get said and put behind us. "You're welcome to fill the vacant space any time, Miss Kronquist. Don't hesitate to wake me if I'm asleep."

She regarded me steadily for a moment. I noted that her eyes were very blue. "But you will never come up forward to bother me in my little cabin, is that what you wish to tell me, Matt? It is my decision?"

"Yours entirely, Ziggy."

"That is good," she said calmly. "I will think about it when I know you better. Now you will tell me about the life jackets and flares and other nonsense the Coast Guard loves so much, so I can show them if they board us, and then you will go and pay the marina while I warm up the motor, and when you come back we will get under way, yes?"

I glanced at my watch. "It's almost lunchtime."

"We can eat as we sail. I will make sandwiches. With eighty horsepower this boat should cruise good at seven or eight knots; if we start now, we can be in Montauk before dark. Those who send me, they want this boat to stop wasting time and money here, where nothing happens, and start moving south, where maybe something does happen."

"Aye, aye, skipper."

"No. You are the skipper. I am just the big stupid Swede girl you bring to pull the ropes, and maybe sleep with. And maybe not. Let everybody guess; it will do them good."

I hesitated. "Well, just let me know how you want to divide up the work on board. As you've probably been told, I haven't had much cruising experience. Hell, that's why you're here."

There were sliding doors port and starboard, open now, letting the breeze blow right through the deckhouse. It blew a lock of blonde hair across her face as she stood by the big wooden steering wheel. She tossed back the yellow strands and looked at me gravely for a moment with those blue Norse eyes.

"The work?" she said. "But the division is really very simple, Matt. I will keep us afloat. You will keep us alive. Okay?"

2

"You were selected because you have had some experience with boats," Mac had told me back in early August.

I remembered that I'd groaned at the time, but not aloud. That's the way it works in our outfit. We're not big enough to support a bunch of temperamental specialists. If you once manage to figure out how to paddle a canoe across a farm pond in the line of duty, you're the resident clipper-ship expert forever after, as far as Mac is concerned.

He went on: "The boat's name is *Lorelei III.* It is an eight-year-old motor sailer, ketch rigged—that means two masts, I believe—displacing about twelve tons. It is currently lying in a slip in the Pilot's Point Marina in Westbrook, Connecticut, about twenty miles east of New Haven. It is being offered for sale, its owner having died last spring. You will travel there and inspect it with a yacht broker. You will also, for appearances' sake, look at some other boats he has lined up for you, but this one will strike your fancy and you will buy it. I am told it needs considerable work. You will have that done and learn how to sail the craft as well as possible in the time available."

"How much time?"

"If your mission is not completed before winter weather sets in, the boat will have to be moved south. You should plan to have it seaworthy by late September."

It seemed to me that he was skipping lightly over a couple of important details that needed further explanation. He was wearing his customary gray suit; and his face was unreadable, as usual, made more so by the bright window behind him through which I could see Washington, D.C., if I wanted to see Washington, D.C. I was more concerned with the familiar, lean, gray-haired gent with the black eyebrows, on the far side of the big desk, who'd called me back from my New Mexico home sooner than I'd anticipated.

I'd hoped to have the whole summer free to train a young Chesapeake Bay retriever I'd acquired in the course of a recent assignment; I'd even hoped, optimistically, to have the autumn free to hunt him. Instead I'd had to leave him with a professional trainer in Texas I'd used before—who'd undoubtedly do a better job of completing his education than I could have, but I'd miss the fun of doing it myself—and rush east to learn that I was about to become a yachtsman.

I asked about one of the details that concerned me: "What did the boat's owner die of?"

Mac glanced at me sharply, annoyed at having his instructions interrupted by a question he'd probably intended to get around to answering later.

After a moment, he said, "Truman Fancher had a heart attack in North Carolina, near a small town called Coinjock, while bringing his boat north from Florida along the Intracoastal Waterway. He was steering at the time. His wife was taking a nap down in the cabin. She awoke when the boat veered out of the channel and ran aground."

"A heart attack," I said without expression.

"That was the official verdict." Mac paused, and went on deliberately. "The boat was refloated without damage and brought to its home marina in Oyster Bay, New York."

"Where's Oyster Bay?"

Mac said, "It's on Long Island but not very far from New York City… That was in June. Early in July, *Lorelei III* was lent to a married couple, friends of the Fancher family, for a weekend cruise. The woman, Mrs. Henrietta Guild, came on board on a Thursday to lay in supplies and make other preparations. Her husband was to join her after work on Friday. When Mr. Nathaniel Guild arrived at the dock on Friday evening, he found the boat dark. Going aboard, he stumbled over his wife's body. She was in her nightgown; she had been killed by several blows to the head. The weapon was apparently the emergency handle for the power windlass, employed to bring the anchor up manually if the electricity failed. Apparently it was kept in a convenient place in the cabin ready for use."

"A weapon of opportunity," I said. "Looks as if whoever did the job didn't come intending to kill. A professional hitman would have brought his own club."

"Perhaps," Mac said. "Or perhaps that is exactly what he wants us to think. At any rate, the body was quite cold, so the crime had presumably taken place the night before." After a moment, he went on. "The family then chartered the boat to a young man named Martin Jesperson, who planned to cruise up the coast to Maine and back."

"New Englanders say 'down the coast to Maine,'" I told him. "Because the prevailing winds blow that way. The hard part is coming back against them, uphill so to speak."

"Indeed? That is very interesting." Mac's voice was dry. "Heading out Long Island Sound, Mr. Jesperson had some engine trouble. He used the radio to call for help, and was towed into the nearest marina. The following day, after a mechanic had solved his problem, he started eastward again; but only a few hours later the Coast Guard was notified that a ketch-rigged vessel was aground on a nearby shoal with nobody visible on deck. The boarding party found *Lorelei III* uninhabited. Jesperson's body was not recovered until the following day. Mr. Jesperson had apparently fallen overboard and drowned. The verdict was accidental death. The boat was returned to the marina. It has, as I indicated, been put up for sale. You will be given the funds with which to buy it."

I grimaced. "A real hoodoo ship, eh? Let me get the history straight. Who was Truman Fancher?"

"He was a wealthy man who had a yacht dealership in Oyster Bay—more a hobby, I gather, than a serious source of income—and was a well-known sailor. He had made an impressive racing record with series of large, fast sailing yachts. However, when well up in his sixties, Mr. Fancher retired from competition, sold his latest racing boat, and bought the comfortable motor sailer that concerns us, in which he cruised Long Island Sound and New England in the summer, Florida and the Bahamas in the winter."

"And he was bringing her up from Florida last spring, when he died." I frowned, thinking it over. At last I said, "Afterward, a surprising number of people seem to've been interested in a dead man's boat; it seems almost indecent the way the poor old bucket was hardly given a chance to catch her breath after losing her owner so tragically. You'd think that, even if they yearned to sail on a boat on which a man had just died, folks would be a little hesitant about approaching the grieving family so soon. The way you told it, Fancher was barely buried and the boat was hardly back in her home slip before people were beating on the door asking to borrow or charter her."

Mac gave me the thin smile that's about as much amusement as he can manage. "Your instincts are sound, Eric," he said. My real name is Matthew Helm, but I answer to Eric on official occasions; and this office is about as official as we get. Mac went on. "You do not need to take the matrimonial bonds of the Guilds too seriously, or their close friendship with the Fanchers. Actually, they were not married, and neither of them was named Guild, any more than Jesperson was named Jesperson."

"I see," I said, although that was an exaggeration. "So we're all phonies together. Well, I don't mind owning a yacht, even a jinxed one, but I hope nobody expects me to impersonate a yachtsman. They speak a special language that I never quite mastered the previous times I had to operate afloat. The jargon is as bad as computerese; just trade RAMS and ROMS for ports and starboards. It's almost impossible to fake. If I pretend to be an old salt, I'll be spotted as a phony right away."

Mac nodded. "So we are making you a book sailor, occupation photojournalist, from the waterless deserts of the Southwest, who has read every nautical volume he could lay hands on—we'll supply you with a suitable, well-thumbed library to bring aboard—and dreamed of sailing alone around the world in the wakes of Captain Joshua Slocum and Sir Francis Chichester, but never actually handled any vessel larger than an outboard fishing skiff. But an uncle died and left you a fairly substantial sum of money, a little over two hundred thousand dollars." The background, apart from the nautical reading and the rich uncle, was fairly close to my own; the photojournalist cover is one I often use by default, when there's no pressing need for me to assume another identity. Mac went on. "You decided to haul your cameras and word processor east and follow your salty dream. It is really amazing how many people have that dream. Even in our cynical profession it seems that a considerable number of the men, and even some of the women, hope upon retirement to buy little cruising boats and sail away into the sunset."

I asked, "Am I supposed to sail away into the sunset on the good ship *Lorelei III*?"

"No. At least not immediately, and if you do go, as I have said, the direction will be south, not west. But first you will spend the remainder of the summer, as I said, just fixing up the boat and learning how to sail it."

I frowned. "What's so special about this particular motor sailer aside from the fact that three people have died on her?" I asked. "Or off her, if Jesperson actually died in the water."

"We have not been told what else makes the boat unique, if anything does," Mac said. "As for the deaths, Truman Fancher may have had a genuine heart attack—he'd had one earlier, but had made a good recovery—but there is apparently some room for doubt. In order to dispel or confirm that doubt, and to find the answers to some other questions, Mr. and Mrs. Guild, so-called, were ordered aboard *Lorelei III* by the agency that has now requested our assistance. That is as much information as we have been given. Our colleagues are operating on a strict need-to-know basis."

I sighed. "And as usual they don't think we need to know very much. I suppose Jesperson was put aboard, officially, to investigate what happened to Fancher and Guild, and I'm going on this jinx ship to investigate what happened to Fancher, Guild, and Jesperson."

Mac nodded. "At least that is the ostensible goal of your mission. And I think you can safely assume that, while Mr. Fancher may just possibly have died a natural death, the individual who clubbed to death the lady calling herself Mrs. Guild was not just a stray seagoing mugger even if he did use a weapon he found on the scene, and the so-called Mr. Jesperson was not really alone on board and did not really fall overboard by accident." He regarded me for a moment. "In support of this assumption is the fact that when Nathaniel Guild recovered from the first shock of finding his 'wife' dead, he smelled propane; the boat was full of it. The master gas valve was open and a hose had been removed from a certain fitting. I'm afraid I can't give you the exact technical details, but a candle was found on the counter in the kitchen—I suppose I should call it a galley. Fortunately 'Mrs. Guild' had left a hatch open that her murderer failed to spot and there was a thunderstorm the night she was killed; the high wind caused enough of a draft to blow out the flame that had presumably been left burning. If it had continued to burn, *Lorelei III* would have exploded violently when the gas rose high enough in the cabin to be ignited."

I said, "Well, if there is something on board that somebody doesn't want found, the simplest answer is to destroy the boat completely. What about the other incident?"

"There was over a foot of water in the cabin when the Coast Guard arrived. The discharge hose of the galley sink apparently leads directly to a valve—I believe they call it a sea cock—in the boat's hull which, open, allows the dishwater to drain into the ocean. The clamps had been loosened and the hose had been pulled off the valve, which was left open, allowing the sea to pour in. And the bilge pump had been turned off. It is assumed that the boat was actually aimed eastward, in the hope that it would sink where Long Island Sound is reasonably deep, but some malfunction of the automatic pilot, which was engaged, caused it to swerve to the north and hit the shoal. The quick response of the Coast Guard prevented it from filling completely. They, of course, immediately shut the sea cock and pumped out the water."

"Just the same, it sounds as if I'm going to have a soggy mess to deal with," I said. "That saltwater never really dries."

Mac said, "We are, as I've said, supplying you with a cover of sorts; if the opposition, whatever it may be, thinks that we, or you, are stupid enough to trust it to keep you safe, so much the better. We are, of course, hoping that it will not."

I nodded. "So I'm not really there just to investigate two or three murders, or even to search the boat for interesting clues. It's also a decoy job. Since the vessel seems to be reluctant to tell us anything, maybe we can get some answers from the people who are haunting it homicidally?" I made it a question.

Mac did not answer directly. He said, "The agency concerned, which has been keeping *Lorelei III* under observation since Jesperson's death, has decided that somebody else should be put aboard. However, having lost two of their own valuable people on this boat, they think it advisable to replace them with more expendable human material from other government sources." He shrugged. "Well, it is what we are paid for, Eric."

A polite name for our organizational mission, which is not publicized around Washington, is counter-assassination. When a government agency starts losing people to somebody too tough for them to handle, they can call on us to take him, or her, out for them, discreetly. But very often we're called in simply because there's a hot spot that needs filling by a gent, or lady, somewhat more bullet proof than the usual run of government employees. This was a fairly typical situation: somebody had come up short a couple of agents and didn't want to risk misplacing any more. Just me.

I said, "If somebody does come for me, what's my reaction supposed to be?"

"Very simple," Mac said. "First, you prevent them from killing you, and from destroying the boat. Then you capture them and call a certain telephone number, and they will be taken off your hands. If you should of necessity wind up with some dead ones, it will be understood, and you will be protected, but live and garrulous ones are preferred. The lady who passed on the instructions spoke in terms of a giant conspiracy; she would like one of the conspirators for interrogation."

I sighed. "Oh, gee, golly, another giant conspiracy, I don't know if my heart can stand it, sir." I yawned widely. Mac did not react to my horseplay, and I went on. "But if I sit on that boat until the cold autumn winds start to blow, and nothing happens, then, you say, I'm supposed to cast off the dock lines and proceed south?"

"Yes," Mac said. "You will head for Florida by a route that will be given you, hoping for trouble along the way. By that time, you should have the boat in good cruising order, and yourself, too."

It was time to bring up another important detail he seemed to be neglecting. I said, "Maybe. But with all the work to be done on this motor sailer, it's obviously not going to be available for boating practice a lot of the time; and I've only got a couple of months. I doubt that even if I had the whole summer to play with it I could turn myself into a real seaman and navigator. Sure, I can fake it—I've done it before; sailing isn't all that difficult—but this is a hell of a lot bigger boat than anything I've ever managed by myself, and if these people feel it's important to get her south in one piece, they'd better give me some help. Cruising alone, little as I really know about it, there's a chance I'll have their expensive bucket on the rocks before I'm out of Long Island Sound."

Mac nodded. "I told our friends that, while you had managed to survive several missions afloat, you could hardly be called an expert seaman. They said it was hoped the operation would be concluded before autumn; but if it was not, they would supply a good hand to help you…"

3

Ziggy Kronquist had the sail up before we passed Duck Island, just outside the river entrance. Again she wanted to do it all herself so she'd learn where everything was and how it worked.

Standing at the wheel in the deckhouse, I had a pretty good view of the operation, forward through the windshield and upward through the large, transparent, overhead hatch that could be slid back like a car's sunroof—well, actually it couldn't, at the moment, since I'd stowed the deflated, folded-up rubber dinghy in the way of it, figuring that this late in the year a sunroof wouldn't see much use. Besides, there was no other convenient place to put the dink. (The little two-and-a-half horsepower motor for it was clamped to the rail aft, if it matters.)

The hatch was designed, not only for ventilation, but for observation: to let the helmsman keep an eye on the mainsail above him. When we left the marina, the big sail was rolled up on its patent furling gear along the aft side of the mast; but as we reached open water, Ziggy started pulling on the outhaul, and it unrolled like a vertical window blind—well, a triangular vertical window blind. The smaller staysail up forward, when she got to it, had no such tricks; it just went up the stay like any normal sail.

I felt *Lorelei III* heel a bit, and then lean farther to a stronger gust as we passed the end of Duck Island and received the unobstructed wind off Long Island Sound. Blocks rattled and creaked as the girl up on deck retrimmed the sails to the new breeze. Down in the deckhouse, I followed instructions and steered us out past the buoy marking the west end of Long Sand Shoal in the middle of the Sound, and then bore off eastward to put us on the course for Plum Gut that she'd punched into the loran.

This was one of the electronic marvels on board that I'd studied but by no means mastered. There was a whole array of gadgetry suspended from the overhead—ceiling to you—above the chart table in front of me: an ordinary radio-tape deck for entertainment, a battery of engine instruments you wouldn't believe, the loran for position, a VHF radio for communication, and a depth sounder for showing how much water was under *Lorelei III*'s six-foot keel. I'd been advised to leave the radio, the loran, and the VHF on at all times, since transistors don't wear out and the warmth would keep the instruments dry and prevent corrosion. Below them, just ahead of the steering wheel, was the dial of the knot meter—seagoing speedometer to you—and the control panel for the autopilot; forward of that was the compass. To starboard of the wheel was the big, old-fashioned, hooded radar; and let's face it, although I'd played with it from time to time, I still hadn't really mastered the knack of relating the fuzzy pattern of blobs on the little screen to what was happening around the boat.

But we weren't using radar at the moment; and the loran was easier to learn. I knew how to get our latitude and longitude out of it any time I wanted them, and the ability made me feel nautical as hell; however, there were a lot of other functions I still couldn't manage without having the instruction manual open in front of me. The one Ziggy had programmed into the machine told me exactly how to get to the buoy off Plum Gut: all I had to do was watch the display and steer to keep it centered. Navigation made easy. After I'd put the ship on her new course, there was more squeaking and creaking on deck as Ziggy trimmed the sails again; then the port deckhouse door slid open and she joined me, a little flushed and breathless, pushing back her windblown hair.

"Hey, you steer not so badly. Is it not a marvelous day? Let me put something on this *förbannade* hair, and then I would like to steer, if you do not mind, but not in this stuffy cabin. I will take it at the outside station… Just a minute." She ducked down the companionway forward and came back immediately, tucking her hair away under a blue bandana. "How do we change over the steering?"

"No problem with the steering," I said. "It's hydraulic, like I said, and works from either station without any switching, but the engine control down here has to be in neutral before you can use the one topside." I pulled back the single lever—throttle and gearshift in one—and the rumble of the diesel died to a low murmur. "You go on up. You don't have a tachometer up there so I'll have to holler at you when you're back to cruising RPM."

I let her know when she had the topside control set correctly. Then I stepped outside—it was three steps from the deckhouse floor up to the side deck—and made my way aft along the narrow walkway, secure inside the substantial teak railing that seemed like considerably more protection than the flimsy wire lifelines to be found on most sailboats. It occurred to me that somebody must have given Jesperson quite a heave to put him over that husky thirty-inch fence.

I climbed a couple more steps to join Ziggy on the raised aft deck, like the poop deck of a Spanish galleon, that was actually the roof of my cabin. She stood at the big destroyer wheel at the rear of the deckhouse. Unlike the varnished, wooden one below, this wheel was shiny stainless steel. There was more wind than I'd thought, and a considerable amount of rigging whine and sea splash.

"She is a good, stiff boat," the girl shouted. "Perhaps she could take the Genoa jib, but it is a very big sail, I think, and I would like to see it first in not so strong a wind. And without the jenny forward we do not need the mizzen for balance aft. I think we have enough sail, yes?"

I yelled, "Lady, I'm a real chicken-sailor; the less of that canvas stuff I have to worry about, the better I like it. Or is it dacron?"

She laughed. "I think you are a fraud, my friend. You steer very good. You know your boat very good. I think you are much better seaman than you say."

"God, don't tell my chief! He'll put me in command of an aircraft carrier next time around."

She laughed again, and stepped over to ease the main sheet slightly, and caught the wheel before the boat could swing off course. She looked spectacular standing there with her strong, bare, golden-brown legs braced against the motion of the boat and some wisps of shining hair starting to blow free of the bandana. She was a little unreal, a painting entitled *The Norsewoman;* but then as I've said the whole situation was unreal.

Mac would keep putting me on these damned boats. The first one I could remember being involved with in the line of duty was a little fifteen-foot outboard I had to learn to launch off a trailer; now I seemed to have worked my way up, somehow, to this great thirty-eight-foot, twelve-ton brute of a motor sailer. You'd think, with my own Viking ancestry, I'd start getting that fine seagoing feeling when I trod the handsome teak decks, and I'll admit that once in a while I did experience a small atavistic thrill, but mostly it was just a very demanding exercise in caution—as a good old New Mexico boy from west of the Pecos, I know I don't really know what the hell I'm doing on these eastern waters, or any waters, so I concentrate on not making any disastrous errors and leave the fancy seamanship to others. Like Ziggy Kronquist.

Presently, we were charging through Plum Gut,

the narrow slot between Plum Island and Orient Point. According to the chart, this was the eastern end of Long Island—well, one of the eastern ends. Since Long Island is forked, there are two. The longer one sticking out into the Atlantic farther south is Montauk Point, toward which we were heading.

We found more wind in Gardiner's Bay beyond the Gut. Spray started slashing aft. I said to hell with it and retreated to the deckhouse; I've spent enough time outdoors that I feel no need to prove how rugged I am by getting wet when I don't have to. After a little, the motor died to idling speed, and Ziggy came in, slamming the door shut, and paused to wipe her dripping face with the front of her T-shirt, casually revealing, among other intriguing things, that she'd done a lot of sunbathing without a top on. She took the wheel and put the engine into gear again and brought it back up to cruising revs, 1,800 RPM.

"Windshield wipers?"

"Right in front of you."

There were three of them, one for each section of the divided windshield, and they could drive you crazy watching them, since they operated independently, totally unsynchronized. They had a considerable amount of work to do now to keep the glass clear. It was getting brisk out there; and *Lorelei III* was heeled over farther than I'd ever had her. With the sails helping the engine, she was also moving faster than I'd ever dared to make her, exploding the short seas that came at her. She felt solid and powerful, and it was an exhilarating ride, but if I'd been doing it I'd have been worrying, as we went roaring past Gardiner's Island and the wind continued to increase, about how much the eight-year-old sails and rigging could take. My gorgeous shipmate apparently had no such reservations; she seemed to be enjoying every minute of it.

"Look, nine and a half knots!" Ziggy pointed to the dial. "We should be picking up the Montauk breakwater soon… Ah, there it is. Come, we had better get her ready for harbor. You can roll up the mainsail and I will bring down the staysail…"

A few minutes later, under power alone, I took us between the breakwaters into Lake Montauk just inside the point, and did a passable job of docking us in one of the marinas—it wasn't hard, after a couple of months of practice, as long as I kept in mind that, having a big, three-bladed propeller that turned counterclockwise in the European fashion, *Lorelei III* backed stubbornly to starboard no matter what you did with the rudder. I'd offered Ziggy the job, but she'd said that I should do it. After all, I was the skipper and should be seen acting as such; she was just the dumb square-head crew.

After we had everything shipshape on deck, I offered to take her to dinner at one of the restaurants in the small town of Montauk, but she said she didn't think the chicken breasts I'd bought earlier in the week should lie in the refrigerator too long, and she wanted to familiarize herself with the galley anyway. She told me to relax in the deckhouse with a magazine or something; but she popped up after a few minutes.

"I found a little bottle of vermouth in the galley. Do you wish a vodka martini?"

I said, "That's what it's for. If you'll join me."

"Ah, I thought you would never ask. Sit still. I am very good with martinis."

Sitting in the red plush cocktail corner in the pleasant deckhouse, with cheese and crackers on the little teak table before us, we raised our martini glasses—actually fairly ugly plastic tumblers that had come with the boat—and drank to a good day's run, a promising start to our voyage south. I had the curtains drawn all around. It was too bad to miss the sunset over the marina, but I can't relax comfortably in a lighted greenhouse when I know there may be hostiles in the growing dark outside. Anyway, the curtained deckhouse, totally private, made for a certain pleasant intimacy. I tasted my martini and thought she'd gone a little heavy on the vermouth, but I'm not very choosy about my booze, and I wouldn't have mentioned it for the world.

"What's the matter with me, Ziggy?" I asked.

She frowned, uncomprehending. "What do you mean? I have made no complain."

"Not you. Those other bastards. I mean, I feel like a wallflower."

"Wallflower?"

"Neglected," I said. "Nobody's tried to kill me. Have I got halitosis or body odor or something?" She looked baffled. I grinned and went on. "Look, a guy named Fancher starts bringing this boat up from Florida; halfway here he falls over dead. A gal named Guild just steps aboard for a couple of days and winds up with brains on her face. A guy named Jesperson inhabits the bucket very briefly and is fished out of Long Island Sound after learning the hard way that breathing water isn't as effective as breathing air. Have I got all that straight?"

She made a face expressing distaste. "You do not put it very delicately, but yes, I believe it is straight."

I said, "Okay; but then a guy named Helm comes aboard and spends two whole months living and working on this jinx boat, awkwardly taking her out for practice runs whenever the repairs allow it, doing his best to look like easy prey, a real stumblebum mariner—it wasn't hard—but in all that time nobody makes a move on him, nobody. It's enough to give a man an inferiority complex. What did those other three have that I haven't got, that nobody wants to murder me?"

"Maybe you have it backward, Matt," Ziggy said after a moment's thought. "Maybe it is what you have that they did not have."

"Like what?" I asked.

"A gun?"

4

She returned from the galley after putting the chicken into the oven. It was an apparatus I'd never used since I'd come aboard, being a frying pan man from way back. All the cooking I know, which isn't much, I learned over western camp fires. Ziggy sat down beside me and picked up her martini.

"I was told that you have the reputation of being a truly dangerous man, and a particularly fine marksman," she said.

I said, "Any good target shot can beat me any day in the week."

"With the targets shooting back? I doubt that very much." She laughed. "I was warned that you are in a different class, shall we say, from our organization of nice little boys and girls playing at coastal security."

"Oh, is that what you're playing at?"

She shook her head ruefully. "I should not have said that; it is a terrible secret. Please forget it."

"Coastal security, what's that? Never heard of it." I grinned. "I suppose the folks who built me up so big were the ones in your outfit who were trying to talk you into coming on a boat on which three people have already died. They were trying to convince you that, in spite of bodies falling to the deck like autumn leaves, you'd be perfectly safe with Sure-shot Helm?"

She smiled. "Something like that, yes."

"And your theory is that the opposition also got to leeward of me and caught a hellish whiff of brimstone and decided they were better off leaving dangerous old me alone?"

"Is it not a possibility?"

I shrugged. "Well, it's flattering to think that my official reputation is so terror-inspiring that it frightens into trembling immobility people who've already committed at least two murders, possibly three. But it doesn't seem very likely; and after all, Guild and Jesperson weren't totally unarmed and untrained innocents, were they?"

She shrugged. "Actually, I believe they did have guns and I know they'd had some training, but they were not very experienced agents. Not like you."

"You make me feel like a veteran of the Indian wars. If you're a real good girl, Grandpa'll show you his scalp collection some time," I said. I frowned. "There's another possibility. I've been told that Truman Fancher was a real gung ho sailor. What about your friends?"

Ziggy said, "They were much involved with sailing in their free time, both racing and cruising. That is why they were chosen to investigate this boat. Of course I was selected for the same reason."

I said, "Your outfit really has a pool of nautical talent available, doesn't it? It isn't every undercover agency—security agency?—that can produce experienced seamen, and particularly seawomen, on demand, time and again."

"But that is only natural, since we are concerned with the shoreline—" She stopped, and laughed. "You are pumping me. Is that the right word, pumping?"

"Pumping is right," I said. "But it's a very reluctant well I'm pumping. Back to the reason nobody wants to kill me. You suggested it's because I'm dangerous; but could it be just because I'm stupid?"

"Stupid? In what way?"

"In a nautical way. Three salty sailors, if we include Fancher, have died on this vessel. But a landlubber from the Great American Desert has survived since August unmolested. Maybe there's something incriminating on board that I just don't see because I don't really know how things are supposed to be on this kind of boat, or any kind of boat… Say Truman Fancher suddenly spotted something new and unfamiliar and disturbing on the yacht he'd gone to a lot of trouble to import from Europe a good many years ago, so somebody fixed up a heart attack for him. Say Henrietta Guild was only on board a day before she heard a sour note in the rigging, so to speak; so she had to die. Say they got rid of Martin Jesperson when he also noticed something offbeat… But Matthew Helm lived on board week after week happily overlooking a peculiarity of his floating home that a real sailor couldn't help but spot, so the people who were watching let the poor dumbo survive untouched. You haven't noticed anything odd about the good ship *Lorelei III,* have you?"

Ziggy shook her head. "So far she seems like a perfectly normal boat, for a motor sailer. She is heavy, of course, and undercanvased, but that is standard for the type. They are not expected to sail in light winds; that is what the eighty-horsepower motor is for. A true sailboat this size would only carry half that power." She glanced at me. "And you have found nothing peculiar? No clues to say why some person feels this boat must be sunk? Nothing suggestive in the ship's log?"

I said, "Fancher's logbook wasn't on board when I got the boat, not surprising considering the number of people who'd had her since he died," I said. "Of course she was a considerable mess when I took her over; everything wet below and lockers busted open and compartment hatches strewn about, along with cushions and carpets and stray gear—I suppose the Coast Guard had to do some hasty exploring, with the cabin knee deep in water, before they found where it was coming from. I had my work cut out for me, getting everything dried out and repaired and put back where it belonged."

"You seem to have done a very marvelous job," Ziggy said, looking around the comfortable deckhouse. "Well, I think there is a little more martini in the pitcher; then I must see about those chickens…"

She was a better cook than bartender; and after dinner

we went ashore to let her make a call from the pay phone in the marina parking lot. She'd started off alone, but I'd told her that could not be permitted; if I was to be responsible for her I could hardly let her wander around in the dark all by herself. She saw my point, but waited until I'd moved out of hearing before she punched in her number. As we walked back out the dock toward the boat after she'd finished talking, she laughed softly.

"I told them you are a big phony," she said. "I told them you could sail the boat perfectly well alone; you were only acting helpless so they would send you somebody female you hoped would share that big bunk with you."

She wasn't looking at me when she said it, and I didn't look at her. "Aw, shucks," I said. "And here I thought I was being so clever."

She said, "I will wash the dishes. "You will dry, yes?"

It was kind of cozy, cleaning up the galley, reminding me of after-dinner sessions with my mother many years ago; although I was very much aware that the lady with her hands in tonight's dishwater was not my mother. Afterward, we had coffee in the deckhouse and listened to the weather report on the VHF radio.

Ziggy said the predicted winds, ten to twenty knots out of the southwest, would make things a little rough on the next leg of our voyage, an overnight crossing to Cape May, New Jersey, since we'd be in the open ocean bashing right into it for almost two hundred miles. However, she'd satisfied herself today that the boat was seaworthy, and the motor sounded fine, and we were under instructions to keep moving south if we possibly could. We'd check the weather in the morning, but if the reports were no worse we'd give it a try.

She said she was a bit tired and we probably wouldn't get much sleep on the long run tomorrow; if I didn't mind she'd turn in now.

"Good night, Matt. It was a good day, ja?"

"Very good, Ziggy. Sleep well."

I watched her go forward, with her long shining hair once more loose down her back, the glorious blond shipmate of every yachtsman's dreams even if she did put too much vermouth in the martinis. I took my coffee on deck and wandered about checking the dock lines, although I was sure that no line secured by Ziggy Kronquist would have the temerity to come unsecured. It was a misty night; the marina lights looked big and fluffy, like dandelions gone to seed.

There was no light from the forward hatch. I wondered if she slept raw, or in a nightie, or pajamas; she kind of looked like a pajama girl to me. I felt a little exposed standing on deck, although the masts and rigging of the neighboring sailboats, and the superstructures of the cruisers and sportfishermen, would have made it hard for anybody to get a clear shot at me. Even a good night sight would only show them the obvious obstructions; they'd never know that there wasn't an unseen rigging wire in the line of fire to deflect the bullet. Anyway, if they'd wanted to go the sniper route they'd already had plenty of better chances. Stepping back down into the deckhouse, I stumbled over one of Ziggy's shoes. I'd been right about her shedding them at the first opportunity. The inimitable Dr. Matthias Helmstein, noted expert on female behavior.

I went to bed in my usual wary fashion; on this voyage I had to worry, not only about assassination, but about concussion. I mean, as I'd indicated to Ziggy Kronquist, the boat looked husky enough outside, but inside she was not designed for gents six-four. The master stateroom, in particular, was low-bridge territory. You could scalp yourself, and I had, going down the steps aft, entering or leaving the little head to starboard, and even getting into the big double bunk—shelves lined the sides and stern of the boat above it, and if you flopped back onto the pillow incautiously you could damn near knock yourself out on the nice teak woodwork overhead. I'd learned to insert myself cautiously, like a sardine entering a can.

Then I lay awake, listening to the small splashing sounds of the waves against the hull. Moved by the night breeze, *Lorelei III* strained gently against her lines. Two couples, not quite sober, stopped to talk some distance down the dock. They said good night noisily, and one couple came past our slip.

"Darling, we seem to know the dullest people on earth," the woman said quite clearly. They boarded a boat farther out the dock, and the marina was silent again.

Time passed very slowly, but I was in no danger of falling asleep in spite of the long day of fresh air and sunshine. Suddenly she was there, at the head of the two steps leading down into my cabin from the deckhouse.

The marina lights penetrated the drawn curtains well enough that I could see the shape of her if not the details. I could certainly see that Dr. Helmstein had got it all wrong. She wasn't a pajama girl. She wasn't a nightie girl, either.

"No," she said when I moved. "Please, no light."

"It's your party."

My voice wasn't as steady as I would have liked it to be. I threw back the covers and sat up, mindful of the overhead shelf, watching the dim, nude, spectacular figure come down the brief steps and make its way to the starboard side of the bunk, the only one available since the other side was built against the boat's hull, which made it a hell of a bed to make up every morning. There wasn't much floor space between the bed and the dresser to starboard, and it slanted up aft to conform with the shape of the boat's hull, reducing the already limited headroom; Ziggy had to duck to reach me.

Looking down at me, she said, "I said I would think about it when I know you better."

I cleared my throat. "And you know me well enough now?"

"Ja, minälskade." She laughed softly. "That means 'yes, my darling' in Swedish."

She sank down on the side of the berth; then she was in my arms, her lips warm and eager, her hands… I caught her wrist left-handed and twisted the point of the knife aside. With my right hand I scooped up the little tranquilizer gun from the bedside dresser and fired it at contact range. She grabbed my wrist but too late to deflect my aim. She was very strong, and I had a hard time controlling her knife hand. The blade that she'd tried to slip into my armpit was the big Sabatier from the rack in the galley; it seemed that I'd found the assassin who liked to employ weapons of opportunity.

There was a testing moment during which we just lay there straining against each other. She was in better condition, but I was bigger and she couldn't force the knife point any closer to me. I let her expend part of her strength keeping the dart launcher twisted aside. It didn't matter since the thing was strictly a one-shot proposition. Suddenly she broke free and rolled away and stood up, or tried to, forgetting where she was. Her head hit one of the wooden battens that held the cabin's elaborate quilted headlining, dazing her for a moment, giving me time to switch on the little bedside light. She crouched there naked, still holding the knife; after a moment, she looked down at the bright little tuft of plastic sprouting from her left breast.

My orders were to take them alive. Using a gun to crease or disable is something that only works in the movies; in a real-life situation, if you try it, you generally wind up with somebody dead, and occasionally it's you. Our armorer had therefore adapted a system used by game departments to immobilize unwanted animals for transport elsewhere. The catch was that, while there are some fairly quick poisons if you want to go all the way, the backroom boys haven't come up with anything reasonably safe that still causes instant unconsciousness in the dosage that can be delivered by a dart. The bear can eat you while you're waiting for him to fall asleep, and the lady can carve you to bloody ribbons…

But Ziggy was looking down at the little brush of plastic fibers that made the dart fly straight, colored Day-Glo orange so you could see your shots. She reached down gingerly and drew a deep breath and pulled it out with her left hand and tossed it aside, still holding the knife with her right. A small trickle of blood escaped from the puncture wound.

She looked at me accusingly. "You knew?" she whispered. "I thought I was very good. You knew?"

"You were very good, and I didn't know, not for sure," I said. "But I'm a pro, sweetheart. I hate to tell you how many times the pretty-lady-in-my-bed routine has been tried on me. I figured, if you stayed in your own bunk tonight, you might be okay; but if you came to me the very first night you just had to be a ringer. I'm not all that irresistible. What happened to the real Siegelinda Kronquist?"

She licked her lips and didn't answer the question. She said softly, "So I was right in hesitating to deal with you; I sensed you were danger and bad fortune for me. But the man said the clients were becoming impatient… I feel strange. Am I dead?"

"No, you'll just sleep for a while. It was you who got the others?"

She looked at me bleakly, and I saw it in her eyes, what had really warned me although I hadn't quite been aware of it: the hunter look, the killer look. I should know it; I've seen it in the mirror often enough.

"Not the old man," she said. "I do not know about that; I was not there. But that stupid woman tripping over her pretty nightdress as she came rushing out of this cabin with her little gun, and the stupid young man so eager to get us into another harbor where he could again… we could again… His girlfriend must have been very uncooperative; he was really eager for it, I had no trouble at all picking him up on the dock and getting him to invite me aboard. I'd studied him, his dossier, of course; I knew he did not swim so good. He was already panicking back there in the wake, drowning, as the boat sailed away from him after I had tipped him over the side. I swim very good. After arranging to scuttle the boat, I swim to the waiting skiff, but this *förbannade* big, clumsy vessel, it will not stay on the course I have set. It will not die! I try to blow it up, I try to sink it, but it will not die!" She drew a long, ragged breath, and went on. "Do you really think you can just shoot me with your little arrow and turn me over to the questioners? Me? Ha, I am a professional, too, my friend!"

She said it proudly, but in her eyes was the gray realization of failure. She'd killed twice, to be sure, but the boat she'd been sent to destroy still floated, and in a moment she would be unconscious, a helpless captive. She was swaying, the drug was taking effect—but it didn't work fast enough to prevent her from putting the point of the big butcher knife against her breast and driving it home with both hands.

5

"Unfortunate," Mac said.

Getting from Montauk, N.Y., to Washington, D.C., I'd discovered, is reasonably simple. You just find a car to rent and drive westward half the length of Long Island to the small town of Islip, from which, strangely enough, there are several flights daily to the nation's capital, roughly two hours away by air.

The view through the window behind Mac hadn't changed much since my last visit, and neither had he. I'd just finished giving him the story in more detail than I'd managed over the phone in the middle of the night. He didn't seem to be particularly distressed about my failure to carry out my mission as specified.

"Unfortunate," he said, "but unavoidable."

"Bullshit," I said. "Thanks just the same, but unavoidable is bullshit, sir. Hara-kiri is not a Japanese monopoly. Falling on your sword when defeated is an old Viking custom. I should have been ready for it; I should have known that was not a girl who would accept failure, humiliation, interrogation, imprisonment…"

"You had no trouble afterward?" Mac asked.

Okay. He was right. Talking about it accomplished nothing. "That depends on what you mean by trouble," I said.

Actually, it hadn't been too bad. Luckily the bedding hadn't got splashed, and washing it off the woodwork had been easy enough. Getting it out of the carpet had been the worst problem, but that indoor-outdoor stuff with a rubbery backing doesn't hold fresh stains too stubbornly.

I'd gone ashore to call the body snatchers first thing, of course, at the same time as I'd made my preliminary report to Mac. I had the cleanup pretty well under control when they arrived to haul away the tarpaulin-wrapped bundle I'd prepared for them, and the girl's belongings. There was no reason to think they'd caused any marina comment; bags and bundles of canvas, large and small, are always being hauled off sailboats, and onto them, even in the middle of the night.

Then I checked out the boat thoroughly to make sure that no items that didn't belong to me had been missed. I'd remembered to send off the shoes she'd discarded in the deckhouse; she'd left nothing else behind but a memory that wouldn't be as easy to erase as her bloodstains. I did a bit more scrubbing; by the time I'd finished, there was dawn outside the deckhouse windows. I went ashore to use the marina showers since the facilities on *Lorelei III*, while nice to have available, were, like everything else on board, a little cramped for a gent six-four. I got into shore-going clothes, grabbed a quick breakfast on the way to the airport, and here I was in front of the familiar desk facing the familiar bright window, telling Mac all about it as usual.

I said, "It wasn't too bad. A forensic genius could undoubtedly discover that somebody'd bled on my boat, but I got it pretty well mopped up. The telephone contact was a woman who identified herself very formally as Mrs. Bell, and called me Mr. Helm. Good for her. In the middle of the night, with a stiff on my hands, I don't want to have to deal with a twittering female dimwit who says, 'Hi Matt, honey-bunch, I'm Bobby, what's your everlasting problem, sweets?"

"Terry, actually."

"What?"

Mac said, "The lady's name is Mrs. Teresa Bell. I suppose somebody calls her Terry. I would not venture to try it myself."

"I know what you mean. Not a warm personality."

"Did she have anything to say?" Mac asked.

"Well, yes. She said she preferred to have me send her live specimens, if it was all the same to me. I said I'd prefer to have her send me nonhomicidal crews, if it was all the same to her. I wouldn't call it love at first sight—well at first hearing, since we've never seen each other. What's her agency?"

"The name has not been revealed to us." Mac smiled thinly. "We are hardly in a position to complain."

What he meant was that nobody knows the name of our outfit, either, perhaps because it hasn't got one.

I said, "The girl indicated that it's some kind of a security organization dealing with coastal problems, whatever that means—maybe true, maybe not. Since she was a ringer we can't be sure how much she really knew about the outfit she was supposedly working for, and how much she was just making up to sound authentic." I shook my head ruefully. "She was quite a girl. It's too damn bad. I could have enjoyed sailing with her."

Mac responded by shoving a stack of file folders across the desk. "See if you can find her in there," he said.

The bundle was bound with very strong half-inch plastic tape put on and sealed by machine. It had a covering sheet indicating that anyone compromising the stratospherically secret contents would be dismembered and cooked piecemeal in boiling oil, or words to that effect. Well, you should see the ones that are *really* sensitive. This was just a routine warning.

I cut the tape with the smaller, and sharper, blade of my Swiss Army knife. There were eleven folders. Each one had the heading DAMAG on the label, followed by a series of numbers that presumably made sense to somebody's computer. She was easy enough to find. She was DAMAG004, the fourth one down. A couple of bad snapshots were stapled to the inside of the folder, along with a small color print of a posed glamor portrait that had been taken when she was a few years younger. The photographer had made her look breathtakingly beautiful, not hard to do.

"This is the girl," I said, turning the file around and shoving it toward him.

"You're certain?"

"Yes, sir. It isn't likely there are two like that around." When he didn't speak at once, I asked, "What's this all about? What's DAMAG?"

Mac said, "I haven't been entirely frank with you." He made it sound as if this were highly unusual, instead of being the normal state of affairs in that office. He went on, "We are, of course, happy to work with our fellow agencies whenever our assistance is requested, but I might not have been so ready to invest several months of a senior agent's time in Mrs. Bell's problem if there had not been reason to believe that it could lead us to an organization with which we have been asked to deal..."

I regarded him rather grimly. Of course I should have known. I once used to hunt with a man who, in a duck blind, specialized in one-shot doubles. He was a superlative shotgunner, and it wasn't enough for him to pick two birds out of a decoying flock and fire twice to drop them both, bang-bang, splash-splash. Most hunters feel pretty good about pulling off a double like that; but what my friend liked to do, and managed more often than seemed possible, was to wait until two birds' flight paths were about to cross so he could cover both with the spread of pellets from a single charge of shot: bang, splash-splash.

No, I'm not that good with a shotgun. Just in case you were wondering.

Anyway, I should have remembered that any time Mac

gets generous and lends me to another agency in the name of interdepartmental cooperation, I should be asking myself just what he's getting out of it. Almost always, he's got a double in mind, and there's another mission on the wing, one of ours, that he hopes to nail with the same shotgun shell: me.

He was still talking: "But you had better glance through two or three of the files and get a preliminary feeling for the people involved."

"Yes, sir."

I retrieved the folder for DAMAG004, the girl I had known as Siegelinda Kronquist. They had quite a bit of stuff on her. I didn't take time to read it all; I just leafed through the various papers until I found the condensed dossier prepared for lazy folks like me:

Larsson, Greta, aka Greta Anderson, Mary Olsen, etc. (for complete list of known aliases consult master file). Uppsala Sweden 59, entered US 64, naturalized through parents. Five-eleven, one-sixty, blonde, blue. Slight accent, often exaggerated for effect. Marginal firearms, excellent unarmed combat, excellent edged weapons, but prefers to operate unarmed employing implements available at scene. W and A, no hosex encounters recorded, sm and sp tendencies suspected. Freelance specializing in B and B. No arrests. Probables: Lionel Hansen, Atlantic City, 83; Margaret Johnson Martinez, Marina del Rey, 83; Laura Pottsweiler, Miami, 85; Carl Gustav Elliston, Bar Harbor, 86...

Well, she'd told me she was a pro. She hadn't been kidding. Although she'd apparently been less than expert with guns, it didn't seem to have handicapped her much, perhaps due to her habit of using whatever was handy—a windlass handle, a good strong shove with her hands, a large kitchen knife, to mention only the cases with which I was acquainted. According to the dossier, she had nine probables to her credit, if credit is the proper word. With the two kills, confirmed by the subject herself, that had not yet been entered into the computer, her total score was eleven, and those were only the ones that had found their way into the record. There could have been others.

I said, "The jargon gets thicker every year. It wouldn't be so bad if they didn't keep changing it. What the hell is W and A? That's a new one on me."

Mac laughed shortly. "It means that the lady was no nun. Willing and able. Hosex refers to homosexuality, sm you can probably figure out, sp means sociopathic, and B and B indicates that she preferred to operate around beaches and boats, in other words seaside resorts and marinas."

I said, "I know I'm old-fashioned, but I thought the English language was kind of nice, back when we used to use it."

I picked a couple more of the files at random. DAMAG006 was a little mustached weasel of a man called Elmer (Snipey) Weiss. I'd heard of him before; I like to keep track of the long-range boys since it's kind of a specialty of mine. DAMAG008, Jerome (Boomer) Blum, was a lean, balding character with glasses who could apparently cook you up anything from a hand grenade to an atom bomb in his girlfriend's kitchen. DAMAG002 was a stout, gray-haired woman named Carlotta (Lottie) Espenshade who specialized in drugs and poisons.

I looked up from the files. "Somebody seems to have made a fine collection of homicidal talent here," I said. "What the hell kind of an outfit is it, sir?"

Mac said, "DAMAG, Incorporated, is what they call themselves, although it seems unlikely that they are a legal corporation. It is thought that the name was originally Damage, Inc., but it was shortened because the truncated form just sounded or looked impressive to someone."

"Damage, Inc.," I said. "Shades of the old Murder, Inc." When he did not comment, I said, "Apparently our DAMAG friends aren't particular what kind of damage they do, anything from killing people to sinking boats, or trying to."

Mac nodded. "Particularly a boat with a certain person on board, when they learn of his presence. One Matthew Helm." He gestured toward the pile of folders. "You did not get to the bottom of the pile, Eric. Examine the final dossier, please."

I dug out the file, DAMAG011, and opened it. "Oh, Jesus!" I said.

"You recognize the name?"

"Roland Caselius? Sure, but he's been dead for so long… Hell, I finished him off myself, way up in northern Sweden."

"How much do you remember about him?"

I said, "Well, I remember clearly that I used half a magazine of nine millimeter stuff on him, just to make absolutely sure nobody'd bring him back to life. As I recall, his espionage activities were the basic reason I'd been sent after him; but the little man was very quick to kill anybody who got close to him, and too damn many people had died at his hands, some of whom I'd kind of liked. Who's using his name?"

Mac said reprovingly, "You're not reading, or remembering, carefully enough, Eric. The first name of the man with whom you dealt all those years ago was Raoul. This is Roland."

"A son?" I asked rather grimly.

People in our line of work shouldn't have families, although I'm in no position to criticize.

Mac nodded. "A son who has apparently inherited much of his father's cleverness. A son who has been brought up to hate America, and a certain American, for tracking down and terminating his father."

I drew a long breath. "Brought up by whom? If Caselius, Senior, had a son he must have had a wife—well, at least a woman—but there was nothing about a woman in the information I was given at the time."

Mac said, "There was a great deal about Raoul Caselius that we did not know; but it appears now that he had been married for some years when he died. The son is in his middle twenties now; he would have been at an impressionable age when his father was killed, receptive to the vengeful message pounded into him by an unbalanced and vindictive mother. She had several years to work on him."

"She's dead?"

"She finally killed herself, leaving a note to the boy saying that he could consider that she'd been murdered, like his father, by wicked America."

I said, "Hell, if the U.S. didn't exist, they'd have to invent it, wouldn't they? Otherwise, who could they blame?" After a moment I went on grimly. "So, having grown into long pants, Roland has organized a fancy sabotage/assassination bureau as an instrument of vengeance. He seems to be an enterprising young fellow."

"He's also quite competent," Mac said. "The Russians used to do a good job of training them, in their unimaginative way."

I said, "That's right, Papa Caselius worked for the Russians. So they kind of inherited the son?"

"They supervised his upbringing after the death of the mother. However, the boy, unlike his father, was not used for espionage; he operated out of one of the departments specializing in wet operations. But after gaining a certain amount of experience he went into private practice, shall we say, presumably with official permission, and maybe even official help, at the dawn of the present era of Muscovite sweetness and light. I think it is likely that we'll find that many land mines like Roland Caselius were left lying around for us to step on by the old guard in Moscow when they saw their power waning."

These undercover services do have their jargon. "Wet,"

for God's sake. I don't know why everybody's so finicky about avoiding the simple word "kill."

I said, "So what wet operation has he got going now, besides his personal vendetta with me, that's got Washington worried enough to call us in? I gather this is something apart from Mrs. Bell's problem. Who's the target whose life I'm supposed to be saving by defanging this DAMAG snake?"

Mac laughed shortly. "You are being very naive, Eric. You know Washington."

I grimaced. "I see. We don't need to know that, so we haven't been told. So I may be risking my life for an anonymous janitor in the State Office Building? Well, he's probably a worthy soul deserving of my protection. Do I gather that somebody feels I'll protect him better by going for DAMAG than by playing bodyguard directly?"

"The city is full of qualified bodyguards," Mac said, "and I suspect some will be employed to cover the potential target, whoever he, or she, may be. However, you have the unique qualification of, more than any other American, being the focus of Roland Caselius's hatred. All you really have to do is put yourself in his path and he'll come after you." He paused, and went on. "The identity of the dead girl confirms what I suspected from the start, that the Arab terrorist conspirators with whom Mrs. Bell is concerned have hired DAMAG to help them. It's your lead to Caselius; use it."

I said, "Arab conspirators? The only opposition I've met so far was blond and blue-eyed; I've met no Arabs yet."

"As a matter of fact, you have spoken with one. Mrs. Bell's maiden name was Othman, and she is fluent in the language, which is why she was assigned by her so-far unnamed agency to set up a task force to investigate this gang and keep it from attaining its terrorist goal."

"What terrorist goal?"

Mac shrugged. "Does it matter? They are always blowing up something. You should stop them if you can, I suppose, but we are more interested in Caselius. Don't let yourself be distracted by the Middle Eastern cutthroats and their glorious plans of anti-American sabotage or whatever. They are Mrs. Bell's concern: DAMAG is yours. I feel your best approach is simple frustration. If DAMAG tries to kill somebody, you keep him, or her, alive. If DAMAG attempts to sink a boat, you keep it afloat. If DAMAG wants it painted green, you paint it red. You want to make Roland Caselius realize that his father's executioner is standing directly in his, Roland's, way; and that there are now business reasons, in addition to personal ones, why you must be removed. We can hope that the personal reasons will lead him to attend to the matter personally… Excuse me." He paused to answer the phone that had started to ring.

Well, it wasn't the first time I'd been asked to poke an angry bear with a short stick, and it wouldn't be the last—assuming that I survived this encounter, of course.

"Yes, Mrs. Bell," Mac was saying. "Yes, he is here… Very well, I will tell him." He put the instrument down and looked at me across the desk. "Mrs. Bell thought you'd be interested in knowing that their missing agent, the real Siegelinda Kronquist, has been located."

"Alive?"

Mac nodded. "Yes, but not in very good shape. She was found this morning, unconscious and in rather battered condition, beside a railroad track in Connecticut. She was at first thought to have wandered drunkenly onto the tracks and received a glancing blow from a train that knocked her into the ditch, where she remained in an alcoholic stupor. However, medical examination showed that she was heavily drugged, and that her injuries were, let us say, more systematic than those that would be inflicted by a locomotive. She is now in a New Haven hospital under observation. She has not yet been debriefed. Well, we can guess what she has to say."

I nodded. "It figures that they grabbed her when she was on her way to join me, probably by rail considering where she was found—there's regular train service all along that shore. They got her seabag and stuff for the other girl to use and took her out behind the tracks somewhere and beat the necessary information out of her—particularly that identification nonsense the other girl worked on me."

Mac said, "At any rate, that girl is out of action for the moment, at least. Mrs. Bell said that she is looking for another agent with the proper qualifications. In the meantime you are to take the boat on south by yourself; they will send you a crew member as soon as they can."

"I don't look forward to it; this one will probably be a

real Captain Bligh," I said ruefully. "Well, it's their boat; if they want to take a chance on my getting it through alone until they can get me some knowledgeable help, it's their gamble."

Mac gestured toward the stuff on the desk. "You will have to memorize the dossiers here; I don't want those yapping mongrels from security snapping at my heels on account of their precious files."

After doing my homework on the files, I caught a flight back to Islip and drove out to Montauk in heavy afternoon traffic. I checked in the rental car, and the man who'd done the paperwork got behind the wheel and drove me to the marina. It had been a long day and I was yawning as I fumbled out the deckhouse key, not hard to locate in my pocket since, along with the ignition key—if the word can be applied to a diesel, which has no ignition—it was attached to a miniature plastic channel buoy designed to keep it afloat if I was clumsy enough to drop it overboard.

Then I stopped yawning abruptly, realizing that the deckhouse door was already open. After a moment, a small dark-haired girl stuck her head out.

"Don't shoot, I'm Lori," she said.

6

She was one of the long-john girls. At least that's how they always look to me, as if they'd forgotten to pull on their pants of a sleepy morning and wandered out of the house in their long winter-underwear bottoms, in this case dull black tights ending two inches above the ankles. Below, white leather boat moccasins with white nonslip rubber soles. Above, a big black sweatshirt that reached well down her hips but still didn't succeed in making her look fully dressed. At least as far as I was concerned, she was still a lady making a public appearance in her BVDs; not particularly sexy—it was not a very stimulating garment—but slightly embarrassing.

The sweatshirt had a hood to keep her head warm, and she might very well need it later in the evening, since she wore her hair too short to provide much topside insulation against the night chill. I was a little surprised, in retrospect, that I'd realized so quickly that she was a girl, since her haircut was strictly boy—or what boy used to be before they all went in for flowing locks. Well, she had a nicely shaped head and pretty ears and if she liked the severe, shorn look, it was her business—as, I suppose, was her underwear. She watched me make my way aboard, taking the standard precautions, which amused her.

"Careful, aren't you?" she said.

I slid the deckhouse door shut behind me, and drew the curtains. It had been a long day, but it was getting toward that time of evening at last. I took a look into the aft stateroom and head, and went forward and checked all the way to the bow. In the forward stateroom, the gear Ziggy Kronquist, aka Greta Larsson, aka DAMAG004, had brought aboard, which had been removed by the disposal crew, had now been replaced by a well-worn seabag, red with rather grubby white straps and handles. So the girl wasn't just a casual visitor; she was moving in as crew. The efficient Mrs. Bell must really have scrambled to get her here so fast—assuming, of course, that the kid wasn't another phony. Returning to the main cabin, I got a bottle of Scotch out of the rack and poured myself a drink.

"One for you?" I asked, seeing her looking down at me from the deckhouse. When she nodded, I said, "Name it."

"Vodka and tonic?"

"It can be done. It shall be done."

Emerging from the cabin with the drinks, I put them on the little corner table. I sat down and gestured toward the settee beside me, but the girl preferred to pick up her glass and perch on the tall stool—the helmsman's stool—that I'd set to one side, out of the traffic pattern, upon reaching port. She sipped her drink and waited for me to start the conversation. I noted that she had big gray eyes, a small straight nose, and even white teeth in a big-enough mouth, all neatly arranged in a rather small, symmetrical face. Actually, she was quite a handsome little girl despite the cropped hair. Her skin was very smooth, and nicely tanned, which these days may be medically negative, but I'm old-fashioned enough to find it visually positive.

I asked, "How did you get in here?"

She reached into a pocket of her sweatshirt and brought out a pair of keys like mine, chained to what looked like an identical plastic float. I frowned at it, got up, and checked in the small locker near the helm. The spare keys were there. I knew I'd returned mine to my pocket, but I reached down and felt for them anyway, finding them right where I'd put them.

"How many keys are there to this bucket?" I asked. "Are they passing them out by the double handful?"

"They didn't pass out this set. It's mine."

She was making me work for it, teasing me, watching me from the high stool. I sat back down and tasted my whiskey, finding myself aware of the length of slim leg being generously displayed in the very snug, mat-black tights. Apparently the garment wasn't totally unstimulating, after all.

"What's a Lori?" I asked. "Who's a Lori?"

She grinned at me a bit maliciously. "You're bright, you figure it out. The keys are really mine; I've had them for years. That should give you a clue."

"Lori?" I frowned again. "Lorelei?"

"Ha, I said the man was bright."

I studied her for a moment and said, "You're too young."

"Too young for what?"

I spoke carefully: "Maybe I was wrong. I figured that Truman Fancher had named the boat—his last three boats—after his wife. *Lorelei I, II,* and *III.* And I was told he was no chicken. And this boat alone is eight years old; he'd have to have married you in the cradle if you've had your name on three of them."

She said, "Keep plugging. You'll get there."

I said, "So, no wife. You were in the cradle, or practically so, when he named the first *Lorelei* for you, his baby daughter. Right?"

She said, "Bravo, I knew you'd make it!"

"Lorelei Fancher?"

She laughed. "Ridiculous, isn't it? Lorelei! I look about as much like a Rhine maiden as Aunt Jemima." She sipped her vodka and tonic. "And my mother died when I was four; and the idea of my stepmother—whose name is Dorothy, incidentally—having a boat named for her is fucking ludicrous. Hell, she hates boats. She was even seasick on the Intracoastal Waterway, for God's sake; they'd done a little bouncing around on one of those wide-open North Carolina sounds inside Cape Hatteras. That's why she was flaked out below when Daddy… when Daddy died."

Lori Fancher was watching me a little too closely

as she talked. I wondered why. It wasn't as if she were telling me anything new and startling; what she'd said only corroborated what I'd heard before.

She went on: "Well, it isn't fair to sneer at her for being seasick, I suppose, it can happen to anybody; but she'd only condescended to help Daddy bring the boat up from Florida because they'd had an awful fight and he'd scared her shitless by showing her the reports of a private investigator he'd hired. He told her he'd kick her out on her ear if she didn't straighten up and fly right, and no court in the world would give her a dime of his money." Lori shook her head. "Poor Daddy, he really loved the sultry bitch, and he was usually so easygoing that I guess she thought she could get away with anything, but she pushed him too far, playing around with that gorgeous greasy-gigolo-type. Roger Hassim, all he needed was a camel and some flowing robes, Valentino would spin in his grave! But of course Dorothy did get away with it in the end, begged Daddy's forgiveness, promised she'd never look at another man—ha!—and showed how she'd turned over a new leaf by insisting on making the spring cruise with him up the waterway—he'd planned to take me—so she could learn, at last, to share with him the sport he loved so much. She even sweetly allowed him to keep his big aft cabin, and condescended to suffer nobly in the cramped stateroom forward—lately they'd had separate bedrooms; old men have to get up at night and of course she couldn't stand being disturbed like that."

I said, "Your stepmother sounds like quite a lady."

"That is *not* the word I would choose!" Lori Fancher snapped. "Where she belongs is in harem pants all drenched with musky perfume popping grapes into the fat sheik's mouth. She's got a figure that won't quit—she makes skinny little girls like me cry in their beer—and black hair almost as long as Crystal Gayle's; that's a country singer in case you don't…"

I said, "I know who Crystal Gayle is; what do you think I am, ignorant?" I looked at her for a moment. "Where are the fuel tanks?"

She frowned, surprised; then she grinned. "Checking up, huh? They're in the engine room right below us, an eighty-gallon tank of diesel on each side of the big mill. That'll take you damn near a thousand miles if you keep the revs down to fifteen, sixteen hundred."

"And the water tank?"

"Tanks, plural. You've got sixty-five gallons under the main cabin sole. Then there's a twenty-five gallon tank under the bunk in the forward cabin. The valve that switches between them is right under that step over there, going down."

"Where's the registration number?" I asked.

She considered getting annoyed at my persistence, but decided against it and spoke like a child reciting its lessons: "*Lorelei III* hasn't got any state registration. She's U.S. documented, like a ship, and the document number is carved on the main beam at the forward end of the engine room. Six five oh nine three one, if I remember right."

It was the correct number in the right place, but I tried one more check: "Where's the switch for the electric windlass?"

She laughed. "Cute, aren't you? The windlass isn't electric; it's a big old manual brute that Daddy… that Daddy was always going to replace but never got around to."

I said, "Well, it's replaced now, I had it replaced, and the main switch and circuit breaker are on the side of the steering console. Of course it's rigged so once the power's on you can work it from up forward."

She glared at me. "Damn you, there's no way I could have known that!"

"I know," I said. "If you had known it, I'd have known you were a phony, just parroting information somebody'd given you this morning. But okay, I guess you're you."

"Well, goody, it makes me feel warm all over, being me." The little girl drew a long breath. "I think I'm supposed to feed you."

"If that's an offer, I accept."

She said, "I'm supposed to help you run the boat, and keep you well fed; and I'm supposed to duck when the shooting starts and let you handle it. You'd damn well better; I'm not much of a marksman… markswoman? Marksperson? Helmsperson? Seaperson? I'm all for women's lib, but I don't know about lousing up the language the way they do. And when they tell me it's insulting to the female sex to call a boat 'she,' I'm with the male chauvinist pigs. *Lorelei*'s a lady, not an 'it,' aren't you, baby?" She patted the steering wheel fondly. "Matt?"

"Yes?"

"What the hell's it all about?"

"Don't you know?"

She shook her head. "I wasn't told a damned thing except would I please dash out to Montauk and help a transplanted cowboy-type take Daddy's boat south, at least as far as Cape May, and make sure he didn't sink her in some stupid, lubberly way."

I grinned. "Gee, thanks lots."

"Come on down and talk to me while I heat up some delicious canned chili, or whatever you've got in the locker. Don't expect any gourmet meals on this Florida clipper, skipper."

I sat at the big table in the main saloon while she started exploring the galley across the way. She knew the boat, all right; she knew about the safety switch for the propane, and she knew where all the storage spaces were, including the sneaky silverware drawer that hid below the stove. She selected several cans from the shelves above the stove, found a skillet and a couple of saucepans, and started assembling something that looked as if it would turn out to be fried Spam with boiled potatoes and canned peas, and canned peaches for dessert. Well, it wasn't as if I hadn't eaten quick-and-dirty meals before and survived. At least I didn't have to cook this one.

I said, "You didn't sign on for a very long voyage, did you? With luck, we should be in Cape May the day after tomorrow, right?"

Lori spoke without turning her head. "I think they'd like me to stay on board longer, at least until they find you somebody else, but the two-hundred-mile open-water jump just ahead of us is the one they thought you really should have help with, and that's all I'm committed to. The rest you can probably manage by yourself if I have to take off. Well, we'll see how it goes." After a moment, she said, "Please understand, it's strictly a job for me. It's what I do, deliver boats. I have my six-pack and I'm working for my hundred-ton license."

I frowned. "Translate. Six-pack? I gather you're not talking about beer."

"Six-pack is what we call the Coast Guard license that lets you skipper a boat for hire with up to six people on board. The hundred-ton license is tougher, but I expect to be ready for it pretty soon. Actually, I don't really need it in the boat-delivery business; but if you're female and not very big it helps to have a lot of impressive papers to wave around."

I said, "If you're in the boat-delivery business, why didn't you deliver this one home, after your dad died? I was told that your stepmother got a commercial crew to do the job."

"She didn't give me time to get down there, damn her!" Lori said with sudden anger. "Dorothy knew I'd have loved to do it. It would have been a way of, well, kind of saying good-bye to… to Daddy, so she hired a couple of local yokels and had the boat on its way north before I could…

"Oh, well. The stepmother-stepdaughter relationship is notoriously poisonous. Are you pro or anti onions?"

"Pro."

After a little, Lori said, "I hope I didn't hurt your feelings by calling you a cowboy. You've really done a good job of restoration; I understand she was in pretty bad shape when you got her. Daddy would approve of you."

"Thanks," I said. I mean, if being patronized by a kid half my size was part of the job, well, I always try to do my duty.

"You didn't happen to come across Daddy's last logbook while you were working on the boat? It seems to have gone missing in all the confusion. I looked for it after… after he died, but I didn't have time to make a thorough search."

I said, "There was no logbook on board when I got the boat."

"Well, it's too bad; I have all the others." Lori shrugged resignedly. "She's such a great old boat; I hate the way she seems to have turned into a jinx ship."

I said, "Well, I don't really believe in jinxes, but there's no doubt that four people have died on board, including your dad."

"And whoever it was who bled all over the aft cabin?" She made her voice casual, but it obviously took a certain amount of effort.

I said, "I thought I cleaned it up pretty well."

"The carpet was damp so I got curious and looked more closely. You missed a few spots. I mopped them up for you." She licked her lips. "I think… I think you'd better tell me about it."

I told her about Ziggy Kronquist-Greta Larsson. Well, as much as she needed to know.

Lori was silent for a little after I'd finished. At last she said, "So that's why you were so careful to check my identity." She eyed me dubiously. "Of course there's just your word for what happened. Maybe you raped her and slit her throat."

"It's certainly a possibility," I said. "How did they get hold of you, anyway?"

"It was a lady named Mrs. Bell. I'd met her last spring when… Well, Daddy's will split everything down the middle, except that Dorothy got the house and I got the boat. This woman called and said she worked for the government. She said they'd had a little problem somewhere down south along the waterway. They were checking all boats that had passed through the area between such-and-such a date and such-and-such a date; and would I mind if they put a couple of people aboard *Lorelei III* to take her where some experts could go over her thoroughly. For certain reasons Mrs. Bell wanted to do it inconspicuously. She wouldn't tell me what she was looking for, but she said it wasn't drugs, and she promised that her people would leave the boat in mint condition. She reminded me that she could easily pull a few strings and get the Coast Guard to do it; and those clowns have never been known to put anything back where they found it. So I checked with the lawyers, and they said all right and, well, you know what happened, first one of Mrs. Bell's people—would you call them agents?—getting murdered and then another one drowning?" She made it a question.

"I've been told," I said.

"That's one reason I put the boat on the market as soon as I legally could," Lori said. "She'd been such a happy ship, but after having so many people die on board she didn't… didn't feel happy anymore, poor old girl. But then, out of a clear blue sky, this Mrs. Bell called me this morning in Newport, Rhode Island, where I'm living now, and said they were hard up for a female nautical expert; it seems they'd run through all theirs. Well, they had one left but she was in the hospital. Mrs. Bell remembered me, and said it was really right in my line, a delivery job, and a boat I knew very well; and would I help them out at double my usual rates—there was some danger involved—until they could get somebody else to take over? Well, I was between engagements, as they say on Broadway, and anyway, as I said, she's a great old boat. I'd hate to think of her getting wrecked because I wouldn't lend a hand. The two-hundred-mile offshore jump from here to Cape May can get kind of mean, and Mrs. Bell made it sound as if you didn't know a hell of a lot about sailing."

I said, "Mrs. Bell was so right."

"Matt," she said.

"Yes?"

Lori was putting a plate in front of me. "I'm not very promiscuous, if you know what I mean," she said.

I glanced at her sharply. "What brought that on?" I asked.

"The way you were looking at my legs, earlier." She went back for her own plate, saying, "And this is a kind of, well, cozy situation, isn't it? I've crewed on plenty of boats with lots of men on board, and there's never been a problem; but here there are just the two of us and I thought we'd better, well, get things settled between us." She sat down on the far side of the big table, facing me bravely.

I spoke deliberately: "Miss Fancher, on my ship—and I seem to own this bucket now after a fashion—you can be as unpromiscuous as you like. That's a promise, even though I do think you have very pretty legs, and the rest of you isn't half bad, either, what there is of it."

It occurred to me that I'd had a somewhat similar conversation with the last girl to occupy the forward cabin of *Lorelei III*.

7

I heard her in the galley before daylight. We'd agreed to get an early start, conditions permitting; and apparently she took her commitments seriously. When I joined her she looked slightly startled, as if she'd forgotten that there was somebody living at the other end of the boat. This morning she was wearing a loose blue T-shirt and wide white shorts—her pants seemed to fit her either too soon or too late, I reflected. No shoes. Her feet were small and brown, with nice straight toes and no nail polish.

"Scrambled okay?" she asked.

"Fine. Anything I can do?"

"“Turn on the VHF and get us the weather. I'll have coffee ready in a minute."

Standing at the stove, she moved aside a bit to let me reach my place at the big cabin table after switching on the boat radio (VHF means very high frequency, in case you're curious) to one of the two NOAA weather stations—National Oceanic and Atmospheric

Administration to you. Administering the oceans and the atmosphere always seems to me like a fairly ambitious project, even for Washington.

Lori spoke without looking around: "You were doing a lot of prowling around the deck last night."

I had a hunch she might have wondered a bit, when she first heard me, if I was prowling in her direction, but it didn't seem diplomatic to ask.

I said, "Somebody's tried to scuttle this boat twice, remember? And me once, not to mention some other characters they actually managed to terminate. I got a bit careless back in that Connecticut marina with nothing happening, but now I figured I'd better start keeping my guard up again. I'll catch up on my sleep while you're chauffeuring us to Cape May."

"Well, let's see what it's going to be like out there."

She put a cup of coffee in front of me, and I sipped from it as we listened to partly cloudy and patchy fog and winds southwest fifteen to twenty knots, seas six to eight feet, small-craft advisory in effect. A thirty-eight-footer does not qualify as a small craft in weather jargon; the U.S. Navy might think otherwise. Lori put plates on the table, stepped up to switch off the radio, and sat down facing me.

I said, "I never could figure out the difference between partly cloudy and partly sunny."

Lori said, "It's about as good a forecast as we're going to get this time of year. I think we should give it a try."

"You're the navigator."

She hesitated. “Well, it’s more or less up to you, Matt. I mean, I’ve been out in a lot worse; but it could be a rough ride for… for somebody who isn’t used to it. If we start now we should pick up the lights of the Jersey coast before daylight tomorrow morning and reach Cape May fairly early in the afternoon, but we’ll have the wind and sea against us the whole way and we’ll have to keep powering into it regardless; there’s no safe place to slip into for shelter.”

This was, of course, just about what her blonde predecessor had told me.

I grinned. “Okay, you’ve done your duty; you’ve terrified me. So let’s clean up the dishes and get the hell out of here.”

Actually, if I’d been doing it alone, I’d probably have stayed at the dock, not because of the unfavorable wind and sea, but because of the morning fog, described by NOAA as patchy. We seemed to have a prize patch sitting right over us. With the deckhouse curtains drawn, I hadn’t realized how thick it was outside. Dawn was struggling to break through the murk but not making much progress. Lori didn’t seem to consider it a serious problem, however; she just helped me clear away the curtains and said that, since she knew the harbor, it might be better if she took the boat out; would I bring in the dock lines, please? When I was back on board she moved us neatly astern until we were clear of the slip, and then sent us gliding forward into the soup, picking up the necessary aids to navigation without any apparent difficulty. Outside the harbor—well, she said we were outside the harbor; you couldn't prove it by me—she turned the wheel over to me, giving me a compass course to steer, while she programmed the loran. At last she cut in the autopilot.

"Watch the loran display," she said. "If you see her sliding off to port or starboard, just tweak Nicky's knob a bit and bring her back. I could use another cup of coffee, how about you?"

I nodded. "Nicky?" I said.

She laughed. "Some people call it Iron Mike or Electronic Eddy, but it's a NECO autopilot so we always called it Nicky. You'll be good friends with Nicky before you get much farther south. Hit the switch and warm up the radar, will you? I'll be back in a minute."

Alone at the wheel with nothing to do, I listened to the electronic whine of the radar beside me and the mechanical rumble of the diesel under my feet and watched the fog swirling past the deckhouse windows. Nicky steered a straighter course than I could have. The shore was invisible somewhere to starboard. The sea was reasonably smooth, but I reminded myself that we were on the north side of Long Island, sheltered from the southwesterly wind; it would undoubtedly be different after we turned Montauk Point and headed out into the shelterless Atlantic Ocean. Lori reappeared and handed me a steaming cup. Presently she switched the radar from standby to on and peered into the hood, studying the screen for a while. She raised her head.

"You'd better take over from Nicky," she said. "There

are a lot of fishing boats ahead."

"Just a minute," I said.

I parked my empty cup, ducked below, and returned with the twelve-gauge pump shotgun I'd brought along—a Remington M870, if it matters—and checked that there was nothing in the chamber and plenty in the tubular magazine. Double-0 buck. Ashore I prefer number four buckshot loads since they carry more pellets for a denser pattern—more effective, I feel, on human targets in the open; but if you have to shoot through a boat, or even just a windshield, the little fours won't penetrate as well as the husky 00s. I shoved the shotgun into one of the clips I'd arranged to port of the companionway, returned to the wheel, and switched off the autopilot.

"Okay, I've got her."

Lori glanced at me uneasily. "Is that… is that necessary? The gun, I mean."

I said, "I most certainly hope it isn't, but with a lot of little boats buzzing around I can't overlook the possibility that one will suddenly make a pass at us and try to toss something inflammable or explosive aboard. It doesn't hurt to have the shotgun there, and it might just possibly hurt not to have it." I looked ahead. Several boats were becoming hazily visible through the fog, and one buoy. "What do I do about this buoy?"

"Leave it to port, reasonably close, and come right ten degrees." She glanced at me. "Daddy was in the Navy in World War II, so we always used right and left rudder for the steering commands, Navy fashion, even if it didn't sound quite as salty as port and starboard helm. I kind of got into the habit. Do you mind?"

"No objection."

The fog was clearing a bit. The sea seemed to be full of small fishing boats, and I felt as if I were conning the battleship *New Jersey* into harbor on regatta day. *Lorelei III* was the biggest thing around. A couple of times, as we plowed through the mosquito fleet, I had to change course to keep clear of little outboards trolling stubbornly without much regard for the rules of the road at sea.

As we rounded Montauk point, still invisible to starboard, the seas grew in size as expected. The main fishing fleet fell astern, although stragglers continued to appear and disappear in the mist. Lori gave me a new course west of south, which brought the wind almost dead ahead. I cut in the autopilot to show I knew how. Plunging into the head seas, *Lorelei III* developed a deliberate pitching motion; spray began to hit the windshield. I started the wipers.

"So far so good," Lori said. "It's too bad we can't use the sails with the wind right on the nose like this; they'd steady her a bit. But now we have about a hundred and eighty miles of this. Say twenty-six hours at seven knots. If it doesn't get so rough we have to slow down. Do we keep on, skipper?"

I said, "You can't scare an old bronc rider with a few little bouncy waves, ma'am."

She glanced at me. "Did you really?"

"Ride 'em?" I grinned. "Hell, no. Any nag that wanted

to buck, I'd pick a soft spot and depart him pronto."

"I don't think I believe you, but here you're not going to be able to get off and walk if you change your mind."

The motion became more violent as the wind picked up. Every so often a solid wave would curl over the bow and come rolling aft to break over the deckhouse as if it were a half-tide rock. The fog seemed to come and go, or maybe it was we who came and went. Even when it cleared temporarily, the day was still dark and misty, with visibility not much over a mile. Nicky did the steering, with only an occasional correction needed to satisfy the loran. There was really nothing to do but hang on, and check that the occasional boat that materialized out of the murk was not on a collision course with us, and watch the seas coming at us.

I peered into the radar when Lori wasn't using it and got so I could pick up approaching vessels on the screen before I could see them. Actually, I was most interested in what was astern; but although there were often blobs back there, nothing seemed to be following us consistently.

Lori fed us sandwiches for both lunch and dinner; there wasn't much hope of getting a plate or soup bowl to retain its contents even though the fancy yachting dinnerware that had come with the boat had rubber inserts to keep it from sliding off the table. At last the darkness of the day turned into the blacker darkness of night. Lori switched on the running lights, red and green up forward, white aft, and white on the mast, indicating a small vessel under power.

"I'm not sleepy yet," she said. "If you want to sack out, go ahead. I think..." *Lorelei III* corkscrewed viciously as a big one passed underneath her; Lori steadied herself and went on. "I think you'll do better in the main cabin. Wedge yourself behind the table and it'll keep you from sliding around. In that big bunk aft you'll wind up on the cabin sole with the mattress for company. The old girl isn't really an offshore boat; Daddy never did figure out a system of bunk boards to keep people from being tossed out of bed when things got as rough as this."

Clinging to the steering wheel as we smashed through another wave, I said, "Just so you admit this is slightly violent. And I don't want to hear about the *real* hurricanes you've been through; this'll do me just fine... Lori?"

"Yes?"

"Keep checking the radar. If anything comes within half a mile and seems to be closing on us, wake me at once."

"Aye, aye, skipper." She hesitated. "Matt?"

"Yes?"

"I owe you an apology. I thought I'd be sailing the boat all by myself by this time, with you moaning and puking below."

I laughed. "It's my Viking heredity. Weak brains and a strong stomach. Good night, Lori. I think two hours on and two off is about right in this stuff, don't you?"

She nodded. "Good night, Matt."

I got my pillow and sleeping bag, some ammunition, and the rifle that was my primary night weapon—the shotgun was intended mainly for daytime use—and wedged myself, as she'd advised, onto the narrow cabin settee, back against the side of the boat with the big table holding me in place. At first it was hard for me to relax; then my body realized that it wasn't really going to be thrown across the boat, and sleep hit me...

"Matt! Matt, wake up, they're coming in fast!"

8

When I reached the deckhouse, it was dark except for the small green-glowing rectangle of the loran display; all the other instrument lights had been turned out. I saw that our running lights had also been switched off. Lori had imposed a full blackout, smart girl. Of course, these electronic days, darkness doesn't give as much concealment as it used to, but there was no sense in making life too easy for the opposition.

Lorelei III was still on autopilot and the smart girl, a shadowy figure except for her gleaming white shorts, had her face buried in the hood of the radar.

She said, "Port quarter, distance three-eighths of a mile, closing fast."

At least I was salty enough to know that a cow may have four quarters, but a boat only has two, and they're both aft. If it's forward, it's off the port or starboard bow.

"Any idea what it is?" I asked.

"'Not really. Well, it's boat-sized, not ship-sized." She

raised her head to look at me. Her face was pale in the darkness, but her voice was steady enough: "Orders, skipper?"

I said, "Take the wheel and cut the autopilot. I'll be on deck, aft. Slow her a bit to reduce the motion so I can shoot and maybe even hit something, twelve or thirteen hundred RPM should be about right. Try to give me a clear field of fire. Any shots forward are risky; we don't want to blow away our own rigging. What I mean is, keep the stern pointed at them as well as you can. That'll also prevent them from coming alongside. If you need more power, use it, but remember I'll be trying to shoot, so the steadier you can hold her the better."

"Got it. Good luck, Matt."

I can never think of any last-minute words of encouragement for the troops; I just said, "Well, here I go."

I already had the rifle. I yanked the shotgun out of its bracket. *Lorelei III* stuck her nose into a wave and gave me a shower bath as I stepped up onto the side deck. Clinging to the teak railing with my right hand and trying to keep the guns more or less dry tucked under my left arm, I made my way aft and crouched at the end of the deckhouse to avoid displaying a recognizable human silhouette.

Shotgun first, I thought. There would be a searchlight and I'd have to get it; and anybody who can hit an eight- or ten-inch target on one plunging boat from another plunging boat, with a single-bullet weapon, is out of my class; this was scattergun country.

I'd mounted another set of gun brackets at the end of the deckhouse; I secured the rifle there. It was a Browning, actually a civilian kid brother of the famous old military workhorse, the Browning automatic rifle, known as BAR. Normally, I'm a bolt-action man where rifles are concerned; it's the most reliable and most accurate type of long gun. However, in considering the conditions I might have to cope with on this operation, I'd decided that trying to manipulate a bolt rapidly while clinging to the gyrating deck of a thirty-eight-foot boat at sea would probably result in both me and the rifle going overboard; and under those shaky conditions just about any gun would have more accuracy than I could use, anyway.

I'd picked the Browning because, unlike many of its type, it accepts some truly powerful cartridges. The one I'd chosen was the heaviest available for the gun, the .338 Winchester Magnum. With a 250-grain slug, it was guaranteed to shoot through a charging African buffalo lengthwise, so I'd figured it ought to be able to penetrate the exterior hull of a fiberglass boat of moderate size, and might even rearrange the interior slightly. The sight was our modification of one of the new commercial laser jobs, throwing a small, sharply defined, red spot out to well beyond fifty yards. We have one that'll operate much farther, and I've used it, but it's an experimental sniper apparatus, bulky and fragile and vulnerable to rain and spray. This production instrument was nice and compact, actually smaller than a normal telescopic sight; and it was supposed to be rugged and waterproof…

The thing came out of the darkness at well over thirty knots. I caught the flash of its bow wave at about a hundred yards; then the dark shape was lunging at us. It was showing no running lights—but suddenly the blinding searchlight I'd been anticipating hit me like a blow in the face. Rising, I braced my hip against the deckhouse, swung the shotgun, and sent one load of buckshot into the glare, and another. The light flamed out. As the other boat rushed at us, aiming to pass us to port, I lowered my aim and used the rest of the magazine to rake the foredeck and windshield with the little round buckshot balls, fifteen balls to the load, each ball just about the size of the bullets Dan'l Boone probably used in his Kentucky squirrel rifle. A couple of insistent fireflies were winking in the cockpit of the oncoming boat; I felt a small shock through my feet as a bullet struck the hull somewhere near me, dispelling any uneasy doubts I might have had: I wasn't pumping a lot of lead at an innocent vessel that had just happened to come by on a near-collision course.

Okay, I thought, two with automatic weapons and one at the wheel. And I was not only supposed to keep them from killing us and sinking our boat, I was supposed to secure at least one live specimen and present it to Mrs. Bell for scientific analysis. Ha!

Then one of the squirt guns stopped firing, and I caught a ghostly glimpse of a man in a white shirt rising in the cockpit over there and swinging his arm in an unmistakable way, but there wasn't a damn thing to be done about it. They were passing us now, and we were already in a hard right turn as Lori kept the stern toward them. There was no way she could make the heavy motor sailer react fast enough for any other kind of avoiding action, so I didn't bother to shout any useless orders; but I lived through several very long seconds until, suddenly, the water boiled up white off the port quarter. It was a considerable relief. I hadn't been looking forward to trying to field the damn grenade falling out of the night sky and toss it back at the enemy, John Wayne fashion.

They vanished into the darkness. I stepped forward and steadied myself in the deckhouse doorway, reloading the shotgun. If I went overboard, I thought, I'd go down like a rock, since my right pants pocket was full of rifle cartridges and the left one bulged with shotgun shells.

"You okay?" I asked Lori.

She looked at me for a moment rather blankly. It had been a rough initiation for a girl who'd presumably been brainwashed, as most of them are these days, to believe in a basically nonviolent world despite all the evidence pointing the other way.

She licked her lips. "Hell, no, I'm not okay!" she said. "Those were *bullets,* I heard them! And what was that crazy explosion astern? And when do I get to change my pants?"

"Good girl," I said.

She drew a long breath and the shock went out of her eyes. She spoke deliberately, straight-faced: "While you were making all that racket, why didn't you get their radar, too? It was right up there beside the searchlight, on that arch over the cockpit."

I grinned. "Some people are never satisfied. I thought I was doing pretty well, just knocking out the light. How do you know I didn't get the radar?"

"It's still transmitting; you can see the funny lines flashing across our screen." She leaned over and put her face against the hood. "They're out there about half a mile… They're turning… Now they're coming back." She raised her head to look at me. "So what do we do for an encore, skipper?"

I wanted to hug her. We meet too many of the helpless ones who just wring their hands and squeal like movie ingénues when things get rough. However, I didn't know the kid well enough yet to maul her, even affectionately; besides, there wasn't time for displays of sentiment.

I said, "You're doing fine. Just keep spinning that wheel and I'll see what I can think up in the way of discouragement."

"Can I help with our searchlight, blind them or something?"

I said, "No, a lot of light will just foul up the crazy laser sight I've got back there; that's one reason I had to knock out their spot." I paused, and we both heard the rumble of big engines approaching fast. I said, "Well, here we go again."

By the time I got back to my poop-deck post, the flashing bow wave was visible out in the misty night, and Lori was turning us hard away from it. I'd traded the Remington for the Browning and switched on the electronic sighting apparatus, aiming skyward to keep my little surprise a surprise as long as possible. Then I made out the dark shape of the hull; when it came within laser range I put the eerie little red dot on it. The temptation was to shoot at the starboard side of the windshield and the helmsman's head that was presumably behind it, but I wasn't that sure of my marksmanship with the deck reeling and the gun barrel waving like an aspen limb in a mountain gale. I held the spot on the oncoming hull instead, to the best of my ability, figuring my angle the way you calculate how to reach the vital zone of an elk with a bullet when the animal won't oblige you with a broadside shot. I waited until things steadied down a bit, and added pressure to the trigger gently. The .338 spewed a long tongue of flame and made a fearful crash in the night, for a moment blanking out all other sounds. The recoil almost knocked me off the deck. It was a hell of a weapon.

The fast-approaching boat swerved violently away from us. I had it pretty well identified by now: one of the big souped-up sports boats that look like forty-foot torpedoes. Overkill. They hadn't needed an ocean racer like that to catch an eight-knot motor sailer, but they purely love those rakish craft, all the nasty people. I'd had one used against me before when a plain old twenty-knot cabin cruiser would have done just as well. The front half of the sleek hull was for humans. The rear half was all machinery. As it turned, my white-shirted opponent rose and made another throw, but this time I knew he'd overestimated his pitching arm; and I concentrated on holding the laser dot on the flank of the vessel as it raced past, and pumping three massive .338 slugs where I thought the great mechanical heart ought to be—well, two great mechanical hearts, since it was a twin-engine job.

Then a rat-a-tat gun was again winking at me from the cockpit. The exploding grenade sent up its boil of white water well astern; no danger there, but a bullet clanged off the aluminum mizzenmast above my head and whined off into the dark. One man shooting now, I told myself, one steering, and one dead or badly wounded if my first, carefully calculated, shot had plowed through enough of the boat straight enough to reach him. I'd better be careful; I had to save at least one alive to keep Mrs. Bell happy. As they showed me their stern I saw, with a sense of satisfaction, that the starboard mill had gone dead; only one propeller was churning the water into foam back there. They disappeared once more into the murky night.

I switched magazines on the Browning self-loader—all right, call it a semiautomatic if you insist on employing that much-abused term. With those big, fat rounds, the gun only held four, counting one in the chamber. I jacked in a fresh cartridge, swung the magazine out again, stuffed a loose round from my pocket into the top, and replaced the magazine in the gun, giving me another four, ready to resume the weird sea battle. Lori was still keeping our stern toward where the enemy had last been seen. I remembered that Admiral Nelson had had a similar problem with his old square-riggers, except that his firepower had been concentrated in his broadside guns so he'd had to keep the enemy abeam as for as possible, instead of astern…

"Matt." It was Lori's voice. "Matt, are you all right?"

I nodded my head to clear it; my ears were still ringing

from the rifle blasts and grenade explosions.

"Coming," I called. I made my way forward and stepped down into the deckhouse. I said, "Come left a hundred and eighty degrees. Idling speed."

She turned to stare at me. "Are you nuts?"

"Don't change the subject. We can discuss my sanity later."

"You're going back after them?"

I shrugged. "That's what we're here for. Can you spot them on the magic machine?"

She sighed. "It's not enough I've got a bitch for a stepmother; I've got to have a loony for a skipper, too!" She looked into the radar. "I've got them. They seem to be dead in the water."

"I put some heavy lead into the works. I think I knocked out one engine. They're probably trying to make repairs."

She was back at the wheel, spinning it counterclockwise. The hydraulic steering took very little effort but required a lot of wheel rotation.

She asked, "What the hell kind of a cannon was that you were blasting them with?"

I showed it to her. "Just a li'l ol' .338, ma'am."

"That's an elephant gun, isn't it?"

"Well, it would do the job, but the Africa boys really like them even bigger." I rubbed my shoulder. "For that amount of recoil, they can keep their damn elephants."

"Matt, look!"

I said, "Hell!"

Lori had made the U-turn I'd asked of her, and there

was a flickering glow in the mist directly off the bowsprit; and I didn't want that lousy overgrown speedboat to burn, dammit. Mrs. Bell, the lady I'd never met, wanted a warm body, not a fried one…

"Get range and bearing if you can," I said, taking the wheel as Lori bent over the radar. "That thing probably carries at least a couple of hundred gallons of high-test; it'll go up like a—"

The explosions lit up the night ahead, first a kind of preliminary flash and bang, then a giant burst of light illuminating the whole misty night, accompanied by a shocking wave of sound. I was aware of Lori licking her lips and swallowing hard. She looked back down into the radar.

"You're right on course," she said. "Steady as you go. A quarter of a mile. Better slow her down." Then she straightened up and drew a long breath. "It's gone. Something was still there for a few seconds after the blast, but now I'm getting no returns at all."

I guess we both had similar mental images of the explosion-shattered hull lying awash briefly before taking the last long dive to the bottom of the Atlantic.

"Take the wheel again, will you?" I said. "I'll get out on the bowsprit with the boat hook and see what I can fish up."

Even at idling speed, the bowsprit was a lively place to be. I clung to the head stay with one hand and held the boat hook in the other, feeling a little like Gregory Peck about to sink his harpoon into the great white whale called Moby Dick. We started to pass scraps of stuff in the water.

I signaled to Lori to cut the power and try the spotlight. The beam picked up more junk ahead as momentum took us forward with the motor out of gear. The sport boat's interior had been dressed up with gorgeous yellow-gold upholstery, velvet or something similar, judging by a couple of floating settee cushions, scorched and soggy now.

Then I saw the unmistakable orange of a life vest. I pointed, and Lori steered us that way, kicked us forward a bit to reach the floating man—who was wearing a white shirt under the gaudy flotation vest—and backed us to a standstill when I gave her the signal. From my uncertain bowsprit perch, I poked and stabbed with the long boat hook and finally managed to snag a life-belt strap, but when I lifted—actually, *Lorelei III* did the lifting, throwing her bow high as she rose to a wave—I saw that this one was not a keeper. His head rolled around with utter limpness; he'd apparently broken his neck when he was blown out of the cockpit. The bounce from the spotlight shining past me gave me enough illumination to see his face, and I knew him. At least I'd seen his picture recently, and read his dossier: Jerome Blum, DAMAG008, specialty explosives.

"There's another one over to port, hanging onto a cushion or something!" Lori had stepped out of the deckhouse to call to me. "What about this one?"

"Dead," I shouted. I freed the boat hook and let a wave sweep DAMAG008 away. Young Mr. Caselius's weirdo organization was losing manpower fast; I hoped he'd find it annoying. "No sense bringing him aboard. Let's go see his pal."

"Matt, be careful. Just because they've got all wet doesn't mean they've turned into nice people."

But the man clinging to a soggy yellow-gold cockpit cushion was no immediate threat; he had only one working arm, and he was badly battered and burned.

"Get down on the swim ladder, aft." That was Lori, behind me. "I'll back us up to where you can grab him."

"Watch that propeller, we don't want to chop his legs off," I said.

She grinned at me, her teeth flashing whitely in her small tanned face. "You do the shooting, Buster. Let me do the sailing, huh?"

A weak voice called plaintively: "Hey, come back, don't leave me here!"

That was the man in the water; we were being blown away from him. Then Lori, back at the wheel, put the spotlight on him and started maneuvering to bring the boat around, following him with the light. It was wet work in those seas, and once I got the ladder on the stern flipped down and myself onto it I was being totally doused every few seconds as waves smashed against the flat surface of the transom; but suddenly he was there off the quarter only some fifteen yards away.

Lori had moved to the outside helm and brought along the biggest flashlight on board since there was no topside control for the spot and it couldn't be trained under the stern, anyway. She backed us skillfully up to the floating man. I spit out half a wave that had just drenched me, reached far out, grabbed the collar of his knit sport shirt, and tested it. It felt reasonably substantial.

"Got him!" I shouted.

The deck lights came on; then Lori was at the stern rail, looking down at us. She called: "He's in no shape to climb that ladder, and I know we can't lift him aboard. Hang on while I rig the sling so we can hoist him." Her face vanished.

"That Staff character, fucking gun-shy bastard calling himself a helmsman!" That was the man I was holding. I had to lean over to hear him over all the splashing. "Fucking Staff crapped his pants when the spot blew out, wouldn't take us close enough… Fucking dashboard exploded in his face. Jeez, must have been some bullet, served the motherfucker right, scared to bring us in close so that big-shot bang-bang genius we'd hired could throw his fucking eggs right."

"Here it comes, Matt." Lori was back at the stern rail with something yellow that looked a bit like a horse collar; a rescue device that had been on the boat when I bought it. "Loop it around him, and I'll crank him up with the mizzen halyard winch. You just kind of guide him… Yell when you're ready."

It took me a minute or two to get the sling into place. "Ready!"

I'd never realized that lifesaving was such hard work; I could see what Lori had meant when she said we couldn't have lifted him aboard by hand. Now she strained at the handle of the powerful winch and I tried to help from the ladder, keeping our awkward cargo from snagging as it rose from the water, and boosting it upward as well as I could. All the time I was uneasily aware that, as Lori had pointed out, this guy was not a friend of ours. He'd tried his best to kill us, he and his gun-shy boatman and his hired blow-em-up artist, and I hadn't had a chance to search him, so there was a distinct possibility that he'd be equipped to try again once we got him aboard.

The trouble with performing a rescue off the stern of *Lorelei III* was that the raised aft deck made it a long haul; not only that, but there was no boarding gate in the stern rail. Our burden had to be hoisted four or five feet from the water just to reach deck level, and then an extra thirty inches to clear the rail, before he could be swung inboard. I got myself aboard when he neared the top. Lori cranked like hell, and I pulled and hauled and kind of rolled him over the rail toward me, and suddenly he was swinging free at the end of the wire halyard, above the teak deck.

"Okay, lower away," I called.

Lori eased him down. I caught him, and spread him out neatly on the well-lighted aft deck, and took the opportunity to run my hands over him. No weapons; but something made me go over him again. Lori came to look down at us, ducking as spray sluiced across the boat.

She said, "Well, I'd better get us back on course before she rolls the sticks out of her… What's the matter?"

I said crudely, "Shit, this son of a bitch is dead."

"But he can't be! I heard him… CPR?"

I said, "He wasn't in the water long enough to need

resuscitation. That's not his problem; the explosion seems to've driven a big splinter of plywood into his groin like a dagger. He just bled to death while we were hauling him aboard."

We were silent for a moment while the wind howled around us and spray drove past us. Maybe Lori was expressing respect for the dead; I was just thinking selfishly that it had been a hell of a lot of hard work wasted. I drew a long breath.

"Okay, you put the show back on the road," I said. "You might as well take it in the deckhouse where it's dry. I've got to see if he's got any ID on him before I dump him."

"Matt, shouldn't we...?" Lori checked herself. It was obvious that she would have preferred to bring the body ashore for a decent burial. I didn't speak, letting her work out for herself the endless complications that would follow. She said quickly, "Forget it. But I'd better stay at this wheel until you're finished. If I'm at the forward station, you could be washed overboard and I'd never know it."

Kneeling beside the dead man, I felt *Lorelei III* begin to move, returning to course and resuming her southwesterly progress, but at reduced speed. The floodlight on the mizzen mast, shining down, showed me a dark aquiline face; it was not one of those I'd studied in Mac's office. The driver's license was made out to Joseph Abdul Arram, of New York City, born thirty-four years ago, height five-eight, weight one seventy-five. He felt heavier than that when I levered him over the stern rail and let him splash into the sea. Then I had to climb down the stern ladder far enough to swing the lower section back up into its stored position. Lori helped me over the rail.

"Everything is under control, skipper," she shouted. "If you're through here, let's get in out of the weather."

Lorelei III was working slowly to windward under power. Even at this reduced speed she was taking a lot of spray; and Mr. Aram's blood was washing away fast. A wave exploded forward and doused us as we made our way to the deckhouse.

I closed the sliding door behind us. Lori went to the wheel and checked the compass, loran, and radar, set the autopilot, killed the glaring deck lights, and turned on the running lights. After the uproar outside, the deckhouse seemed very quiet and peaceful. I reached up to switch on one of the cabin lights overhead. Lori turned at the wheel, squeezing her wet hair back with both hands, although there wasn't much of it to squeeze. Her drenched T-shirt and shorts were plastered to her small body, and a dark wet area was forming on the carpet around her bare feet. Suddenly, she was hugging herself and shivering uncontrollably.

"C-cold," she said. "S-should have p-put on oilskins. Somehow n-never think of it, s-s-steering from in here where it's so nice and dry… Oh, Jesus! D-don't look at me. Some k-k-kind of idiot reaction…"

She turned away, hunched over the steering wheel, her shoulders shaking. I hesitated, but I'd kept my hands to myself long enough; I went over and turned her around, and she threw her arms around me and clung to me desperately.

She gasped, "S-scared, I was so d-d-damned scared..."

"Who wasn't? Join the Cowards' Club, Miss Fancher."

"You didn't look very scared, damn you!" she said angrily.

I said, "I've had a lot of practice at putting on my hero act."

"Well, you sure fooled me!"

"And you fooled me," I said. "I was afraid I had some kind of a kooky superwoman on board. It's nice to know we're both perfectly normal."

She giggled and, after a moment, looked up at me, her lips slightly parted in her sea-wet face. The invitation was obvious and could not be refused, not that I had any desire to refuse it. It was quite a satisfactory kiss, as kisses go. I was glad to discover that she knew where the noses went; she wasn't quite as young and inexperienced as she sometimes looked.

After an interesting exploratory interval, she said, a little breathlessly, "Well, it t-took you long enough to g-get around to that!"

"You wanted to be unpromiscuous, remember?"

She laughed. "You shouldn't believe everything a g-girl t-t-tells you." She hesitated, and went on. "There's nothing on the radar, and we're not moving very fast; the boat can take care of herself for a little while. Let's g-get us the hell out of these wet c-clothes and into a dry b-b-bed."

There was some stiffness in her attitude. Clearly she wasn't used to offering herself to strange men, and wasn't certain she was doing it right or, in spite of the kiss, that I even wanted her; but after dealing with death there's almost always the impulse to reaffirm life in the most direct way possible. However, I'd come to like and respect this girl, and I hesitated to take advantage of her impulses in this, to her, unfamiliar situation.

I said, "Just for the record, I'm pretty old for you, and I'm kind of a mean guy."

She laughed again, relaxed now, knowing that she hadn't misread me or approached me wrong. "I love old, mean guys. Come on, I'm freezing, Matt. I'll catch pneumonia if you make me stand here dripping while you struggle with your lousy c-c-conscience. You know it's g-going to lose, anyway."

It did. It's really not much of a conscience.

9

We raised the misty lights of the New Jersey coast just before dawn. Instinctively, I checked the depth-sounder—when you suddenly see indications of land ahead, you want to reassure yourself that it isn't sneaking up on you from below, also. But we were still a good many miles offshore, and the instrument, betraying its origin, showed a depth of some fifty European meters, which agreed with the charted soundings, at our loran position, of around twenty-five nautical fathoms, which my conventional brain managed to translate to about a hundred and fifty good, old-fashioned U.S. feet. The standardization of seagoing units of measurement leaves something to be desired. Anyway, with a two-meter, or one-fathom, or six-foot draft—take your pick—we weren't in any immediate danger of running aground.

I leaned over to call into the cabin, "Land ho!"

Lori came up, wiping her hands on a rag. She was wearing ratty blue jeans that had recorded on them a long history of boat painting and repairs. For a change, the pants were neither too large nor too small, but she had on a white shirt she must have inherited from King Kong, that had also received its share of indelible boat-yard stains. She looked at the dim chain of lights off the starboard bow. It wasn't brightening very fast since, on our southwesterly course, we were closing with the land only gradually. She checked the loran, and the chart, and nodded.

"We're a little behind our original schedule, but we should make it to Cape May with plenty of daylight to spare," she said.

Under normal circumstances I might have made some kind of a crude joke about the breathless sexual activities that had contributed to the delay; but she was a very serious little girl this morning, and instinct warned me that it was not something she cared to be kidded about.

"How are you coming with the repairs?" I asked instead.

Her conscience hadn't let her spend too much time in my arms afterward; she'd felt compelled to get up to the bridge to make sure we weren't ramming anything and nothing was ramming us. When we were dressed again, in dry clothes, we'd checked the boat out thoroughly before bringing her back up to cruising speed. We'd found four bullet holes in the hull, plus an insignificant groove in the mizzenmast; not many hits considering the number of shots that had been fired at us. None of the bullets had hit any tanks, machinery, or instruments. Lori had taken over as damage control officer while I functioned, temporarily, as helmsman and navigator.

Now she reported: "I've patched all the interior holes that showed. As soon as we have a little more light, I'll mix up a batch of gelcoat and fill the outside ones. I don't think we need to inflate and launch the dinghy; I can work hanging over the side, if you'll hold my ankles."

I said, "I'll be more than happy to hold your pretty ankles, ma'am. Call on me anytime."

It wasn't the right thing to say, or perhaps it wasn't the right way to say it.

Lori hesitated, and spoke without looking at me: "Matt."

"Yes, Lori?"

"It wasn't me," she said.

"What wasn't you?"

She turned to face me, and licked her lips. "That girl last night. She wasn't me. That's not grammatical, but you know what I mean. The cold-blooded bitch who calmly helped to kill three men without a qualm wasn't me. The crazy nympho girl thrashing around in that big bunk with you wasn't me, either. Or I, if you want to be picky." She drew a long, ragged breath. "I… I don't know where that weird creature came from, Matt. I… I've never acted like that before, never! I don't know what happened to me. I'm not like that, I'm not!"

She stared at me blindly for a moment; then she turned and ran down the brief steps out of sight. A few moments later I heard her banging at something forward that probably didn't need banging, at least not that hard.

As I've said, they're brought up to believe the myth

that they're nonviolent people living in a nonviolent world. It shocks them terribly to discover, when they grow up, that the world isn't at all the peaceful place they were told; but what really throws them is the discovery—made by some of them, at least, the ones with survival value—that they aren't the peaceful people they were told, either. The old self-preservation genes are still right in there pitching, and the adrenaline still flows when the glands are properly stimulated, and certain other juices also get secreted with fairly predictable results. But these aren't at all the calm and safe and civilized lives they were promised in the beautiful, nonviolent dreamworld they were led to expect, and the whole business upsets them dreadfully…

Daylight wiped out the coastal lights and didn't give me a visible shoreline to take their place for a couple of hours; then little strips of gray appeared along the western horizon. Lori came up with some two-part goop she mixed up and colored to the right shade of off-white to match the hull. We slowed the boat way down while she hung over the port gunwale to fill in the bullet holes, and I held her legs to keep her from falling overboard.

"I'll sand down the patches when they've had a chance to harden," she said, after I'd hauled her back up to the deck. There was more girl there than you'd think, looking at her; but I already knew that. She went on: "Now I'd better make some breakfast or the skipper will court-martial me."

She was trying for the light touch; but our relationship

wasn't what it had been. After breakfast, she took the helm—well, she took over supervision of Nicky, who had the helm—while I washed the dishes and cleaned up the galley and went aft to shave.

"You'd better get up here," Lori called as I was finishing my face. "We've got company."

I dried myself and grabbed my shirt and stepped up into the deckhouse, pulling it on.

"Where?" I asked.

"Starboard quarter." She pointed. "It's the Kokaine Kops. Better put the artillery out of sight unless you want to answer a lot of silly questions." She shook her head uneasily. "I wish I'd had a chance to sand down those patches, but if they board from starboard maybe they won't notice."

I took the shotgun and rifle below, cased them, and set them in a locker where, if discovered, they'd look innocently stowed, I hoped, and not guiltily hidden. Back in the deckhouse, I watched the white Coast Guard boat bearing down on us, without pleasure. I remembered that, when I was a kid, the local sheriff and his deputies were our friends, and we were always glad to see them because we knew they were nice guys who were there to protect and serve us. Nowadays, it seems that law-enforcement is concerned mainly with snooping after so-called illicit substances. The snoopers are always very self-righteous but not always very nice; and protection and service are well down their list of imperatives.

This is, of course, most true and most obvious with the

U.S. Coast Guard, which used to be a fine rescue service beloved by everyone on the water. Now all the reports I'd read and heard indicated that it has turned into an arrogant, drug-sniffing, seagoing Gestapo with constitutional powers land-bound cops only dream of, which it doesn't hesitate to flaunt. I'd been hoping I'd have no occasion to check those reports first-hand because I didn't think I'd enjoy the experience.

It looked like a moderately large, rather squatty sport fisherman; but it had the standard slanting red stripe, and after using the bullhorn to order us to heave to, it disgorged a boarding crew that came charging up to us in an outboard-powered inflatable… I can't tell you much more about it; I had to put my mind into a holding pattern at that point. The trouble with my racket is that we often do get pushed around by dictatorial characters with uniforms and guns, and we learn to act properly humble, but that's the enemy met in the line of duty. It's hard to maintain the same meek and respectful behavior when the people who are brandishing weapons on my boat, and making a mess of her below looking for some dumb crap I've never used in my life, are supposedly on my side, ha ha…

"Well, they're gone," Lori said at last. "Here. Have a nice martini."

"What?"

I drew a long breath and saw her standing there. I'd been watching the striped white boat, now pulling away fast, estimating how far I would have had to lead it if I'd had a pretty little cannon, a three-incher would do just fine, with which to blow it out of the water. Of course, with a proper ship-to-ship missile, lead is not involved; the whizbang just homes in on the designated target, *kaboom*... Hell, a man can dream, can't he?

"Thanks," I said to Lori, taking the glass she offered.

"It's a little early in the morning, but you looked as if you needed it." She hesitated. When she spoke again, there was an odd note to her voice. "You did real good, skipper. You didn't kill a single one of them."

"How much of a shambles did they leave below?" My voice sounded strange and distant.

"Never mind that, I'll take care of it." After a moment, she went on in a carefully expressionless voice. "That's what you were thinking, wasn't it? I could see it in your face."

I said, "What was I thinking?"

"You were thinking how you would kill them."

I said, "Hell, no. Killing them was nothing; that kid next to me was practically making me a present of his weapon, and it was loaded. Grab it, chamber a round, and if I timed it right when they were bunched, I could have had them all down in a few seconds, the ones over here. The problem was the mother ship. Ramming it, *Lorelei* would have had to hit it just right, aft of the cabin, where she'd ride right up over the cockpit, to roll it under and swamp it. I figured the collision would probably wipe out our bobstay and maybe our whole bowsprit, but the inner forestay would keep the rig from going over the side. That part of it was okay, the big question was, would she accelerate fast enough to get over there before they woke up and threw those big motors in gear… What's the matter?"

She licked her lips. "Matt, you're talking about the United States Coast Guard!"

I said, "Sweetie, I'm a pro. To me one bunch of clowns with guns in their hands is the same as another bunch of clowns with guns in their hands, I don't care what kind of monkey suits they're wearing or whose government they're supposed to be working for. To me, they're all just problems in extermination. If they don't want to be, they can leave the guns home."

Lori licked her lips. "That… that's a terrible way to live!"

I said, "It's the only way, baby. The alternative is dying, which is undesirable."

"No," she said. "No, it's just your only way."

I said irritably, "Well, if it wasn't my way, and if I hadn't been ready last night, if I hadn't figured out in advance how I was going to kill anybody who came at us out there with hostile intentions, we'd both be dead now, right? And this morning, how did I know… Hell, anybody can paint a silly pink stripe on a boat and put on an idiot sailor suit. Anyway, even genuine government agencies get funny orders sometimes."

"That's absolutely paranoid!"

I said, "Now you've got it. In my business, only the paranoid survive."

She started to speak again, presumably to continue

the argument, if that was what it was; but she checked herself. After a moment, she just said, "You'd better get us under way again, hadn't you?"

The low shore came gradually closer as *Lorelei III* plugged along at a steady eight knots. We saw large numbers of tall buildings over there, one collection of which, according to the chart, was Atlantic City. The binoculars showed, in addition to the high-rise stuff, an amusement park complete with roller coaster and Ferris wheel. A little after three o'clock in the afternoon we spotted the sea buoy off the Cape May entrance far ahead; an hour and a half later we were inside and docked in the South Jersey Marina. After the lines had all been secured to Lori's satisfaction, and fenders placed at all possible points of contact, we made ourselves drinks to celebrate our heroic ocean crossing.

Sitting beside me on the corner settee, Lori spoke abruptly: "You shouldn't have any trouble with Delaware Bay, Matt; but the Cohansey River about halfway up is a place you can duck into if you have to. At least you can anchor behind the little island at the mouth, but I think you can get six feet through the entrance at any reasonable tide, and there's plenty of water inside. Then you have the Chesapeake and Delaware Canal; you'll stop halfway at Schaefer's Canal House. Watch the currents there; they can be fierce, either way."

I said, "Watch the currents, yes, ma'am."

She sipped her drink—another vodka and tonic, I noticed—and went on without looking at me. "On

Chesapeake Bay you may have trouble with the loran. Don't panic, it isn't the set going bad; it's just the big navy transmitter in Annapolis blasting away and scrambling everybody else's electronics. South of Norfolk the water can get pretty thin in spots. But even if you do bottom out occasionally along the waterway, and most people do, if you handle this boat right, you shouldn't have any trouble getting off. The natural instinct, when you feel the keel hit, is to stop and throw her into reverse and try to back out of there. Wrong! You've got eighty horsepower and a three-bladed propeller almost two feet across; so throw the rudder hard over toward deep water and slam the throttle all the way forward. Use everything she's got. It's generally soft mud, and with all that power driving that great big prop you can probably blast on through if you don't let her lose momentum..."

"Lori," I said.

"Another thing," she said. "Crossing those big North Carolina sounds, don't hug the channel markers too closely. The channel isn't really there, it's well off to the side, usually several boatlengths, you have to kind of feel for it with the depth-sounder. Remember, it's a dredged channel and those big dredges aren't going to work right up to the marker posts, they're going to give themselves plenty of room..."

"Lori," I said.

She looked at me for a long moment. Her eyes were strange and bright—with unshed tears, I thought, but I could have been mistaken.

She said, "I only promised to navigate you as far as Cape May, Matt; and we're here. Let's just leave it at that. As soon as I finish my drink and change my clothes, I'll haul my seabag ashore and call Mrs. Bell; she said she'd get transportation to me if I decided I wanted to leave the boat here."

10

The woman said, "I'm Mrs. Bell. May I come aboard?"

I'd been nursing a drink down in *Lorelei III*'s main saloon; and shame on you if you call it a salon. (The only place you find salons afloat is on cruise liners—beauty salons.) I'd been telling myself it was great to have my boat all to myself once more. No more oddball dames cluttering up the ship, terrific. Right?

Then somebody rapped on the hull, and I palmed my .38 as I stepped up into the deckhouse to investigate. When I saw an unarmed and very respectable-looking female figure standing on the dock—any woman wearing nylons and high heels in a marina, where the boating ladies all run around bare-legged in tattered Topsiders, can't help but look respectable as hell—I returned the weapon to its inside-the-waistband holster, dropped my shirt over it, and went out on deck for a better look.

I can't say that my first view of Mrs. Teresa Bell surprised me, since I'd made no attempt to visualize the individual to whom I'd spoken on the phone. Trying to picture people from their telephone voices is a waste of time and imagination. What I saw now was a sturdy woman of medium height who could have been any age from a mature thirty to a well-preserved fifty. She had thick and rather coarse black hair carefully sculptured about her head. There was a single streak of gray that she apparently emphasized for drama instead of concealing it for youth. She endured my inspection without showing any signs of impatience, perhaps because she was using the interval to take stock of me, too.

"Permission granted," I said at last, in answer to her request.

She said, "I'll need a ladder. I'm not dressed for acrobatics."

"Just a minute."

I stepped up on deck and got the ladder off the deckhouse, where it had been secured, alongside the folded rubber dinghy, for our offshore jaunt; and hung it over the side at the boarding gate. Mrs. Bell was wearing a black suit with a rather short, narrow skirt. The jacket was also short and snug; it buttoned high enough, with small, round, cloth-covered buttons, that no hint of a blouse showed, assuming that one existed. There was some decorative black piping down the front. The nylons were black, as were the dressy pumps. The legs and ankles were very good for a bureaucratic lady who was no sylph; the-feet were quite small. I seemed to be noticing female feet recently, I reflected; maybe I was developing a foot fetish.

I said nothing about the spike-heeled pumps; I wanted to find out if she knew enough about nautical protocol to spare my teak decks without being asked. She did, pausing at the ladder to slip the shoes off. She passed them up to me, with her purse. Then she worked her tight skirt upward to give herself legroom, quite unself-consciously, and swung herself up the ladder in an effortless manner, indicating that her gray hairs were either artificial or premature, no evidence of senility. She spent a moment adjusting her clothes and patting her hair into place.

I gestured toward the open door facing her, and she stepped down into the deckhouse. I followed her, slid the door closed behind me, and returned her shoes and purse.

"Mr. Helm…"

"Just a minute," I said. "I think a little privacy is indicated. Sit down and make yourself comfortable. You can be deciding what you want to drink."

I closed the other door, pulled the side and rear curtains over the deckhouse windows, and went through some gymnastics to reach over the chart table and snap into place the cloths that covered the windshield, noting as I did so that the sun was almost down. The last sunset I'd seen—or would have seen if the dismal weather at the time hadn't obscured it—had occurred a few hours before Lori and I were attacked at sea. It seemed a long time ago. I switched on the overhead lights and turned to my guest.

"Well, what about that drink?" Then I thought of something. "Maybe I'm out of line. I remember now, you're the Arabia lady; and Muslims aren't supposed to indulge in alcohol, right?"

She said, "Bourbon, with a couple of ice cubes if they're available, please."

So much for the ethnic niceties. I was interested to learn that she knew enough about small cruising boats to know that ice couldn't be taken for granted; but of course *Lorelei III* was a very high-class yacht, complete with refrigeration. After accomplishing my hostly duty, I sat down on the section of the corner settee she wasn't occupying, and raised my glass to her.

"It's a pleasure to meet you, Mrs. Bell. I was starting to wonder if I've been talking to a computerized telephone voice."

She said, "You create difficulties for us, Mr. Helm; you really do."

I studied her across the corner of the little table. I saw a dark-skinned businesswoman whose expensive clothes made the best of her stocky figure. Her features were bold, with full lips and a rather large, arched nose that gave her a hawklike appearance. Her eyes were brown, large and lustrous and intelligent.

I said, "Tell me about your difficulties, Mrs. Bell."

She tasted her bourbon cautiously, nodded approval, and took a less careful sip. "You're hard on your crews. One girl commits suicide, and another runs away from your boat in tears." When I didn't respond to that, she went on. "What did you do to the child out there, anyway?"

I said, "She discovered out there that she's a very brave

and sexy little girl; and she hates it."

Mrs. Bell frowned. "Is that supposed to make sense?"

"Do little girls ever make sense? Or big ones, either?"

"I'm afraid you're a male chauvinist, Mr. Helm," the woman said. I gathered that she didn't entirely disapprove of male chauvinists. She went on, "Miss Fancher said you were stopped by the U.S. Coast Guard. Why?" My reaction brought another frown. "Why do you laugh?"

"You keep asking these unanswerable questions. Why don't little girls make sense? Why does the Coast Guard stop people? Hell, they stop people because they've got the power to stop people at will—unlike the poor shore-bound cops who have to show cause and get warrants—and it makes them feel big to throw their weight around. I have a new policy where the U.S. Coast Guard is concerned, ma'am. I call it zero tolerance."

Mrs. Bell looked at me sharply and said, "The girl said you displayed some hostility toward the boarding party; it was one of the things that seemed to disturb her. But you will not get involved in a feud with another government agency while you are working for me. I forbid it!"

I looked at her for a moment and sighed. "Finish your drink, ma'am," I said, "and get the hell off my boat."

"What?"

I rose and slid open the deckhouse door. "Good-bye, Mrs. Bell."

She was on her feet, also. There was something fierce and regal in her face as she confronted me, and her angry brown eyes were quite beautiful; she was a dark Eastern princess about to snap her fingers to summon the eunuch executioner with the big beheading sword. Then she laughed and, surprisingly, patted my cheek.

"Down, Rover," she said. "I suppose 'forbid' was the unacceptable word. I apologize. Is that satisfactory?"

I drew a long breath. It was nice, for a change, to meet a lady who knew her way around our world. I nodded.

She said, "I don't envy the man you work for, running a kennel of half-tamed wolves like you. Of course, that is what it takes, but doesn't one ever go for his throat?" When I didn't speak, she went on. "Well, shall we sit down and get back to business?"

"I'll freshen the drinks," I said, sliding the door shut.

I felt a little foolish, as if I'd overreacted, but they often try it, and if you don't stop it at once you're stuck with it for the duration. "Forbid," for God's sake! I poured her another stiff shot of bourbon; she'd drained her glass before handing it to me. Returning, I put the drinks on the table and resumed my place on the settee.

I asked, "Did you check to see if there had been any reports of an explosion at sea at the latitude and longitude I told you over the phone?" I'd given her a quick report when I called the contact number immediately after Lori had left the boat.

She nodded. "A commercial fishing vessel had seen and heard it, distantly, and turned to investigate. They picked up a life ring—actually, I believe, one of those horseshoe-shaped buoys—and a dead body in a life jacket. There was a boat's name on the ring or whatever you call it. *Hot Mama.* We're having it traced, but the boat was probably stolen so I don't expect its registration to tell us much." She glanced at me. "There was no report of another vessel seen in the area, if that's what interests you. Or of gunfire. We are also trying to trace the man. There was no identification on him."

Well, that figured. The other dead man had packed a wallet, but he'd been an amateurish terrorist type. The hired blow-up man from DAMAG, smart enough to get himself into a life jacket when things started going wrong, had also been smart and professional enough to leave his IDs on shore. I hesitated. The files I'd been shown by Mac had been given a pretty high security rating, but I have a perverse reaction to security; those bastards will make you shit your pants to prove that you have a need to know where the john is. Anyway, the woman beside me undoubtedly had plenty of clearance, and I saw no reason to let her waste a lot of time and manpower finding out something we already knew.

I said, "His name was Jerome Blum, also known as Boomer, and he was the egg man."

"Egg man?"

"He was the guy who was supposed to lay the eggs… throw the grenades. Actually, he was a quite a high-powered big-bang expert from DAMAG… You know about DAMAG?"

"Of course. They are the specialists who have been hired by this terrorist organization because it is mainly composed of uneducated fanatics incapable of dealing with technical matters, or even performing routine assassinations beyond what can be accomplished by hosing down a neighborhood with automatic-weapon fire."

I nodded. "Well, when they needed somebody handy with grenades, I guess Blum seemed like the logical man for them to use, even though they'd presumably hired him for more serious explosive work."

"How do you know this, Mr. Helm?"

I said, "Golly gee, ma'am, I thought I just heard you ask a foolish question, but I must have been mistaken. You don't look like a foolish lady."

She laughed. "Very well. Jerome Blum, aka Boomer. I'll pass it along. Thank you."

I said, "There was another floater. His wallet is on the window ledge behind your head. A guy named Joseph Abdul Arram. A third man on board the speedboat presumably went down with it; at least we saw no sign of him afterward. Arram, dying, referred to him as Staff."

"That would be Mustapha Kiral." She was studying the contents of the still-damp wallet. "These two we know. They have worked together before. Very dedicated, very dangerous, but like most of them, uneducated and not very intelligent. A man named Roger Hassim supplies the education and intelligence for the gang."

I frowned. "Hassim? Mrs. Fancher's boyfriend?"

"Oh, Miss Fancher told you about the family troubles?"

"That her stepmother had a lover, yes. Not that she was working with terrorists."

Mrs. Bell spoke severely: "You must not say that, Mr.

Helm. Mrs. Fancher is a wealthy woman with a high social position. Lovely young wives of elderly rich men are often foolish about handsome young men; and you should see this one, he is really spectacular. Of course Mrs. Fancher is being terribly deceived and has no idea whatever that her beautiful paramour is involved in wicked plots against the United States of America, Heavens no! You are risking an action for slander if you suggest such a thing." Mrs. Bell smiled crookedly. "I'm going to get the goods on that sultry bitch, Mr. Helm; but I have to be very careful how I go about it. My position isn't strong enough to allow me to tackle all that money head-on."

I said, "Well, anyway, I'm sorry I couldn't save you a live one out there, but I didn't figure I'd be doing you any favor if I hauled the remains ashore and made you bury them."

"You were correct," Mrs. Bell said. "However, it was another thing that distressed the little girl, your callous manner of dealing with the dead." The woman glanced at me. "Of course she's in love with you; and she desperately doesn't want to be, considering what a wicked person you are." She gave me a chance to comment on that; when I didn't, she said, "The question is, who can we get to help you now?"

I said, "How about you helping me a little, Mrs. Bell?"

She looked startled and gestured toward her smart city costume. "My dear man, I'm hardly dressed for boating, and while I have done a considerable amount of sailing, my schedule is much too full…"

I laughed. "I didn't mean help me on the boat, although you're welcome any time."

She wasn't amused. "Then what kind of help did you mean, Mr. Helm?"

"Information-type help," I said. "For one thing: do you have Truman Fancher's logbook? Or do you know who does? People keep asking about it."

She asked sharply, "What people?"

"The girl who called herself Siegelinda Kronquist, for one. Greta Larsson. Just a casual question. Very casual. And Lori Fancher had all her daddy's other logs and wondered if I'd found the last one; she hated to leave the collection incomplete, for sentimental reasons."

Mrs. Bell said, "No, we do not have that book. We would very much like to see it. If you find it..."

"Just what would I be looking for? A dime notebook or something the size of a telephone directory?"

"Fancher bought fairly expensive hardcover notebooks to record his experiences with his various boats," Mrs. Bell said. "His daughter showed me some of them. About eight inches by ten inches, and three quarters of an inch thick, trimmed with red leather or something similar."

I shook my head, "A pocket notebook I could just possibly have missed, tucked away somewhere. But I've done enough work on this boat that I don't think there's much chance of my having overlooked a bound eight-by-ten-inch volume. What do you think the book would tell you, besides where *Lorelei III* was on what date? Or is that what's important?"

She said, "You do not need that information, Mr. Helm."

I sighed. "Good old need-to-know! Okay. Next, have you been down in the engine room to examine the bilge of this boat? It's accessible—part of it, anyway—through a couple of hatches next to the engine box; actually, they're the ones you'd stand on while working on the engine."

Mrs. Bell said, "I haven't examined the area, but one of my people did, the woman operative going by the name of Guild, who was bludgeoned to death a few hours after she reported to me by phone. I'd asked her to search the boat for hiding places. She said that the least accessible space of any size on board was the one you just mentioned."

"Good for her," I said. "It's roughly twelve inches by twelve inches by four feet. There are, of course, all kinds of lockers in the various cabins under the seats and bunks, and some are even larger; but they're readily available to anybody who happens to be looking for a sail cover or a piece of twine. As your girl said, this is the most inaccessible storage space on board. Fancher apparently used it for storing extra engine oil, extra antifreeze, that kind of stuff. He presumably kept a little of everything in a more accessible place for day-to-day use. Recovering from a recent coronary, he wouldn't be likely to wrestle all those heavy hatches and go poking around in the bilge unnecessarily. Somebody could toss out his reserve supplies and use the storage space for something else, and there was a very good chance that the old man wouldn't discover the substitution."

Mrs. Bell frowned. "Something else? What something

else were you thinking of, Mr. Helm?"

I shrugged. "With Boomer Blum involved, the chances are good that we're dealing with something explosive. You could stuff quite a big bang into that space."

"Yes, that was our idea, too." She frowned. "Would there be any problem getting it in and out of the engine room?"

"None whatever," I said. "The boat is designed so you can replace the whole engine if necessary; just open the hatches and slide back the sunroof and hoist it right up through the deckhouse into the open air. If you haven't got a crane, you can use the main halyard and its winch."

"I see."

I glanced at her. "There's one more piece of information you can help me with, maybe, Mrs. Bell."

"Yes?"

"What's holding things up?"

"What do you mean?"

I said, "*Lorelei III* came up the ICW last spring. If something was hidden in her bilge, it was presumably taken off her then. Yet you people are still worrying about it some five months later, so apparently it hasn't been used yet, whatever it is. Who's waiting for what?" I looked at her face and sighed. "Okay, don't tell me. I don't need to know. Right?"

Mrs. Bell shook her head. "It's not that. We simply don't have the information. That is why we're so interested in Fancher's logbook; we hope that, if we can find it, it will give us an indication of where *Lorelei III* might have unloaded her secret cargo, which in turn will give us at least a hint of what target these fanatics have in mind… You're absolutely certain the book is not on board?"

"Absolutely is a big word," I said. "I'll just say that the chances of its being on board are very small, and if it is on board it was probably reduced to a soggy, illegible mess when the cabin was flooded. But I'm not handing out any absolutelies, no, ma'am."

"Fancher's daughter says that he often kept the book by his bunk in his cabin—the aft cabin—when the boat was not underway."

I said, "When I was drying things out, I had everything open that could be opened without a wrecking bar, including all the compartments in the aft cabin. If there's anything hidden back there, it's built into the woodwork or the fiberglass hull."

"Hassim and Dorothy Fancher seem to believe it's still on board, somewhere. That is presumably why they want the boat destroyed."

I said, "Which brings up the question: why didn't they sink it while they had it??"

Mrs. Bell said, "I think that's readily explained: Mrs. Fancher had a dead husband on her hands. I suppose she considered giving him a Viking funeral, burning his boat with his body on board, but if anything went wrong and arson was suspected she'd also probably find herself accused of his murder. It was too big a gamble, so she reported the death to the authorities like a good wife—widow—and sent the boat home with a delivery crew, planning to attend to it later."

I said, "Lori Fancher thinks she used a hired crew out of spite; but obviously she wouldn't want the kid spending a week or two on board, if there was something incriminating there. And then, before she could do anything about the boat up in Oyster Bay, you started sending your agents around. Maybe that's when she panicked and got hold of DAMAG and told them to deal with the situation, or got Hassim to hire them for her."

Mrs. Bell said, "Let's hope she and her terrorist lover are persistent and send yet another crew to do the job, DAMAG or Arab or whatever. But if you are to cope with them, I had better find somebody to help you sail this boat."

I said, "It plays better with a woman, but it will work with a man. You've got the guy who was playing husband to the dame who was blackjacked to death, don't you? I think he was calling himself Nathaniel Guild at the time."

Mrs. Bell shook her head. "He's really not much of a sailor; the woman had the nautical expertise on that team."

"What about the real Siegelinda Kronquist? Has she recovered from her ordeal yet?"

Mrs. Bell shook her head. "She is still not well enough for our purpose. She wouldn't do, anyway. I keep telling them in Washington that their screening methods are quite inadequate; Kronquist is a prime example. You can't rely on girls like that; they'll do anything, say anything, to save their pretty faces and avoid a little pain."

I said, "What I want is somebody to relieve me at the helm and help with the dock lines; she doesn't have to be a torture-proof heroine for that. She does know her way around a boat, doesn't she?"

"Oh, yes, she's a good sailor, but..."

"That's all I need. If she's ambulatory, send her along."

Mrs. Bell's eyes narrowed. "My dear man, don't you start trying to tell me what to do; I can be just as temperamental as any government assassin."

I grinned. "Okay, I apologize, very humbly. I'll rephrase my suggestion: Dear Mrs. Bell, will you please be so kind as to send me the girl, I need somebody and I think she'll do just fine. Pretty please?"

Mrs. Bell shook her head. "I really don't think she's suitable... Well, I'll give it some thought. I'll find you somebody. Is there anything else we should discuss?"

There wasn't, and I accompanied her to the ladder, handed down her shoes and purse, and watched her step into her pumps and walk away up the dock, a competent adult lady who had a lot going for her, if you liked competent adult ladies.

11

An evening study session with the charts told me that I had a fairly long run to my next planned stop on the Chesapeake and Delaware Canal, so I rose at five next morning and was under way by six. Leaving the marina, I turned *Lorelei III* into the brief Cape May Canal, that lets you cut across the southern tip of New Jersey from the Atlantic Ocean to Delaware Bay, saving you a long, tough sail down around the cape and its outlying shoals.

I found that, while I kind of missed the company, and the competence, of my former girl navigators, I rather enjoyed handling the boat by myself for a change, although the weather had me slightly worried. It was another gray fall day, and the NOAA weather report had promised scattered showers and southerly winds in the fifteen-to-twenty-knot bracket, the same stiff breeze we'd bucked for almost two hundred miles coming down from Montauk; but on the northwesterly run up Delaware Bay it should be favorable, for a change. However, sailing by myself, inexperienced as I was, I would have preferred a bright sunny day and a flat calm.

Emerging from the short canal, after first slowing down to let a ferry of some kind turn into its dock near the entrance—I guess it runs across the mouth of the big bay, between New Jersey's Cape May and Delaware's Cape Henlopen—I headed out across the coastal flats, in some twenty feet of water, on a course that converged with the deep big-ship channel off to the west and would join it fifteen miles up the bay. On this hazy day, it was like taking off across an ocean; the distant Delaware shore was not visible.

With a brisk wind on the quarter, it would have been a good time to hang out some sails. Either of my departed female nautical experts would undoubtedly have been right out there pulling the strings, but I was busy enough getting the loran zeroed in on the next significant buoy up by something called Miah Maull Shoal, and the autopilot settled on the proper course; I didn't need any flapping Dacron distractions. Besides, it had started to rain, and I was quite comfortable in the deckhouse and had no yearning whatever to get out into the weather and wrestle wet sails and haul on wet ropes—excuse me, lines. The big Ford diesel was doing just fine without wind assistance, thank you.

The seas picked up as we came out from the land, giving us a roller-coaster ride, and Nicky had to work hard to keep us headed in the right direction. An hour passed, the rain stopped, and I switched off the windshield wipers and relaxed a bit. It was beginning to look as if Delaware Bay wasn't going to hit us with anything we couldn't handle. I started thinking about setting a couple of sails after all, just to prove they didn't intimidate me...

"*Lorelei III, Lorelei III,* this is *Bartender:'*

It's pretty standard to cruise along with the VHF radio on, tuned to channel sixteen, the emergency and contact channel; and it's also pretty standard to ignore the constant gabble that comes out of the speaker—boatmen, not to mention boatwomen, seem to be lonely folks forever looking for somebody to talk to—until you hear your own boat's name spoken. As a matter of fact, it took me a minute or two to wake up to the fact that somebody was calling me.

"*Lorelei III* this is *Bartender.* Come in, *Lorelei III.*"

I looked around, puzzled. There were a couple of big ships in sight moving along the hazy horizon to the west, following the deep channel over there; but I could see no boat nearby that could be calling.

"Come in, *Lorelei III*!"

I pried the microphone out of its bracket above the chart table. "*Bartender*, this is *Lorelei III.*"

"Switch to seven-two."

Once you've made contact, you're supposed to get off sixteen and do your talking on one of the other channels. If you don't, the Coast Guard will break in and scold you for tying up the emergency and calling circuits.

I said, very nautical, "Seven-two, aye aye."

Channel sixteen comes on automatically when you turn

on the VHF, but it took me a minute or two to remember what buttons to push and knobs to twist to change the red sixteen glowing in the little window to seventy-two. By the time I had the proper channel tuned in, the other boat was already calling me on it, impatiently.

"Come in, *Lorelei III.*"

I picked up the mike I'd put down. "This is *Lorelei III.*"

"Cap'n, I have a crew member here missed you at the marina, you took off so early." Out on the water, everybody calls everybody "captain," particularly over the air. "She hired my boat to bring her out to you."

Apparently Mrs. Bell had found somebody to send me sooner than she'd expected—well, if I took the message at face value. I wondered if, assuming it was genuine, she'd decided to use the Ziggy Kronquist, after all.

"Where are you, *Bartender*?" I asked.

"Two-three miles astern of you. Got you in sight, I think, cap'n. White ketch with a pilothouse east of Brandywine Shoal?"

"Affirmative," I said.

"If you just come back on a reverse course slow and easy I'll bring the lady right out to you."

I hated to turn around and lose time and miles backtracking, but I didn't have a choice. If the still-unidentified female really was my crew of the day, or week, or month—I hoped she'd at least last a little longer than the previous two—I could use the help; and if she wasn't, if perhaps she didn't even exist and the whole thing was a trap, well, that was why I was out there, doing my stupid-sailor routine so traps could be sprung on me. Wasn't it?

I said, "Roger, captain. Come alongside to port when you get here, she can board a little easier from that side."

I sounded salty as hell, I thought, maybe a little too salty for the nautical stumblebum I was supposed to be. *Bartender* acknowledged the instructions and signed off—*Bartender*, for God's sake! I've given up trying to figure out how they pick their boat names. Of course the real reason I preferred to have him make his approach to port was that that was the side on which the gun brackets were located. I took over the helm from Nicky and sent us back toward Cape May. Heading more or less into the wind made things considerably rougher and wetter on board, even at reduced speed.

I set the autopilot again and went below to get out the two weapons I'd used the other night, bringing them up to the deckhouse. Before stowing away the rifle, earlier, I'd replaced the laser sight—that might have made the Coast Guard curious—with a standard 3x—9x9 variable telescopic sight that had raised no eyebrows. Now I set it to 3x, since you can't use much magnification shooting from an erratically moving boat. I loaded the rifle fully, checked the safety, and clipped the weapon into place. I loaded the magazine and chamber of the shotgun and snapped it into its clips beside the rifle, again with the safety on, not that I have implicit faith in safeties. A safety will do its job practically all of the time—but it's that "practically" that can kill you.

Having prepared the heavy artillery, I checked the smaller stuff I had hidden around the boat in various places the Coastie snoops had missed. After all, I'd had two months to work on the problem, and the places where you hide weapons aren't the kind of places they'd been looking for, the kind where you hide drugs—a space that can hide a folding knife, or even a .25 automatic, won't hold enough happy-dust to make anybody rich. Then I returned to the deckhouse, bracing myself against the boat's pitching. Nicky was having an easier time holding course since we were going to windward, but *Lorelei III* was making wet work of the short, steep Delaware Bay chop.

I started the windshield wipers again, but I couldn't spot an approaching boat through the glass, and of course there didn't have to be one. Somebody could be calling me from a distant helicopter, setting me up for a minisub small enough to operate submerged in these shallow seas; a homing minitorpedo could be heading my way any minute. But I wasn't really expecting such an elaborate sci-fi attack. So far, DAMAG had sent against me one pretty lady with a knife, and one souped-up sport boat with some grenades; young Caselius didn't seem to favor very far-out techniques, where homicide was concerned.

I uncased the ship's big binoculars—7 x 50s, if it matters—and stepped up into the port doorway to scan the bay ahead more carefully, and there it was: a husky outboard craft about twenty-five feet in length heading straight at me—well, as straight as the seas allowed. Actually, it would yaw widely on occasion as it surmounted one of the larger waves, letting me see that it was white with a blue stripe, and had no cabin, just a steering console in the center of the big cockpit. There were fishing rods in various holders, and two big motors on the stern. Having handled a boat somewhat like it once or twice in the past, I could appreciate the skilful job the helmsman was doing, surfing along with the steep chop; but he'd have a slow rough ride pounding back to Cape May against the wind after making his delivery.

Looking up from the binoculars, I realized that we had another squall approaching fast. For a few minutes, I thought *Bartender* would reach us first; but when the outboard was a hundred yards away it disappeared behind a gray curtain of rain. Moments later we were also in the soup, flying blind. I closed the deckhouse doors against the stuff blowing in and thought, as I had before on this mission, that this was a hell of a spot for an innocent boy from the Great American Desert. Lightning lit up the murk momentarily; the sound effects followed loudly.

Bartender appeared out of the pouring rain, dead ahead. I pulled *Lorelei III*'s throttle back to idling speed, just enough power to allow Nicky to hold the course. I stepped over to port and opened the deckhouse door and the boarding gate, as the outboard swung around and came alongside. It was wet out on deck. I stood ready to reach back down for the shotgun if necessary, but all that happened was that a very wet woman in white slacks and shirt picked up a dusty-pink suitcase in one hand and a ducky little matching dusty-pink cosmetics kit, or whatever, in the other, and moved to the rail.

A suitcase, for God's sake! Even I knew that nobody with any sailing experience brings a suitcase onto a boat, because there's never any place to stow the bulky thing—that's why duffel bags were invented. I wondered where the hell Mrs. Bell had found this female landlubber, and why she'd bothered to send her to me. Of course the dame didn't have to have come from Mrs. Bell. The phony Ziggy Kronquist hadn't.

After seeing the impractical luggage, I wasn't a bit surprised at the high-heeled white pumps. In spite of them, the woman managed the crossing in reasonably agile fashion, with some help from me, after passing her bags over first. She dove for the shelter of the deckhouse without thanking me for my assistance. *Bartender*'s skipper gave me a farewell salute and gunned his big outboard motors. I noticed that they were Yamahas, a hundred and fifty horsepower each, which sounds like a lot but is actually rather conservative by today's standards.

As I joined her in the deckhouse, the woman said, "My bags! They're getting all wet out there on the deck!"

I said, "So haul them inside and close the door. I've got to get this train back on track."

I stepped over to the steering console, flipped Nicky's switch to off, spun the wheel, and brought us back to the northwesterly course the loran said would bring us to the buoy up by Miah Maull Shoal. I reset the autopilot and turned to face my dripping new crew, if that was what she was. Even if she was, I had the distinct impression that, unlike her predecessor, this one wasn't really committed to feeding me well and keeping me happy.

She was a slender female in her late twenties or early thirties… Correction. The waist was slender, but what was above and below it wasn't. She was actually a rather voluptuous dame, looking more so in her drenched clothes. The trouble with taking the modern feminine styles to sea is that they may look fashionable dry, but they look totally ridiculous wet. A gal in snug wet jeans is just a gal in snug wet jeans; but a female in the voluminous shorts currently in vogue looks pretty silly with all that loose stuff plastered to her, as Lori had demonstrated; and a dame in a pair of the baggy pleated slacks that look terrifically smart in *Vogue* becomes a real clown after being doused with rain and sea-water.

My new shipmate was trying to pull the clinging bunches of sodden cloth away from her legs. Her wet shirt, clearly expensive, with some nice embroidery down the front, was coming out at the waist, and her hair was escaping from her natty little sailor cap—well, some dainty landlocked designer's idea of what a sailor cap should be.

She gave up the futile attempt to resuscitate the drowned crease of her pants and straightened up to look at me. A strand of wet dark hair trailed across her face, and after trying instinctively to brush it aside, she made a little sound of annoyance and yanked off the cap and shook it all loose. Having a handsome long-haired woman release her confined locks artistically is always good for a small sexual charge; they invariably make it look like a surrender of sorts. I saw that the hair was really long, and glossy, and black…

She's got a figure that won't quit… and black hair almost as long as Crystal Gayle's, Lori had said. So I knew what I had, although I still didn't know why I had it.

"Mrs. Dorothy Fancher, I presume," I said.

12

Lori Fancher's stepmother said, "I think we can postpone getting acquainted until I've put on some dry clothes." She picked up her two cases, large and small, and turned to go forward, to the cabin she'd occupied, according to Lori, when sailing with her husband.

I said, "Hold it a minute."

"Mr. Helm, I'm sopping wet. Just let me go downstairs and..."

I said, "I'm pretty damp, too, and it isn't killing me. I don't want you wandering around my boat until I've done a little checking. Just stand right there and drip on the carpet, if you please."

That brought a gasp from her. She drew herself up to protest, but aborted the angry words with an effort that was obviously painful. A lurch of the ship threw her off balance. She braced herself against the side of the deckhouse with the hand that held the cosmetics case. Steady once more—well, as steady as the antics of the boat allowed—she set down both bags and watched me tuning the VHF to a new channel. I picked up the mike.

"Marine operator," I said. "Marine operator, this is *Lorelei III,* Whiskey Alpha November 8855."

Like most boatmen, I'm sloppy about using the boat's call sign when talking to other boats, but I feel constrained to identify myself properly, at least on the first try, when calling the Coast Guard or the marine operator, just in case somebody out there is feeling official.

Waiting, I noted that the rain squall had passed. I switched off the windshield wipers. The big ships in the main channel—three in sight at the moment—were closer than they had been, but the loran computer said we still had thirty-seven minutes to go to Miah Maull Shoal at our present rate of progress. Backtracking to meet *Bartender* had cost us about an hour. However, we still had plenty of time to make Schaefer's Canal House in daylight, if there were no more delays.

The loudspeaker remained silent. I had the VHF tuned to the public correspondence channel listed for the area in the cruising guide I was using, but it was an older book, and those listings aren't always up to date, anyway. Well, I couldn't spend all day working my way through all the possibilities, but sometimes they monitor channel sixteen. I hit the button that put the set back into its original mode.

"Marine operator, marine operator, this is *Lorelei III.*"

Mrs. Fancher said, "I'm freezing to death. How long are you planning to make me stand here?"

I remembered another cold, wet female who'd come

into my arms in this deckhouse. Well, Lori seemed to have decided that she was better off away from me, smart girl. Any girl is better off away from any man in our line of work. I had no impulse to take the stepmother into my arms, which was odd, come to think of it. She was a good-looking woman with most of her feminine defenses washed away temporarily, but she didn't do a thing for me, at least at the moment.

I said, "I really doubt that hypothermia is imminent, ma'am."

She drew another sharp breath and started to speak hotly, but checked herself again, glaring at me. There was something familiar about her anger, reminding me of another dark-faced lady, not quite so voluptuous, who'd also considered sending me to the guillotine—well, the headman's block—without anesthetic. This one was younger and sexier, but the smooth dusky skin and the big dark eyes were the same, definitely originating somewhere south of the Mediterranean. Mac had said Mrs. Bell's maiden name had been Othman; I wondered what Dorothy Fancher's had been. I remembered Lori's words: *Where she belongs is in harem pants... popping grapes into the fat sheik's mouth.*

There was still no sound from the VHF. Either the operators were all on their morning coffee breaks, or they weren't interested in channel sixteen, or the nearest station was out of reach for my old set. I stuck the mike back into its bracket; to hell with it.

Mrs. Fancher asked, "Whom were you trying to call?"

"The lady I'm working for currently. I had two questions to ask her, the first being if she'd sent you."

Mrs. Fancher said, "You could have asked me. I would have told you she hadn't."

I said, "But if you'd told me she had, I'd have had no way of knowing you were lying."

"You're working for that government snooper, Theresa Bell, aren't you? Or should I call her a snoopess?" Dorothy Fancher laughed shortly. "Heavens, I wouldn't let her send me across the street for a hamburger! Nobody sends me anywhere, Mr. Helm."

I said, "How nice for you. I keep getting sent to all kinds of oddball places, like the middle of Delaware Bay. Where did you meet Mrs. Bell?"

"She was nosing around after my husband died… *Two* questions, Mr. Helm?"

I spoke deliberately, watching her: "My second question was more of a request. I wanted to ask Mrs. Bell to make sure, since you were on board, that there was a thorough autopsy if I should be found dead on this boat of an apparent heart attack, like the late husband you just mentioned."

Dorothy Fancher stood quite still for a moment, staring at me. Then she made a sharp hissing sound—strangely, it didn't put me in mind of a cat, but of a resident swan I'd once startled unintentionally in the Connecticut marina where I'd spent the last couple of months. It had responded with the same angry hiss, ready to go for me with its beak. Swans can be dangerous, lovely as they are; they've been known to kill children and dogs. The dark lady facing me didn't bear much physical resemblance to a swan, but her impulses were similar: she took a quick step forward and tried for me with her nails. I blocked her strike left-handed, and put a short, hard, right-hand punch just below her ribs. She doubled up and went back against the corner settee and sat down hard on the end of it, hugging herself.

"Thank you," I said. Breathless, she gave me a furious, strangled look. I said, "I was looking for an excuse to demonstrate that I'm not a gentleman. Thank you for being kind enough to give it to me."

She was still incapable of speech, which was probably just as well. I took a quick look around. Nicky was still doing his job. We didn't seem to be hitting anything, and nothing seemed to be hitting us. I stepped below just long enough to grab a large beach towel out of the locker in the aft head. When I returned, Mrs. Fancher was taking some short experimental breaths and rubbing her diaphragm area tenderly. I dropped the towel on the settee beside her.

"Get undressed," I said.

She glared at me and managed to croak a few words. "My dear man…!"

I said, "You wanted to get out of those wet clothes. So get out of them."

"If you think for one moment…!" Her voice was improving.

I said, "Mrs. Fancher, this is not a debating society. I didn't invite you on this boat; since you chose to come aboard, you'll play by my rules. Either you strip or I'll strip you. And if I have to knock you unconscious to do it, you'll be out like a light before you know it."

She said scornfully, speaking without effort now, "Well, you've certainly proved that you haven't any scruples about hitting a woman!"

I grinned. "You dames want it all your own way. You can kick us and slap us and claw our eyes out, but just let us deliver one good, clean punch to the solar plexus and we're unspeakable beasts. Well, what's it to be?"

I knew damned well what it was going to be. No woman with those eyes and that figure would ever be truly embarrassed about taking her clothes off in front of a man. In fact, she'd enjoy every minute of the performance—once she'd made the proper, modest, ladylike protests, of course.

Dorothy Fancher got to her feet deliberately, facing me. She made quite a pretty production of unbuttoning and peeling off her wet shirt. She wore something flimsy under it that didn't conceal the fact that her breasts were as impressive as those of the first lady who'd come aboard *Lorelei III* recently. I thought again about Lori, who was cute as a button but not particularly well endowed. Well, two out of three ain't bad. Mrs. Fancher had stepped out of her pumps. She didn't seem to be wearing any stockings. Her ecdysiac performance was somewhat handicapped by the motion of the boat, and by the fact that there's no really seductive way of climbing out of a pair of trousers—skirts can be disposed of much more sexily. But she got the job done with reasonable grace, and straightened up to face me in a one-piece silk-and-lace confection called, I believe, a teddy, don't ask me why. With her long black hair, she was something to see in the cabin of a boat going downwind in that steep Delaware Bay chop with the autopilot working hard and the big diesel shaking the sound-absorbing hatches under our feet.

I half expected her to ask to be allowed to stop there; but I didn't know my lady. I'd asked for it and I was going to get it, the full treatment. Extricating herself from a few ounces of lacy wet lingerie took her longer than shedding shirt and shoes and pants—and the sad part was that the beautiful routine was pretty well wasted. I'll admit to a few minor stirrings, but, dressed or undressed, she simply didn't arouse me in any important way. Maybe, as a blond Scandinavian boy, I was a racist at heart—if heart was the proper word here—and just didn't react to dark Mediterranean girls. Or maybe economical little Lori had spoiled me for the abundance that confronted me as the last vestige of clothing dropped away. But *Lorelei III* certainly did seem to be making a collection of spectacular ladies.

I kicked the fallen clothes aside, and picked up the big towel, and put it into the woman's hands. "Dry it off and cover it up while I do some piloting," I said.

We were approaching the main ship channel. I was aware of the woman behind me, toweling herself vigorously, angrily, as I studied the situation. A big tanker was coming toward us, heading down the bay to the ocean, and I didn't want to have to worry about dodging it, or a freighter I saw coming the other way. A quick check of the chart told me that there was plenty of water for *Lorelei III*'s six-foot keel if I just ran a quarter mile or so outside the channel where the ships, much deeper, couldn't go.

When I turned from resetting the loran and the autopilot, Dorothy Fancher was wrapping the towel around her like a sari.

"If Mrs. Bell didn't send you, why did you come?" I asked.

"Lori said you needed somebody. You ought to be ashamed of yourself, Mr. Helm, robbing the cradle like that." Dorothy Fancher laughed shortly. "No, she didn't tell me. But it was obvious every time the child mentioned your name that she'd slept with you and was in love with you and wished to heaven she'd fallen in love with a nice normal cannibalistic serial killer instead. So of course I had to see this monster who had my pretty little stepdaughter in such a state; and she said you needed a crew." She shrugged. "I'm not much of a sailor, Mr. Helm, I think it's a very stupid sport, but I have steered a boat—this boat, as a matter of fact—and helped with the dock lines; and after all, what does it really matter to you whether or not I put poison in my husband's soup?"

"Did you?"

She laughed again. "As the American children used to say in the school I went to: 'That's for me to know and you to find out.'" She took a precautionary tuck in the towel, which had begun to slip. "Since you don't seem to want to take advantage of my nudity to rape me, dammit, may I put some clothes on, please?"

"Just a minute."

I picked up the wet stuff on the floor and went through it. In the shirt pocket I found a comb, which I put on the table. In the pants, she carried a soggy wad of Kleenex, which I dropped into the wastebasket, a flat little leather wallet, which I tossed onto the chart table, and a small case holding three keys: a car key—Mercedes, if it matters—what looked like a house key, and a small ornate gold key that, when I tried it, opened up the dusty-rose cosmetic case.

"It works on the suitcase, too," the woman said.

I asked, "Is there anything in here you absolutely need, Mrs. Fancher? Heart pills, insulin, anything like that?"

"No, but all my makeup…"

She stopped, as I hefted the case, glanced at her, dumped the contents onto the table, and examined the satin-lined interior. The supposedly secret compartment in the bottom was a joke; even the Coast Guard could have found the .25 automatic and its spare magazine. It was a real little sex pistol, nicely engraved, shinily nickel-plated, with gorgeous mother-of-pearl grips—the slipperiest stuff in the world to hold, but very pretty to look at. If you like pretty guns.

"I suppose it's no use for me to say that it wasn't intended for you," Dorothy Fancher said. When I didn't speak, she went on. "I think you're judging me on the basis of what Lori has told you. Please don't forget that stepdaughters have hated stepmothers since the beginning of time."

There was no answer needed there. I checked the .25 and found that it carried a full magazine in the butt but no round in the chamber, a good way to leave it. I pocketed it, along with the extra magazine; then I picked a packet of hairpins from the pile of stuff on the table and laid it aside, scooped the rest back into the satin-lined case, gathered up the wet clothes and shoes on the floor, slid the port deckhouse door open, and threw it all into the sea. I heard her gasp behind me.

"What in the world do you think you're…!"

Her voice trailed off as she realized that her belongings were gone and no protests or recriminations could bring them back. I spent a moment closing the boarding gate in the rail that I'd opened to let her come aboard. Leaving the deckhouse door open, I picked up the dusty-pink suitcase and put it on the little table. The key, which I'd retained, worked the lock, just as she'd said it would. I opened the bag. It held a lot of dainty garments that did not seem to have been designed for cruising in a small boat.

I said, "Tell me what you want to wear. Something tough and practical, if you brought anything like that." She didn't speak or move. Her face was stony; clearly she wasn't going to play my games anymore. I dug around a bit and said, "Okay, I'll do the picking. Two outfits should do it; and I don't think you're going to need any dresses…"

Even after I'd laid aside the stuff I'd selected, I couldn't close the bag for the clothes that, no longer folded neatly, were overhanging the edges, but I hinged one part down over the other, clamlike, took it all across the deckhouse, heaved it out, and slid the door closed. Through the deckhouse windows I saw that the floating suitcase survived one wave but was swamped by the next. Some bright stuff remained on the surface, but it soon became waterlogged and disappeared from sight. Turning, I spotted the cap and sunglasses she'd laid aside after coming aboard. I checked them over carefully and added them to the stuff I'd saved out for her.

Mrs. Fancher broke her stony silence at last. "I hope you're enjoying yourself, Mr. Helm."

I said, "You'll feel better, dressed. Or maybe I'll feel better when you're dressed."

She said sharply, "Funny joke! I seem to have about as much effect on you as a side of beef in a freezer. If it wasn't for Lori, I'd think you were homosexual." She let the towel drop and, watching me, found and stepped into a pair of panties. She grimaced. "It's terrifying, the way the man can hardly contain his raging lust at the sight of my nude body! Are you going to tell me why you threw my things overboard?"

I said, "If you like. I can think of only three possible reasons why you're here, Mrs. Fancher. The first: you actually came to assist me in running the boat, as you claim. I'll work on believing that, but since you obviously hate boats, and since I can think of no reason for you to want to help me, let's try the next possibility: that you came to kill me."

"Why would I want to kill you?"

I said, "Hell, I don't know, but there have been two attempts on my life since I started on this job; why shouldn't you be planning the third?" I shrugged. "There's a lot of stuff on this boat you can use for homicidal purposes if you put your mind to it, but I pretty well know what it is, so I figure I can watch out for it. But I didn't want to have to cope with any weirdo explosives or exotic poisons you might have brought with you, not to mention daggers and guns, and in order to make sure nothing like that was hidden on you, or in your luggage, I'd have had to pretty well rip everything apart, after which it would have been no good to you, anyway. So it seemed simpler just to deep-six it."

She'd picked the long-sleeved shirt, of the two I'd saved for her, and put it on. Now she held out a wrist; clearly I was supposed to button the cuff for her. I did.

She said, "And the third possibility, Mr. Helm?" I said, "Well, unlikely as it may seem, you could have come aboard to seduce me."

13

Mrs. Fancher had me button the other shirt cuff for her. Then she pulled one of the pairs of pants I'd selected, managed to fasten them up without my assistance, and stepped into the low white boat shoes I'd found in her suitcase. The white linen trousers were, like the pants she'd worn aboard, cut fashionably full, and the shirt was also a loose fit—I had a feeling that the voluptuous, dark lady was actually making a statement that had nothing to do with style, retaining some vestige of the flowing garments of the desert-dwellers from whom she sprang.

I remembered Mrs. Bell's close-fitting costume with its spectacular display of sheer black nylons, perhaps another statement, rebellious this time. Like the Muslim-forbidden bourbon. But it seemed ironic that the sexier lady wore the more modest clothes.

Dorothy Fancher opened the packet of hairpins I'd saved out for her, did some work with the comb, wound the heavy black rope of her hair around her head in a practiced way, and pinned it into place.

"Truman, my husband, never did figure out a place to put a mirror in this deckhouse for me. I must look like a washerwoman." When I said nothing, she laughed. "All right, *don't* tell me I don't look like a washerwoman. But why would I want to seduce you, Mr. Helm?"

I said, "It's the logical next step, isn't it? I mean, if the man presents a danger, and if a couple of attempts prove that he's too tough to be taken out with knives or grenades, just render him helpless with love, the old Samson-and-Delilah routine."

She studied me for a moment. "This is strictly beside the point, but why do you find me repulsive? Most men don't."

I took a little time to formulate my answer. At last I said, "Repulsive is not the word, Mrs. Fancher. You're a very handsome lady and I think you're even pretty bright, really quite an attractive person; but the fact is you scare the hell out of me."

She looked at me sharply. "I frighten you? You don't look like a man who's easily intimidated."

I said, "Of course I'm totally fearless in the face of death—I mean, that goes with the territory. We're all intrepid heroes in this business, and if we aren't we certainly don't admit it. But this isn't a question of life or death, it's a question of… Well, I know that if I went to bed with you, you'd eat me up, no dirty pun intended. As you probably devoured old Truman Fancher. I wouldn't stand any more chance against you than you'd stand against me if you tried to use that cute little pistol you brought aboard. Pistols are my business. Sex is obviously yours. And I'm not dumb enough to try to compete with a pro in his or her line of work."

She smiled faintly. "Isn't that just a long-winded way of calling me a whore?"

I shrugged. "We professionals are always sadly misunderstood, Mrs. F. So you're a whore and I'm an assassin, if you want to make with the loaded words."

When she had nothing to say to that, I turned away from her and checked the view ahead through the windshield, all clear so far. The depth-sounder said we were running in seven meters of water, over twenty-one feet. Plenty. The little wallet I'd taken from her pants still lay on the chart table. It was wet outside, but when I picked it up I found it quite dry inside. I glanced through the cards it contained. Most were made out to Dorothy A. Fancher; but there was a worn old Social Security card that gave her name, presumably the maiden name I'd wondered about, as Dorothy Ayesha Ajami. There was also a sizeable wad of bills.

"Ayesha," I said.

"Do you find it an odd name?" she asked.

I said, "Hell, no. I'm an old H. Rider Haggard buff. I guess *King Solomon's Mines* was his best-known book, but *she* was pretty great, too. She-Who-Must-Be-Obeyed, the beautiful, all-powerful, immortal queen of the secret land behind the mountains. Her real name was Ayesha."

"It's a fairly common Arabic female name." After a moment Mrs. Fancher went on, "Actually, I grew up as

Ayesha Fatima Ajami. Our religion frowns on mixing Islamic and infidel names. However, it was decided that I would… function better if my name sounded more Americanized, so I had it changed legally. Speaking of books, I picked 'Dorothy' out of *The Wizard of Oz.*"

I said, "Function better doing what?" Then I looked ahead and saw that the buoyage off the port bow didn't look the way I had it memorized. I said, "Let's postpone this discussion until we're safe in port, or we may never get there. Why don't you make yourself useful and construct some sandwiches? The arsenic is on the top shelf and the strychnine is in the locker under the sink."

She said, "As a matter of fact, I didn't poison my husband, Mr. Helm."

I said, "Well, in that case, you'll find the bread on the galley counter and the flatware… Hell, you probably know your way around this boat better than I do."

"To my sorrow, I probably do." She made a wry face. "Spending a couple of hundred thousand dollars to live in a space the size of a shoe box! If a slum landlord tried to rent out an apartment this small, that rocked on its foundations at the slightest breeze, the housing authorities would have him thrown in jail."

I got the problem of the buoys straightened out with the aid of the binoculars and the chart—we'd just come a little farther than I'd expected. Apparently we had the tide with us, giving us an extra knot or so over the ground. I made, and imbibed, a prelunch martini. Mrs. Fancher refused to indulge, another ethnic statement like her voluminous pants, no doubt. I couldn't help wondering what it would be like to take your race so seriously; any time I start getting cocky about my Aryan origins I can't help remembering that Adolf Hitler had the same idea.

Mrs. Fancher served up sandwiches, Swiss on rye, and coffee. With the current and wind behind us, we roared up Delaware Bay, following the main channel now that I could give my full attention to the traffic. My handsome shipmate cleaned up the galley, which surprised me a bit; I wouldn't have guessed that housekeeping was a big thing with her. She returned to the deckhouse to sit silently in the cocktail corner. The bay grew narrower as the afternoon progressed.

"What's that?" Dorothy Fancher asked at last: I hadn't been aware that she'd come to stand beside me.

The wasp-waisted towers ahead were unmistakable. I checked the chart. "Salem Nuclear Power Plant, it says here," I said. "Why, do you plan to blow it up?"

Her laugh was slow in coming, frighteningly slow. She hadn't expected the joking question, and she hadn't been ready for it. Remembering the empty bilge compartment that should have been full of engine oil and antifreeze—you could pack some very interesting stuff into that space—I had a sudden tight feeling in my chest; and it was very hard not to look at her.

"Don't be silly," she said belatedly. She went on quickly: "You've got the wrong girl, mister. I'm just the babe who poisons husbands, remember? They die like flies around me, poor dears. But I'd never dream of blowing anything up. I'm a tidy person; explosives are much too messy and noisy."

Not Salem, I thought. It was just a coincidence that we'd happened to pass it today and I'd happened to ask about it in a kidding way. Not Salem, but something like it, something nuclear, say something southward that *Lorelei III* had passed along the waterway, probably while Truman Fancher was still alive. Something near which the mysterious cargo had been off-loaded and left waiting for reasons yet unknown.

Of course we hadn't actually passed Salem yet. The wind was picking up, and as we approached the distinctive towers the seas funneling up the bay were becoming so steep that Nicky was losing control; I had to switch him off and take over. Steering a boat running fast downwind in a stiff breeze is a real test of helmsmanship. I was just barely good enough to hold *Lorelei III* when she tried to round up sharply into the wind—"broach" is the technical seagoing term. "The slow hydraulic steering, while it provided plenty of power, made it hard to respond in time and necessitated a lot of wild cranking of the wheel. We charged past the wasp-waisted towers and up the narrowing waterway.

After a while, sweating over the wheel, I said, "Take the binoculars and see if you can spot the entrance buoys of the C. and D. Canal, please. I've got my hands full here."

"What would you do without me?" Mrs. Fancher asked dryly. She studied the view ahead. Presently she said, "There they are. You're right on course."

I remembered something and said, "You're supposed to be vulnerable to seasickness. With this violent motion, you should be on your knees in the head, heaving up everything and hoping to die."

She didn't respond to that, and the buoys were coming up fast. I made the turn, and *Lorelei III* took a wave broadside that burst right over the deckhouse. I held her steady as the wipers cleared the windshield and let me see again; then we were gliding through the entrance into the calm water of the canal with the boat just heeling slightly in response to the wind that continued to buffet the masts and rigging. An hour later, with the low sun shining through cracks in the cloud layer to the west, we were docking at Schaefer's Canal House, having come just about half the distance between the head of Delaware Bay and the head of Chesapeake Bay. The current wasn't as bad as Lori had led me to expect—it presumably varies with the state of the tide—and with Mrs. Fancher to throw the lines as I brought the boat alongside, and a man coming over from the fuel pumps to catch them, we had no trouble getting tied up for the night; but by the time we had the boat properly secured it was almost dark.

"That was a pretty hard run. We'd better check the engine in the morning—remind me," I said, noting the time of our arrival in the log I'd started on a pad of lined paper I'd found on board, since the ship's official logbook was missing. "That's assuming you're planning to stay on board, of course… What is it?"

I looked around to see her offering me a glass, on

a tray no less. She made a little curtsy. "Your evening martini, captain. If you hadn't thrown all my pretty things overboard, I could have served you more glamorously."

I said, "Maybe that was what I was afraid of."

Setting the tray aside, she followed me to the settee, sat down beside me, and watched me take a sip from the glass and nod approvingly.

"You're a strange man," she said. "It's a wonder you've survived so long in that savage world of yours. How do you know I didn't doctor that drink?"

"Or the cheese sandwich I had for lunch? Or the coffee?" I grinned. "Well, I made sure you didn't bring aboard anything odorless, tasteless, and lethal, didn't I? There's some toxic stuff in the paint locker, and I had to fight off some roaches that were taking over the boat when I came aboard, but you haven't had time to read all the labels; and I can't think of anything available that I couldn't smell or taste before it killed me. Anyway, I'm gambling, now, that my third guess was correct, and you didn't come aboard with homicide in mind."

She said ruefully, "I wish you'd decided that before… I really didn't have any explosives or poisons in my luggage. Just some very nice and expensive clothes and a perfume that was guaranteed to drive any man mad with passion. Well, looking on the bright side, they might as well be at the bottom of the sea, since obviously they'd have had no effect on you whatever."

I grinned. "But you're still in there trying, aren't you? Washing my dishes, humbly bringing me my martini, calling me a strange man... Flattery, flattery. All men love being waited on, and all men love being called strange men almost as much as they love being called dangerous men. As you know perfectly well. Are you planning to stay on board and work on me for a while?"

"Until you get tired of watching me make a fool of myself, throwing myself shamelessly against the solid rock of your integrity." She got up and walked to the starboard door, on the side of the boat that lay against the dock. It was open to the night air, and she stood looking out, breathing deeply. "The clouds are breaking up; it's going to be a beautiful night," she said. After a moment, she went on. "Truman considered the restaurant here one of the best along this coast; he said they have a Long Island duck that's quite fabulous, and their fish is also excellent. May I repay you for your hospitality by inviting you to dinner, Mr. Helm?"

I said, "You have finally found the way to my heart, Mrs. Fancher: I'm a sucker for duck. I accept with pleasure. But may I make a suggestion?"

"Of course."

I said, "You may be a pro in some respects, but no pro in my line of work would ever stand like that, silhouetted against the light."

She said, "I can't think of anybody who'd want to shoot me, except perhaps you if you feel your purity endangered by my irresistible charms, or a duck dinner." She turned her head to look at me. "You're a clever man, Mr. Helm."

"And strange, don't forget strange."

She said, "You're perfectly right. I did come aboard to seduce you. Those high-powered professionals Roger had hired were obviously a total waste of money."

I remembered Lori saying that a gorgeous greasy-gigolo type named Roger Hassim had caused trouble between her father and stepmother—Truman Fancher had even used a private detective to obtain evidence of the relationship, as I recalled. But it was no time to ask distracting questions about stray lovers.

Dorothy Fancher was saying, "You wouldn't think destroying one clumsy motor sailer would be much of a problem, but their woman fumbled it twice; apparently she was quite good at killing but not so good at sinking. Then you came along and she died, and the man who followed her died, along with two of ours who'd been drafted to run that ridiculous, overpowered speedboat. Four dead, six if you count the two killed by the hired blonde, and nothing accomplished! It was getting to be a bad joke. It was time to try a different approach, *my* approach. I was going to make you quite mad about me, my helpless slave..."

She stopped talking. An odd, dark streak had suddenly appeared on the side of her forehead just below her glossy turban of black hair; the cough of the silenced weapon outside followed immediately. I was on my feet, disentangling myself from the comer table, as Dorothy Fancher collapsed bonelessly on the brief steps leading up to the deck.

14

In order to get out of the deckhouse, I had to step over her. I did it without taking time to see how badly she was hurt—if she was dead, there was nothing I could do about it; and if she was alive, with a head wound, depending on its severity, she'd need either a brain surgeon or a Band-Aid, either of which could wait a few minutes. With the help of a weathered piling, I hauled myself up to the boardwalk, a couple of feet above deck level, gambling that the kind of people who would shoot at Dorothy Fanchers were not the kind of people who'd hang around and shoot at Matthew Helms. No shots came.

Schaefer's is not the standard marina with finger piers and boat slips; you merely tie up to a very long dock that runs parallel to the shore at the side of the canal. It's built a little ways out from the bank where the water is deep enough even for the biggest yachts; and it's connected to the shore, and to the frame building housing the office, restaurant, and showers, by several short bridges or crosswalks. A couple of sailboats lay ahead of us, and half a dozen assorted vessels, power and sail, were tied up astern, including one floating three-story power-palace over sixty feet long.

The dock was well lighted, and I had no trouble spotting the running figure heading for the nearest bridge to shore—actually, the guy seemed to be handicapped in some way: he was limping badly and not making very good progress. He made a clear target under the lights. I had my short-barrelled .38 Special in my hand, but the range was long for a snubby. Anyway, I felt I could probably run down a cripple without arousing the neighborhood with a lot of noisy gunfire, so I took out after him.

He was even slower than I'd thought, and I was closing the distance rapidly as we came off the crosswalk and into the lighted parking lot—except that by this time I knew that I'd made a mistake: even limping badly, the figure ahead of me ran like a woman, not a man. She glanced back and I saw that there was something odd about her face; she seemed to be wearing a peculiar white mask. She was still carrying the weapon she'd used on Mrs. Fancher, an automatic pistol, probably a .22, the barrel of which looked quite long since it was extended by the silencer. However, she made no attempt to bring it around to shoot at me; in fact, when she heard me getting close, as we came into the cleared area beyond the shoreline brush, she simply stopped and raised her hands and let me come up behind her and take the lifted weapon from her.

"Turn around," I said.

She turned. It wasn't a mask; it was a white bandage; actually there were two of them, one on each cheek, symmetrically placed. She was a moderately tall young woman with a rangy, almost boyish figure and short blond hair, potentially attractive, but she looked as if she'd suffered a serious recent accident. In fact, the last time I'd seen such a beat-up female was a few years before, when my daughter-in-law had survived, just barely, the bomb that had killed my older son. This girl wore a normal shoe, a brown loafer, on her right foot, but the left foot was bandaged and stuffed into what looked like a man's felt slipper. The two last fingers of her left hand were also bandaged, and immobilized with a splint. Then there were the facial bandages; and of course I was being stupid. Accident, hell.

"It's about time we met, Miss Kronquist," I said.

She was breathing hard from the run. She was wearing blue jeans and a high-necked navy-blue jersey, a sensible costume for night operations. She waited until she'd stopped panting so hard before she spoke. "Take a good look, Mr. Helm! This is what they did to me for trying to protect you!"

I asked, "What are you doing here, Miss Kronquist?"

She drew a long breath and let the anger go out of her voice. "You might as well call me Ziggy, everybody else does. I don't blame them; who wants to wrestle with a mouthful like Siegelinda?" She licked her lips. "I was looking for a job, Mr. Helm, but I see the position has already been filled."

"Well, I'm Matt, and you seem to have done your best to create a new opening, Ziggy," I said.

She said calmly, "It wasn't my best; it wasn't a good shot. I think I just grazed her. I... I guess I don't make a very good murderer. Although I prefer the word 'executioner.'"

I said, "Let's move over there, under the trees." I led her to a picnic table, and she sank down on one of the built-in benches. It was obvious from the way she moved that her attempt to flee had done her damaged foot no good at all. There was less light here, some distance from the dock and the buildings. I asked, "Did Mrs. Bell send you?"

Ziggy Kronquist gave a bitter little laugh. "Mrs. Bell thinks I'm a terrible sissy, a total loss to the organization. After all, I only let them cripple one hand and one foot, and slash my face a couple of times. I'm just a hopeless sniveling weakling; I... I gave in and talked before they could b-blind me... Oh, Jesus!" She put her elbows on the table and buried her bandaged face in her hands. When she spoke again, her voice was muffled. "Why the hell did I want to be a glamorous girl field operative, anyway? Glamorous? God, look at me! Why didn't I just stick with my research and my computers? And now I probably can't even go back to punching a computer keyboard, the way they've mangled my fingers!"

A power yacht even larger than the big one at the dock glided slowly past. It looked like a miniature cruise ship, blazing with lights. Well, it undoubtedly had a professional captain who'd come through here a hundred times and could run the canal blindfolded. The girl had found a handkerchief with her unbandaged hand and was mopping her eyes.

She sniffed, put the hanky away, and said more calmly, "In answer to your question, no, Mrs. Bell didn't send me. She's still looking for somebody else, somebody brave and strong, to help you. But in the meantime... I knew you'd got to Cape May, which meant you'd probably stop here next, and I told her I was coming here to see you whether she liked it or not."

"Why?" I asked.

She hesitated. "Well, I owe you an apology, don't I? I really held out as long as... I'd really had all I could take. But I did... did talk, and Mrs. Bell said I almost got you killed. I'm sorry."

I said, "I'm still here; don't sweat it."

"Mrs. Bell said you'd asked for me in spite of everything. She thought it was pretty dumb of you, and she wasn't about to be a party to any such foolishness. But I hoped if I came here, even without orders from her... I don't really want to go back to those lousy computers. At least not until..." She stopped.

I looked at her for a moment, and said, "Revenge, Miss Kronquist... I mean, Ziggy? You don't want to retire from the fray, or be retired from the fray, until you've settled with the people who damaged you so badly?" She didn't answer, but the answer was in her silence. I said, "Well, just hold everything for a little, vengeance-wise, please. I need that woman alive—I hope she still is in spite of you—until I can learn what she and her friends are up to. I presume that, since you shot her, she's the one responsible for your injuries."

Siegelinda Kronquist said, "I'd recognize her voice anywhere!"

"Voice?"

"Well, it was the man who... who tortured me; and he had a couple of dark-faced gofers who helped him tie me down on that old iron bed. We were in a kind of rundown shack near the railroad where they'd grabbed me. But gradually I became aware of somebody watching from the doorway beyond my head, and then she... she started making suggestions. You could just feel her licking her chops, enjoying every minute of it, the sadistic bitch. I never saw her face, but I'd know her voice anywhere, with that hint of an accent."

I said, "So you'd have a hard time identifying her in court. A good defense lawyer would throw so many accents at you, you'd have a hard time spotting a Tayxas caowboy." I regarded her critically. "Well, let's skip that for the moment. I didn't realize they'd left you in such bad shape, when I asked Mrs. Bell to send you to me. Aren't you being optimistic to even think of working on a boat yet?"

She said, "Mister, I've seen a little of your record, and I'm willing to bet that with just one hand and foot I'm a better sailor than you with two of each. How far am I going, to have to hike on my busted toes, anyway, going down the waterway on a thirty-eight-foot motor sailer? I can certainly manage a steering wheel—I just drove my car from Washington, D.C.—and throw a line; maybe I can't do any heavy, two-handed hauling, but you look pretty strong in a skinny, rawhide sort of way, and we're not going to be setting any racing sails, so how much beef do we really need on board?"

I said, "Okay, say you've convinced me; but as you pointed out, yourself, the position you're plugging for is filled at the moment."

"That female rattlesnake!"

I glanced at the gun I was still holding, the one I'd taken from her. It was the old assassination weapon that was once standard in a lot of undercover services and still keeps turning up regularly: the beautiful, now obsolete, .22 Colt Woodsman with the usual silencer—nowadays we're supposed to call it a sound suppressor for reasons that escape me, but it was still a silencer back when this gun was made.

I said, looking at the handsome old weapon, "You seem to have come prepared to deal with her."

She licked her lips. "I… I just knew that if I managed to talk you into taking me along, sooner or later I'd come across one of them, either her or that lovely torture-happy Arab Apollo of hers, Roger Hassim. So before I left Washington I managed to sneak a gun out of the historical section of the Armory without anybody seeing me, and buy a box of .22s. The hard part was finding the lowspeed stuff that would work with the silencer; everybody seems to stock nothing but high-velocity .22s nowadays. But I didn't expect to find the woman so soon. It… it took my breath away, literally, when I walked out the dock hoping just to get a chance to talk with you, and heard her voice in the deckhouse, talking with you. I knew it instantly, of course; and I stood there with my silly mouth open… And then it was as if a computer program had taken over and I found myself running—well, hobbling—back to the car and getting the gun out of the trunk and checking the magazine and jacking a cartridge into the chamber and sneaking back to see her standing there in the doorway, a lovely target… But as I told you, it wasn't a good shot. I didn't take my time the way I should have; I rushed it; I didn't wait to catch my breath. The whole thing had taken me by surprise and I wasn't… wasn't ready, psychologically."

"Maybe you never will be ready, psychologically," I said. "Some people are never ready to kill."

The girl shook her head with sudden violence. "No, I'll be ready next time. She's got to die!" Ziggy Kronquist drew a long breath, looking up at me. "You don't understand! That's not a woman, it's an animal. They all are; at least they're not really human the way we understand human. They don't laugh at funny jokes, they laugh at pain; and if it's pain that cripples and disfigures, so much the better! She and that beautiful Hassim freak! He was like a kid tormenting a small animal for fun, and she was egging him on: she'd tell him what joint to crunch with his ugly pliers, or where to slice next with his pretty little knife, and he'd do it very carefully and stand back so she could appreciate the marvelous effect he'd achieved. They thought it was hilarious when I moaned and sobbed and shrieked in agony. They thought it was delightfully comical when I… when the pain got so bad that I… I wet and d-dirtied myself; oh, look at the ridiculous infidel girl making such a disgusting mess of her expensive slacks, ha ha, try the other finger, now the face, now the other cheek, now the eye…" She stopped and drew a deep, ragged breath. "That's when I screamed that I'd tell them what they wanted. That silly ID business about the weather in Maine and Connecticut. I'm sorry, sorry, sorry if it made you a lot of trouble, but I just couldn't let them… I just couldn't help myself!"

I said, "You understand that even if I wanted to, I couldn't take you aboard right now."

She drew a long breath and said, "Thanks for listening. I didn't really mean to use you as a father confessor."

I said, "Welcome to the club, Ziggy. I can tell you one thing, it won't be any better next time; it's not something that improves with practice."

After a moment, she smiled faintly. "Gee, thanks lots, Matt. That's really a great big help!"

"Here," I said, "you may need this for protection. Just don't use it for anything else until I give you the all clear."

She looked at the pistol I put into her hand. She started to ask a question, but changed her mind and, sitting there, slipped the magazine out of the butt of the gun. Then she jacked the cartridge out of the chamber, fed it into the top of the magazine, and reinserted the magazine into its slot, working quite efficiently in spite of the splinted fingers. She lifted her jersey and wedged the gun inside her snug waistband. The demonstration, indicating that she knew firearms and was careful with them, helped to confirm the decision I'd made.

I said, "Assuming you're right and the woman isn't too badly hurt, I'll try to keep to the schedule I've been given. That means we'll be in Annapolis, Maryland, tomorrow night, Port Annapolis Marina. Then, continuing south, Solomon's Island on the Patuxent River the following night, Zahniser's Marina. Then a night at anchor in Fishing Bay, off the Piankatank River; then Tidewater Marina in Norfolk, the official beginning of the Intracoastal Waterway. I don't know what's going to happen, I just hope something is. There's not much you can do while we're under way—don't try to trail us in another boat, there's no way of doing it without being spotted, and I want her to think she's got me all to herself—but if you can manage to keep up with us in your car and stay handy in the evenings to make sure nobody sabotages the boat when we go ashore, and see who else is interested in us, if anybody, it could be useful."

She studied my face for a moment. "Thanks, Matt," she said quietly. "Thanks for taking a chance on me in spite of the way I… I'll try to do a good job for you."

"Not too good," I said.

She frowned. "What do you mean?"

I said, "You've got nothing to prove. If it gets dangerous, back off. A dead girl is no damn good to me."

She grinned. It was a pretty good grin despite the bandages. "Mister, don't you know you've got yourself a certified coward here? If you don't know, ask Mrs. Bell, she'll be happy to tell you. Well, you'd better get aboard and hold the female monster's head. Just watch out she doesn't bite you, they say those rabies shots are rough..."

15

When I came aboard *Lorelei III,* Mrs. Fancher wasn't lying where I'd left her and had half expected to find her, possibly dead even though Ziggy had called it a grazing shot. Predicting what bullets are going to do to people is not an exact science. However, the woman was very much alive, sitting at the top of the steps leading down into the galley, where she could reach the paper-towel dispenser mounted on the nearby bulkhead. She had a strip of the toweling draped over her shoulder and tucked into the collar of her shirt to protect it, and a bloodstained wad pressed to her head.

"I think the bleeding has stopped," she said without looking around. "Bandage it for me, please, but be careful. Considering how few clothes you've left me, I can't afford to get blood on them; it's very hard to get out."

I squeezed by her—I seemed to be spending a lot of time climbing over her, but she still did nothing for my libido—and got the first-aid kit and a clean washcloth out of the galley. I wet the washcloth under the tap. Turning back to her, I found her watching me. The pupils of her lovely, unreadable, brown eyes were exactly the same size, which is supposed to be a good medical sign.

"No dizziness, no double vision?" I asked.

"Only a headache," she said. "I was just stunned for a moment; I was never really unconscious. I presume you caught the girl with the gun, since at present she is incapable of running very fast."

"You saw her?"

"At the last moment, yes. The one who calls herself by that ridiculous name. Ziggy."

I said, "You're not as bright as I thought. You help to maim a girl and scar her for life—and then you tell me you can't imagine anybody wanting to shoot you!"

"So she recognized me? I thought I had kept well out of her sight."

"She recognized your voice."

Mrs. Fancher shrugged. "I suppose I underestimated her. It's hard to take them seriously, these modern American children. They are all taught from infancy that they are supposed to be safe, that they have a God-given right to be safe, as if any deity, yours or mine or theirs, could be bothered with such a minor thing as their physical safety—their spiritual salvation is, of course, quite a different matter. But what kind of training for life is that, particularly for our kind of life? When they make the dreadful discovery that this is not really a very safe world, the shock is more than they can bear. The young woman was so very noisy and messy under interrogation that I did not think she could possibly find the courage to retaliate even if she did manage to identify me. It seems that I was wrong. What did you do with her?"

I said, "What do you think I did? I gave her back her weapon, of course, and told her to try to shoot straighter next time."

Mrs. Fancher gave a short bark of laughter. "And undoubtedly, after hearing what she had to tell you, you think I am a very terrible person."

I said, "Hell, I knew you were a very terrible person the minute I saw you. Hold still now."

Standing down in the galley, I was in a good position to work on her as she sat on the steps above me, when she leaned forward a little. It was a brief furrow in the smooth, dark skin at the side of her forehead, an inch below the hairline. As she'd said, it had already stopped bleeding. I left the groove itself alone, I just washed around it cautiously and taped a small dressing over it; then I used the damp washcloth to clean the rest of the drying blood off her face. I picked up all the bloody paper and stuffed it into the garbage can under the galley sink, rinsed out the washcloth and hung it up to dry, and put away the first-aid kit.

"I don't suppose you feel up to hiking over to the restaurant for dinner after all that," I said. "I'll take a rain check on your invitation and see what I can cook up for us here."

She shook her head cautiously. "No, just find me a

couple of aspirins or Tylenols and I'll be all right. It's really just a scratch."

I grinned. "It's hell what some folks will do to avoid having to eat my cooking."

One good thing about getting rid of her belongings was that I didn't have to wait for her to dress for dinner. After washing down the pain pills I brought her, with water from the galley, she let me help her up to the dock, and over the crosswalk to shore. I saw her look around a bit warily.

"It's all right," I said. "I told the kid not to shoot you again until I was finished with you."

She laughed and took my arm to cross the big parking lot. When we entered the restaurant, we found that it was by no means full; but in spite of her modestly loose-fitting costume Dorothy managed to get the attention of what male customers there were. I doubt that any of them even noticed her bandaged forehead as she walked past; they weren't looking at her face.

We were given a pleasant window table with a good view along the canal, which seemed to be lighted almost as well as a city street; but the desolate, marshy land across from the canal house dock, that we'd seen coming in, was now hidden in darkness. Two pilot boats were tied up below us, painted orange for identification. Even as we were being seated, one of them cast off its lines and pulled out. I'd been told that they guide the ships through in two stages, and that Schaefer's is where the Maryland pilots take over from the Delaware pilots and vice versa. I ordered another martini to back up the one I'd been served so graciously on the boat that I'd never got to finish.

When the waiter had delivered our drinks and departed, I said, "I hate going out with dames who don't drink. They always look so damned smug and disapproving as they sip their lousy Perrier water."

She laughed. "I'm sorry. It was not my intention to look disapproving, although, of course, my religion does disapprove of alcoholic beverages."

I said, "I'm not much for religion. Particularly a religion that says drinking a glass of wine is a terrible sin but spoiling a pretty girl's face is perfectly all right."

Mrs. Fancher said calmly, "They were clean incisions with a very sharp blade; Roger keeps his weapons well. A plastic surgeon can probably erase the scars with very little difficulty. And not that it matters, but the girl was not really very pretty."

I said, "Maybe your pretty isn't my pretty. Talking about pretty, tell me about Roger Hassim. The kid said he's a very beautiful man, for a practicing sadist."

Dorothy said, "You are trying hard to make me angry, aren't you?"

I said, "I'm trying to give you the impression that I don't really like you much, and that I doubt that I'm going to be very fond of any of your friends."

"Why would you do that?"

I said, "Well, that way I can maybe kid you that I'm an honest man; if I pretended to adore you and love your religion and admire your beautiful boyfriend, you'd know me for the bar I really am. Tell me about this lovely, toe-crushing, finger-cracking, face-slashing Hassim bastard. Does he make a full-time career of mutilating women, or does he have some interesting sidelines like murder or arson or robbery—or sabotage?"

She didn't rise to that bait. She just said, rather stiffly, "I do not think you are really in a position to disapprove of the interrogation we conducted. I know you must also have questioned people rather drastically when it was necessary."

She was, of course, perfectly right; and the fact that I don't laugh and giggle when I have to work somebody over for information doesn't really make me a better person. But the attitude of moral outrage was, I felt, useful at the moment; if I could needle her enough, perhaps she'd get angry enough to let slip something that would prove helpful.

I said, "You still haven't told me anything about this Roger character. All I really know about him, aside from the fact that he loves hurting people, is that he screws other men's wives."

Dorothy said, undisturbed, "My husband was an old man. I was very good to him, I made him very happy whenever he desired me, something no other woman had been able to do for several years before he married me; but the women of our race have always had effective methods of pleasuring men, even quite elderly men. He should have been satisfied with that. It was unreasonable of him to expect me to wait around unfulfilled, a woman like me, for the few times a month he was… interested. I was always available when he wanted me; he should not have asked for more." She paused, and went on. "Roger does what he must for his people. Our people."

I said, "Oh, one of those."

She said, "You should be able to understand people like Roger and me."

I frowned. "Why the hell should I?"

"You're not so far from your roots, either, Matthew Helm," she said. "Not like these mongrel Americans who have long since forgotten the blood that bred them. We know that you have been back to your native land more than once to renew your ancient ties that the soil from which your family sprang..."

I almost laughed; she made an occasional visit to Scandinavia, mostly in the line of duty, sound like a pilgrimage to a holy shrine. Well, it's a nice enough place, and some of my Swedish relatives are pretty nice people—and some aren't—but my spiritual ties, if any, bind me to the vast sunny expanses of the southwestern United States where I was brought up, not to the misty little country from which my folks emigrated a few years before I was born because they could do better for themselves over here... I was aware that the woman across the table had changed the subject.

"...and you are not really interested in Roger, anyway," she was saying.

I said, "Tell me. I'm interested in my interests."

She said, "Roger Hassim is nothing to you. Please don't try to convince me that you feel you must punish him because he was unkind to a not particularly attractive young woman you met for the first time less than an hour ago. What you truly want—the person you really want—is a certain rather dangerous young man, a Soviet-trained killer, who hates America and bears a grudge against one American in particular, you, because under orders from Washington you shot his father to death some years ago." She regarded me steadily across the table. "I can give you Roland Caselius. For a price, of course."

It took me by surprise. In my mind, I'd filed this business under two separate headings: the murky Arab terror operation that was mainly of interest to Mrs. Bell, and the straightforward DAMAG mission—R. Caselius, find and neutralize—that was my concern. I'd certainly hoped, as had Mac, that one would lead me to the other, that was why I was here; but I hadn't really expected a participant in one to go out of her way to help me to the other, even at a price...

The waiter saved me from having to respond immediately, and when he left, after taking our orders, Dorothy seemed to have forgotten Caselius. She said, "I do not seem to be as good a judge of people as I thought. In addition to misjudging the girl, I also seem to have underestimated you, or at least your powers of resistance. And I definitely underestimated my elderly husband."

"In what way?"

"I thought... I should have remembered that the old ones can be sly and dangerous. Even when you think you have them totally infatuated... It's not like dealing with a lovesick boy, who will reject all suspicions of his beloved as unworthy and degrading. Truman surprised me once by hiring a private detective; but I thought I'd convinced him that Roger was just a brief aberration and I truly regretted it and intended to devote the rest of my life to making it up to him, my wonderful husband. Why, I was even willing to live for several weeks in that cramped little cabin on that ridiculous little boat just to be with him. Greater love has no woman, ha!" She grimaced. "Actually, I would never have dreamed of subjecting myself to such an ordeal, but Roger saw how *Lorelei III* could be utilized for our purposes. However, we couldn't risk having my snoopy little stepdaughter on board sticking her nose into everything, and the only way to get her off the boat was to put me on it."

Well, I was learning a few things, and I had a hunch I was about to learn more. I couldn't help wondering why the lady was confiding in me so generously. The arrival of the salads silenced her only briefly.

Then she continued her recital. "As I say, old men are sly. I thought I had convinced Truman of my wifely devotion; I certainly made every effort to prove it during the endless boring waterway trip from one little buggy, miserable anchorage or marina to the next. He seemed contented enough, and he was delighted by the sights along the way, as if he hadn't made the same voyage so many times before! He was forever pointing out to me new wonders… I must say that those creepy mangrove swamps down south leave me quite cold, and I've seen a deer, and while the dolphins are mildly entertaining, I am not a bit enchanted by the obese manatees that Truman went ecstatic over, the couple of times we managed to get a glimpse of one—the ugliest animal on earth, and so enormous! I had a vision of one bumping a hole in the boat in its moronic, friendly way. But of course I pretended to share my husband's childish pleasure. Apparently, my pretense wasn't good enough…"

The arrival of our dinners interrupted her. The duck lived up to its advance publicity, and I allowed it to keep me busy for a while. It seemed best not to act too eager to hear the story she was so eager to tell me.

"Well, what happened?" I asked at last.

"He caught us unloading," Dorothy said. "I had put something into his evening coffee, enough that I was certain it would keep him asleep all night no matter how much noise we made, first moving the boat to the proper location, and then unloading, and finally returning to the original anchorage…"

"Unloading what?" A little stupidity seemed to be indicated, and I went on. "You mean drugs?"

She shook her head irritably. "Don't be ridiculous! If we want drugs, we have people who can obtain them at the source; we don't need to carry them around in the bilge of a yacht. I think you have a fairly good idea…"

The waiter came by to ask if everything was okay. Somebody should teach them in waiter school not to be forever interrupting the customers' conversations with that foolish question.

"Go on," I said to Dorothy, after telling the man that everything was just wonderful.

She said, "Truman came stumbling out of his cabin just as we were hoisting it out of the engine room and up through the open skylight. He must have got some of the drug before he poured out the coffee when I wasn't looking; and of course, with his heart, he wasn't supposed to drink coffee at all. Maybe that's why he got rid of part of it, remembering his doctor's instructions; but I think it's more likely that he suspected… Anyway, he had enough sedative in him that he was quite groggy, and he just stood swaying in the doorway, whatever you call it on a boat, staring at us. There it was, hanging in the deckhouse, and I was helping to guide it upward, wearing the greasy old coveralls he used when he worked on the engine. There were several of Roger's men helping, and Roger himself… I think it was the sight of Roger, whom I'd promised never to see again, that did it. He started to say something, and then his face changed and he put both hands to his chest and bent over, gasping with pain. I knew it was another heart attack, of course; I'd seen the first one…"

I said, when she paused, "So he died very conveniently for you."

She shook her head. "No, he didn't die, not then; and it would actually have been very inconvenient to have him do it there, calling attention to that neighborhood… I got him below. We saw that he was very sick, but we decided that the best thing to do was keep him alive, sedated if necessary, as long as possible while we got him, and the boat, as far as possible away from the critical area. I won't tell you how long he lasted. Maybe it was just a few days, maybe it was weeks. In any case, it was not a pleasant cruise. He was a very tough old man, and I was beginning to be afraid we might have to expedite matters. We were getting pretty far north, but one morning his heart finally gave out for good. We set up the charade you know, running the boat aground at the side of the channel there in North Carolina and having me supposedly wake up from my seasick nap to find my husband dead on the deckhouse floor under the big steering wheel. I used the radio to call for help, sounding very frightened and desperate, and everybody was very kind, very considerate, and there were no awkward questions at all—except, of course, from my stepdaughter, who was certain that I had murdered her father. Well, perhaps I had in a way, perhaps he would have recovered and lived a few more years if we'd taken him to a hospital. However, you will note that I did tell you the truth. I did not poison him."

She looked very attractive sitting across the table in the pleasant restaurant, a handsome, civilized, dark lady chatting with her escort and sipping occasionally at her innocent Perrier water as she coped with her duck. She was, of course, as Ziggy Kronquist had said, a monster. Well, we meet such a lot of them in the business.

I suppose some people would be horrified at the thought of poor old Truman Fancher lying helpless and drugged, with a failing heart, in the master cabin of his own yacht as it raced northward—well, as fast as you can race in an eighty-horsepower motor sailer—to get a suitable distance north, while his beautiful, sexy wife hovered over him hoping he'd keep breathing long enough, but not so long that she'd have to expedite his departure with a pillow.

Lori would, of course, have been horrified. I don't horrify so easily. Still there was definitely something about the woman that activated certain warning circuits inside me—maybe I should call them the monster-warning circuits—keeping me from responding to her sexually; it was as if she wasn't a real human woman.

I cleared my throat and said, "What about his logbook? Were you afraid the last entry would tell the world where *Lorelei III* anchored that night, before you moved somewhere else to unload your cargo? That would still be fairly close, wouldn't it?"

Dorothy Fancher gave a short laugh. "Close? He had the exact position! My husband was a seaman, Mr. Helm. Awakening from a drugged sleep, seeing a strange object being hoisted out of the bilge of his boat, not to mention seeing a man he hated, he still automatically noted the loran reading from his cabin doorway." Strangely, she sounded quite proud of the elderly husband she'd allowed to die without medical attention. "He not only noted the position, he remembered it even after falling unconscious with a coronary. And wrote it down in the log later, when we thought he was helpless in his bunk; and hid the book and told me about it. He said it was concealed where we would never find it, but somebody else would; and when I said he was bluffing, he smiled his wicked old smile and closed his eyes—he was getting very weak—and read off the figures from memory, quite correctly! We searched and searched but found no traces of the book. Of course we couldn't be too drastic. I knew that with her father dead, my stepdaughter would inevitably accuse me of his murder; we couldn't risk the additional questions that would have been asked if the authorities had found, not only a dead man, but a badly damaged boat. So I sent *Lorelei III* up to Oyster Bay before little Lori arrived; and we've been trying to get rid of the boat and that damned logbook, wherever it may be hidden, ever since!"

It had been quite a recital; and I still wondered why she'd told me so much. I drew a long breath. "Okay, what's the deal?"

She was watching a large freighter glide past in the canal. "What did you say, Matt?"

"You offered me a bargain," I said. "Roland Caselius at a price."

"Oh, yes," she said. "Of course, originally I hadn't expected to have to bargain. Since those stupid killers Roger hired had failed to cope with you, I would simply hitch a ride on your boat and drive you mad with lust to the point where you would be happy to do anything... Well, I have already told you. Oh, dear, it's a terrible blow to my vanity to meet a man on whom I have so little effect!" She dabbed delicately at her lips with her napkin. "So I must offer a trade instead. The arrangement would be simply this: I help you carry out your mission, and you give your word not to interfere with mine."

The dessert, when we got to it, was almost as good as the duck.

16

When we left the restaurant, a night mist was again making halos around the lights. Like the land of my ancestors in northern Europe, it was another damp damned part of the world. I hadn't seen a truly clear, starry night since I left New Mexico.

The phone booths, a cluster of three, were located in the parking lot—if you want to flatter them by calling them booths. I refer, of course, to the fresh-air installations that have taken the place of real booths, merely protecting the equipment and to hell with the customers. Thanks loads, AT&T.

From the one I chose, I could watch *Lorelei III* at the dock among the other boats, unmoving in the quiet night. I guess the seafaring life was leaving its mark on me: I was getting so I just liked to look at my boat. She wasn't pretty, as boats go—no motor sailer is—but she was sturdy and businesslike. We'd left the lights on in the deckhouse, and she had a friendly, cozy, comfortable look, lying there.

I could wish that I were just taking her for a pleasure cruise down the ICW, perhaps with a competent and compatible sailing friend—little Lori Fancher had written me off, but I remembered that Ziggy Kronquist was supposed to be an expert sailor and, if you looked past the splints and bandages, seemed like a reasonably bright and attractive girl, Dorothy Fancher to the contrary notwithstanding. Despite her injuries, she'd probably make a good shipmate.

But instead of cruising for pleasure I was playing dangerous games on board with a very wicked lady whose eventual intentions, where I was concerned, were undoubtedly homicidal.

"You can go on to the boat if you like," I said to the wicked lady, waiting nearby. "I'm just going to clear things with my chief in Washington."

"That's all right, I'll wait," she said.

Well, on second thought I'd just as soon have her where I could see her, instead of opening sea cocks or mixing up roach-powder cocktails on board. Having kind of committed myself to letting her come along, I felt a little like the cowboy who'd lassoed the bear and couldn't quite figure out what the hell to do next.

I had no trouble reaching Mac; we seldom do. I brought him up to date. Dorothy had moved off a short distance to perch gingerly on one of the low pilings along the seawall, after carefully checking it out for dryness and cleanliness for the sake of her white linen pants. I wondered if Ziggy Kronquist was watching from out in the dark somewhere. I could see no sign of her, but if she was any good, I wouldn't.

"You agreed to the lady's terms, of course," Mac said.

"Well, naturally," I said. "I mean, what's a minor atomic holocaust or two when you can nail a dangerous chap like Caselius?"

Mac said, "I owe you an apology, Eric."

Startled, I said, "What the hell for?"

He spoke carefully. "I am afraid I thought you were rather jumping to conclusions when you decided that the planned terrorist activity would be nuclear in nature, merely on the basis of the expression on a lady's face. However, we've received some information that pretty well confirms your guess."

"What information?"

Mac said, "I thought it odd that the life of a valuable specialist like Jerome Blum would be jeopardized on an operation that required only a reasonably strong pitching arm. On a hunch, I suppose you would call it, I requested an instant autopsy on the body. It turns out that Mr. Blum was a very sick man. Apparently his employers felt that, since they were about to lose him anyway, they might as well risk him at sea and get some use of him. And perhaps he went without protest, hoping to be killed, as he was. Radiation sickness does not give an easy death."

I whistled softly. "So friend Boomer had been playing around with uranium or plutonium or whatever! But, hell, I thought the guy was supposed to be an expert; you'd think he'd take all the necessary precautions."

"He was an expert with materials like dynamite, Semtex, plastique, or gelignite," Mac agreed. "But just how many civilian atom bomb experts are there? Apparently, after dealing so long with conventional explosives, Mr. Blum failed to treat the new materials he was handling with the proper respect."

I said, "All the blow-'em-up boys have the secret ambition to, just once, construct a Big One. We met another guy like that some years ago over in the Bahamas, remember?" I frowned. "So I may have guessed slightly wrong about Dorothy Fancher and her friends. It's the weapon they plan to use that's atomic, not necessarily the target they plan to use it against."

Mac said, "It doesn't take much training to make such a bomb, these days; you can buy a how-to book on any newsstand."

"Sure. *Hiroshima Made Easy.* I've just had a very interesting discussion with the lady in question..." I told him about it. "So the gadget Boomer Blum constructed for these people, at the cost of his own life, is presumably waiting somewhere near the area of its intended use. The questions are: where and when? You haven't heard of any recent terrorist activity along the East Coast, have you?"

"Nothing of the sort has been reported."

"If the thing has been in place for months, what are they waiting for?"

Mac didn't answer my question. He said, "I suppose you will have to help Mrs. Bell put a stop to this nonsense, although sabotage is not really within our designated field of operations."

I said, "Sir, I have given my sacred word not to interfere."

He spoke rather wearily. "I am told that a sense of humor can be useful to an agent, but I find yours a bit feeble at the moment, Eric." What he meant, of course, was that nothing is sacred in our business, particularly promises. He went on. "But don't let this distract you from your primary mission. How does the lady say she'll set up the touch for you?"

The Mafia calls it a hit. One of our fellow agencies likes to call it termination with extreme prejudice; well, they've always been wordy bastards over in Langley. We call it a touch.

I said, "Her idea is that she'll make contact with DAMAG again and point out that she and her associates have made a sizeable down payment on a boat-sinking—DAMAG asks for 50 percent of the fee up front—and *Lorelei III* is still floating like a cork. She'll say, either refund our deposit, Mr. Caselius, or get on your horse and earn the balance of your dough—and you'd better give it your personal attention this time, buddy, we've had enough of your incompetent underlings! And just to make sure it gets done, she'll say, she'll be right there to blindside that Helm clown if he turns out to be too much for him and his DAMAG dimwits again."

"She intends to remain on board?"

"Of course. She tells me she'll be there to help me against dangerous Mr. Caselius, just as she's undoubtedly told him she'll be there to help him against dangerous Mr. Helm. Obviously she's going to double-cross one of us. I'll be very much surprised if it turns out to be young Roland."

The lady under discussion was examining her fingernails in the light of an overhead lamp, as if to demonstrate that she was taking no interest whatever in the conversation.

Mac changed the subject. "Exactly what have you agreed to do in return for the lady's assistance?"

"Nothing," I said. "Like I said, I've simply promised non-intervention. I've agreed to attend to my own affairs and not interfere in hers. Of course I'm expected to ignore the fact that she more or less murdered her husband—well, that's cop business anyway and no concern of ours. Mostly I'm supposed to forget the gadget that was unloaded from *Lorelei III,* and give Mrs. Bell no help in finding it."

Mac said, "Does she really think you'll look the other way while she and her terrorist friends perform an act of nuclear terrorism, just because she offers you assistance in carrying out your own mission?"

I said, "Well, there's something else in favor of our cooperation. She feels that we are kindred spirits in a way—an ethnic way."

He said irritably, "That makes no sense at all. If I remember correctly, your parents were Scandinavian. Hers were Arabic—well, there have been many political rearrangements in that area and the Middle Eastern country they came from no longer exists. I'd have to check the dossier to give you the current name. But the two of you are about as far apart ethnically as it's possible to get."

I said, "You're looking at it from the wrong end, sir. You're looking at what we are, ethnically; she's looking at what we aren't, ethnically. And neither of us is a mongrel bastard of a melting-pot American like you, sir. We're the first generation of our families to be born here, and we haven't forgotten where our parents came from. We know our ancestors across the sea, we remember our proud ethnic heritage, we have worshipped at the old shrines, and our blood is pure, not the racially mixed-up mess of hemoglobin that pumps through your lousy Yankee veins, sir."

He started to make some kind of a protest, but checked himself. "Does the woman really believe this?"

I said, "She believes it fanatically, and so do the people she's with; and there's no worse fanatic than an ethnic fanatic. Even the religious fanatics can't compete; and of course these people have that, too. The question is whether she believes I believe it. I doubt that she really does. However, for her purposes I don't have to be sincere in my belief; if I'm pretending, it will do just as well. Just so I play along with her and give her, and her associates, time to carry out their preparations. At the proper moment, of course, she'll snap her fingers and somebody'll split my skull with a nice ethnic scimitar—I'm sure they wouldn't dirty their hands with a lousy infidel-type Bowie."

"What kind of preparations?"

I said, "I don't know, sir. I don't know what they're

waiting for, what's holding up the fireworks. But she's obviously come aboard to keep me feeling that I'm accomplishing great things by deceiving her and therefore will keep Mrs. Bell from lowering the boom… And these fanatics do tend to judge others by themselves. She may really think that I'm a possible convert; that nobody whose family hasn't been corrupted by many soft generations here in America could possibly admire this country. Since she hates the fact that she was born here, and can't conceive that anybody wouldn't rather be an Arab than an American, she figures that I, in more or less the same ethnic situation, although from a different part of the world, must go in for the same kind of ancestor worship. I confess that I've encouraged her. Upon coaxing, I did admit unpatriotically that I wasn't too proud of my parents' adopted country and actually thought Norman Schwarzkopf was kind of a jerk."

I heard him make a surprised sound at the other end of the line. "What in the world has General Schwarzkopf got to do with this?"

"Everything," I said.

Actually, it had turned into a weird dinner conversation at the end. I suppose I should have known, considering her origins, that the Gulf War would enter into it somehow. That was rather awkward for me because, unlike most of my countrymen—judging by the press and TV—I found it at the time a rather boring exercise in the deployment of military machinery and didn't follow it very carefully. Now that it had joined a lot of other U.S.

military excursions as ancient history, I'd forgotten most of what little I'd seen and read about it. I'm a low-tech assassin, or counterassassin; that kind of elaborate hi-tech homicide doesn't interest me much.

After claiming me as a fellow refugee from Americanism, Dorothy had asked, "Are you really proud of 'our' country's glorious triumph in the gulf? Proud of slaughtering a quarter of a million 'gooks,' or whatever the soldiers called them, at the cost of a few dozen men? Is that a brave victory to boast about?"

I thought her figures were a bit off, but it didn't seem advisable to correct her. I said, "Well, I thought it was kind of like watching Mike Tyson knock a high school welterweight out of the ring. No, I can't say it made me particularly proud."

"That is because you are not one of them, not one of the millions of soft fools who, safe in their living rooms, with those idiotic yellow ribbons tied to their front doors, licked their lips eagerly as they watched the bombs and missiles explode on TV, and drooled happily at the sight of the charred bodies—not really human, of course, just a bunch of yapping Islamic dogs who'd had the effrontery to do in Kuwait exactly what America had done in Grenada and Panama—but such behavior is not permitted to us lesser, subhuman breeds!"

I said mildly, "Well, I don't know about all that, but I didn't think friend Saddam was much of a prize."

"He was deceived, tricked into believing that America would not interfere if he corrected the unjust boundaries imposed upon his country… If America did not want Saddam Hussein to have the Kuwaiti oil fields, and if she had the courage to take them away from him and keep them for herself, well, that is how international politics work, and the strongest wins. So it has always been. But instead of being honestly ruthless—a thing that could at least be respected—she had to hide behind the pretense of defending democracy in Kuwait… Democracy in *Kuwait*? That reactionary sheikdom? How can anyone respect such hypocrisy? We cannot fight this great flabby country and hope to win, but that does not mean we cannot fight and do as much damage as we can so they will remember those broken buildings and blackened bodies that they found so entertaining on their little screens. We will see just how entertaining they find them in real life…!"

When I had finished reporting the conversation, Mac was silent for a while. I watched another freighter glide past beyond the dock and the tied-up boats, which looked very small by comparison.

Mac spoke at last, tentatively. "It seems that Mrs. Bell still, after several months, has no knowledge of the target date. What clues are there to the target area?"

I said, "As you'll recall, the boat was put aground in the North River near Coinjock, North Carolina; that's where Dorothy sent out her Mayday and put on her tearful-widow act for the rescue services. It's only a couple of days' run south of Norfolk, Virginia, the start or finish—anyway, the northern end—of the Intracoastal Waterway. But knowing where Fancher's heart finally gave out for good is not much help. Dorothy was very cagy about how many days it had taken them to get there from the spot farther south where she first assisted him into the bunk he never got out of."

Mac said, "I believe the Intracoastal Waterway is over a thousand miles long, although the extreme southern part runs along the coast of Florida and probably doesn't concern us."

I said, "Great. And Coinjock is in North Carolina, so we can forget Virginia. That's two ICW states eliminated, leaving us only three to worry about, and between six and seven hundred miles of canals and rivers. Dorothy seems to be figuring on having us at least start to retrace the route while she's setting up Caselius for me, or vice versa. I suppose she's heading us southward because it keeps us in landlocked waters where we'll be an easier target; I guess the boys and girls don't want another sea battle offshore. They didn't do so well in the last one."

Mac said, "The problem is, even if you get clear back down to the place where Truman Fancher had his first heart attack—well, actually his second; his first on the boat—how will you know it when you see it?"

I said, "Barring some other kind of a break, I can only hope Dorothy will betray herself, as she did once before."

"Does she know you are calling me?"

"Sure, she's sitting twenty yards away, watching me talk with you. I told her I had to phone my boss and sell him on our deal." After a moment, I went on. "She happens to be a very arrogant woman who is sure she can fool me.

Just as I happen to be a very arrogant man who is sure he can fool her. It makes for some great double-talk, sir."

"To be sure," Mac said. "I will report your situation to Mrs. Bell."

"Tell her that, although I've finally managed to come up with a live specimen, I'm not delivering Mrs. Fancher for interrogation because I think she's got too many lawyers on tap for us to deal with, with no more evidence than we've got. I can get more out of her by kidding her along while she's happily kidding me along. Besides, this is a real tough female, and I doubt that she could be made to talk even with heavy pressure."

"I will pass the word. Be careful, Eric."

"When am I not?"

I heard him snort, unimpressed, as he hung up. I stood there a moment trying to read the time on my fancy digital watch, which had the advantage that, unlike some old-fashioned timepieces, it didn't glow in the dark unasked and make a target of me; however, I had to remember which little button to press to illuminate the display when I wanted it lit. Time: twenty-two hours, fourteen minutes, and fifty-seven seconds—ten-fifteen p.m. to you.

Something was wrong.

Schaefer's Canal House was almost quiet. I heard the car of some late diners driving away from the front door. The back of my neck itched. I knew suddenly that I'd misread the situation, kidding myself that the lady would make her move eventually.

Eventually, hell. She'd insisted on going out to dinner

tonight in spite of a dented skull. She'd kept me listening to her revelations until the restaurant was closing and the parking lot was empty…

Something was very wrong right now.

17

I've been in the business too long to disregard that look-out-buddy-they're-closing-in-on-you feeling. Playing with my trick watch, I stalled, standing more or less sheltered by the island of pay phones in the center of the parking lot.

Question: *What the hell is haywire here, anyway?*

Answer: *Dorothy.*

She was still sitting on her piling, apparently fascinated by her fingernails. So why was she pretending she hadn't seen me hang up the phone? She wasn't the patient type; you'd think that, after being kept waiting while I made my call, she'd be on her feet ready to go.

Nothing moved in the wide, lighted, empty parking lot designed for busier times of the year, or around the restaurant behind me, or in the grove of trees with its picnic tables ahead of me on the bank of the canal. I reminded myself that I couldn't safely assume that, just because the opposition hadn't gone the sniper route before, they'd renounced it forever. Of course I could be simply suffering from a case of secret-agent midnight paranoia. We're always seeing snipers in the dark. The trouble is, of course, that quite often they're actually there.

I said, "Okay, Dorothy, let's get aboard."

"Well, it's about time!" she said.

She rose, brushed off the seat of her linen slacks fastidiously, tucked in her silk shirt neatly—and turned and dove into the canal. It was rather shocking. You don't expect a handsome, neatly dressed lady, who's just taken you to a fancy restaurant and treated you to a fine duck dinner complete with cocktails and wine and polite conversation, to end the evening by jumping into the water with all her clothes on.

On the other hand, it made some kind of sense: if there was to be shooting she'd want to get the hell out of the line of fire, anybody's fire. Clearly she'd weighed her choices and decided that the C. and D. Canal was the safest place around, and to hell with her clothes and hairdo.

I sprinted after her. I mean, my fastidious dinner companion wouldn't have deliberately got herself all wet putting distance between us unless something very dangerous was about to happen in my vicinity. Training and instinct told me to hit the dirt because a rifle bullet was about to come from somewhere, looking for me. Dropping flat was the textbook response; but the fact was that I'd make almost as easy a mark prone under the lights in the bare parking lot as I did upright. So I ran; at least I could give the guy a moving target instead of a standing one.

I also yelled, "Okay, Ziggy, take him!"

I had no real hope that the girl, if she was even within hearing, was in a position to help me, but the idea that I had reinforcements at hand might make the marksman a bit nervous... Then the gun in the trees went off, sounding like a salvo from a battleship's main battery. It threw a flame you wouldn't believe, looking like a great round ball of fire since it was aimed directly at me, which was a damn good thing. It should have been aimed a little ahead of me to allow for my forward motion. As it was, fired with insufficient lead, the massive load of buckshot ripped up the graveled parking lot behind me as I sprinted toward the water.

I'd been thinking in terms of a rifle, perhaps with a fancy modern night sight of some kind, or perhaps a submachine gun, although it was long range for the kind of pistol cartridges those weapons employ. Instead, what I had to deal with was just a plain old-fashioned shotgun, but judging by the booming report, it was a shotgun even heavier than the substantial twelve-gauge I had on *Lorelei III.* Say a long-range ten-gauge Magnum, just the medicine for sky-high ducks and geese, and stupid government agents.

Running hard, I heard a feminine voice I recognized raised in a warning cry, and some weak plopping sounds: so Ziggy was actually present and had joined the fray. The roaring boom of the shotgun was repeated, but no pellets came near me. I had a disturbing vision of the crippled girl, with her lousy little silenced .22, going up against that monstrous cannon in response to my shout, disregarding my previous orders to back off if things got dangerous. Perhaps she was trying to demonstrate that, although she'd once cracked under interrogation, she wasn't a total coward.

It seemed to take me forever to get across the open space, but I couldn't actually have spent much time at it because Dorothy hadn't got very far out from the seawall when I made my own dive. I hit the water hard and came up fairly close behind her. Oddly, in this age of windmilling crawl-stroke swimmers, she was a tidy breaststroker, moving herself along competently but not very fast, with her soaked white clothing swirling around her, and her long black hair, loosened, streaming behind her. I could probably have caught her, although my swimming abilities aren't much better than my sailing abilities; however, away from the shore my head would make a perfect shotgun target, and grabbing the lady and holding her in front of me for protection didn't appeal to me. It wasn't a matter of chivalry; it was just that I don't like betting my life on somebody's sentimentality. Maybe there was a hard guy behind the shotgun, ready to pay the price in dead dames for dead Helms. We never play that hostage game; I wasn't going to count on anybody else doing it.

I turned away, therefore, and paddled clumsily back to the seawall—I don't recommend swimming with shoes on—where I found the water only waist deep. Standing up, I pulled out the .38, shook the water out of it, and prepared to blow away anybody who shoved a ten-gauge over the edge above me. I saw the sleek, seal-like head of the swimming woman disappear among the slimy, weed-grown pilings of the offshore dock.

"Matt!" It was a girl's voice, sounding rather distant from down where I stood. "Matt, are you okay? Matt?"

"Yo!" I called back.

"It's all clear, but please get up here."

"Coming."

I threw a final glance at the dock, but the darkness underneath it was impenetrable and I could hear no splashing. To hell with Dorothy Ayesha Fancher. I guess I was rather relieved to be rid of her; she wasn't a safe or comfortable houseguest—well, boat guest—and we were probably better off having her stirring up her mischief elsewhere.

I waded a short way along the seawall. I had to crouch to remain covered as the bulkhead became lower to my right. Then came the moment of truth when I had to straighten up and show myself, remembering that it could easily be a trap. After all, the girl who called herself Ziggy had broken once and revealed an ID code that might have got me killed; she could now be calling me to my death with a shotgun muzzle against her spine.

I reared up, hauled myself over the low wall, rolled several yards inland, and wound up prone, gun ready, facing the trees ahead. The light in among them wasn't as good as out where I was, but I could see the girl by one of the picnic tables aiming her silenced pistol at a man lying on the ground. I started to pick myself up to join her, but something moved among the trees…

"Ziggy, look out!"

My shout came too late. A second man rose out of the brush behind her and swung something at her head. She went down. I fired, as the dark figure over there picked up the .22 that she'd dropped. I'd held high for the head to keep the bullet away from her, and the distance was too great for that kind of marksmanship with a snub-nosed .38. I missed and took aim again but did not fire; it would have been just another hope shot without much chance of connecting. As the man straightened up, his face moved into a beam of light from one of the parking-lot lamps, and even at that range I knew him. In Mac's office I'd seen photographs of him as a younger man; and far up in northern Scandinavia a good many years ago I'd known, and killed, an older man with very much the same features, a man named Caselius. His father.

Roland Caselius seemed to be taller than Raoul Caselius had been, but he was still not a big man. He was wearing dark clothes, slacks and jersey, and he moved like a young man in good condition. With Ziggy's .22 in his hand, he looked my way for a frustrated moment—both of us holding firearms that were inadequate for the distance between us—then he raised the pistol barrel in a kind of duelist's salute and turned away and lost himself among the trees.

I kept myself from charging after him. If he wanted to get away, and had transportation handy, pursuit was a waste of time; with his head start, he'd reach his car long before I could catch up. And if he didn't want to get away, if he decided this was a good night for avenging Daddy after all, he'd have too big an advantage if I blundered heedlessly into the darkness of the little woods after him. I waited, reloading the fired chamber of my revolver.

At last I heard a car start up and drive away, and I saw Ziggy stir and sit up, groping for her pistol. Not finding it, she stood up shakily, feeling her head. I was surprised at the strength of my relief at seeing her relatively undamaged—well, except for her earlier injuries. Hell, I'd only spoken to her once for a matter of minutes.

"Matt," she called. "Matt, where are—?"

She stopped abruptly. Looking around, she'd caught sight of the man on the ground. She stared at him for a moment and turned away, and bent over. Even at the distance, I could hear her being violently ill.

I rose and hurried over there, taking a chance that Caselius might, after driving off a little way, come sneaking back. I was motivated by a growing sense of urgency. While a shot or two might have gone unremarked in these rural surroundings, we'd put on enough of a firefight that somebody must have called a policeman or constable or sheriff or whatever law-enforcement official operated locally. When I reached her, Ziggy was wiping her mouth with a Kleenex.

"It's Roger Hassim. I… I never shot a man before," she said shakily. "And I did a lousy job, he's still alive, just lying there looking up at me… Oh, God, here I go again!" She turned away, retching. I stepped over to the body. Hassim was still alive, but that was about all that could be said for him. I suppose it was too bad in a way: as I'd been told more than once, he was, or had been, a very beautiful creature indeed. He had a face off an ancient frieze, Egyptian or Abyssinian or whatever, such as I'd once seen in a museum, but with the racial characteristics subdued. It had only a trace of the beaky, hawklike look that Mrs. Bell had a lot of and Dorothy a considerable amount; it was simply a remarkably handsome male face cast in bronze—well, the skin could just have been heavily suntanned but wasn't.

The torso, in light slacks and a sport shirt, had obviously been terrific, also, but three .22-caliber bullet holes—two in the chest and one in the left side of the neck—had apparently destroyed some critical operating circuits, and the man simply lay there looking up at us with big liquid eyes.

"I'm sorry," the girl said, coming up beside me. "I was hiding over there, watching. I didn't have a clear shot when you yelled, I couldn't keep him from getting off that first one. And then it took me three to put him down."

I said, "You did fine."

The lovely man on the ground just watched us with his beautiful brown eyes.

Ziggy went on: "When I shouted to distract him, he tried to bring the gun around to shoot me, but my first bullet made him let one go prematurely that just blasted splinters off the top of the table. Even so, he kept trying, and almost made it. I missed my second shot altogether, trying to shoot too fast. Then I managed to hit with the next two, and he went down at last. God, for a while I thought those damn little bullets weren't doing *anything*; I was beginning to think I'd have to beat him down with the gun barrel!"

Reaction had her talking too much; but she'd earned the right. The man on the ground made an involuntary moaning sound and choked it off.

I spoke to Ziggy. "This is the guy who worked you over?"

"Yes, of course. I told you. Roger Hassim."

"Do you want to finish him off?"

"What... Oh, God, no!" She licked her lips. "It's funny how often I've dreamed of killing him, but..."

I sighed. "Then I guess I'll have to."

I started to raise the .38; then I saw the big shotgun lying on the ground beside the picnic table with the buckshot-splintered top. I picked it up. It was what we used to call, in our technical innocence, an automatic shotgun; nowadays, in the interest of accuracy, we've got to say semiautomatic or self-loader. They're commonplace in twelve-gauge, but there are only a few that take the big ten-gauge shells, perhaps only the one. I haven't checked the catalogs recently. It had been loaded with the legal waterfowl-hunting limit of three shells; there was still one in the chamber.

I aimed and fired; the gun spouted its impressive tongue of flame, made its ferocious blast of sound, and pushed me back a step with its heavy recoil, fortunately a long, strong push rather than a sharp blow. At this range, the massive load of buckshot, where I'd aimed it, tore Roger Hassim wide open, disemboweling and castrating him. It did not kill him instantly; he had time to look down weakly at the ugly wreckage of his body, and raise his eyes to me, shocked and accusing. Then the lovely brown eyes filmed over, and he was dead.

The girl grabbed me by the arm and started shaking me. "No! she cried. "No, even if I hated him, I didn't want… You didn't have to do it like that! Oh, that was dirty!"

It takes them awhile to understand that dead is dead, whether you're drilled neatly through the head with a little .22 bullet or ripped wide open by a massive ten-gauge load of buckshot.

I said, "Come on, let's get out of here."

"Damn you, Matt Helm, I'll have nightmares…"

Her insomnia was no concern of mine; I just took her by the arm and hurried her away. When we were out of the trees, I stopped her.

She blurted, "Why did you…?"

I said, "For Christ's sake, Kronquist, snap out of it. I'm beginning to think you're the total loss I was told you were. Remember that there are two kinds of animals that walk on two legs, *thems* and *usses*. What's lying back there was a *them*, not an *us*, and what happened to it was of no significance. Now get over to one of those phones and call Mrs. Bell while I head for the boat and warm up the diesel; we've got to get out of here before the law arrives. Tell Mrs. Bell to get here fast and clean up after us. Then come running and help me cast off… Oh, here. "I gave her my revolver. "You may need this; Dorothy Fancher's around somewhere. Last seen swimming in the canal, but she could be armed if she's managed to climb aboard one of the boats out there and steal a weapon."

"All right, Matt."

Her obedience was mechanical, and she turned toward the phones stiffly, moving like a zombie. I dug Dorothy Fancher's little .25 out of my hip pocket for something to carry. Now that the evening's emotional peak was past, I hoped, I had the self-conscious feeling you always get, muddy and wet, in a world full of clean, dry people—well, almost full. I couldn't afford to forget the other soggy specimen, female, that was somewhere around. I headed toward the nearest crosswalk and was almost there when Ziggy's voice hit me.

"Matt, no!"

I turned to see her running toward me in her halting way. "What—"

"You can't go out there!" She stopped in front of me, panting. "I… I'm sorry, I'm all shook up, I almost forgot. While you were in the restaurant with that woman, a man boarded *Lorelei III* carrying something; he didn't have it when he came ashore. I was starting to leave my hiding place to go inside and tell you when I realized that another one had come into the trees with that great big shotgun; he kind of had me trapped in that awkward spot. I… I figured, if I tried to slip by him, and he got me, there wouldn't be anybody to warn you about the boat, so I'd better just wait."

I said, "Hell, I should have known. That's why Dorothy waited around while I made my phone call; she wasn't about to go on ahead and board a booby-trapped boat. It must have been young Caselius you saw, the same guy who got you from behind."

"I saw him leave; I thought he'd gone for good," she said.

"How long did he spend on board?"

"Not very long. Ten minutes at the most."

I said, "Okay, go call Mrs. Bell. Tell her the situation."

Ziggy interrupted: "It's probably a bomb, isn't it? I'll ask her to send an expert."

I shook my head again. "We haven't got time for that. We've made enough of a racket that somebody must have called it in; there has to be fuzz on the way. If they catch us here, it'll take Mrs. Bell days to pry us loose. I'll go aboard and see what I can find. If he only spent ten minutes out there, he couldn't have done anything very elaborate or hidden it very well." I shook my head ruefully. "The old double whammy. Mrs. F gave me a lot of crap about how she'd come to seduce me; but it was all just a smoke screen for this. Even after being creased by a bullet, she insisted on taking me to dinner on shore so Hassim and Caselius could set it up. I guess she figured that if I managed to escape the shotgun ambush on my way back to the boat, I'd be feeling so smart that it wouldn't occur to me to take any precautions going aboard."

"Matt, you can't... Do you know anything about defusing bombs?"

I said, "Sure, I know the red wire is negative and the black one is positive, or is it the other way round?" When she started to speak again, I said, "Go on, dammit, make your phone call. And don't come out to the boat until I signal all clear, okay?"

She hesitated, and said reluctantly, "All right, Matt."

I was only vaguely aware of her walking away; I was forcing my feet, squishing in their wet shoes, to move me out across the little wooden bridge to the long dock—I guess I'm really not very fond of high explosives. Then a left turn. Then eleven steps, and a smart right-face; and I was confronting the sliding door that would admit me to *Lorelei III*'s deckhouse.

Everything looked perfectly normal. There didn't seem to be any odd wires attached to the door; and Ziggy had said Roland Caselius had actually gone aboard. If she'd seen him just crouching on the side deck wiring up a whizbang, she'd presumably have mentioned it.

Okay, you'll be needing both hands for this, so put away the peashooter... Now step aboard very lightly, don't rock the damn boat unnecessarily. Key in lock—how did he manage that? Well, it's a simple lock, easy to pick. Click. Key back in pocket. Now slide back the door very gently. No loud bangs, goody. Still no dangling wires...

I looked at the familiar interior. The lights were on, as we'd left them. I took stock of my indicators. One corner of the carpet not fully tucked away under the wooden molding, check. Helmsman's stool set aside not quite parallel to the side of the deckhouse, check. Unless he was very good indeed, with a photographic memory, he hadn't moved out the furniture and pulled up the carpet and visited the engine room and done his stuff down there, and then put everything back exactly as I'd left it—well, in ten minutes, he'd hardly had time.

On the other hand, the teak top of the little corner cocktail-and-breakfast table, just a friction fit on its metal pedestal, was now exactly square with the boat. I'd left it slightly cockeyed. Obviously he'd bumped against it and carefully squared it up the way he figured a tidy seaman like me would have left it. Encouraging. He could make mistakes. And the black tape marker on one of the steering-wheel spokes—it helped me center the rudder when I was maneuvering—that spoke was in the upright position instead of being lined up with one of the corner screws of the console…

I stood for a moment longer trying to get into the mind of Mr. Roland Caselius, coming aboard my boat, vengeance in heart, bomb in hand. I remembered the jaunty salute he'd given me ashore, before turning away. Sure. Why should he indulge in a risky long-range pistol duel when he had a lethal surprise waiting for me here? He was probably sitting in his car a quarter of a mile away, hoping to hear a big bang and see a burst of light above the trees.

Ten minutes, I reflected. Something simple. He could have knocked against the table on his way to just about anywhere on the boat, but why had he messed with the steering wheel?

Well, why not, stupid? Isn't the steering console where practically all the ship's electrical connections are located?

I stepped down into the deckhouse at last. No pressure-sensitive gadget hidden under the carpet blew my foot off. I lowered myself cautiously to kneel in front of the wheel, and looked at the little plywood door below it that gave access to the bottom of the console and the two big master switches inside, one for the engine battery and the other for the two batteries that, wired in parallel, provided light and refrigeration. There was a lot of other wiring higher up inside the console; but if you wanted to work on that, you had to remove the steering wheel, take out half a dozen long screws—make that seven by actual count—and pull off the whole front panel of the console; but that was more than a ten-minute job in itself.

I reached out cautiously, and my hand retreated of its own accord. Chicken! I made myself reach out again. I found the catch with my finger and swung open the little plywood door, and nothing blew, and there it was…

"Matt."

Startled, I jerked back and hit my head on the little table behind me. Ziggy stood in the doorway.

"Jesus Christ!" I said. "Don't sneak up on a man like that. I told you to stay on shore, dammit!"

"Don't be silly, I want to help," she said. Apparently Roger Hassim's gruesome death was forgiven, or at least shelved for the moment. "What can I do?"

Well, if the fool wench was bound she was going to get herself blown up proving she was really a very brave girl after all, who was I to stop her?

I said, “Come around me carefully. Get the flashlight from the ledge behind the settee, and some paper towels from the galley, and a roll of black tape, electricians tape, from my toolbox over there… Okay. Now hunker down beside me and shine the light in here so I can see what I’m doing.”

I couldn’t help wincing as the flashlight beam hit the thing; but apparently it wasn’t photosensitive. It just lay there, inert, at the bottom of the console.

Ziggy cleared her throat. “It… looks just like a bomb, doesn’t it?”

It did look just like a bomb, not the round black anarchist kind from the comic strips, with the sputtering fuse, but the crude four-sticks-of-dynamite-taped-together kind, with a couple of wires coming out of it. Both wires were black. Well, I don’t suppose polarity means much to a detonator; it’ll happily take its current in either direction.

“A little higher,” I said.

Crouching beside me, Ziggy directed the light upward while I craned my neck to see where, in the incomprehensible tangle of colored wires that ran the boat, the black ones ended. Okay. Two alligator clips, not very far up. What were they hooked to? Don’t ask; I didn’t. I disengaged myself cautiously, although it didn’t seem likely, now, that the thing was going to be set off by movement. Some water from my wet clothes had dampened my hands, and water is an electrical conductor.

I didn't want any electrical conductors dripping around, so I dried my hands carefully on the paper towels Ziggy had brought me. I picked up the roll of tape.

"What's that for?" she asked.

I said, "I want to tape those clips as I take them off, so they don't accidentally make contact with each other."

She said, "I shouldn't think that would set it off. It obviously has no battery of its own; I can't see any, and why bother with little dry cells when you have twelve volts and several hundred ampere hours handy in the boat's big batteries?"

I said, "Who's defusing this damn bomb, anyway?"

"Sorry."

I reached up and disconnected one clip, and nothing happened. I brought it out cautiously, letting it touch nothing on the way, and wrapped rubbery black tape around it—probably quite unnecessary, as Ziggy had said, but tape's cheap. I brought out the other clip the same way, for the same treatment. Easy. Hey, where's the nearest bomb-disposal squad, and do they take hero-volunteers?

I said, "It doesn't seem to be attached in any other way, does it?"

"No."

"Then I guess I'm safe in lifting it out now," I said. "Well, we'll soon know."

I lifted it out. It wasn't attached, and it didn't explode. I coiled the wires carefully and taped them to the already tape-wrapped bundle of dynamite sticks.

"Do you want me to throw it overboard?" Ziggy asked.

I studied the thing. It could, of course, have a timing device in addition to the contact wires; it could be booby-trapped in a dozen ways, and I wouldn't know the difference. On the other hand, it's only on TV that the hero makes a habit of throwing away useful weapons he encounters in the course of his adventures, or leaving them behind, and DAMAG hadn't shown any great flights of imagination so far, although I had to admit this double-barreled effort tonight had been fairly ingenious.

I said, "You never know when a few sticks of dynamite will come in handy."

I put the bundle away at the bottom of a nearby locker and stowed the tape in my toolbox, reflecting that from the amount of stuff I'd accumulated in there over the past couple of months, working on the boat, you'd think I was a mechanical genius.

Ziggy said, "What I really came for was to tell you that Mrs. Bell says she'll take care of everything if we just get clear and keep going. Oh, and I saw Mrs. Fancher crawl ashore way up ahead of us; she looked like a giant muskrat or something with all that wet black hair. And there's a siren coming… Well, it's getting pretty close now."

"To hell with the woman. Let's vacate these premises as instructed. Take in the lines while I fire up the mill."

Ziggy didn't move at once, and I realized that she was waiting for me to start the engine. She obviously wasn't quite sure that we'd cleaned up the premises; Caselius could, for instance, have shoved one package way up inside the console and then left a second one, more obvious, down below for us to play with. I didn't think he'd had the time, or was that tricky, but I could be wrong. Well, we couldn't hang around here forever…

I made myself reach out deliberately and turn the key. The big diesel rumbled into life beneath our feet with no more noise than usual. Ziggy winked at me and swung herself up to the side deck and down to the dock, managing quite gracefully in spite of her injured foot. Moments later she was back, tossing the last line aboard.

"Okay, you're free, skipper, take her away."

The approaching siren was quite close now, but as we were gliding away I heard another sound from the shore: an eerie, wild-animal howl that belonged out in coyote country, not in these civilized eastern surroundings. Ziggy, securing the gate in the boat's rail, heard it, too; she looked around questioningly. I made sure we were headed in a safe direction for the moment, centered the wheel, and joined her out on the side deck where I could hear better.

The wailing sound came again. I recognized it now; it was a human—a female human—shout of mindless grief. The woman called Ayesha was mourning over the mutilated body of her lover.

18

It was the first time on this cruise that I had managed the boat from the upper control station, although I'd watched three different female navigators operate back there. Ziggy, the latest nautical lady to handle the big stainless-steel wheel, had held it while I got into dry clothes, and for an hour more of slow progress—the night mist had thickened into real fog—but presently I noticed that she was trying not to wince whenever she had to make a course correction. I got her to admit that her splinted hand was hurting her, and took over, under her supervision.

It was tough steering for an inexperienced helmsman. At times I thought the bowsprit was going to disappear completely into the murky darkness ahead, tinted red and green by the boat's running lights. However, as I've said, the canal was illuminated like a city street; the lights, set on wooden posts in the water near the bank, were close enough together that upon reaching one we could generally make out the vague glow of the next.

Looking on the bright side, any police boat sent after us would have trouble finding us in this thick stuff. Well, with radar, in such narrow waters, maybe not a lot of trouble; but at least the fog should hold off the boys in blue long enough for Mrs. Bell to get them called off altogether.

"Better come left a bit," Ziggy said, "you're starting to lose depth again."

"Left, aye, aye," I said.

The outside steering station had the advantage of giving the helmsman a clear view; under these lousy conditions of visibility we didn't need the added handicap of steering from behind glass. However, there were drawbacks. In addition to being totally exposed to the weather—there was no real rain, but we'd both put on oilskins against the penetrating dampness—the upper station lacked instrumentation: no knot meter, no tachometer or engine gauges, no loran, no radar.

Fortunately, the one instrument that did exist back there, besides a steering compass, was the one that was essential to tell us when we were getting too close to the bank: a depth-sounder. Unfortunately, it had apparently been an afterthought, installed in a space that just happened to be available, quite low on the bulkhead under the wheel. Even Ziggy had had to crouch to read it; with my greater height, I almost had to go to my knees, each time taking my attention off the canal ahead longer than I liked—if the lights of another boat came at us out of the foggy blackness, I'd have to react instantly to have any hope of avoiding a collision. We'd therefore put Ziggy on one of the seats back there that afforded a good view of the illuminated numbers, and given her the duty of calling them out to me.

"Good, you're back to twelve feet," she said.

The digital instrument, clearly a later, high-tech American addition to this Finn-built boat, also differed from the old-fashioned rotary flasher in the deckhouse in that it did not read in meters.

Ziggy's voice came again: "I… I want to apologize."

"What the hell for?"

"I guess I'm just not used to seeing mangled bodies—well, besides my own. But considering the way I've spent months thinking of the gruesome deaths I'd inflict on that sadistic bastard if I ever got the chance, I can't believe that I acted like such a sentimental jackass… But why do it like that? I'm not criticizing," she added hastily. "I'm just curious. I don't think that you, unlike Mr. Hassim, go around mutilating people for fun."

I said, "Well, those .22-caliber holes you put into him weren't necessarily fatal. We had to be rid of him permanently, for one thing because he was the visible leader of this Arab terrorist gang. With him gone, Dorothy Fancher, the unseen partner up to now, can't hide behind him anymore; she's got to come out of the closet and take control. That'll make Mrs. Bell's job easier. And my job is Caselius. Dorothy didn't seem very impressed with him and his DAMAG outfit when she talked with me. Now that she's in charge, she might have fired the whole crew—but not now, not after the crummy way I finished off her boyfriend, not a chance. She's going to join the Hate Helm Club, of which Caselius is a charter member, and keep him around to help her feed the vengeance fires; there's nothing like a common enemy to make a couple of people bosom friends."

"I see... Nine feet. Better come left a little."

"Left, aye, aye."

We glided through the murk for a while, in silence except for Ziggy's voice calling out the soundings; at last she raised her head and looked around.

"I do think it's clearing a bit."

I realized that, although we hadn't reached the next light, I could see the one beyond it; I could also see ghostly trees and bushes along the shore to starboard in the diffused light of dawn. There was a sound astern. Looking over my shoulder, I saw a large yacht coming out of the mists, gaining on us rapidly. It was another junior-grade cruise ship in the sixty-foot class, like the one I'd seen docked at Schaefer's. I'd read somewhere that while little boats were hard to get rid of these recession days, big ones were still selling pretty well.

Apparently the vessel astern had been, like *Lorelei III,* creeping cautiously through the fog from light to light; but now that the visibility was improving she was putting on speed, swinging out toward the middle of the channel to pass us. Unlike the one at the canal house, which had had a cabin aft, this vessel had a rather low cockpit back there, in the middle of which was set a large and elaborate fish-fighting chair. It seemed like a hell of a lot of boat to take out trolling for little fish, or even big ones, and I'd have hated to be the captain who had to maneuver all thirty-some tons of her when the owner hooked into something energetic.

She was really a floating skyscraper; not only was there a flying bridge above the deckhouse, but there was another control station way up in the tall tuna tower above that, reached by a rudimentary ladder that made me dizzy just to look at it. However, the helmsman wasn't up in the spindly tower this morning; he was apparently satisfied with the visibility from one story down. The flying bridge was actually a little plastic greenhouse, reasonably well protected from the elements by transparent curtains all around, a common sight this uncertain time of year. The helmsman, kind of blurred in his elevated cellophane box, gave us a friendly wave as he went by. *Gulf Streamer*, from Fort Lauderdale, Florida.

The fog had thinned to the point where I could now see both sides of the canal, which was widening as we entered the headwaters of the Chesapeake Bay. Soon it was no longer a canal, just a buoyed channel through a widening estuary. I ran the throttle forward; it was a real pleasure to feel the old girl come to life again after the endless hours of barely making steerage way. Suddenly, miraculously, we ran out of the fog altogether and found the morning sun shining brightly. We shed our foul-weather gear and shifted control to the lower station.

Chesapeake Bay turned out to be a navigational nightmare. The U.S. armed forces were ganging up on us. Lori had warned me that the loran might not work properly here because of the navy's powerful radio station at Annapolis, and it didn't; but she hadn't mentioned that the Coast Guard had scrambled practically all the buoys on the bay—at least this upper end of the bay—so that their numbers, and sometimes even their locations, didn't correspond with what was printed on my charts. Without a navigator, I might have been in serious trouble; however, Ziggy knew the area, and eventually, in spite of the obstructive efforts of the U.S. government, we found our way into open water.

By late afternoon we'd motored under the impressive spans of the Chesapeake Bay Bridge—it's actually two separate bridges, eastbound and westbound—and entered the Severn River a few miles below it, passing the navy antennas that were scrambling our loran, a real forest of them on the point. We docked in Annapolis where, years ago, I'd really commenced my nautical career by submitting, with a dozen other eager young agents from carefully unidentified agencies, to a short course in small-boat seamanship designed for spooks who might have to get their feet wet.

Today, my docking maneuver was performed quite smartly, if I do say so myself; a credit to my Naval Academy training, all two weeks of it.

"I think we'd better have another fender here… No, a little farther aft. There, that does it."

When I heard the familiar voice, I'd just finished adjusting *Lorelei III*'s dock lines with Ziggy's help. I hadn't really studied my surroundings except to mark down in my mind, as I always do, the potential danger sectors from which a sniper could operate, and to note that we'd been directed to pull in astern of the oversize sportfisherman that had passed us earlier in the day. Now I looked that way, to see a small figure on the dock giving instructions to a red-haired young man on the yacht's deck above; he was securing an inflated rubber fender—we salty seamen don't refer to them as boat bumpers—roughly the size of the Goodyear blimp. I moved that way. With the problem solved to her satisfaction, Lori Fancher turned to greet me.

I said, "I didn't recognize you, hiding up there behind all that plastic, when you passed us this morning."

"And you were probably calculating just how far you should lead me if you had to shoot me," she said dryly.

"Natch, what else," I said. I looked at the impressive powerboat. "A delivery job?"

Lori was wearing skinny, faded jeans and a loose blue sweatshirt, neither very clean. There was a smudge of grease on her cheek, but she was still a very attractive little girl, and I knew a moment of regret. Well, there are always the ones who make you wish you were a better person and had led a better life; and there's never a damn thing to be done about it.

She nodded in answer to my question. "It was on the answering machine when I got home. They want her in Lauderdale for the winter, so I got hold of Billy, who's sailed with me before—" She indicated the young man now hosing down the decks, "—and took off." She looked past me at Ziggy, who'd come up to join us. "Hi, I'm Lori Fancher."

"Ziggy Kronquist."

The two girls didn't shake hands, which didn't mean anything; girls often don't. But there was a moment of wary appraisal, while Ziggy obviously wondered just what my relationship with this salty, grubby, tanned little female might be, and Lori just as clearly wondered where I'd found this lanky beat-up specimen and had I slept with her in that big aft bunk on *Lorelei III*—not that Lori gave a damn, heavens no; it was just something a girl kind of liked to know about a man she'd slept with herself.

"That's quite a boat you've got there," Ziggy said, nodding toward the big sportfisherman.

"As I was just telling Matt, I'm delivering her to Florida," Lori said. "Yes, she's not a bad boat, if you like big powerboats and are in a hurry… Oh, this is Billy Barstow."

Red-haired Mr. Barstow looked sloppy and comfortable in threadbare jeans cut off raggedly above the knees and a knitted green sport shirt with paint on the front and a rip at one shoulder. He was a chubby, freckled young fellow; and with that curly bright hair and a truly sweet and friendly grin he was seemingly just the kind of happy crew member you'd want to have on board—but like an attractive blond girl I'd met not too long ago, also an ideal shipmate at first glance, he was just a little too good to be true.

If you looked hard, you realized that he wasn't chubby

at all; what was there was two hundred pounds of solid muscle. If you looked even harder, and knew what to look for, you could see that the nice-boy-next-door grin was belied by the cold and unsmiling and watchful gray-green eyes. I knew what to look for, and I knew that I wasn't ever going to be happy with cheerful, friendly Billy Barstow behind me, even if he was supposed to be one of the good guys. I mean, I'm supposed to be one of the good guys, too—well, kind of—but Mac sometimes gives us some pretty weird instructions. How did I know what kind of orders Mr. Barstow was operating under?

"If you want to go out and have something to eat with your friends, I'll keep an eye on the boat, skipper," he said to Lori after the introductions. "Nice to meet you, Miss Kronquist, Matt."

He swung himself back aboard *Gulf Streamer* in a rubbery, effortless way, and grabbed his hose and long-handled brush, and went back to washing down the hull. It's a compulsion with powerboat people, I've noticed; they start scrubbing the minute they tie up to a dock. Sailboat folks don't seem to be quite so obsessed with getting the salt off soonest; and as a matter of fact the *real* sailors, the ones who cross oceans, apparently don't have this terrible fear that a little residual seawater is going to eat big holes in their boats, perhaps because, after thousands of sea miles, it hasn't.

Ziggy said, "I want to check the engine, Matt. It was a fairly long day's run. Anyway, I haven't even seen our power plant yet, and I'd better learn how to get at it."

Mindful of her broken hand, I started to offer to help her with the heavy hatches, but checked myself, realizing that *(a)* she was being nice and deliberately giving me some time alone with a girl she saw I liked, and *(b)* she wouldn't thank me for calling attention to her infirmities by acting solicitous.

Lori said, "Well, Matt, since things seem to be under control on both our ships, suppose we important sea captains hike over to a nice restaurant I know down along the creek, just a few blocks from here..."

I told Ziggy not to work too hard while I was playing hooky; and Lori waved farewell to Billy, very industrious with hose and brush.

I asked Lori, "Where did you find that one?"

"Billy? Oh, Billy's always somewhere around. I've used him on other deliveries. He's a doll."

"Unlike me?" I said.

She glanced at me sharply. "Definitely unlike you, Matt. You're a lot of things, some bad, some good, but a doll you are not."

I asked, "How long is always?"

She frowned. "What do you mean?"

"I'm just curious. How long has Mr. Barstow always been somewhere around?"

She hesitated. "Matt, I..."

I sighed. "I hate to call a nice girl a liar, Lori, but I do not believe that bouncing redhead is just a helpful chap you've known since the two of you shared pacifiers in the playpen. After a moment, I went on. "You showed good sense by walking out on this screwball operation after completing the short delivery that was all you'd really contracted for. I wish you'd continued to stay the hell out of it. You almost got killed once associating with nasty people like me, wasn't that enough?"

She spoke dryly: "There's nothing that makes a girl's day like having a man act overjoyed to see her." When I didn't respond to that, she went on. "I really don't understand what you're trying to say, Matt."

I said, "I'm trying to say, and saying, that William Barstow, Esquire, is definitely not a doll, any more than I am. Do you think we don't know each other, sweetheart? Do you think a wolf doesn't recognize another wolf? Do you think a rattlesnake doesn't recognize another rattler? I could smell that guy in the dark."

She started to speak quickly, and stopped, saying, "Here we are."

It was a big, bulky, gray-painted wooden building, apparently a converted boat shed of some kind, set on pilings out over the creek, so-called, a tributary of the Severn. In arid New Mexico we'd have called that much water a river in its own right. There was a dock out front for customers arriving by boat. Inside, the place had a very high ceiling; far up there, the old beams and rafters were visible. The light was medium dim, pleasant after the strong fall sunshine outside. There were red-checked tablecloths on the heavy wooden tables.

After being seated, Lori said grudgingly, "All right, I really haven't known Billy very long, but he seemed nice enough… I guess I'll have a vodka and tonic."

"And one vodka martini," I said to the waitress. To Lori, I said, "I'm not trying to run the guy down."

"Calling a man a rattlesnake isn't running him down?"

I said, "From a fellow rattlesnake, it could be a compliment, He looks like a fairly tough young fellow, and if you're going to follow me and *Lorelei III* around in that junior-grade destroyer escort, I'm glad you have somebody on board who may be able to handle the trouble you're asking for. But don't try to kid me he's a just childhood playmate."

She drew an uncertain breath. "I didn't realize that he was… I'm not very bright about people, I guess."

I said, "Mrs. Bell wished him off on you, didn't she?"

"Actually, the whole idea was Mrs. Bell's," Lori said. "That was the message on my answering machine when I got home to Newport: I was to call her at once. She sent me right back over to Montauk to skipper this boat along the same route as before, again at twice my regular rates; she said she wanted you to have reinforcements available. Billy was on board when I got there."

When we returned to the marina after a pleasant meal, Barstow was still polishing away at *Gulf Streamer* in the fading evening light. He greeted us as if he were truly happy to see us, and gave Lori a hand to help her aboard, lifting her up to the deck without apparent effort. She invited me aboard for an after-dinner drink, but I asked for a rain check. There was no real reason why Ziggy should have come to the deckhouse doorway to welcome me home, like a loving bride, but the fact that she wasn't in sight made me uneasy.

I walked down the dock and stepped up to *Lorelei III*'s side deck. The slight roll of the boat in response to my weight should have alerted anybody on board to my arrival, but Ziggy didn't appear or call a greeting. I drew a long breath and palmed the .25. Then I caught a hint of tobacco smoke drifting out the open door. Okay. No professional waiting in ambush is going to alert the quarry by smoking; and amateurs seldom shoot you without doing a lot of talking first. I parked the firearm and stepped down into the deckhouse.

The first thing I saw—in fact I had a hard time not felling over it—was an expensive, leather-bound duffel bag or sea-bag of heavy green canvas, with a polished brass plate displaying the initials T.O.B. The second thing I saw, seated at the corner table, was Mrs. Teresa Bell. I remembered being told that her maiden name had been Othman. She was again wearing a dark, snug, dressy black suit; this one let a triangle of white blouse show. There were again sheer black stockings and high-heeled black shoes. A .38 revolver I recognized lay on the table in front of her.

I looked around. "Where's Ziggy?" I asked.

Mrs. Teresa Othman Bell tapped the long ash of her cigarette into a coffee mug she must have got from the galley, and said, "I hope you don't mind."

"Tobacco smoke?" I shook my head. "No, ma'am. I don't expect to live long enough, in my line of work, to die from secondhand emphysema. You haven't said where Ziggy's got to."

Mrs. Bell gave me a hard, challenging look. "I sent Kronquist away. I told you I did not want you to use her. I cannot afford to have this already fouled-up operation further jeopardized by inadequate personnel." She gestured toward the weapon on the table. "I relieved her of that. She said it was yours. I feel that unreliable young lady is better off without firearms."

She was clearly expecting an argument; but there was nothing to be gained by getting into a fight with her, so I merely shrugged.

"So?"

Mrs. Bell spoke calmly: "You once invited me aboard to assist you, if you recall, Mr. Helm. Well, here I am. If you would be so kind as to put my bag into the forward cabin while I finish my cigarette, I will change into a more suitable costume; I just drove down from Washington."

Her eyes still challenged me, slightly amused how as she waited to see if I had the gall to tell her I didn't want her on board. But there was something else in her handsome, dark, predatory face. Behind the show of amusement, Mrs. Teresa Othman Bell was a worried woman.

I realized that considerable pressure must have been exerted on this high-powered executive lady to drive her to the desperate expedient of leaving her Washington command post and joining the troops in the field. Apparently there were reasons why she could not afford, professionally, to have this operation go wrong, so she was taking over its management in person. It explained the presence of Lori and Billy Barstow with the big, fast sportfisherman. They were not really escorting *Lorelei III* south to give me support and assistance, as Lori had been told; they'd been sent along primarily to look after the interests of their commander in chief, riding with me.

I said, "On this ship we carry our own bags, ma'am. And the crew does the cooking."

She laughed, and crushed out her cigarette, and rose. "As you wish. You are the skipper. Well, up to a point."

19

I guess I was getting hardened to having strange women living at the other end of the boat; my rest was not disturbed by speculations about whether this one slept in a nightie, pajamas, or none of the above. In the morning, when I emerged from my stateroom aft, she was already working in the galley. I had to admit that I had no complaints about the industriousness of the crews I'd had on board: even Dorothy Fancher had done a good job on the dishes.

My breakfast eggs were nicely scrambled, neatly mounded on the plate, and surrounded by a tidy fence of four bacon strips, one more than I usually allow myself, but I can be persuaded. The coffee was, shall we say, undistinguished, but that wasn't the cook's fault; there was nothing but instant on board. She joined me at the big table in the main saloon with her own plate and cup. I noted that she, also, had bacon, although I seemed to remember that it was a no-no for Arabs as well as Jews. I recalled that she hadn't taken the anti-alcohol attitude of her forebears seriously, either. Or perhaps she took the traditional Muslim prohibitions very seriously indeed, seriously enough to rebel against them at every opportunity.

She didn't ask how I'd slept, or if my breakfast was satisfactory—if I didn't like the food she'd prepared, her attitude said, I could damn well spit it out and cook my own.

She said, "I want us to get under way as soon as possible, Mr. Helm. I've decided not to stop at either Solomon's Island or Fishing Bay, as originally planned. I want us to head straight for the start of the Intracoastal Waterway at Norfolk, at the best speed we can manage. We should be there tomorrow morning."

I studied her across the big table. She was wearing a piratical red-and-white-striped jersey and crisp white cotton trousers that, I was pleased to see, were not fashionably baggy; they were just plain, straight pants. Her black hair was neatly brushed with the streak of gray prominently displayed. She'd worn considerable makeup the previous evening; presumably that was her business face. Her boating face, this morning, displayed hardly any cosmetics. Nevertheless, even without them, her dusky skin looked smooth and clear; I revised my estimate of her age downward a bit.

"Tomorrow morning?" I said. "That means running all night."

"Yes."

I shrugged. "It's okay with me, I'm all caught up on my sleep. But I hope you remember that we've got that souped-up navy radio station sitting right on top of us blasting the loran off the air. It'll have to be mostly eyeball navigation, and it'll be mostly up to you. I have trouble enough finding my way around the water in broad daylight."

"It's no great problem," Mrs. Bell said. "Actually, night piloting is easier in some respects. Chesapeake Bay isn't all that narrow, particularly south of here, and the bad spots are well marked with lighthouses. We should have a favorable wind, judging by a weather report I listened to—after you turned in last night. It ought to be a fairly easy run."

"May I ask, what's our hurry?"

She smiled thinly. "There isn't any, really," she said.

I frowned, feeling stupid. "Then why—"

She said, "But they don't know that, do they?"

After a moment, I whistled softly. "Right on, baby!"

"I prefer not to be addressed as 'baby,'" she said.

"Yes, ma'am," I said, "Sorry, ma'am."

She started to speak sharply, obviously to tell me that she also preferred not to be addressed as "ma'am," but checked herself.

She said instead, "You see it, don't you?" When I nodded, she said, "Tell me what you see."

I gave it a bit of thought before I spoke. "Well, while she was on board here, Dorothy Fancher got a pretty good idea of the schedule you'd set me—I made no secret of it—and she'll have passed it along to Roland Caselius and his DAMAG goons, male and female. So they all know where to expect us the next two nights, right?"

Mrs. Bell said, "If you tell me that I'm trying to elude

them by doing something unexpected, I'll be disappointed in you, Mr. Helm."

"Elude, hell," I said. "You're smart enough to realize that there's no way of eluding them. It's one of the controlling factors of the situation: they *know* we'll be heading down the Waterway. They know that if they lose us on the Chesapeake, all they have to do is race ahead and wait along one of those narrow rivers or canals further south and pick us up again as we go by. Anyway, you're obviously not trying to lose them; you're trying to find them—and tease them into jumping right into your lap. Our laps. What's the matter, do you have problems in Washington? Are they bugging you for quicker action?"

"My Washington problems are none of your business." Her voice was stiff.

"Sure," I said. "But you're obviously trying to light a fire under the opposition by making it look as if we'd suddenly got hold of something… I mean, there I was, loafing along happily according to my easy schedule, a mere forty-fifty miles a day, content to have a partially disabled young lady for crew. Suddenly you appear out of the blue, along with a fast escort vessel. You boot the poor, handicapped girl off my boat and take her place… and then *Lorelei III* starts charging south at full throttle, running day and night, as if she suddenly knew where she was going and was in a hurry to get there. It seems likely that our friends—well, enemies—will draw certain conclusions, right?"

"That is my hope."

I said, "You hope they'll think we've finally found the missing logbook with the magic position written in letters of fire—well, numbers of fire. You hope they'll figure that, if we know where we're heading at last, they'd better really pull up their socks and get this damn boat sunk, but fast."

Mrs. Bell nodded. She drew a long breath. "On second thought, I will tell you something about my situation: this is an act of desperation on my part, Mr. Helm. I am counting on you to help me, because you want that man Caselius and this may bring him in to you; but of course Caselius means nothing to me or those above me."

"They're making things rough for you, are they?"

She spoke evenly. "It is always rough for a woman in Washington, particularly a woman of an unpopular race. When things go wrong… They are saying that I have accomplished nothing to secure the area for which I was made responsible, and that it was clearly a mistake to select a foolish minority female for the position simply because it might involve Arabs and she spoke Arabic and had the best performance record in the department." She grimaced. "The fact is, Mr. Helm, that because it is the only thing I can think of to do, and because mission instinct tells me to do it, and because this operation will probably be taken away from me in a very few days, anyway, I am going to take this clumsy motor sailer and drive it down Chesapeake Bay like a speedboat and hope I startle somebody into action besides the fish." She drew a long, ragged breath. "So you will now run quickly over to the boat ahead and tell your little friend Lorelei—what a name!—what we are going to do. Tell her, and Barstow, to be careful; if we do manage to get somebody upset with us, they may decide to dispose of our escort before tackling us. Then you will come back here on the double and take this boat out of here, because I have not yet had an opportunity to learn how she maneuvers. Well, go on, snap into it!"

It didn't seem to be the right time to remind her that she'd told me I was the skipper here, or to point out that I wasn't really subject to her authority, anyway, and who the hell did she think she was, ordering me around like that, Captain Bligh?

"Yes, ma'am," I said meekly, and made a hasty departure.

Outside the boat, with its still-drawn curtains, I found full daylight, although the sun had not yet appeared and might not make it at all: it was another damp, gray morning. When I reached *Gulf Streamer,* Lori asked me into the deckhouse. It was about twice the size of the one on *Lorelei III* and looked even bigger because, to my surprise, the forward end was not cluttered up with a steering wheel, engine controls, and navigation instruments; only a well-equipped bar. Apparently the big sportfisherman could only be managed from the flying bridge or the tuna tower.

"Coffee, Matt?"

"Thanks."

I took the mug she offered me. It had a leaping sailfish on it. Billy Barstow was sitting at the table nursing one with a leaping marlin. Well, I thought it was a marlin; the dorsal fin was somewhat smaller in relation to the fish. Lori's mug had some kind of tuna on it, not leaping. She'd changed from her grubby engine-fixing clothes into the floppy white shorts and blue jersey I'd seen before. Barstow was still in his torn shirt and cutoffs. I had a feeling the relationship here had deteriorated significantly: Barstow wasn't his bright and bouncing and super-smiling self. Maybe he'd made a pass and got slapped down. I passed on Teresa's message.

The red-haired man said resentfully, "Christ, Ma Bell sent you over to tell me to be careful? What does the old biddy think I am, a dumb school-kid with her the fucking teacher?"

I said, "I've got some spare artillery if you need it."

"Look, you stick to your fucking business and I'll stick to mine; I don't come on a job without bringing what I'll need."

That was two fights I could have had in the space of a few minutes. I passed it up. If I didn't watch out, I was going to turn into a pacifist.

"Sure," I said mildly. "Well, we're off. See you at sea."

"Maybe you'll see us and maybe you won't, but we'll be there," Barstow said.

Lori looked unhappy but didn't say anything. Well, he was her crew; she had to get along with the surly bastard. I wasn't exactly distressed by the fact that she must have lowered the boom on him pretty hard; I just hoped for her sake that she'd be able to keep him in line for the duration. She didn't see me out; but as I walked back toward *Lorelei III,* I heard my name called, and looked back to see Barstow making a show-off vault over the sportfisherman's rail and landing lightly on the boards of the dock below.

I waited for him to reach me. He stopped in front of me, clearly annoyed that he had to look up a bit; he was heavier, but I was taller. It would help, I thought, but not enough. He was not only strong as a bull, but he probably knew the *Hah-Hah* stuff, and I never go up against one of those bare-handed. If he came, I'd simply have to kill him. It seemed like something that should be avoided if possible—at least at the moment.

He said, "I don't like hotshot agents who talk against me behind my back."

I wanted to say that all I'd done was call him a snake, but that would not have been diplomatic. I said, "I'm sorry, I thought she knew you were one of Mrs. Bell's operatives. I didn't mean to spill any beans."

He was disconcerted by my placating attitude. He said irritably, "Hell, that little girl was just as sweet as she could be until you talked to her. I had her just about ready, but now she wont give me the time of day. Shit!"

I was interested to learn that her recent experiences on board *Lorelei III* seemed to have turned Lori against not just one particular undercover operative, but the whole sinister breed; well, it was a good way for her to be. We don't as a rule bring a lot of happiness to our ladies. Barstow glowered at me in a frustrated way, clearly wanting a fight. He glanced around to see if Lori was watching; if she had been, he might have worked himself up to it. But she was not in sight, smart girl, and he wheeled abruptly and marched back to *Gulf Streamer* and swung himself aboard.

Mrs. Bell had the deckhouse curtains cleared away and the diesel warming up when I joined her after casting off all but the bow and stern lines. She stepped out to deal with those, and I managed to get us out of there without hitting anything. I took it easy until the engine temperature was up; then I raised the revs to eighteen-fifty. We were logging eight and a half knots through the water as we passed the radio towers at the mouth of the Severn.

"Is this as fast as she will go under power?" Mrs. Bell asked.

I said, "Just about. At nineteen hundred the engine temperature starts to climb."

"Well, as soon as we make the turn down the bay, we'll set the sails and see if they help." She glanced at me. "If that is all right with you, Mr. Helm."

Some people can apologize and some can't. I knew that she was deferring to me now because she'd thrown her weight around earlier. It was as close as this rather arrogant woman could come to saying "sorry."

20

I'd started this cruise with a female navigator who looked like a reckless young Viking and sailed like one. My present nautical adviser looked like a staid middle-aged businesswoman; but when it came to hanging out the canvas, she also turned out to be a throwback to her wild seafaring ancestors. Timid Arab tradesmen sailing on a dhow with Mrs. Teresa Othman Bell in command would have pissed their burnooses for sure.

As we emerged from the Severn River into Chesapeake Bay, we set the little mizzen, hoisted up its mast in traditional fashion, and rolled out the considerably larger mainsail from the tricky furling gear mounted along its taller mast, forward. The brisk wind was out of the northeast, off the port quarter when we turned onto the course that would, some time early tomorrow, bring us to Norfolk if we survived the weather, the folks trying to sink us, and Mrs. Bell.

"How big is that jenny?" she asked, looking forward.

"About four hundred square feet," I said. I added uneasily, "It's a lot of sail."

Actually, the Genoa jib, roller-furling like the mainsail, was almost big enough to wrap *Lorelei III* for mailing. Twice as large as the mainsail, it was by far the largest sail on board—a spinnaker would have been even larger, but apparently Truman Fancher hadn't wanted to wrestle one of those monstrous kites and its man-killer pole on his retirement boat, for which I was grateful. The jenny was bad enough, a vast expanse of rather stiff, slick Dacron that was, at the moment, safely wound around the head stay that supported the mast up forward with the help of the inner stay, on which the little staysail could be set—which is what I would have done if I was doing it. That is, it's what I would have done if I had messed with the sails at all in this fairly stiff breeze, which was unlikely.

"We'll just give it a try and see how she handles," Mrs. Bell said. "You get on that starboard sheet; I'll ease off the furling line."

We were standing side by side at the topside steering station. The day was still gray, now with a bit of a drizzle, which seemed to be customary in these parts at this time of year, and I was wearing my cheap yellow oilskins—I hadn't seen much point in blowing a lot of money, even if it wasn't my money, on foul-weather gear that was only, I hoped, going to have to last me through this one seagoing mission. My companion's expensive waterproof pants and jacket were orange-red and, hood up, made her look like a gaudy teddy bear. *Lorelei III* was coasting along easily on autopilot under the two conservative sails already set, with the engine throttled back to keep things reasonably steady while we worked on deck.

"Yes, ma'am," I said.

I gave the sheet three clockwise turns around the big starboard winch on the deckhouse top, to make sure it didn't get away from me when the strain came on.

"Any time," said the stocky lady in red beside me.

I hauled away, the winch clicked and clattered, and a small triangle of Dacron appeared reluctantly at the other end of the boat; then the wind caught that, and the jenny unrolled with a rush that was only slightly retarded by Mrs. Bell's efforts to brake it with the thin control line that ran from aft clear out the bowsprit to the roller-furling drum. It started flapping in a heavy, jerky manner and shaking the whole boat.

Mrs. Bell secured her little line and said, "Here, I'll tail that sheet for you."

I passed it to her; that left me free to use both hands on the crank of the powerful, geared winch. As the sail came in, it stopped flapping and filled with wind. The boat assumed a considerable angle of heel.

Mrs. Bell said, "That ought to do it... You'd better take a look below and check to make sure all the ports are closed."

"Yes, ma'am."

Hanging onto any grips I could find, I made my way into the deckhouse and checked out the boat from bow to stern, finding all openings safely shut. Increased noise and more violent motion told me that Mrs. Bell had brought the engine up to cruising RPM. Back in the deckhouse, I saw that the knot meter needle was hitting nine and a half knots. I remembered that we'd been making eight and a half before setting the sails; I couldn't help thinking that we'd done a lot of work for a gain of just one lousy nautical mile per hour, but I guess sailing fanatics are all speed-crazy in a kind of microscopic way. Hell, the America's Cup boys will spend a million dollars to gain a tenth of a knot.

When I stuck my head out the windward door, I saw that Mrs. Bell was working hard at the wheel aft, having switched off the autopilot. She yelled at me to stay below where it was dry, and relieve her in an hour, so I made myself a cup of instant coffee, with some difficulty—I had to hold the pot on the stove—and took it up into the deckhouse to watch the misty, gray view slide past the rain-spotted windows. A bulky container ship moving up the bay was passing us well off to port. At the moment there was no sign of *Gulf Streamer.*

I spilled a little of my coffee as the boat lurched violently. There wasn't any real sense to this, I reflected wryly: the hawk-faced bitch back aft was simply abusing my poor old boat—of course, her outfit had put up the money for it, but the name on the document was mine and the work of rehabilitation had been mine—because she was worried about her job and mad at the world. If Caselius and Dorothy Fancher came to sink us, they'd come, I was sure, whether we were charging along spectacularly with all sail set or just cruising placidly under power.

They didn't come. Nobody came. Nothing came except more wind and a few more large ships that materialized out of the murk ahead or astern, passed us, and dematerialized astern or ahead. Occasionally, we'd catch a glimpse of *Gulf Streamer* in the distance, and oddball flashes on our radar indicated that she was keeping track of us on hers.

I took my turns at the wheel. It was hard work, and late in the afternoon, with the wind still rising, I almost lost her twice; clearly my growing skill as a helmsman was not keeping pace with the increasing demands of the situation. Or perhaps the situation was getting out of control—after all, *Lorelei III* was not a racer; she wasn't designed to be driven this hard. The second time, it was a toss-up whether or not I was going to be able to avoid a broach; the boat swung almost broadside to the waves before the rudder took charge at last…

It happened without warning. There was a sharp crack up forward, as loud as a gunshot, and the Genoa took off skyward. I didn't have time to analyze what had gone wrong; I was too busy getting the boat back under control. Then Mrs. Ball was on deck shouting commands.

"Cast off the jib sheet… Ease the main… Head straight downwind and try to blanket that jib so I can secure it…"

It became clear that a tired elderly fitting at the end of the bowsprit had broken, turning loose the headstay and the Genoa's rollerrfurling gear as well as the sail itself. After I'd slacked off the sheet, the flailing jenny was still attached to the boat by two of its three corners. The substantial wire halyard held the head of the sail firmly at the masthead, and the little quarter-inch control line connected its furling drum, which had broken off with the rest of the apparatus, loosely to the bowsprit. Mrs. Bell had made her way forward and was trying to use that flimsy line to haul the lower corner of the sail—tack, to you—down within reach.

Sweating at the wheel, I tried to find the wind angle that would give her the most assistance, but trying to blanket a four-hundred-square-foot jib with the wind shadow of a two-hundred-square-foot mainsail is not really a profitable occupation. But suddenly it worked, for a moment—the wrong moment. The flapping Genoa lost its wind and collapsed, and a corkscrewing lurch of the boat sent the heavy roller-furling drum, several pounds of steel and aluminum, slashing through the air like a giant mace.

Mrs. Bell saw incoming and tried to get out of its way, but she'd been thrown off balance and didn't quite make it. The swinging drum caught her a glancing blow across the head, and she went down to hang limply across the rail like a shapeless red sack, threatening to flip over into the rushing bow wave. I threw a hasty look over my shoulder: *Gulf Streamer* was visible on the horizon, but she was at least three miles away. Even if I called her in by radio, she'd never arrive in time to help if the woman went overboard; and the chances of my making the pickup in this wind, single-handed, with the Genoa going berserk aloft, were nonexistent. I'd already yanked the engine control back to neutral to slow things down a bit, but Mrs. Bell was teetering up there very precariously, and I didn't think I had time to get *Lorelei III* tracking straight under autopilot, or properly heave to, so I could leave the wheel and run forward...

So I did the thing that you are warned never to do on a sailing vessel going downwind in any kind of a breeze: I jibed the damn boat all standing.

I spun the wheel to starboard and everything went to hell. The wind got behind the sails. The mizzen boom came slashing across where my head would have been if I hadn't ducked. The mainsail came crashing across between the masts like a great swinging gate. I had no idea what was happening to the idiot jenny aloft; I was just hanging onto the steering wheel trying to stay with the boat, on that high aft deck, as she went over on her ear and slewed up into the following wave, which broke right over her.

Then she was lying there kind of shaking herself like a wet dog, with water sluicing off the decks; and the masts were still standing. I was proud of the rugged old girl, surviving a jibe under those conditions. The sails were flapping thunderously, all except the Genoa, which, on this tack, was mostly plastered high up against the forward rigging by the wind.

And up in the bow the formless orange-red sack was no longer draped over the starboard rail—it lay sprawled on the foredeck where the bulwarks and lifelines would keep it from going over the side. Okay. So if you have something hanging precariously off the starboard bow that you want back on board, and you can't get forward to attend to it yourself, all you have to do is heel the boat hard to port and smash her into a big wave and hope it'll do the job for you. Who ever said seamanship was difficult?

I drew a long breath and found that, as far as I was concerned, unconscious was a hell of a good way for Mrs. Teresa Othman Bell to be, letting me run my boat for a while without her breathing down my neck. I didn't need expert advice about what came next, it was obvious even to a New Mexico cowboy: all I had to do was stabilize the vessel in a reasonably safe attitude, drag the unconscious woman into the cabin, and then get rid of that crazy sail aloft. Simple.

I quickly learned what I suppose generations of lone sailors had learned before me, that a good boat isn't going to disintegrate because of a little wind or a few flapping sails or some water washing along the deck or even a broken rigging wire or two; and that if you don't panic—ha!—and just keep solving one problem at a time and ignore all the other shit going on around you, eventually you'll get it all worked out…

"Need any help?"

The bullhorn almost made me jump overboard. It was Lori Fancher's voice, electronically distorted and magnified; and there was *Gulf Streamer* right on top of us. The girl was at the flying bridge controls and Billy Barstow was balancing on the sportfisherman's high, plunging bow ready to make a flying leap between the boats—but in that sea, even with all Lori's seamanship, there was no chance of making the transfer without some boat contact. There would be at least minor damage and possibly a major smashup. Anyway, I didn't want the red-headed clown on my boat.

I waved them away. "Stay clear," I shouted. "Just stand by."

"Where's Ma Bell?" That was Barstow.

"She's okay," I yelled, and pointed to the cabin.

For all I knew, I'd dumped a dead woman down there—I hadn't taken time to check—but to hell with him. And her. I was aware of relief as *Gulf Streamer* pulled away and left me alone to deal with my next problem: how to work the Genoa, which I'd got under some kind of control, loose from the tangled mess it had made. It was late in the day now, and I was racing against darkness; but at last it was done, and everything else that needed doing was also done, and we were blowing downwind quite peacefully, considering the weather, steered by the autopilot.

Standing at the wheel aft, I looked down the length of my little vessel with a certain amount of satisfaction. Behind me, the jenny and various busted and twisted parts of its furling gear made a rather untidy pile lashed down on the aft deck, but otherwise she was shipshape. The jib halyard was secured to the end of the bowsprit and set up taut to replace the headstay, which was lashed to one of the starboard shrouds minus the roller-furling drum, which I'd got rid of by chopping it off with an enormous bolt-cutter that old Truman Fancher, bless his experienced seaman's soul, must have put aboard specifically for the purpose of cutting away damaged wire rigging in an emergency. The mizzen and mainsail were furled, and I'd set the staysail forward, figuring that the little sail pulling from the bow would make life easier for the autopilot—as well as the woman below, if she was alive—than the big motor pushing from the stern.

I patted the shiny steering wheel and spoke to my boat. "Okay, old girl, be good: I'll give you a course as soon as I figure out what it is."

I made my way into the deckhouse and found no woman on the carpet where I'd left her; it seemed that these dames with damaged heads simply wouldn't stay where you put them. There was only a damp spot on the rug and Mrs. Bell's foul-weather gear, looking like something shed by a large, red bug. Then I heard a sound forward that I recognized—without the motor running, the boat was reasonably quiet in spite of the wind outside. Well, if she was alive enough to vomit, she'd last a little longer without my help.

Daylight, such as it was, was going fast. I switched on the tricolor masthead running light, all that was required under sail, and snapped on the chart-table light, and frowned at the chart spread out beneath it. I was going to have to figure out just how far we'd come, and in what direction, since the last position recorded by Mrs. Bell, and I had to decide where we should go from there; and I was very much aware that I hadn't had a hell of a lot of practice at dead reckoning. After making a rough estimate of our position, I grabbed the parallel rules to lay out a tentative course, remembering that the after-guards on the old square-riggers used to make a big mystery of navigation to prevent mutiny on board: if you could kid the dumb sailors forward into believing that they'd never get home without the genius officers aft to show them the way across the oceans, they weren't likely to take over the ship no matter how often the cat-o'-nine-tails was employed or how rotten the bully beef became…

"Don't forget the variation, about nine degrees west."

Mrs. Bell was standing on the steps leading down into the main saloon, looking gray-face and shaky.

"Yes, ma'am," I said.

I'd already made allowance for the local compass variation, necessary because there are only a few places in the world where a magnetic compass points to true north and Chesapeake Bay isn't one of them.

"You'd better switch on the running lights," she said. "Well, without the motor running, all we need to be legal is the three-color masthead light."

"Yes, ma'am," I said. "How are you feeling?"

"I'm all right," she said, and collapsed on the steps.

It was as good a place for her as any. I looked at my lightly penciled course line and had no faith in it; it was based largely on guesswork. Without much hope—it had been displaying nothing but gibberish earlier in the day—I switched on the loran, the landlubber's friend. To my joy, some good-looking numbers started coming up on the little dual screens; apparently the U.S. Navy's disk jockeys were taking a dinner break or something.

With a firm latitude and longitude safely written down on a scrap of paper—I reminded myself to pick up a real logbook in Norfolk to replace Truman Fancher's missing mystery volume—I used the loran computer to give me a new course south. I was pleased to see that my previous guesswork, while off by a few miles and degrees, had erred in the right direction and would not have run us aground.

I tweaked the autopilot knob until the steering compass showed us to be on the new course. Then I went topside to see, while there was still light enough to see by, how things looked up there. They looked okay, but I trimmed the staysail slightly to compensate for our changed heading. There was enough wind that the little sail was pulling us along at an easy two to three knots. I stood there for a moment, feeling pretty good; I was discovering that playing sailor could be kind of fun—if you were allowed to work it out for yourself without a lot of expert advice and assistance.

When I came below, Mrs. Bell was sitting on the steps where Mrs. Fancher had sat only a few days ago, also with a trauma-induced headache. Mrs. B had her head in her hands, but she raised it to look at me.

"If you've got the jenny off, you'd better secure the jib halyard up forward in the place of the broken headstay. I don't think that inner forestay is strong enough to take the full strain indefinitely."

"Yes, ma'am," I said. "Let me look at your head."

She said, "When we get down near Norfolk you want to

give Old Point Comfort a reasonably wide berth. There's actually enough water close in, but with this wind the seas will get sloppy near shore; it's better to stay… Ouch!"

I said, "You've got a good-sized lump there, but I don't feel any dents in the skull, and the hood of your jacket seems to have saved your scalp; there's no external bleeding. Let me see your eyes." I held her face steady for a moment, and released her.

"What was that for?" she asked.

"Maybe I just like to stare into your lovely eyes, sweetheart… I know, I know, I mustn't call you 'sweetheart.' I never knew anybody so damned sensitive about what they were called. You're welcome to call me Squarehead Helm any time you feel like it, us Scandihoovians don't insult as easy as you Ayrabs." I grinned, and went on. "If one pupil is smaller than the other, it means something. I don't know what, but yours are the same size, so it doesn't matter."

Mrs. Bell said, "Actually, you don't know what the hell you're doing, do you?"

"Correct. And since I don't know what the hell I'm doing, I'm going to call in *Gulf Streamer* and get you aboard somehow, even though it's a sloppy night to make the transfer. With those big engines, Lori will have you in a Norfolk hospital before morning.'"

"No!" Mrs. Bell spoke the monosyllable violently.

I regarded her for a moment. "Look, lady," I said, "I have a hard enough time putting up with you when you're in good health. Puking all over my boat and maybe going into convulsions, you'll be unbearable and I'll have to shoot you."

She said, "Damn you, don't call me 'lady'!"

I said, "There you are. Just like I said, unbearable."

I reached for the microphone of the VHF. She rose and caught my arm. She licked her lips and made what was obviously, for her, a tremendous effort.

"Please," she said.

It came out awkwardly; it was a word she clearly hadn't used for a long time, if ever. Having been brought up to consider "please" and "thanks" and "sorry" as just about the three most important words in the English language, I always wonder how some people get along without them.

"Why?" I asked.

She licked her pale lips. "If I wind up in a hospital, they'll put me on sick leave, those bureaucratic apes in Washington; and by the time I'm pronounced well again, they'll have me back sorting useless papers in some little office that doesn't amount to anything."

I said, "It isn't working, you know."

"What do you mean?"

"The opposition isn't reacting to our mad dash south," I told her. "If they'd been watching at all, hoping to stop us, they'd have made their move when the headstay went adrift and we were helpless to maneuver. We've seen nothing, and there's been nothing suspicious on our radar. We're playing to an empty house, Mrs. Bell." She didn't speak. I said, "Well, it's your concussion and your subdural hematoma, if any. But you'd better lie down and take it easy for a while; we've got a long night ahead of us."

She looked at me for a moment longer. "Thank you," she said at last.

If she didn't watch out, she was going to turn practically human.

21

We reached the southern end of the Chesapeake around noon next day and sailed past another lighthouse—as Mrs. Bell had said, the damn bay was loaded with them. This one was at the mouth of the James River, into which we had to turn to find the big anchorage of Hampton Roads and the busy port of Norfolk.

I'd unrolled the mainsail to keep us moving when the wind eased after midnight; now we glided across the flats inside Thimble Shoals Light and found the ship channel just south of it. The depth-sounder was acting up, showing confusing little red flashes all around the dial, but Mrs. Bell—briefly awakened—had told me that was perfectly normal, they all did it occasionally, disregard. However, after the behavior of the loran farther north, it did make me wonder a bit about all this electronic navigation. Maybe those old boys heaving their leads and piloting by their compasses hadn't been so dumb after all.

The morning had cleared, and the Chesapeake capes

guarding the entrance to the bay, Henry and Charles, were visible on the horizon to port; the Atlantic Ocean lay beyond them. Ahead was the mainland of Virginia. To starboard was Old Point Comfort and Hampton Roads. There were several ships in sight, and I wasn't about to dodge through that traffic under sail, so I turned *Lorelei III* into the wind and got everything neatly furled; then I started the motor and headed in.

Perched comfortably on the helmsman's stool at the lower steering station, I was feeling pretty good. Mrs. Bell had spelled me from one to three; and any sinister undercover character who can't get by on two hours of sleep had better turn in his trench coat. And I had a pleasant sense of accomplishment: I had this nautical nonsense licked. Several times before I'd managed to fake my way through a seagoing operation; but this time I felt that I'd really mastered some of the fundamentals, at least enough that, mostly without help, I'd got the old bucket clear down the Bay in the dark, under sail, in moderately breezy conditions, without capsizing her or hitting anything solid…

The squatty forty-footer with the silly pink stripe took care of my euphoria in a hurry. I'd seen it emerge from the land ahead and recognized the shape of it, similar to that of the sister ship we'd encountered farther north. I let myself hope naively that this one was going to pass us by and go on about its business, but when it was almost abeam it slowed, turned, and headed for us. When I got the heave-to command, I threw the engine into neutral, let *Lorelei III* coast a short distance, killed her way with reverse, and stepped up onto the side deck as the rubber boat approached.

The previous boarding party had been commanded by an NCO of some kind—I'm not too strong on the navy and Coast Guard ranks and ratings—but the young fellow in charge here seemed to be an officer. A sailor up forward secured the painter to one of *Lorelei III*'s lifeline stanchions and then held onto it to keep the boat alongside. There was a small rat-a-tat gun with a straight twenty-round magazine slung over his shoulder, and another handy to the second sailor managing the outboard motor.

I spoke to the officer: "One of your boats checked us out off Cape May. What kind of contraband do you figure we could have picked up on Delaware Bay or the Chesapeake?" He was a rather handsome boy, if you like boys. He had nice brown eyes in a nicely tanned face and nice brown hair, cut quite short, of course, according to the custom of his service. He also had a nice automatic pistol of some kind in a nice snap-top canvas holster from which he could probably have pried it by next Wednesday, by which time I could have filled him so full of holes with my .38 that, as the old country saying had it, you'd have thought his papa was a sieve and his mama a colander…

It's a natural phenomenon, I suppose. Maybe fighting pit bulls hate killer Dobermans. The FBI is reputed to hate the CIA and vice versa; and I've heard that any tough street cop hates both indiscriminately. Certainly we who work in the shadows detest the whole arrogant pack of law-enforcement clowns with their snappy uniforms and shiny badges, or three-piece suits and fancy IDs. As I've said before, the enemy fuzz is bad enough; God save us from the supposed friendlies.

The young officer asked suspiciously, "If you came down the Chesapeake, what are you doing way out here?"

It was clear that, seeing us heading in the ship channel, he'd thought—hoped—that we'd just come off the Atlantic in our husky motor sailer, with a heavy payload of illicit substances (love that jargon!) picked up, say, in Bermuda.

I said mildly, "I was told it gets sloppy around Old Point Comfort with the wind in this direction, and my crew isn't feeling too good, so I stayed out a bit to keep her comfortable. I'd appreciate it if you didn't disturb her. We're heading for the Tidewater Marina in Norfolk; if you want to inspect the boat, I'll be glad to have you do it there."

He said, "We won't be heading back to Norfolk; we're being transferred..." He checked himself; his orders were none of my damned business. He gestured, and said curtly, "Open the gate and let us aboard."

Instead, I stepped back inside briefly and lifted the big hinged chart table to take a leather folder from the bin underneath. We have our fancy IDs, too, for use when it's necessary to impress the peasants. Returning to the deck, I found myself looking into the muzzle of one of the toy squirt guns: the bowman had come aboard with his piece. We're trained to deal with that situation rapidly and lethally; it took a lot of willpower to check my instinctive reaction.

"Oh, relax," I said mildly, instead of sweeping the gun barrel aside and putting three .38s into his guts—no, make that two .38s, leaving one for each of the others and one to spare; you don't want to shoot your gun empty if you can help it. I extended the ID case to the officer, still in the boat. "The lady below and I are doing special work for the U.S. government," I said. "I must warn you against searching this boat."

He glanced at my ID, unimpressed, and handed it back. "The fact that you're government employees doesn't give you any exemption, mister… All right, Zawicki, let's get on with it."

The man already on board opened the gate in the rail and unsnapped the lifeline below it… I switched myself off, as I had on the previous occasion. Everybody makes such a big goddamn fuss if you do shoot the bastards, even when they're asking for it; hell, Lori Fancher had flipped her little lid because I'd merely thought about it. The alternative was just to go away a small distance and hover there while they played their idiot dope-hunting games on board. Half an hour later they reembarked in their little rubber speedyboat. The young officer threw me a worried look as he departed. He was clearly wondering why I'd made such a fuss about a search when there'd apparently been nothing to find—could he have missed something? I was aware of Mrs. Bell coming to stand behind me.

"What was that all about?" she asked.

I said softly, "It's really too bad. A nice-looking

young fellow like that committing suicide. I suppose somebody'll miss him."

She said, "Damn you, Helm, I told you I wanted no feuds… What crazy thing did you do? I didn't see you plant anything on them."

I was watching the cutter, if that's what the Coast Guard still calls its mini-warships, roar away seaward. It would again have made a lovely target for the right weapon; real sporty, like a live-pigeon shoot in spades.

I said, "Oh, I haven't done it yet. And it may never happen. But I wanted to know."

"Know what?"

I said, "My chief likes us to be nice and polite to other government departments—as long as they're nice and polite to us. But you saw how much cooperation and courtesy I got out of those boys, even though I was just as sweet as sugar the whole damn time."

She said dryly, "I noticed you didn't sound at all natural. But I don't understand—"

I said, "We may encounter some more of them farther south. I went through that routine because I wanted to know how I stood with them. I told the son of a bitch, in the nicest way possible, that I was a fellow government-employee on a mission. I even told him there was a sick lady on board and let him know that they'd had their freebie—that I'd already put up with their search nonsense once, up around Cape May. Well, he wouldn't listen. One of his men even held a gun on me. Okay. Great. Terrific, in fact. They've had their warning. If we meet down south and they get in the way, I won't have to worry about being nice to them; I can just go right through them. It's a big load off my mind." I drew a long breath and let the anger go out of me. "How are you feeling?"

She hesitated, wanting to discuss it further, but decided to let it go and said, "My head hurts a bit, but I'm all right, otherwise. I don't think my brains are seriously scrambled."

"Well, you'd better lie down some more; I can bring her in from here."

Mrs. Bell gestured shoreward. "Over there, you turn south into the Elizabeth River; it's well marked. You'll see the marina to starboard after you've passed most of the commercial docks and navy installations; it's just beyond buoy thirty-six, which is the official Mile Zero of the Intracoastal Waterway. The entrance is pretty narrow, and you have to make a hard turn to port just inside, so don't take it too fast… Well, you'd better call me when you've got it in sight; you'll need help with the docklines, anyway."

Sailing through Norfolk—well, powering—was quite an experience. I mean, even though I was getting used to handling her, *Lorelei III* still seemed like a lot of boat to me, but the stuff along both sides of the wide channel, lined with docks, gave the poor old girl a serious inferiority complex. This was particularly true when we got past the commercial shipping to the navy installations and had to move aside for a submarine heading out with the help of a couple of tugs. I'd always thought of subs as fairly small, but this thing was enormous, particularly when you realized that most of it was invisible under water. That is, it seemed enormous until we passed an unbelievable aircraft carrier that could have picked up the sub and used it for a dinghy.

Then we were through the main harbor. Feeling independent when I reached the marina, or maybe perverse, I took *Lorelei III* through the entrance without calling Mrs. Bell, made my sharp turn to port successfully, and motored up to the fuel dock, figuring that there'd be an attendant to give me a hand with the lines, as there was. I topped up the tanks with diesel and water, careful to stick the right hose into the right hole. My crew came on deck as I was finishing up. I saw that she'd taken time to comb her hair and fix her face. Her pirate jersey showed no signs of her ordeal, and if her white cotton pants were a bit wrinkled, cotton pants are born that way. She was a tough dame, I reflected; nobody looking at her would have guessed that she'd almost had her brains knocked out only a few hours earlier.

"Have you inquired about a rigger?" she asked me.

I shook my head. "I thought you'd probably know whom to call for the repairs."

"As a matter of fact, I do," she said. "I don't suppose we can get anybody here this evening, but if I call now maybe we'll see some action in the morning."

I said, "Okay, why don't you go find a phone? I'll take care of things here."

We'd already been assigned a slip. With the help of one of the marina hands, I put *Lorelei III* into it, alongside a high, fixed finger pier that, since the tide was low, was about six feet above deck level. Fortunately, there was a ladder. Mrs. Bell showed good agility when she came aboard half an hour later to report satisfactory progress; apparently the blow on the head had not affected her coordination.

In the morning, the sail and rigging doctors she'd summoned held a consultation over the patient and prescribed some minor patches on the Genoa, a whole new head stay and furling gear, and three weeks of bed rest—well, marina rest—while the new stuff was being fabricated. Mrs. Bell wasn't having any of that, and went off to talk it over with somebody.

Returning, she said, "I'm having the repaired sail and the new gear shipped to a marina near Savannah, Georgia, when they're ready. You can have the installation done there."

I looked at her. "I can?"

She said, "It's close to six hundred miles, not too far from the Florida border, about two weeks at a normal rate of progress for this boat. If anything is going to happen, it'll happen before then; and in any case it isn't likely I'll be with you that long. I'll either succeed in solving this problem and go back to Washington in triumph, or I'll fail and be recalled in disgrace. In the meantime, we'll just carry on like this. The mast isn't going to fall down, and we won't have much use for the sails south of here. There isn't enough open water to worry about. We'll be under power the whole way. We'll take off in the morning."

"Yes, ma'am," I said.

She looked at me for a moment. "You saved my life,

didn't you?" she said. When I shrugged, she went on. "I was completely unconscious; I had no idea… I just met Barstow and the girl on the street. He said you lost control and lucked out. She said it was a fantastic piece of seamanship: you deliberately threw the boat into a crashing jibe and washed me back aboard just as I was about to go over the side. Two prejudiced sources, one against, one for; but I know which one I believe, and I thank you."

I said, "Hell, thank old *Lorelei*; she did all the work."

Mrs. Bell smiled. "What I'm really driving at is that you can't decently continue to address a lady whose life you've saved as 'ma'am,' even if it does amuse you in some obscure way. Suppose you try Teresa for a change. I… I prefer that to Terry."

"I'll try to respect your preferences, Teresa."

She frowned a bit, looking at me. "You do find me amusing in some way, don't you?"

I said, "No, I find you a bit intimidating and I'm trying bravely not to show it. You know, like a little boy whistling in the dark? Truly competent ladies always scare me."

It occurred to me that I'd said something-similar to another woman who'd served *Lorelei III* as crew, for totally different reasons. But it was the wrong thing to say here. Mrs. Bell—excuse me, Teresa—made an angry grimace.

"Competent?" she said. "If I was competent, would I be here? See the high-powered lady administrator playing deckhand on a silly little yacht! If I was truly competent, Matt, I'd have had all this straightened out weeks ago. Now all I can do is take a boat ride and hope people continue to try to sink the boat; but we've had no action at all since I came aboard, except that I managed to stupidly get myself hit on the head." She drew a long, ragged breath. "And the terrible thing is that this truly competent lady can't think of a single useful thing to do except just keep on going—and hoping."

22

Coming from the dry wildernesses of the high Southwest, I found the wet wildernesses of the low Carolinas quite impressive. I hadn't realized that there was so much desolate, uninhabited land in the super-civilized East, if you want to call that soggy stuff land. The damn marshes went on forever, it seemed, with the ICW marker posts, with their bright little numbered signs, blazing a trail through mazes of swampy lagoons and still, brown creeks and meandering rivers—and great, wide-open sounds that looked like fine sailing water but were barely deep enough to float a canoe except in the dredged channel.

The swamps and sounds were connected by long, ruler-straight, man-made canals through slightly higher and drier ground that still didn't seem to attract much habitation beyond an occasional shack or fishing camp.

I encountered my first lock on the first day out of Norfolk, but it hardly qualified me to tackle the Panama Canal, since the change in water level was less than six inches. It turned out to be the only one along our route—I checked in the guidebook—but bridges we had always with us. The main highways were seldom any trouble since they were usually carried over the ICW on the standard sixty-five-foot-high spans, but the smaller roads crossed on drawbridges that had to open for us, some on demand but many according to schedules that seldom synchronized with *Lorelei III*'s eight-knot rate of progress: if you hit one right, you'd be too late or early for the next. That meant jockeying around in the channel for up to an hour waiting for the bridge tender to get around to pulling his levers or pushing his buttons. I learned a lot about ship handling in tight quarters.

We reached Coinjock, North Carolina, the small town just south of which Truman Fancher's heart had finally given out for good, and started backtracking the old man's final voyage. In Belhaven, North Carolina, we sat out a one-day gale. Just north of Beaufort, still in North Carolina, I cut a little too close to a channel marker and, although supposedly in deep water according to the chart, hit bottom quite heavily and threw Teresa, who was standing beside me, against the chart table almost hard enough to knock the wind out of her—almost, but not quite; she still had breath enough to snap out some orders.

Remembering what Lori had told me, I paid no attention. We were grinding to a sluggish halt on the unexpected and uncharted shoal. Before we lost all momentum, I threw the wheel hard over toward the center of the channel where the deep water ought to be—to port, if it matters—and rammed the engine control clear up to the stop. After a couple of dragging bumps and lurches, with her diesel roaring and her big three-bladed propeller leaving a trail of churned-up mud astern, *Lorelei III* started to pick up speed again. When she was definitely running free, I straightened her out and brought the tach needle back down to cruising RPM.

Teresa drew a long breath, rubbed her bruised diaphragm, and said, "Well, that's one way of doing it!"

I said, "Lori Fancher told me that was the way her daddy did it; and what was good enough for old Truman is good enough for me."

"Well, don't try it if you ever run aground along the Maine coast; you'll rip your boat wide open on the rocks." She glanced at me and gave a little half-embarrassed laugh. "Matt."

"Yes, Teresa?"

"I'm a bossy, know-it-all bitch, aren't I?"

I shrugged. "I've met worse." I grinned. "I can't remember exactly when."

She said, "You've been very patient."

Something in her voice made me look at her sharply. She was wearing another pirate jersey, this one striped blue and white, and clean blue jeans that were neither sexily tight nor fashionably faded: just a tidy, durable costume on a tidy, durable lady. It surprised me to realize that we'd been together for over a week, working our way down the ICW from Norfolk, and that it had been an okay week.

When I first met her, I'd have said that if I was ever

condemned to put up with this arrogant dame for any length of time I'd commit suicide or, more probably, murder. Instead, living at the ends of the boat and meeting, in the middle, we'd got along quite well in a very polite, very businesslike manner; the manner of two intelligent, adult people enduring a forced association who know it will work a lot better if minor irritations are suffered in silence and open disagreements are carefully and diplomatically avoided.

I said, "Patience is part of the training, ma'am."

She smiled. "What I'm trying to say is, thank you, Matt. It's been nice. Of course that's the trouble. It wasn't supposed to be nice. There should have been limpet mines on the hull, torpedoes in the water, and machine guns in the night."

I said, "Sorry about that, but we've still got—"

She shook her head quickly. "No. It was a desperate move on my part, and let's face it, it didn't work. And I was tired enough to let myself waste too much time just relaxing and resting and enjoying the boat ride. Now I'd better go back and face the music. It'll look better that way than if they have to send for me. We'll be in Beaufort tonight. It's a sizeable town, and Morehead City is right next door; I'm sure that between them they have an airport with reasonable service to Washington. I'll take a plane out in the morning..."

Several blasts on a boat horn from astern interrupted her.

Glancing around I saw *Gulf Streamer* coming up on us

fast. Lori was up on the flying bridge.

The bullhorn spoke with her amplified voice: "*Lorelei III,* ahoy. Billy just got a call on the cellular phone. Mrs. Bell is wanted in Washington soonest. There will be a plane for her at the Beaufort-Morehead City airport; we're to run her there with quote all possible dispatch end quote. Give us a call on seven-two when she's packed and ready, and we'll come alongside."

Teresa waved her arm out the door to signal that the message had been received and understood. *Gulf Streamer* fell back. The woman in the doorway stood there a little longer, looking away so I couldn't see her face. It was quite expressionless when she turned at last.

"Well, it looks as if they beat me to the draw," she said quietly.

I wanted to say something helpful and sympathetic; but she wasn't a lady who encouraged sympathy. I just said, "Yell when your seabag's ready. It looked pretty heavy; let me wrestle it out of there."

She smiled crookedly. "On this ship we carry our own bags, remember?"

I said, "On this ship, I'm the skipper; I make the rules. And break them… Teresa."

"Yes?"

I cleared my throat. "Anybody you ever need killed, you know where to call."

She looked at me for a moment. Then she stepped forward and kissed me lightly on the lips and turned and disappeared down the companionway. A few minutes later

I watched *Gulf Streamer* pull ahead, white water boiling out from under her stern as Lori fed the power to the oversize twin diesels. Mrs. Teresa Bell stood in the cockpit beside Barstow. She glanced aft and raised her hand to me. It was not really a farewell wave; it was more a salute like that given by the Roman gladiators marching in to face the lions: Hail, Caesar, we who are about to die, etc.

I reached Beaufort late that afternoon and found myself back in civilization. The city marina was right in the middle of town, opposite an anchorage area holding a considerable fleet of boats. I inserted *Lorelei III* into her assigned slip, with the expert assistance of the dock master. He was as good a hand with a rope as I've seen, east or west: he could flip the loop of a heavy dock line over a distant piling like a rodeo cowboy lassoing a running calf. With the boat secured, he pointed me toward the nearest pay phone.

Mac listened to my report and said, "You seem to have lost contact. We may have to approach the Caselius problem from another direction."

"Do we have another direction?" I asked.

Mac didn't answer my question. He said instead, "If Mrs. Bell is correct, and she is to be replaced upon her return to Washington, I suppose we will soon receive official notification from her successor, and be advised how he, or she, wishes us to proceed. Since any new incumbent, in any office, is likely to make a point of rejecting the policies of a predecessor wherever possible, it may be that the boat will no longer be considered relevant to the terrorist problem with which that organization is concerned."

I said, "It's my boat. I've got papers to prove it."

"Meaning?"

"Meaning that I can do what I damn well please with it," I said. "Frankly, I think Teresa—Mrs. Bell—and her associates have given up on this approach too soon; and now you seem to want to quit it, too, sir. But with all due respect, I don't think we've lost contact at all. I think those Arab crazies, including Dorothy Fancher, and their hired DAMAG goons, including Roland Caselius, are right out there watching *Lorelei III* move steadily south toward the critical area. They just don't have the stomach for any more frontal attacks, by sea or by land; the Battle of Montauk Point and the Battle of Schaefer's Canal House cost them too many people. But, hell, Mrs. Fancher isn't going to give up now, not with her beautiful lover dead with his beautiful balls shot off. And Caselius isn't going to forget his poor dead daddy."

"What are you suggesting, Eric?"

I said, "I don't think we need another direction, sir. I think the direction we're heading is perfectly swell. If Mrs. Bell's outfit decides on a different approach, and still wants our assistance, maybe you can find somebody else to give it to them. I'd like to keep right on sailing—well, motoring—down the ICW. I think young Mr. Caselius and I have a rendezvous not too far ahead. I gather that those secretive folks in Washington do still want him neutralized."

"Yes, indeed."

"And they still won't identify the DAMAG target

they're trying to protect?" I said. Mac didn't respond to that question, and I continued. "Well, in this case I'll cheerfully risk my life for the White House doorman, or whoever, since even if I were willing to leave Caselius alive, the chances of his being willing to leave me alive are practically nonexistent. It's a job I'll have to do eventually; I might as well get it done."

Mac said, "But the question is, is this the best way of doing it?"

I said, "Hell, wherever the sensitive point may be, down south of here, it's got to be somewhere reasonably near the Waterway, so I can't miss it by too much if I just follow the channel markers, even if I may not know that I'm there when I get there. But I don't figure Dorothy Fancher and her fanatics will let me get too close to their secret spot, not as long as there's even a remote chance that I have Truman Fancher's logbook lying on the chart table in front of me open to the exact latitude and longitude. There's no reason for them to risk it, and every reason for them to dispose of the boat and me with the help of their hired DAMAG experts, as soon as they've figured out a safer way to do it than they've managed so far. The fact that they've held off for a few days doesn't mean they've given up; it just means they're cooking up something very fancy."

Mac said dryly, "All of which is just guesswork, of course."

I said, "We don't call it guesswork, we call it instinct, sir."

I heard a short laugh at the Washington end of the line. "As it happens, I have seldom lost money gambling on an experienced operative's mission instinct. Very well, Eric. As the U.S. Navy likes to say, carry on. If Mrs. Bell's people object, I will deal with them."

"Thank you, sir."

He said, "However, if they decide to withdraw your escort vessel, there is nothing I can do about that."

I said, "*Gulf Streamer's* not around at the moment—I don't know where they took her—and frankly I hope she stays away. I'm just as happy without Mr. William Barstow breathing down my neck; he's not one of my favorite colleagues. As a matter of fact, it might be a good idea to run a check on him. Apparently he's been giving the little Fancher girl a hard time, and he's kind of a schizo personality anyway, a hardheaded pro one minute and an oversexed slob the next. His record should be interesting; I have a hunch it isn't exactly snow-white."

"Very well, Eric. Report in when you can."

"Yes, sir."

After dinner, obtained from a can—Dinty Moore beef stew, if you must know—I opened the big chartbook for the area to see what lay ahead; I hadn't done my navigational homework beyond Beaufort. In North Carolina, the U.S. coastline turns a fairly sharp corner, called Cape Hatteras, and begins to angle southwest instead of southeast. Proceeding directly from Norfolk to Beaufort, we'd cut the corner; the ICW had brought us straight down its well-marked channels almost fifty miles inside Cape Hatteras and the Outer Banks.

But now we were back on the shores of the Atlantic Ocean—actually for the first time since Cape May, New Jersey, having spent the intervening time on the inland waters of Delaware and Chesapeake bays—and I saw on the chart that the waterway ahead followed the coast, protected from the open sea by a string of barrier islands broken by occasional inlets that, the guidebook said, were apt to be troublesome because of the strong tidal currents that rushed through them. Those currents, the book warned, if you weren't careful, could carry you into shoal-water difficulties; particularly since storms often changed the bottom, scouring out new channels and silting in the old ones in an unpredictable manner…

"Pssst! *Lorelei* ahoy!"

I had the deckhouse draperies closed for privacy and the doors open for ventilation. Since there was no wind to flap the curtains tonight, the two purposes did not conflict seriously. The voice had come from the side of the boat away from town; it had been very soft, but I'd recognized it. I released the butt of the .38.

"Ziggy, what the hell?" I whispered.

"Oh, damn this lousy hand…! Help me with this dinghy, please, Matt."

I debated turning out the deckhouse lights, but that would have told watchers on shore, if any, that something was up, so I just slipped through the curtains and stepped up to the side deck. She was standing right below me in a tiny white plastic boat that didn't approve of upright passengers; it wanted to slide out from under her and dump her into the harbor. With one hand splinted, she was having trouble holding the little craft in place while she secured the bowline, or painter, to a lifeline stanchion.

I took the painter from her and tied what I hoped was a seamanlike knot. I opened the boarding gate and got the ladder off the deckhouse and hooked it over the rail. She got herself aboard in a rather stiff-legged fashion.

"Where'd you get the dink?" I asked.

"Stole it," she said. "I didn't want them to see me coming out here to talk with you."

"So let's get under cover," I said.

In the cabin, I turned to face her. She'd thrown back the hood of the buttoned-up foul-weather jacket she was wearing—standard marina costume, rain or shine—but as always the gauze and tape still made her face somewhat anonymous. I noted once more that she had blue Scandinavian eyes—with a name like Kronquist she could hardly help it—a slightly tip-tilted nose, and a soft mouth devoid of lipstick. The visible features were promising; I suppose it was only normally ghoulish to wonder just how badly she'd been spoiled, beneath the dressings, by the sharp blade of a dead man's knife.

I said, "First, one question. You said you didn't want *them* to see you coming here. So I'm really under surveillance?"

Ziggy nodded. "Oh, yes, you've got some nice shadows ashore; I had a hard time staying clear of them."

"Well, that's a relief," I said. "A lot of folks seem to feel that, since I haven't been shot at recently, there's nobody following me around."

Ziggy was looking down at the chartbook lying open on the table. "You're going to have trouble with those damn inlets, Matt. I've had some experience with them, so I thought I'd try to persuade you to take me back aboard as a pilot, now that T. Bell seems to have left you." Ziggy looked around. "She's gone, isn't she? I've been watching since you came in; she wasn't on deck to help with the dock lines, and there's been no sign of her on board."

I said, "She was recalled to Washington; she went ahead on *Gulf Streamer.*"

"That's the big sportfisherman we saw in Annapolis with your little girlfriend and Curly Red Barstow on board? Well, I didn't see them come in, but I wasn't looking out for them particularly; and those gold-plated power-palaces all look alike to me, I'm a sailboat girl at heart. And of course there are other places besides the city dock here where she could have landed and got a taxi to the airport, over in Morehead City, for instance."

I hesitated, watching her, and asked, "Have you run the Waterway recently, Ziggy?"

"Two years ago. We brought a custom forty-footer up from Palm Beach; actually, we took her clear to Newport, Rhode Island."

I said, with a glance at the chart, "Well, it does look as if I could use a pilot, and I certainly need somebody to blame when I run aground. It might as well be you."

23

Ziggy said dryly, "It's really best not to try to sail where the birds are wading, Matt. Their legs aren't *that* long."

I'd missed spotting a channel marker that we were supposed to round, and failed to make the indicated turn. Moments later, I'd seen the long-legged white birds standing in the water thirty yards ahead, letting me know I was in the wrong place, but we'd bounced against the bottom a couple of times before I got us out of there and found us the deep channel again—well, four meters deep according to the flasher, call it twelve feet, practically an ocean abyss in that part of the world.

I said, "Don't be mean; we can't all be genius navigators."

The previous night we'd just turned the borrowed dinghy loose to drift through the marina with the tide, hoping that it would bump against the boat of an honest citizen who'd secure it and get it back to its owner. In the morning, we'd risen early and motored out of Beaufort's sizeable harbor and back up the big-ship channel to the ICW, which carried us south past Morehead City and along a dredged channel that ran down a long, shallow sound. A mile or so off to port was the low island that sheltered us from the open sea.

It was pretty well covered with beach cottages that looked very vulnerable, perched on that skimpy sandbar on the edge of the wide, potentially violent Atlantic. Well, in California they built their mansions on the San Andreas Fault; here they stuck them on little barrier islands that just asked to be swept clean by any serious hurricane. But who was I, in my line of work, to criticize other folks for living dangerously?

Now we were back in the coastal marshes. The chart continued to show solid ground of sorts between us and the ocean—more barrier islands, sometimes supporting other beach communities; but most of the structures we saw along the Waterway were either duck blinds or fishermen's shacks. We passed several inlets; at each one, the piloting got tricky, as promised, with sudden currents and winding channels, but Ziggy seemed to sense where to find the navigable water.

Which was more than could be said for me; toward the end of the morning, I managed to put us onto the mud in a tricky spot where the channel turned out not to be where the chart said it was. Lori's ungrounding prescription failed to work. I turned the controls over to Ziggy, which I should have done before things got sticky, and she managed to wiggle us loose by judicious employment of prop and rudder.

"You're pretty good at that," I said when we were clear. "I suppose you can't leave me sitting in the mud just anywhere; you've got a definite place you're supposed to deliver me."

She was perfectly still beside me for a long moment. "I... I don't understand, Matt."

I said, "Don't try it, Ziggy."

There was another lengthy silence. When my companion spoke again, her voice was strained. "I... I don't know what you're talking about."

I said, "What happened? Did they catch you and go to work on you again?"

Another long pause. "How did you know?" she whispered at last.

I said, "Hell, I'm a pro, baby. I suspect everybody. I even suspect a poor bandaged girl you'd think had the most compelling reasons in the world for hating the folks who crippled and scarred her. What was the idea of that elaborate stolen-dinghy drama? Did they figure that if they had you go to such lengths to hide your presence from them I couldn't possibly suspect you of working for them?"

She licked her lips. "Matt, I—"

I went on. "You lost your .22 at Schaefer's Canal House. Before sending you away so she could take your place, in Annapolis, Mrs. Bell confiscated the .38 I'd lent you as a substitute. I'm just mean enough to suspect young ladies who aren't supposed to have any firearms but button their jackets up tightly on a warm evening nevertheless: what could they possibly be hiding? And I don't trust girls who've only hurt a foot, and have been getting around on it quite gracefully, but suddenly behave as if the whole leg were stiff when they swing it over a boat's rail: what long object could they possibly have tucked into their pants to make them so awkward?" I spun the wheel to negotiate a turn in the channel. Without looking at her, I said, "You slipped it under the settee cushion as you came aboard yesterday. Get it and lay it on the chart table, please."

She said with sudden anger, "Have you been playing with me ever since I came aboard, all the time knowing that I…? Oh, that's dirty, Matt."

I said, "Look who's talking about dirty. And why should I antagonize a good pilot? Get the gun, please."

She turned away, and I heard her at the corner settee. A moment later the familiar old Colt Woodsman, with the sound suppressor we're no longer allowed to call a silencer, was lying in front of me. It was, of course, conclusive evidence against her, it had last been seen in Roland Caselius's hand. There was no reasonable way she could have got it back innocently.

Her brief anger had evaporated. "I… I'm sorry, Matt," she whispered.

"What happened?" I asked.

She licked her lips. "I… I'm just a complete, utter coward, after all, just like Mrs. Bell always said! I simply couldn't go through all that… all that pain and humiliation again! I couldn't stand the thought of having any more ugly things done to me. Living inside the freak they've already made of me is more than I can bear. I think… I think something broke inside me when they… when they ruined me like this, Matt."

"How did they catch you?" I asked. "They didn't. Just because I… just because I'm yellow doesn't mean I'm stupid. I wouldn't have let *them* catch me. It was that red-haired creep."

"What red-haired creep?" I frowned. "You mean Barstow? He trapped you for them?"

She nodded. "That's right. Bill Barstow. He came up to me on the street right there in Beaufort while I was watching the Arab goons who were watching you. He said he wanted to show me something so I could tell you about it; he didn't want to be seen contacting you directly. Well, he waved an ID at me, and of course I knew who he was, anyway; everybody in the organization knows Curly Billy, particularly the girls. I had no reason to suspect… Anyway, I went with him. He took me out to *Gulf Streamer.* She was anchored way up the harbor in Beaufort where she couldn't be seen from the city dock where you were; but he had that red rubber boat with an outboard motor they'd carried on the foredeck. We climbed aboard the sportfisherman, and he opened the pilothouse door for me, and there they were, lying on the cabin sole all tied up; your little girlfriend and Mrs. T. Bell. I tried to duck out of there, but he was right behind me; he just laughed and got me in some kind of a crazy grip, he's strong as a horse. He squeezed on my neck in a funny way, and I blacked out. When I woke up, I was tied up, too, laid out on one of the settees in *Gulf Streamer's* deckhouse, and the Arabian Nights lady was there—Mrs. Fancher; she has a kind of full-blown Scheherazade look, don't you think?—with a youngish man, kind of medium-sized but very fit, you know the kind, just bursting and bouncing with muscles and fitness, and handsome in a tough, mean, crew-cut, Nazi way. Mrs. F called him Rollie, dear."

"Roland Caselius," I said. "He's the guy who sneaked up behind you and hit you on the head and took your gun after you shot Roger Hassim... So our Dorothy has found somebody to take Hassim's place in her affections."

"And her bed," Ziggy said. "I mean, you can tell. She's got him hooked; and I'd say, from the way she looks at him and touches him, that she's found him very satisfactory, too, although she's enough older that she's not totally helpless with rapture, if you know what I mean."

I frowned. "What about Barstow? Did you gather that he was a recent recruit? Or was he a sleeper of long standing, planted in our government by the Russians years ago, say, and taken over by Caselius when the Evil Empire collapsed?"

"Well, I got the impression that Caselius had something heavy on him, maybe that, but there was also a question of lots of lovely Arab oil money, not to mention the girl."

"What girl? Lori Fancher? "

Ziggy laughed. "Who else? It isn't like he'd be leching after our tough old Mrs. Bell, is it? It seems Miss Fancher had hurt his crummy little feelings; so he'd made her part of the price, a bonus on top of several hundred grand in a numbered bank account on one of those islands that still keep financial secrets... I'll get some Judas money, too, if I follow orders, gobs of beautiful money to hear them tell it, maybe even enough to pay some high-priced specialists to make me human again with fingers and toes that all work and a face that doesn't frighten... Oh, God, I just *hate* sniveling cowards who do nothing but gripe, gripe, gripe about their miserable existence!"

Her second encounter with her torturers seemed to have thrown her into a real tailspin. After a moment, she gave a choked little sob and, leaving the wheel untended, stumbled down the companionway, bumping against the knife rack in passing. She was crying hopelessly as she made her way forward. I suppose she needed sympathy and reassurance, but for the moment I was too busy taking control to do anything about it.

There was no sound from below, and I found myself remembering the noise of Ziggy bumping against the knife rack, that in retrospect hadn't sounded quite like a simple bump. I leaned over to look down into the galley, and saw a gap in the rank of knives. The missing item was the big Sabatier that the first Ziggy Kronquist, the phony, had planned to stick into me, and had wound up sticking into herself. I'd been tempted to get rid of it on that occasion, and then I'd told myself firmly that I was not a sensitive fellow and I wasn't going to discard a fine, sharp blade because it had once had a kind of blood on it for which it had not been designed. The stuff washes off, dammit.

Now I said irritably, "Oh, sweet Jesus Christ!"

I looked around. The Waterway was reasonably wide at this point. There was no traffic ahead or astern. I threw the engine into neutral and set the autopilot so the boat would stay in the middle of the channel as long as her momentum kept her moving. After that the wind or current might drift her into trouble, but she wouldn't hit it very hard. I went down the steps quickly and made my way forward.

I found the damn girl in the head compartment up there—toilet to you. It was a tiny cubicle just big enough to hold a throne and a sink, and she was sitting on the cover of the former with her left arm held over the latter. The big butcher knife was in her right hand. In order to expose the artery, she'd pulled away some of the tape that was wrapped around her left wrist to hold the finger splints in place.

There was some blood in the sink, but although she'd sliced herself twice, neither cut was very long or more than skin deep. Technically, I believe they're known as hesitation marks. It generally takes a suicide at least a couple of tentative tries before he, or she, manages to make the big, reckless incision that really opens up the arm or the throat and lets the life out. Face averted, the girl didn't look at me as I took the knife from her.

"Come on, Ziggy," I said.

"Useless!" she breathed. "The no-good bitch hasn't even got the courage to kill herself! Gutless Ziggy, Secret Agent Zero, the nothing girl!"

I said, “Come on before the damn boat drifts off into the swamp.”

After a moment she drew a long breath. “Oh, all right. I’ll be with you as soon as I put something on it so I don’t drip blood everywhere, ugh.”

“Sure.”

I left the knife in the galley sink—I didn’t think she’d try using it again—and scrambled into the deckhouse to find that *Lorelei III* was well out of the channel but still afloat with a few inches to spare. I engaged the gears and headed us cautiously toward the gaudy green rectangle of the nearest mark; we churned up some mud but made it. I told myself that one day I was going to sail out on the ocean where the bottom was a couple of miles down and all I had to worry about was storms and whales; this skinny-water navigation was too nerve-racking for a timid landlubber like me.

“How about a nice vodka martini on the rocks, skipper?”

It was my masked navigator, emerging from the main cabin with a clean white bandage on her wrist and a well-iced glass in her hand. I glance at my watch and saw that it really was about time for my prelunch libation.

“Thanks,” I said.

“Where are we?” Ziggy asked, coming to stand beside me. I showed her our position on the chart. After a moment, she laughed. “Do you know what those people expected me to do, Matt? They wanted me to… to get the drop on you and take over the boat.” She giggled. She seemed to have come to terms with whatever had been bothering her, and sounded almost happy. “Can you imagine it, Matt? I told them they were crazy, hadn’t they ever read your dossier? I told them I had about as much chance of making an experienced professional like you do what they said—novice me and my little twenty-two!—as I had of flapping my arms and flying; you’d just take the silly gun away from me and spank me like a baby. Or… or shoot me dead.”

“What were you supposed to do after you took over the boat?” I asked.

“I was supposed to make you turn up one of the side channels ahead, at West River Inlet. The river leads back to one of the anchorages in the marsh that’s recommended by the guide. I was supposed to make you drop the hook there; then they’d come aboard and take command. Of course, if you resisted, I… I was supposed to shoot you dead and run the boat in there myself, but I got the impression that Mr. Caselius didn’t really want me to.”

I finished my martini and set the glass on the chart table. I said, “No, he wouldn’t. There’s a little personal matter between us; he wouldn’t want you to deprive him of the fun of dealing with me himself.”

It was, of course, strictly a phony scenario; even Ziggy had found it laughable. Even if she hadn’t told them, Dorothy Fancher and Caselius would have known, when they gave her back her gun, that there wasn’t a chance in the world that she could carry out their instructions. And if they knew my capabilities, I had a pretty good idea of theirs. In particular I knew that Roland Caselius was a belt-and-suspenders man. There had been that shotgun ambush backed up by a hidden dynamite bomb. So what was the backup he'd arranged for the .22 Woodsman that, in Ziggy's hands, wasn't very likely to do the job it had been sent to do here…?

Steering, I blinked as the red channel marker that was gliding by to starboard seemed to go unsharp for a moment. I saw Ziggy watching me oddly, and suddenly I knew exactly what kind of suspenders young Mr. Caselius had picked to help his belt keep his pants up, figuratively speaking. I had a moment of regret. She'd had a rough time, and she was a nice enough girl when she wasn't feeling sorry for herself. However, she'd know the rules by which we operated; she'd know they gave me no choice. Perhaps, unable to do the job herself, she was deliberately inviting me to do it for her.

I took the silenced .22 Woodsman off the chart table and fired four times as the mists closed in.

24

Coming awake, I first checked my surroundings as well as I could without opening my eyes. There seemed to be a body beside me, which didn't surprise me greatly. Hell, one had been there when I went to sleep, why shouldn't it be there when I awoke? Then the body beside me stirred and poked me with a sharp elbow.

"Look, it's a big bed; you don't have to take up all of it!"

It was a female whisper, but it was not, of course, Ziggy Kronquist's whisper. I opened my eyes and found myself lying beside Mrs. Teresa Bell on the double bunk in *Lorelei III's* aft stateroom. The door to the deckhouse was closed, as I seldom kept it, since it made the cabin seem very small and reminded me of the somewhat claustrophobic fact that the door was the only exit.

Up forward, each compartment had an overhead hatch through which you could haul yourself out on deck in an emergency. There was no such hatch aft; and while portholes across the stern and along both sides of the stateroom provided good ventilation, they were too small to accommodate anything but a monkey. It wasn't something I spent long, wakeful nights brooding about, but I'll admit that I'd mounted a moderately large fire extinguisher near the foot of my bunk to help me fight my way out of there in case fire in the engine room, just forward, should threaten to block the doorway.

The motor wasn't running. *Lorelei III* seemed to be motionless, either aground or anchored in calm water. The sunlight at the curtained cabin ports was quite low. I'd drunk my doctored martini at just about noon; apparently I'd been out for several hours. As I watched, the angle of the sunlight on the curtainfolds changed very gradually. Okay. We weren't aground, we were swinging lazily to an anchor.

I determined that my ankles were lashed together with the thin white Dacron cord I'd bought a generous supply of when I was replacing the boat's original, well-worn flag halyards; and my wrists were tied behind me, presumably with the same tough stuff. I turned my head and saw that the woman beside me was similarly bound. I squirmed myself a little distance away from her.

"Thank you," she breathed. "I've been trying to push you off ever since they threw you in here practically on top of me, but you just keep rolling right back against me, like a newborn seeking its mama's breast."

That required no comment. I asked, "What's the situation?"

"We're anchored just off the waterway. That is to say,

Gulf Streamer is anchored and we're tied up—rafted, if you want the nautical term—alongside. On the other side of *Gulf Streamer* there's another powerboat rafted. About thirty-five feet; one of the standard plastic power cruisers somebody stamps out with a cookie cutter. I just caught a glimpse of it when they dragged me across from *Gulf Streamer* and dumped me in here."

I asked, "Did you see anybody on the strange cruiser?"

Teresa laughed shortly. "There were men all over her; she seemed to have a crew like a Barbary pirate; and as a matter of fact most of them probably have relatives in that general part of the world, by the looks of them."

"Some of Dorothy Fancher's playmates."

"It was a couple of them who hauled me over to this boat and kind of dumped me down the deckhouse steps. I landed on you and Kronquist, lying there. I thought you were both dead, but after they'd picked me up again and tossed me into this stateroom I heard somebody say that you were only unconscious due to knockout drops the girl had fed you, but you'd managed to shoot her before you passed out."

I examined it and found that I could live with it. Well, I'd had practice. I was helped—although I shouldn't have needed help—by the fact that there had been no hatred in the dying girl's eyes; I'd done for her what she'd been incapable of doing for herself.

"You sound disapproving," I said.

I felt rather than saw her head shake. "Not of the shooting; quite the contrary, Helm. I've always wondered if your chief's gang of secret assassins—sorry, I understand you like to call yourselves counterassassins—was as tough as everybody claimed. I'm happy to see that you live up to your advance billing and obey your own ruthless rules."

"Then why the disapproval?" I asked.

"Well, you don't seem to temper your ruthlessness with a great deal of intelligence, allowing a girl to slip you a drugged drink… Shhh, here they come."

I'd felt the boat rock slightly as somebody—more than one somebody—stepped aboard. The cabin door opened, and Mrs. Dorothy Fancher entered. Her long black hair made a neat turban around her head, and she'd found some new clothes to replace the ones in which she'd gone swimming in the C. and D. Canal. Today she was wearing big brown trousers, narrow at the waist and ankles and voluminous elsewhere, of the kind of thin cotton stuff that comes pre-wrinkled. Her brown shirt, constructed from the same crinkly material, hung loose over the pants and had long flowing sleeves. How a woman could look voluptuous in that sloppy-floppy getup was a mystery, but she managed. She was followed by Roland Caselius.

I'd seen him once before, of course, just out of pistol range at Schaefer's Canal House at night; but this was the first time I'd got to study him up close in good light. As Ziggy had said, although not one of the overmuscled bodybuilders, he was clearly a fitness nut, nicely tanned, with clear blue eyes and cropped blond hair and a springy, bouncy way of moving. Okay, I told myself, so you don't mix with him even though you've got some advantage in weight and reach. You blow his brains out with a gun or gut him with a knife. Fairness is for Boy Scouts.

He was wearing a knitted blue sport shirt and stiff new jeans that didn't look right on him. I remembered that he came from Germany. It's funny about Europeans, they generally have problems with Mr. Levi Strauss's sartorial invention. They yearn for blue jeans, they'll rob and kill for them, but when they acquire their precious denim and put it on they seldom achieve the casual-cowboy look they dream of; they almost always manage to look as if they would really be happier in tailored gray flannel with a pinstripe.

There wasn't much room at the foot of the bed, but I noticed that the man and the woman managed to stand even a little closer—bodies touching—than the circumstances required: two large predators in love. Roger Hassim would be spinning in his grave.

Caselius said, "So. The important lady bureaucrat and the dangerous government executioner!"

I said, "Like father, like son. All mouth."

His hand twitched; he would have slapped my face if he could have reached it. However, the head of the big bunk was a long way from the foot where he stood, the floor space and headroom alongside were limited, and the overhead shelf across the stern helped to make slapping access difficult. He decided to forgo the pleasure, temporarily.

He shook his head and said, "It was unwise of you to remind me of the fine man you murdered so many years ago, Mr. Helm, although it's not likely I would forget your ancient crime, having just disposed of one of your more recent victims. But I will deal with you presently. In the meantime… Mrs. Bell?"

"Yes?"

"Mrs. Fancher would like to know what new information you obtained that led you to leave Washington so suddenly in order to take charge of this operation in the field."

Teresa said, "I don't know what you mean… Well, I learned that Helm, here, had taken the Kronquist girl aboard against my orders. I couldn't let him jeopardize the whole mission by depending on a crew I knew to be unreliable. Things weren't going well in Washington, anyway, so I arranged for *Gulf Streamer* to provide support; then I drove to Annapolis, kicked Kronquist off the boat, and took her place. Nothing mysterious about it."

Dorothy Fancher said to Caselius. "This is a waste of time. Whatever she learned, or thought she had learned, it was obviously wrong or she would not be here. Probably she was only bluffing, trying to panic us by acting as if she had the information; and as you may recall, we were a bit disturbed until she betrayed so clearly that she had not read the figures written in my husband's log." She grimaced. "The old fool! What did he think to accomplish by writing down that loran position, even if he had managed to read it before he collapsed? And where did he hide the book? Not that it matters now."

Caselius said, "As you say, it does not matter now. And it would be better if you allowed me to conduct the interrogation my own way, dear lady. It is always advisable to allow the subject to first trap himself, or herself, in irrelevant lies before proceeding… But very well. I will get to the point. Mrs. Bell, we are interested in anything you can tell us about the Richard ceremony scheduled for this weekend."

"Richard?" Mrs. Bell sounded puzzled. "Ceremony? I don't know what you mean!"

Dorothy put her hand on Caselius' arm. "We already have all the necessary information, Rollie, dear."

Caselius was watching Teresa. "I would like to hear it confirmed… Well, Mrs. Bell?"

"I really don't know who you mean. Or what you mean."

Caselius studied her bleakly for several seconds before he spoke again. "Mrs. Bell, I was well trained in dealing with stubborn people, and I have considerable experience in interrogation. We will be back shortly. Think about it. You can save yourself considerable pain by cooperating." He looked at me. "There is nothing for you to think about, Helm; you cannot change what is in store for you."

He turned and ushered Dorothy Fancher out of the cabin. Despite the unbecoming brown clothes, she made an interesting picture going up the steps. Although I still felt no desire for her, I could enjoy watching an exit—a very female exit—well performed. The door closed.

After a moment, Teresa, lying beside me, made a sound of disapproval. "Tied hand and foot with death staring him in the face, the hero operative who's been assigned to help me can think of nothing better to do than antagonize the opposition unnecessarily and ogle a female rump—a somewhat oversize rump at that!"

I said, "I wasn't so much interested in the rump dimensions as in the rump action. And needling friend Caselius is not unnecessary; the more I annoy him, the longer he'll want to play with me before he kills me. Who's Richard?"

Teresa's response was irritable. "I haven't the slightest idea. I never heard of him before."

I said, "Goddamn it, Terry, this is no time to play your damned Washington security games! Who the hell is Richard and what kind of a ceremony is he putting on or participating in or whatever?"

"Matt, I don't know, I swear it! And I asked you not to call me Terry."

She sounded convincing, but in that crazy city on the Potomac they learn how to make even the wildest lies sound convincing. But if she did know, she obviously wasn't about to tell me.

I said, "Well, I certainly don't know any fucking Richards that could possibly…"

"What is it?" Teresa asked when I stopped, frowning.

I said, "Something's trying to come through, the name rings some kind of a feeble bell way back in… No, I can't get hold of it." I grimaced. "So your man Barstow was actually working for Caselius. That's some manpower pool you've been tapping! We'll skip that first homicidal agent of yours I met, since she wasn't really your agent; but then there was the true Ziggy Kronquist who was a very nice girl who'd have made some accountant or insurance salesman a wonderful wife, but who had no business whatever being in this racket, dammit. And the careless dame who let herself be brained with a windlass handle, and the lovesick swain who let himself be shoved overboard. And now there's this oversexed Barstow clown, who turns out to've been, probably, a sleeper working for the Soviets while we still had Soviets. Or maybe he's simply for sale to the highest bidder. I wouldn't say you've put together a really major-league team, Mrs. B, unless there are some hot players in the lineup that I haven't met."

She said, "There aren't. I think I told you. When this mission came up, so clearly suited for me with my top efficiency rating and my special language qualifications, they didn't dare pass me over and risk being accused of discriminating against women and minorities. So they gave it to me—and also gave me the sweepings of the stables to work with, even including one male operative whose sexual proclivities had already proved embarrassing elsewhere, and whose security clearance was being reviewed for cause. But what they forgot was that traitors can be very useful, properly employed. I put Barstow on that sportfisherman precisely because his loyalty was questionable. And when he came charging up and said that I was wanted back in Washington ASAP, ha ha, I went on the boat with him like an unsuspecting female idiot who really expected to be delivered to the nearest airport. I let myself be overpowered and tied up and dragged around like a sack of potatoes—and the man I was counting on to rescue me, and deal with the opposition, was letting little girls feed him knockout drops instead of tending to business!"

I was getting a bit tired of that nonsense. I said, "For Christ's sake, Teresa! I'm here, aren't I? Where would I be if I'd thrown that loaded drink in the girl's face?"

The woman beside me was silent for several seconds. "Do you expect me to believe that you *knew*...?"

I said, "You used yourself for bait; do you think you're the only one who ever had that idea? I didn't know it was a Mickey Finn, no; I just hoped it was. The kid was under orders to deliver me to Caselius. He had her thoroughly intimidated. I'd taken her gun away, but I was sure he'd provided her with an alternative, and I much preferred being knocked out by a Mickey to being clobbered with a sap, or that damned windlass handle—she might not know her own strength—so I sure as hell wasn't going to analyze any drinks she handed me, or be slow slugging them down. I was fairly sure that Caselius wouldn't have her feed me anything lethal. Those retribution kids all have to keep you alive long enough to tell you just how painfully they're going to avenge dear old dad, before they do it. Now everything is rosy, and Caselius is very happy about the way he put one over on me, and there's a dead girl to prove how terribly surprised I was by those knockout drops and how strongly I resented them. So he's not likely to suspect that I'm exactly where I've been trying to get ever since I left Washington, right next to him."

"A helpless prisoner!" Teresa said.

I laughed. "Lady, I spent two months working on this boat. And I wasn't just polishing the damn teak..."

I stopped as *Lorelei III* rocked again, minutely, to signal the arrival—or rearrival—of our visitors.

The woman beside me spoke without expression. "Well, here they come again. Wish me luck, my friend."

I said, "I recommend screaming very loudly. Don't be brave and spit in his eye, that'll just stimulate his Torquemada impulses. Since you have no information to give him, give him some nice agonized howls and moans and whimpers instead. Maybe he'll get so tired of listening to your racket that he'll decide that you really don't know anything and to hell with you."

Teresa Bell said, "I thank you for the advice."

I said, "Sure. And you'll do as you damn well please. Incidentally, where's Lori Fancher?"

"The little girl is probably having a bad time right now on the other boat, having been left to the tender loving care—with emphasis on the loving, I'm afraid—of William Barstow, Esquire. But I must say that her problems do not concern me greatly at the moment..."

Then they were entering the cabin, Dorothy Fancher in the lead as before. She was holding in her hand a blue object I recognized: it was the big butane lighter I kept at the stove, one of the refillable jobs designed for use with charcoal grills, that can be adjusted to produce anything from a small candle flame to a real blowtorch spout of fire.

So the sexy Arab lady was going to do the honors, and it was going to be a toasting session rather than a slicing session. I didn't look at Teresa Bell, lying beside me. I remembered that she'd scorned Ziggy Kronquist for breaking under heavy interrogation. I wondered if she was also remembering that, now that her turn had come.

25

On instructions from his sexy associate, Caselius pulled off one of Teresa's boat shoes—the left one, if it matters—and white cotton socks. Dorothy made a dramatic production of snapping the trigger of the butane lighter and adjusting the flame to its maximum length, about three inches.

Then Caselius turned up the left leg of Teresa's jeans very neatly and got a good grip on the ankle. Dorothy leaned forward eagerly, the flame shot out, and there was the familiar smell of overcooked meat…

I'd been there myself, of course. I had the scars to prove it. With that stink in my nostrils I found myself remembering very clearly a titled Swedish gentleman—actually a distant relative of mine; I said they weren't all nice people—who'd supervised the use of a knife-sharpening steel heated in the flame of a gas stove. There had also been a rather handsome lady in Brazil who'd been very good at keeping a cigarette burning brightly in spite of repeated contacts with human flesh, my human flesh. And far back in my checkered past, I recalled, back home in southwestern U.S.A., I'd encountered a couple of folks with original ideas about employing a soldering iron…

"What day is the ceremony, Saturday or Sunday?"

"Who is scheduled to attend?"

"What time of day will the presentation be made?"

The questions were punctuated by the trigger clicks and the leaping tongue of flame and the stink of burning. The interrogation continued:

"What time will the guest of honor arrive?"

"Will the ceremony take place on Sunday?"

"Will the ceremony take place on Saturday?"

"What time of day…?"

Caselius said quietly, "That is enough." When Dorothy snapped the lighter on again, he seized her arm and spoke more sharply. "I said, enough!"

Dorothy Fancher's long black hair had loosened, untidy about her perspiring face. She looked like an angry witch interrupted at her satanic witch work, as of course she was.

"Let me go!" she protested, "I'm going to make the stubborn bitch give me at least one civil answer if I have to burn her to a cinder!"

There was no sound from the woman lying beside me, and no movement. There had been none throughout. Far from taking my advice about screaming loudly, she'd maintained total silence: no squeals, gasps, grunts, whines, or whimpers, and certainly no words. Caselius had long since released his grip on her leg since it wasn't required. She hadn't struggled, she hadn't even flinched, she'd just lain there, soundless and unmoving.

It was unreal. It'd thought at first she must have suffered an immediate blackout of some kind, maybe even a heart attack brought on by the pain; but her eyes had remained open and alive, and her breathing was steady. I must admit that I felt a small pang of professional envy. As I've already said, I've been there, but although I can generally refrain from shrieking if it's indicated, I've been known to twitch and thrash around and put considerable strain on the restraints provided, and maybe even moan rather loudly when it hurts enough; such total control put this woman out of my class.

"She is not going to answer," Caselius said. "She will die without speaking. It is a recognized phenomenon; it was discussed in training. There are not many such, but their silence cannot be broken in this manner. With drugs, perhaps, but we do not have the drugs." He shrugged. "It does not matter. We have the information we needed: she does not know. I have been watching her; I have watched many being questioned. She is playing a game with us. She has nothing to tell us; she really does not know what we are talking about; her organization has apparently not been informed, so it is nothing to worry about. We are wasting time. Put that torch away."

Dorothy Fancher said hotly, "You forget yourself, *Mister* Caselius! Don't think you're suddenly in charge here just because we… Basically, you're just a hired hand, so don't try to give me orders!"

"A thousand pardons, Mrs. Fancher!"

Caselius's accented voice was stiff and formal. He released Dorothy's arm, turned sharply, mounted the steps leading to the deckhouse, and was gone. A slight movement of the boat indicated that he'd stepped off it onto the larger vessel alongside.

"Come back here!" Dorothy Fancher shouted after him; and then in a different tone, "Rollie, I'm sorry, I didn't mean… Allah, these men and their sensitive feelings!"

She looked down at the butane lighter, and at Teresa. She threw the lighter angrily onto the bed and started away; then she checked herself and came back and retrieved the implement and hurried out. A small rocking motion let us know that she, too, had left *Lorelei III.* I felt the woman lying beside me let her breath go out very slowly and carefully.

She whispered, "In case you were wondering, Matt, that was… that was just no fun at all!"

"I know."

After another pause, her voice came again: "Well, I suppose you do. I suppose it's a normal occupational hazard. And it's a good career move, isn't it? Every bureaucrat should have a little field experience on record, don't you think? But I don't quite know how I'll describe this in a resume."

I knew she was talking to take her mind off the pain. I said, "I owe you an apology."

"Apology?"

"I was told that you were kind of rough on the Kronquist girl after she'd folded under interrogation. At the time I assumed you were just another pantywaist LMD operator telling us field personnel how brave we should be. My humble apologies."

"Accepted," she whispered. "LMD?"

"Large mahogany desk."

She gave a small, strained laugh, and was silent for a little. From her carefully controlled breathing I knew that she was still fighting the throbbing agony of her foot.

After a moment, she said, "It's too bad that female didn't leave the lighter on the bed. We might have been able to use it to free ourselves."

"Don't sweat it," I said. "I told you, I did a lot of work on this boat. Can you stand up if you get the chance?"

"She only burned it; she didn't chop it off. I can walk on it. Just get rid of these ropes. I'll be all right."

I said, "Well, I don't want to make a move until we have a little time to ourselves… Here they come again."

Caselius entered first, this time. Dorothy remained on the steps, behind and slightly above him. She'd put her heavy black hair back into some kind of order and mopped her sweaty face. She licked her lips, watching, as Caselius took a revolver from his waistband—my little five-shot Smith and Wesson .38.

Caselius said, "I was planning to make you pay a somewhat higher price for the murder of my father, Mr. Helm, but the courage of your companion has brought you a quick death. I could undoubtedly demonstrate that you are not so brave, but that would tarnish the matchless performance of Mrs. Bell. It will be enough for me to know that I have done my duty by my parent and you are no longer walking the earth. Good-bye, Mr. Helm."

He raised the short-barreled pistol and cocked the hammer. Well, I'd been here before, also; but it's never a good place to be. I watched his eyes, bracing myself to roll aside at the final instant. There was hardly anywhere to roll, and not much to do when I got there, but what the hell, I might as well die moving as lying still…

"No!"

Dorothy pushed Caselius's arm upward; for a moment I thought the revolver was going to fire and blow a hole in the ship's aft deck, above us. Then Caselius freed himself and let the hammer down. His impulse was clearly the same as that of any marksman—I won't venture to speak for the markswomen—interrupted while concentrating on a shot: to slap the interfering idiot across the room. However, he managed to control himself and spoke quite mildly.

"Pushing the arm of a man holding a cocked pistol is not very intelligent," he said.

She said harshly, "It's too easy!"

Caselius said, "Dead is dead, dear lady."

Her voice was fierce. "This is the man, you told me, who shot down your father in cold blood! He is also the man who brutalized the body of my dying lover Hassim, mangling him horribly with a big shotgun in the last moments of his life. And the woman is of our race, but she has chosen to side with the imperialistic American tyrants; she is a traitor to our people everywhere. Such individuals do not deserve quick and merciful deaths."

Caselius shrugged. "So what is your wish?"

Dorothy looked around the cabin. "Neither of them is small enough to pass through one of those little portholes; they can only escape by the door. Make certain of their ropes and knots, and nail the door shut. When we scuttle the vessel off shore they will have time to repent their sins and commend their souls to whatever strange deities they worship, if any, as the boat carries them to the bottom." She turned to the nearest porthole, the only one open at the moment, and closed it, dogging it down firmly. "Now the water will not come in too fast. There will be a bubble of air trapped in here for them to breathe for a while, as they watch the sea slowly rise to drown them… You disapprove?"

Caselius shrugged again. "I do not favor these elaborate homicidal procedures…" He raised his hands quickly. "You do not have to remind me, dear lady. I have taken your money. As you have already pointed out, you are the hirer and I am merely the hireling. It shall be done as you desire."

"Make certain the man has nothing with which to cut himself free. He is said to wear a special kind of belt…"

"I have already removed his belt, with its ingenious buckle. I will check the bonds of both prisoners… You are certain that the pilot you have summoned really knows how to negotiate the nearby inlet even in the dark, knows the tides, and is aware that this boat has a six-foot keel, much deeper than his motorboat? It would be awkward if morning found us hard aground on a shoal within sight of land."

She said stiffly, "Paul Rashid is one of the best pilots on this coast. You will steer this boat, following him closely."

"As you wish."

"I will stay with you, but Paul also wants to put a lookout with us, stationed in the prow, to make certain that, operating in the dark without lights, you don't lose him or, for that matter, run him down."

As an old salt—well, a new salt—I have a negative reaction to people who refer to the pointy end of a boat by the flossy, archaic term, prow, instead of the currently accepted term, bow. I've never heard a *real* sailor speak of a prow. Well, that's the kind of superficial stuff that goes through your mind in a crisis, keeping your surface thoughts busy while the real self-preservation plans are forming at the deeper levels of your consciousness.

"I will be glad to have a lookout forward," Caselius said.

"But we are wasting time. Tell Captain Rashid to get ready, and give Barstow his instructions…"

Dorothy hesitated. "I think we have had enough of Mr. Billy Barstow. He is really a disgusting person, and not reliable: a man who can betray once, can betray twice. Paul has men to spare, he can provide a crew for the sportfisherman. Barstow has served his purpose. Give me the silenced pistol, please. I believe it still holds a few bullets, enough."

I also react negatively to people who talk about bullets when they mean cartridges. Those hunks of lead are not self-propelled, dammit. But then, Mrs. Dorothy Fancher wasn't likely ever to become one of my favorite people.

Caselius passed her the .22 Woodsman. He said, "I recommend a brain shot with such a small caliber, even though our professional executioner, here, chose another target."

"You men are not the only ones acquainted with firearms, my dear," the woman said. "There will be no trouble. That human goat is too busy with the girl; he will die in a state of goatish bliss..."

I found myself wondering if Barstow was being killed because he'd made a pass at Dorothy—or because he hadn't, insulting the lady by preferring a younger girl. Then she was gone. Caselius checked our bonds carefully, and tested the cabin door, which opened inward. He ran his hand over the smooth surface.

"It is a handsome teak," he said. "I regret to have to damage it; however, since the boat is to be sunk I suppose it makes no difference. Good-bye again, Mr. Helm. I would have preferred to do it my way, but I work for money these decadent days, and must obey those who pay me."

The door closed behind him. Moments later, the starter kicked the diesel into life; it settled down to idling speed. There were sounds of activity and shouted commands that I couldn't decipher but probably involved the casting off of the line securing us to the larger boat alongside.

I thought I heard the rumbling exhaust noise of more powerful motors, presumably the kind that would drive a standard twin-screw power cruiser abut thirty-five feet long. That sound faded as the other boat pulled away; then it was wiped out altogether by the noise of our own motor being brought up to cruising RPM.

"Well?" Mrs. Bell said.

I said, "Take it easy. That's a pro we're dealing with. He hasn't spiked the door shut yet; he's going to check us again before he does. Just pull up a blanket and make yourself comfortable."

Actually, the blanket and top sheet had been removed from the bunk; Caselius hadn't bothered to take away the bottom sheet, however, perhaps because it was a custom job fitted to the oddly shaped mattress that conformed to the awkward angles of the boat's stern, and couldn't be yanked off so easily. The diesel slowed markedly. It was still in gear, however; I could hear the inch-and-a-half shaft rotating directly under us, still turning the big three-bladed propeller, but quite slowly.

"What's happening?" Teresa asked. When I didn't answer at once, listening, she answered her own question. "We must be feeling our way through the inlet. Those channels shift with every storm, and the Coast Guard has to move the buoys accordingly."

I said, "I'm glad somebody else is doing the navigating; I hate that shallow stuff. How's the foot?"

"Don't ask stupid questions. If you've ever had it done to you, you know how it is."

"Sorry."

"No, I'm sorry. I didn't mean to snap at you. My foot is just fine, Mr. Helm, it merely hurts like hell. Don't give it another thought."

I said, "You're quite a girl, Terry."

"I am definitely not a girl and haven't been one for quite a few years. And I don't like to be called Terry. Apart from that, the compliment is appreciated... *Now* what are they doing out there?"

The motor had sped up again, in fact the high resulting noise level indicated that Caselius had shoved the throttle clear up to the stop, not good for the machinery if he kept it there too long, but as he'd pointed out, if the boat was to be sunk anyway why worry about the woodwork, or the rings and rods and valves and bearings? *Lorelei III,* driven hard, was meeting a certain amount of wave opposition and smashing through it bravely. I felt a surge of affection for the sturdy old craft, and hoped I could bring her out of this safely, although it seemed unlikely at the moment. The racket made it necessary for me to shout in Teresa's ear.

"I'd say we're clear of the shoals and heading out to sea."

"And you still don't think we should do anything? Just remember, I'm not very good at swimming without water wings a hundred fathoms down."

"I'll keep it in mind."

It grew dark in the cabin with its curtained portholes. Our headlong progress continued; I sensed that the boat was taking a certain amount of spray, and even an occasional sheet of solid water, over the bow. It would not be pleasant for anybody riding the bowsprit, but presumably, now that the tricky piloting was past and we were out in open water, the lookout provided by Captain Paul Rashid had retired to the shelter of the deckhouse, making three people there. Given time to get free and reach a hidden weapon or two, I could probably have dealt with them; but if I was interrupted before I was ready Caselius would either shoot us or, at least, secure us in a much less favorable position. It was too much of a gamble, I decided; better to wait.

I said to Teresa, "Now you'd better roll over on your side and I'll kind of back up to you so you can reach my wrists. Pick at my knots desperately, scratch my wrists, break a couple of fingernails if you can..."

"Wonderful!" she said. "They fry my foot and now you want to mangle my hands; there won't be anything left of me if this keeps up... Wriggle a bit closer, please."

The cabin was dark now. *Lorelei III* was pitching and jolting as she stormed through the night. Teresa started clawing energetically at my bonds, drawing blood in the process, as instructed. Working blindly behind her, in the dark, with her own hands bound, she wasn't likely to accomplish much, but we'd be expected to make some effort...

The cabin door opened. A flashlight beam hit us. Behind the glare, the deckhouse was dark, of course—under way at night you don't impair your vision with cabin lights. Besides, running without the legally required navigation lights, they wouldn't want any brightly illuminated ports or windows to betray their presence. The flashlight approached warily. I'd rolled onto my back as if to hide my wrists, and lay there looking innocently up at the bottom of the shelf overhead. I heard Caselius laugh.

"Show me, please," he said.

"Show you what?" I asked.

Then I sighed and turned to display my scratched wrists and, perhaps, some pulled-out whiskers of rope, if Teresa had managed to achieve that much.

Caselius inspected the knots with the aid of the flash and said, "Well, the lady might manage to free you, given time. Unfortunately you will not have that much time. Good-bye once more, Mr. Helm."

I said, "You say as many good-byes as an opera star."

"Give my regards to my father. Tell him I sent you."

Then he was gone. The door closed. Presently, over the sound of the motor, I heard a buzzing noise and realized that he was using the cordless drill from my toolbox to make pilot holes in the door for the spikes or screws with which he intended to secure it, since he'd have to angle them into the door frame and they might not take the proper direction without guidance.

"Matt, for God's sake, what are we waiting for?" Teresa breathed in my ear.

The drilling stopped, and the door swung open, and the flashlight beam hit us again. I heard Caselius laugh. The door closed. A hammer began to work out there. I waited a little longer, in case he was being very tricky indeed; but the pounding continued, sealing us into our teak-lined, red-plush-upholstered coffin.

The hammering stopped. The engine slowed again. There was a jolt as another boat came alongside. *Lorelei III* reacted minutely to the weight of several people leaving. Then there was nothing but the slow rumble of the engine and the easy motion of the boat driving lazily now, presumably under autopilot, into the moderate seas of what was presumably the open Atlantic Ocean…

26

"Matt, I think we're sinking!"

I said, "Well, I certainly hope so."

"Is that supposed to be funny?"

I was working as we talked; I'd been hard at it ever since I'd convinced myself that Caselius was finally committed to nailing the door shut and didn't intend to take another peek at us. The first thing I'd done was change places with Teresa in the big bunk—an intimate but sexless maneuver—to get at the side of the boat. I'd located with my fingers, behind my back, one of the little hideouts I'd constructed while putting *Lorelei III* back into commission. I was trying to get it open, not as easy a task as it had seemed some weeks ago when I'd tested it without ropes on my wrists.

I said, "If we weren't sinking, that *would* be something to worry about... Damn, my fingers are half-asleep!"

"Do you enjoy talking nonsense?" Teresa asked.

I said, "Hell, if we weren't sinking, it would mean that

Caselius didn't follow that Arab witch's orders to scuttle the boat but rigged something fancy instead, like one of the late lamented Jerome Blum's tricky little bombs, atomic or otherwise. But now all we have to worry about, I hope, is an open seacock or two."

"All right," she said, "but let's not have any race prejudice on this ship, mister."

Startled, I asked, "What the hell brought that on?"

"I'm an Arab witch, too, don't forget."

I said. "Hell, I've got nothing against Arabs; just don't ask me, as a good Swede, to tolerate those awful Norwegians, Finns, and Danes..."

One of the obvious possibilities for which I'd prepared *Lorelei III,* since I'd been instructed to use myself as bait, was exactly this one: that I'd be taken prisoner on my own boat and kept in this cabin, probably tied up in this bunk. (I'd also made arrangements in the deckhouse, main saloon, and forward cabin in case I wound up there.) The sides of the aft stateroom were nicely sheathed with inch-and-a-half strips of tongue-and-groove teak, fastened to the outer hull with shiny little stainless-steel screws, each with its shiny little stainless-steel washer. The fastenings were carefully lined up to make a regular pattern against the dark wood. Groping behind me with my bound hands, I'd already found the second strake up from the mattress. I'd located a certain screwhead and washer, and pushed them a certain way to release the invisible catch I'd rigged with help from a real ship's carpenter sent by Mac.

Now I was trying to find another of the gimmicked

screws farther forward. I got it at last, and released that catch also, enabling me to pull out a two-foot strip of teak that wasn't as tongue-and-grooved as it looked. Still working by feel behind my back, I deployed the knife blade I'd fastened to the fiberglass hull beneath it. The problem with freeing your bound wrists if you manage to promote a knife, is finding somebody to hold it for you. I hadn't been certain of having company; I'd therefore hinged the hidden blade in such a way that I could swing it out and lock it firmly into place. I did that now. Once it was done, cutting my hands free was easy, although I managed to acquire another nick on one of my wrists, in addition to Teresa's scratches.

Finished, I folded the knife blade back against the hull before proceeding; it was long enough and sharp enough to spear me painfully if a roll of the boat should throw me against it. I found and freed the flat little Russell folding knife I'd taped under the same strip of sheathing. It was actually just a skeleton of a knife: two flat, grip-shaped pieces of steel protecting a razor-sharp three-and-a-half-inch blade, total thickness about a quarter of an inch. I used it to liberate my ankles and deal with Teresa's bonds. Another hiding place nearby yielded a .38 to fill my empty holster, not that it was needed at the moment, I hoped.

"I won't ask how you did all that," Teresa said, "but now you'd better produce another miracle to get us out of here, fast. I think there's already water sloshing around at the foot of this bunk."

There was. I stepped into it and tested the door, but

Caselius had done a solid job, and it was obvious that tugging on the handle would only get me, if I could pull that hard, a broken handle. As far as miracles were concerned, I had tools hidden away that could cut us an escape hole, but they'd been selected more for ease of concealment than for speed of operation, so I unclipped the big fire extinguisher at the foot of the bunk and, a bit reluctantly—no sailor likes to smash up his own boat—took a tentative swing with it. The sturdy teak door bounced it right back at me. Aware of the water around my ankles, that seemed to be rising with frightening rapidity, I swung my impromptu battering ram with all my strength. The door panel splintered. Moments later I'd beaten most of it away, enough to let me squeeze through.

Up in the deckhouse, the growing sluggishness of the boat's response to the sea was noticeable. I hurried to the wheel and hit the bilge-pump switch in front of it. The little red indicator light came on to signify that the pump was operating, but to make certain Caselius hadn't sabotaged it in some ingenious way, I opened the sliding door to port and leaned far out to look at the outlet in the ship's side, spouting water in a satisfactory manner.

"What's the matter? Isn't it working?"

I hadn't been aware of Teresa behind me. Turning, I saw that she'd put her white sock, but not her shoe, back on the blistered foot.

I said, "It's doing fine. What kind of shape are you in?"

"Why keep asking?" she said irritably. "I'm in terrible shape, I'm suffering dreadfully, ain't it awful? But I'll be in even worse shape if I drown. Tell me what to do."

I hesitated. I didn't like the idea of sending her to wade through the half-flooded cabin; but as she'd said, drowning was even less attractive.

I said, "Okay, if you're up to it, you can grab the flashlight off the shelf over there and go forward and find whatever sea cocks Caselius has opened up there, and close them. Do you know where they are?"

"Yes, I checked them out like a conscientious crew member when I started sailing with you. One big red valve under the galley sink and several under the passageway forward. But he probably sabotaged the engine room, too."

"That's where I'm heading. Watch where you shine the light; keep it away from the portholes. We don't want to show any signs of life in case they've still got us in sight.

"Aye, aye, skipper."

I got a spare flashlight, and a screwdriver and a pair of pliers—with those two tools, and perhaps a hammer, you can fix 95 percent of what goes wrong on a boat; for the other 5 percent you need a big toolbox full of iron and a mechanical or electrical genius to go with it. I remembered to switch on the saltwater wash-down pump so I wouldn't have to climb back out of the hole to do it later; but at the moment, of course, it was simply pulling water from outside the boat and spewing it out on deck to run back into the sea. An odd sweetish smell made me glance at the engine's instrument panel. The temperature gauge was reading in the danger zone. I started to reach for the kill button and pulled my hand back: the pumps were electric and drew quite a bit of juice, so the diesel had to be kept running to keep its alternator charging the batteries.

When I yanked open the big hatches, after pulling the carpets aside, I was greeted by a stronger stink of ethylene glycol. The motor was fresh-water cooled—actually, it used a fifty-fifty mixture of fresh water and antifreeze—and the heat was transferred to the ocean by a saltwater-cooled heat exchanger. It was clear that Caselius had pried the hose off the exchanger's seawater intake, letting in the ocean to help fill the boat and at the same time leaving the engine to overheat and, eventually, if *Lorelei III* stayed afloat that long, self-destruct.

The water level was creeping up the side of the lead-lined engine box. Fortunately, the control valves I wanted were outside the box so I didn't have to dismantle that. I lowered myself into the water and found, and turned, the lever of the Y-valve that switched the wash-down pump to pumping from the bilge instead of the Atlantic Ocean.

That got as much water going out of the boat as we could manage without resorting to the manual pump, which wasn't very effective. Now to tackle the water coming in. I groped around until I located, well submerged, the big gate valve for the raw-water intake. As I'd guessed, the hose had been disconnected and water was gushing into the boat. The reluctant handle seemed to turn forever before I got it closed. By the time I had the hose back in place, firmly clamped, and the valve open again, I was thoroughly soaked.

"All secure forward, skipper." Teresa was looking

down into the engine room. She looked as wet as I felt; her pirate jersey was sodden, and her gray-streaked black hair was plastered to her skull as if she'd just emerged from a swimming pool. She went on, shouting over the noise of the engine. "He had two hoses off. I didn't try to replace them; I just closed the sea cocks as you said. How are you doing down there?"

I reported everything under control, which was not quite true: the motor had undoubtedly boiled away a lot of coolant which should be replaced, but to do that I'd have had to stop the mill and wait for its temperature to drop, which wasn't practical at the moment. I climbed out of there. When I had the big hatches closed, I realized that my companion had disappeared. There was a gleam of light in the aft cabin. Looking through the framework of the splintered door, I saw her sitting on the bunk with the flashlight lying beside her. Even though it was aimed away from her, I could see that she was pulling on her shoe over the stained and sodden sock.

I said, "For Christ's sake, Terry, what are you trying to prove? To hell with your iron-woman act; now that we've things more or less under control, we've got to clean up that foot and bandage—"

"Is a wet bandage any better than a wet sock? There's no way I'm going to keep my feet dry, the way this boat is at the moment. Anyway, you'd better stop worrying about me and start thinking about where we're going, skipper. At the moment I believe we're still heading for Europe, or maybe Africa."

I said, "Okay, but first I want you to lie down on that bunk—"

She said angrily, "Damn you, will you stop worrying about me? I'm perfectly swell. I toast my feet in the fire every morning before breakfast because I hate cold toes."

I said, "Relax, I'm not being solicitous. I just want you to shine that flashlight on the underside of the shelf across the stern. When Caselius was holding his flash to check my knots, the light reflected off the white bedsheet and I thought I saw something scratched into the wood that I hadn't noticed in all the weeks I've slept in that bunk. Check it out for me, please."

"Aye, aye, skipper." Lying on her back, she pushed herself aft and aimed the flashlight upward. Her voice reached me after a little. "There's something here, all right. Some faint numbers."

"Can you read them?"

She took a moment to respond. "They look as if they were written with a ballpoint pen, but of course there's no ink because those things don't work upside down. Does 365046 mean anything to you?"

"Not at the moment. Is that all?"

"No, there's another one… Wait a minute, I missed a decimal point. 3650.46. And 7617.82."

"Let me get something to write on—"

"Matt!"

"What's the trouble?".

Her voice expressed self-disgust. "How stupid can we get? It's a position, of course! To hell with that mysteriously missing logbook, *this* is where Truman Fancher wrote down the loran reading he saw. Are you ready?"

"Fire away."

"Latitude thirty-six degrees, fifty point four six minutes. That would be north, of course, although he didn't bother to mark it down. And longitude seventy-six degrees, seventeen point eight two minutes west..." Her voice trailed off, and came again. "Thirty-six? But that's crazy, Matt!"

"What's crazy?"

"I don't know about the longitude, offhand, but latitude thirty-six fifty has got to be over two hundred miles north of us. I haven't really been keeping track, it's not as if we'd been navigating the open ocean. Who checks latitude and longitude in these canals and rivers? But we're south of Beaufort, North Carolina; we must be down around latitude thirty-two or thirty-three by this time. What's a degree of latitude, anyway, sixty miles?"

I said, "How would I know a thing like that? You're talking to a dumb landlubber, remember? Well, you figure it out; I'd better check things topside."

Outside the deckhouse, it was a black night, starless and moonless, with a stiff breeze from the southwest. There were no lights visible in any direction; we had the Atlantic to ourselves, which was actually a good thing, but I couldn't help feeling a bit lonely on my little boat in the middle of all that dark ocean—also, wet as I still was, rather chilly. Looking on the bright side, water was spouting from the bilge-pump outlet in a reassuring manner, and running along the deck and over the side from the gushing wash-down faucet; *Lorelei III* was beginning to feel bouyant and seaworthy once more.

When I reentered the deckhouse, Teresa was standing at the chart table. She'd turned on the red light above it that was supposed to let you navigate without spoiling your night vision. She hadn't dried off much yet, either, and her jeans and jersey clung in wet wrinkles to her sturdy figure. It occurred to me that she was the third dripping dame I'd entertained in *Lorelei III*'s deckhouse. It also occurred to me that, while of course I prefer them young and slim and blond, given my druthers, somebody with different tastes might find that strong adult body and dark hawklike face and dramatic gray-streaked hair not unattractive. There certainly was nothing missing in the courage department.

Theresa looked around. "This is perfectly ridiculous!" she said.

"What's ridiculous?"

Some water dripped from her hair onto the chart in front of her. She wiped it away with a towel she'd found somewhere, and squeezed the lank strands back from her face.

"It doesn't make sense!" she protested. "Truman Fancher sailed up from Florida, and had a heart attack when he saw his wife and her friends unloading something from his boat—we think a peculiarly nasty homemade bomb—at a certain spot down along the waterway. At that point he's supposed to have sneaked a peek at the loran and jotted down the reading in a logbook that was never found. Then the sick old man was brought further up the ICW in a fairly helpless condition. He finally died just below—*south* of—Coinjock, North Carolina. Have I got it right?"

"That's what we've been told," I said.

"Then how does it happen that the position he went to a lot of trouble to scratch over his bunk is fifty miles *north* of Coinjock? A spot he's not supposed to have reached at all on this trip except perhaps in a coffin? A spot we're supposedly looking for here, way down south, that we've actually been getting farther and farther away from every day!"

"Show me."

Teresa put her fingers on the chart. "Right there, Captain Helm, sir. The place where you and I stopped several days ago and left some rigging to be repaired. The Tidewater Marina, Norfolk, Virginia!"

27

It seemed very quiet with the engine stopped. *Lorelei III* lay hove to on the port tack. I'd unrolled about half the mainsail to hold her steady—well, as steady as a thirty-eight-foot boat can be offshore on a breezy night—while I waited for the overheated mill to cool, and patched up my reluctant crew.

"I just got that damn shoe on and now you want to pull it off again. I tell you my foot is just fine!" Teresa protested, trying to rise from the deckhouse settee as I knelt before her. "Why don't you let me worry abut my foot? We're wasting time!"

I said, "We've got it to waste. Just sit still and drink your drink." A little stimulant had seemed indicated; and I took a sip from my own glass—and set it aside, hearing the happy sound, or cessation of sound, I'd been waiting for. The automatic bilge pump had cut out, indicating no more water to pump. I went over and shut off the manually controlled wash-down pump and returned to my patient. I said, "Hang on now, while I get this sock off."

Fortunately, being wet, it hadn't stuck. I didn't comment on the mess that was revealed when I got it off. What the hell, it was just a burned foot; and it wasn't the first burn I'd ever seen. If she could take it, I could.

Teresa protested. "Look, we've got to get on the radio and—"

"Take it easy," I said. "Think about it, Terry. Who're we going to call on that VHF and what are we going to say—with the whole world listening, including Dorothy Fancher and Roland Caselius? They're bound to have their ears on, aren't they?"

"I've asked you not to call me Terry," she said. "And we'll simply call the Coast Guard—"

"And tell them to send somebody to thirty-six degrees north and seventy-six degrees west and pick up a nice little atom bomb mislaid by a careless yachtsman?"

"Well, why not?" she asked. "If they check the records of the Tidewater Marina, they can find out what slip Truman Fancher's boat had last spring. The bomb is probably right there, most likely invisible under water, lashed to one of those big barnacled dock pilings... Ouch!"

I hadn't thought the word was in her vocabulary; but apparently she didn't feel compelled to play the complete stoic in front of me alone. Wading around in the flooded cabin hadn't done her foot any good; and I was using a pair of surgical scissors from the first-aid kit to trim away the broken blisters.

"You're going to say all this over the air?" I said, "And

what will Fancher, Caselius, and Co., do when they hear their precious secret revealed to the world?"

"What do you mean?"

I said, "Do you think Dorothy is going to let months of risk and labor just go down the drain? At present she seems to be waiting for something to happen in Norfolk—a ceremony of some kind that she wants to disrupt—but if you announce over the air that all is discovered, isn't it likely that she'll rush to the nearest phone and call her man or woman in Norfolk and say 'go baby, go,' however that reads in Arabic? She promised me shattered buildings and blackened bodies. Do you really expect her to give up altogether, just because the timing isn't quite right? I mean, she's a real damager; if she can't have the scenario she's planned, she'll just wreck the city of Norfolk out of pure anti-American spite. And she'll have time enough to do it. Even if the Coast Guard believes you—remember that they're plagued with a lot of phony distress calls, and you'll be asking them to accept a real weirdo—and even if they react instantly, it's going to take them a while to get the right kind of bomb expert to the right place."

"But we can't just sit here…!"

I said, "We sure as hell can, for a while. They indicated that the ceremony, whatever it is, isn't scheduled until this weekend. Two o'clock on either Saturday or Sunday. It would be nice if they'd told us which, but you can't have everything. This is only Thursday. We don't have to rush; we've got time to do it right."

"Do what, if we're not going to call the Coast Guard?"

I shook my head. "I didn't say we shouldn't call them. I just said we shouldn't tell them stuff over the VHF that'll send the opposition into a nuclear convulsion. Remember, they don't know we've found those elusive numbers that old Fancher did *not* write in his logbook; and we won't tell them over the air. Actually, we have a choice. We can try to get ashore and find a telephone from which, without being overheard, you can call either the CG or, preferably, somebody you know in Washington with real clout who knows you and won't ask a lot of dumb questions and can get things moving in Norfolk. That sounds good; the trouble is that I don't like the way this shallow coastline looks on the chart. It's a lee shore with this breeze, which keeps getting stronger; and I have a hunch that by the time we get close to one of those inlets there are going to be breakers clear across it. I know I'm not man enough—seaman enough—to run that stuff. If you think you can handle it, okay, we'll give it a try."

Teresa shook her head. "No, I don't know this coast either; but I do know that most of the inlets change so often, with storms and tidal currents, that it takes a local, like Dorothy's Paul Rashid, to keep track of the shifting channels."

I said, "So we go to Plan B. We do call the Coast Guard; but we make it a simple distress call, just what our friends would expect to hear from us, if we managed to cut ourselves free before the boat went down. We hold off on the important stuff until the CG gets here and we can explain things face to face without the whole world listening… Now where are you going?"

"What do you mean? I'm going to make the call, of course!"

I said, "Mrs. Teresa Bell, you are the hastiest dame I ever met. Sit down and relax and have another drink."

"But—"

"Sit, goddamn it! My God, how did you ever get anything done in Washington, the way you keep going off half-cocked? Today is Thursday. We've got until Saturday, maybe even until Sunday; what's the everlasting rush? Stay put while I fill your glass—and you ask yourself what the opposition's reaction to *this* broadcast is going to be."

When I returned, she took the drink I offered her and said, "I suppose you mean that, when they hear they didn't sink us after all, they'll come charging back out to finish the job."

I said, "Maybe not Dorothy. She doesn't like either of us, and I was kind of mean to her lover, but she's had her fun with you, and the girl who really killed Hassim is dead. With the big bang coming up, Dorothy may just grab a ride north so as not to miss the sight of the beautiful mushroom cloud scheduled for the weekend. But Caselius has a vengeance hanging fire; he'll be out here, you can bet on it."

"Even after the Coast Guard has been summoned?"

I said, "According to the loran, we're only twelve miles from the nearest inlet, the one they probably used to bring us out here—and to get back in again. So Caselius has been through it twice with Paul Rashid; unlike us, he knows the channel. If he commandeers *Gulf Streamer,* as he probably will, at twenty to twenty-five knots it can be here in considerably less than an hour. Unless the Coast Guard just happens to have a cutter nearby, there's not a chance in the world they can get here that quickly. He'll have plenty of time to sink us, if we let him; after which he can run that overpowered sixty-footer ashore and disappear before the Coast Guard pops over the horizon… Do you want this goop on it?"

"What?"

I held up a tube of ointment. "It's for burns, it says here, antibiotic and anesthetic and everything."

"All right, put it on; maybe it will at least keep the bandage from sticking." After a moment, Teresa asked, "What can we do about it? If anything."

I said, "We'll be kind of outclassed, with that three-story, two-thousand-horsepower fishing machine coming at us, but at least we can start by lying here hove to without disturbing the airwaves until our little eighty-horse mill has cooled enough that I can open up the radiator—if that's what you call it on a boat—and pour water and antifreeze into it without being scalded to death or cracking the block. Trying to outmaneuver *Gulf Streamer* isn't going to be fun under any circumstances; I sure as hell don't want to have to try it under sail alone."

She was silent for a moment; then she asked, "Matt, how did we get everything so wrong?"

I said, "Get, hell. It was given to us. We believed everything Dorothy Fancher told us—mainly me—about

Truman Fancher's last cruise. Actually, I have a hunch Jerome Blum's bomb wasn't even put aboard *Lorelei III* in Florida, as she told me. It was probably put aboard just south of Coinjock, N.C., and that operation was what the old man saw when he woke up unexpectedly, that gave him his heart attack. At least that's the way I figure it now. From there it's only a couple of days' run to Norfolk—well, it took us two days; actually you could make it in one if you pushed hard. So they raced fifty miles north and planted their radioactive mushroom tree. But the old man wasn't quite as sick as he pretended; he knew that his boat and his sexy wife were involved in something lousy, and he'd been playing possum in that big bunk, waiting to learn more about it. In Norfolk, he saw the gadget being hauled out of the engine room. In that aft cabin, he couldn't see much through the ports, so he didn't know where the hell he was, but he could read the loran; and he scratched the position on that overhead shelf. But he was afraid somebody might spot it, so as a diversion he simply dropped the logbook, that he often kept on the dresser by his bunk when not under way, out one of the open ports. When Dorothy realized that it was missing and started raising hell, he gave her the song-and-dance about what he'd written in it and how well he'd hidden it. It kept them from looking for anything else; and after the way she'd betrayed him I don't suppose he minded giving her something to worry about."

Theresa said, "Don't make that dressing so bulky I can't get my shoe back on… But why did they go to all that trouble to use *Lorelei III.* Why not just use a boat of their own?"

"Respectability," I said. "At least I figure that must have been the reason. Truman Fancher was a well-known yachtsman and his motor sailer had been shuttling up and down the Waterway for several years after he retired from racing. He was probably well known in that Norfolk marina. And criminals do tend to be paranoid, and minority criminals think the world discriminates against them, and maybe it does. I suspect they felt that if a cheap power cruiser manned by a bunch of dark-skinned bums came into Tidewater, everybody'd be watching it suspiciously wondering what they planned to steal; but if it was just old Fancher and his *Lorelei* on his twice-yearly Waterway pilgrimage nobody'd pay any attention—the fact that he didn't appear on deck probably wouldn't even be noticed with his wife doing the honors—and they could unload their whizbang at leisure, unobserved." I shrugged. "And the next day, having planted their firecracker, they raced back south."

"Why? Why didn't they just continue up Chesapeake Bay?"

I shrugged. "They had a dying man on board—and if he didn't manage to die of his own accord, when they were ready for it, Dorothy was right there to help him with a pillow, I'm sure. Obviously, after what he'd seen, he couldn't be allowed to survive and tell about it. But if, after they reported the death, and presented the body, it became known that they'd been in Norfolk and kept on going, they'd be asked why they hadn't got the sick old gent into a big-city hospital when they had the chance. This way, Dorothy could claim, as she did, that they were out in those endless Carolina sounds and marshes south of Coinjock when Truman had his coronary and he'd refused to let her radio for help: he didn't need any lousy helicopters, he'd insisted that he could by God make it to a Norfolk hospital under his own power. Of course, if somebody wanted to unravel their itinerary, witnesses could probably be found—the lock keeper at Great Bridge, for instance—who'd seen them going both ways, but nobody thought to investigate, not even Lori Fancher, so they got away with it."

Teresa nodded. "Well, I guess it's plausible. What are you doing?"

"I don't want to put that wet shoe on it; I'm getting a Baggie to tape over it to keep it dry, at least for the time being."

"Matt?"

"Yes?"

She was frowning. "Why Norfolk? It's not all that big and important a city. If they'd just kept coming north a few more days, they could have had Washington, D.C. Or Baltimore. What's in Norfolk that makes it such a desirable target for a bunch of Arab terrorists?"

I shrugged. "Well, it's a big harbor, and it has a lot of shipbuilding... Oh, Jesus Christ!"

"What's the matter?"

"That goddamn carrier!"

"What goddamn carrier?"

I said, "You were asleep below when we came past all the navy stuff. There was a sizable submarine heading out; right afterward, there was an obscenely enormous aircraft carrier in a dry dock or something. I mean, the thing was the size of the island of Manhattan. And the Tidewater Marina wasn't more than a mile or two beyond it."

"You think—"

I said, "Something's been nagging at my memory. It just came back to me. Guess what the name of that overgrown flattop was."

She licked her lips. "The Richard something?"

"Well, you're close." After a moment, I went on. "In case your memory is faulty, let me give you a little refresher course in American history, ma'am. Back in 1779, if I remember rightly—anyway, during the revolution—a U.S. ship under the command of a nautical gent called John Paul Jones tackled a British convoy that was escorted by the frigate *Serapis.* Jones took a pounding at the start of the battle, enough that the Britisher asked him to surrender. Jones responded with the deathless words: 'I have not yet begun to fight!' After which he managed to capture the *Serapis* and the rest of the fleet, becoming our first great naval hero. His ship had a funny name for a Yankee privateer: the *Bonnehomme Richard.*"

Teressa drew a long breath. "And that was the name of the aircraft carrier you saw?"

"That was the name," I said. "What do you bet her crew refers to her as the *Big Dick?*"

"Ha ha." She finished her drink and set the glass aside.

"And you think she's the target? But you say the marina is over a mile away."

"Something like that."

She frowned. "Is a little homemade bomb, even if it is atomic, going to hurt a big warship that far off? Those ships are built to withstand bombs and gunfire right up close, aren't they?"

I said, "As far as the ship itself is concerned, maybe a blast at that range won't do more than shake her up a bit. But we're talking about a ceremony, remember, which is almost bound to be staged out on that great, wide-open flight deck. As I recall, at Hiroshima, people caught in the open even a couple of miles away from ground zero didn't find it a very healthy experience. And one reason Jerome Blum slipped and doused himself with plutonium or whatever is that he was instructed to make his boom-boom just as dirty as he could."

"Dirty? Oh, you mean with radioactivity." After a moment, Teresa said, "I still wonder what made them pick that particular target; that particular carrier."

I said, "I think the real question is: what kind of a ceremony is planned on board and who's going to attend?"

"Of course, it doesn't really matter," she said. "Regardless of who's involved, we've obviously got to stop it."

"You do," I said. "It's not in my contract. I was hired to keep this boat afloat, not to save some lousy VIPs from radiation poisoning… Relax. Just kidding. But in order to be sure to stop it, we've got to survive long enough to get the word out, which means that our immediate problem is Caselius. So we won't go on the air until I've got this boat in reasonable fighting trim. But I don't need any help getting things organized on deck and attending to the motor when it cools; you might as well lie down and rest a bit. I'm going to need you sharp and healthy when the action starts. Use the big bunk aft; it's more comfortable."

"Well, all right, I guess I do feel a little shaky." She laughed shortly. "If I were younger and prettier, I'd have some reservations about a man who was forever trying to get me into a bed."

I looked at her for a moment, and said, "You're a brave and handsome lady and you don't need to fish for compliments."

"I wasn't—" She stopped. After a moment, she said, "Thank you, Matt. Wake me when it's time."

"Yes, ma'am."

28

I'd checked that the shotgun, and the rifle with its laser sight reinstalled, were secure in their brackets at the upper steering station. The ammunition was in my pants pockets, rifle cartridges left, shotgun shells right. The mainsail had been furled again: I didn't need the hassle of trying to trim sails during the violent maneuvering I anticipated. The engine, once more fully supplied with a proper mixture of water and antifreeze, seemed to have come to no harm; it sounded fine, ticking over gently, in gear, as the autopilot guided us slowly shoreward.

I sat at the swaying deckhouse table trying to construct a Molotov cocktail with a sting. I'd emptied a bottle of Chardonnay into the galley sink—with regrets, although at five bucks a fifth it was hardly what you'd call a great wine—and filled it with gasoline from the red two-and-a-half gallon can kept on board to supply the inflatable dinghy's little outboard motor. I'd jammed a strip of rag into the neck, along with the cork, and left about six inches hanging out. I'd got out Romey Blum's neat little four-stick dynamite bomb, taped the bottle to it, and then taped the butane lighter from the galley on top of everything, aimed at the rag, which I tacked down with tape so it would be sure to receive the flame. In theory, with the cloth well soaked with gasoline, all I had to do was pull the trigger of the lighter to set it on fire, and heave the whole mess onto the other boat. The bottle would break and release the gas, the burning rag would ignite that, and the heat of the blazing fuel would set off the dynamite. Well, it was a pretty theory.

Blum had designed his bomb to be detonated electrically, of course; but I knew that if I started monkeying around with batteries and wires and blasting caps that I knew nothing about I'd blow myself up for sure; and I couldn't think of a gadget that would make reliable electrical contact on impact, anyway. A good hot fire ought to do the job; and even if the dynamite didn't go off, well, a lot of blazing gasoline would at least embarrass the enemy. If I could get the thing aboard.

I stowed the super-Molotov cocktail at the aft steering station, beneath the overhang of the deckhouse. Then I stood for a moment watching my little ship idling westward; without any canvas up, she was rolling heavily in the quartering seas. I couldn't help remembering that I'd spent a lot of time and effort to get her back into shape; in the process I'd developed considerable respect and affection for the sturdy old vessel. I didn't like to think of the broken headstay, the soggy carpets below—

I'd got the sea salt out of them once but it hadn't been easy—and the smashed door. It was no way to treat a good boat, and she'd probably suffer worse damage before the night was over.

I patted the big destroyer wheel before going below. "Sorry, old girl. We've got no choice. It's the bloody Battle of Midway and pretty soon we'll have the big Jap carriers coming at us."

In the deckhouse, the only lights were the reddish glow of the compass, the two greenish rectangles of the loran display, and above them, a big red sixteen showing in the channel-selector window of the VHF radio. I turned up the volume, but there was no chatter over the air at the moment; perhaps all the lonely nautical conversationalists had gone ashore for the night. I debated using Mayday and decided against it. This was between Caselius and me. I didn't want any innocent vessels to come charging nobly to the rescue. The Coast Guard, okay. Like me, they'd been hired to shoot and get shot at occasionally.

So quit stalling, hero. I took the mike out of its clip and pressed the transmit button.

"U.S. Coast Guard, U.S. Coast Guard, this is motor sailer *Lorelei III.* Our position is..." I read the lat-long coordinates off the loran. "We have an emergency, we have an emergency. I repeat, this is thirty-eight-foot motor sailer *Lorelei III,* Whiskey Alpha Hotel eight eight five five, with engine failure and a bad leak, two persons on board, calling U.S. Coast Guard. Our position is..."

I read off the figures again and released the button. I'd

expected a wait, but the boys were on the ball. A young male voice responded promptly.

"Vessel calling U.S. Coast Guard, switch to channel twenty-two Alpha."

"Twenty-two Alpha, aye, aye."

I had no idea what Alpha signified, but I'd listened in on Coast Guard conversations from time to time and I knew it was what they always said. I also knew, having tried it, that putting a plain old number twenty-two into the VHF channel-selector window would bring them in fine, fuck Alpha. I twiddled the knobs and pushed the buttons accordingly.

"This is *Lorelei III*."

"This is the U.S. Coast Guard..."

With contact established on the new channel, I was ordered to put life jackets on everyone on board, after which we were off on the usual bureaucratic information-collecting, form-filling-out routine: description of boat—size, color, number of masts, horsepower of engine (when functioning)—registration or documentation number, where from, where to, names and home addresses of all on board, nature of emergency (I made up something dramatic here that, I'm afraid, varied significantly from the truth) and did I consider it life-threatening.

"Not right away, no, sir," I said. "We have two electric pumps and they're pretty much keeping up with the leak at the moment, but with the engine out, the batteries won't last forever, and I don't think we'll be able to keep her afloat with the little manual bilge pump alone."

"It will take about three hours for us to reach you. Can you hold out that long?"

"All we can do is try."

"Stay tuned to this channel and report any—"

"Coast Guard, Coast Guard." A male voice that I recognized broke in. "This is *Gulf Streamer,* sixty-two foot sportfisherman off Little Pogie Inlet. We can reach the vessel in distress in about half an hour and stand by until you get there…"

I listened to the exchange, as they went through the same bureaucratic hassle as before and, with all vital statistics duly recorded, doubtless in the right color ink on the proper paper—well, okay, it's probably punched into a computer nowadays—settled my future between them, finally asking me if I approved, which of course I did. With everything arranged, I returned the mike to its clip, grinning.

It was nice to meet a young man with principles. I remembered that Roland Caselius had been brought up in a country that considered a saber scar no disfigurement but a mark of honor. He could have stayed off the air and tried to catch me unawares; instead he'd deliberately warned me he was coming for me. Obviously he saw himself engaging in some kind of a romantic nautical duel with his daddy's murderer. His boat had the advantage in power and speed and there was nothing he could do about that, but he'd felt obliged to inform me that he was taking no other advantages; he wasn't going to sneak up on me in the dark like an assassin. Well, like me.

Of course, not being stupid, he was also, undoubtedly, quite aware that he'd probably bought himself a little more time to finish us off. The Coast Guard wouldn't be in quite so much of a rush to rescue us, knowing that somebody was standing by to save us if our boat did go down.

I went aft to wake up my crew, and found her sleeping so heavily that turning on the overhead light didn't arouse her. I suppose I should have told her to change into dry clothes, but she was a strong-minded lady and I doubted she'd have appreciated having a man instruct her how to dress. At any rate she lay on her back on the stripped bunk in her damp jeans and jersey. I regarded her for a moment. In repose, her dark face was softer, almost girlish—it was not the face of a pretty girl, but pretty is a dime a dozen. Well, her looks were fairly irrelevant at the moment. I leaned over her.

"Wake up, Teresa." Receiving no response, I shook her gently. "Come on, wake up!"

Her eyes remained closed. I had a moment of panic, thinking she might have died on me, but investigation showed that she had a steady pulse and was breathing regularly.

I shook her more roughly. "Up and at 'em, Terry!"

There was no response. I drew a long breath, realizing at last that I was seeing the little death of total exhaustion: she'd expended too much of herself, during interrogation, in her grim battle against pain. With her iron self-control released at last by a couple of drinks, the machinery had simply shut down for self-repair.

I lifted her off the mattress as carefully as I could

and wedged her into the space between the bunk and the dresser so she wouldn't be thrown across the cabin if *Lorelei III* took a bad roll. She did not react in any way to being hauled around. She was so far out that I doubted that even a bucket of cold water would bring her around, and if it did work it might do serious psychological damage. And if it didn't, it might give her pneumonia. To hell with it; I'd just fight the Battle of Little Pogie Inlet single-handed.

Returning to the deckhouse, I switched on the white masthead anchor light; I'd be expected to give the Coast Guard something to home in on—something, but not too much, considering the precarious state of my batteries. Then I switched off the autopilot and put the transmission into neutral, leaving the engine idling. In the dark, the exhaust would probably not betray us, and Caselius might get careless, seeing us lying there without any way on, apparently powerless and helpless. I checked the radar and had no trouble finding him, a sizeable blob between us and the shore, moving our way rapidly. His radar was on, throwing odd curving patterns of lines across the screen, and he undoubtedly had a good picture of us, too.

I went on deck and looked around, thinking I'd never seen such a black and empty night sea. No ships, no stars, no horizon, just an occasional gleaming crest marking a big wave rolling in from the southeast... I sat down to wait, occasionally checking my watch. At last I spotted a flash of whiteness downwind. A few seconds later I caught another on just about the same bearing, and still another. Okay. *Gulf Streamer* was coming for us in fine style, blasting through the big ocean rollers, throwing lots of spray and, no doubt, giving her passengers a very lumpy ride in spite of her size.

I rechecked my weapons, as you do—not necessarily a sign of nervousness but, on the other hand, not necessarily not. I returned the shotgun to its clip and retained the rifle, turning on the laser sight and pointing it skyward. I made certain that my superbomb hadn't slid out of position; but instinct told me that Caselius would be cautious on his first pass no matter how helpless we looked; he wouldn't come within shotgun range immediately, let alone grenade-pitching range. I'd have to coax him in somehow…

Instinct was wrong. He came roaring in quite straight, so I began to wonder if he had kamikaze intentions—his boat was big, but it wasn't a battleship; it wasn't big enough to let him ram a husky twelve-ton motor sailer at flank speed without doing fatal damage to his own vessel. But at the last moment, I saw the shadowy, onrushing craft change course a bit, and I realized that I'd goofed badly: this could have been my chance, he was going to pass within half a boatlength. I could have dropped my bundle right into his cockpit—or, if I'd had the shotgun in my hands, I could have blasted him off his flying bridge with a spreading load of buckshot, but in the dark I couldn't see him clearly enough up there behind all the plastic to put a single rifle bullet where it would do the job.

There was a man on the foredeck and another in the cockpit. They opened fire at well over fifty yards, but *Gulf Streamer*'s motion was too violent for them to hit anything at that range with their lousy little squirt guns. At forty yards I heard a couple of bullets strike *Lorelei III*'s hull. I picked the foredeck man, the easiest target, figuring I'd probably only get one shot before they were past. At thirty yards, I managed to get the red dot on him in spite of the violent motion of the oncoming boat and the rolling deck under my feet. I saw him look down at himself and see red death shining on his shirt; the heavy .338 bullet smashed through him before he could take evasive action. Then, as I was swinging to throw a shot at the cockpit man, moving away rapidly now, *Gulf Streamer*'s wake hit us.

I should have anticipated it, of course. In our previous nautical encounter, wake hadn't been much of a problem: a light sportboat, planing on top of the water, doesn't dig that big a hole. However, coming down the waterway, I'd become acquainted with the uncomfortable wakes of some rude powerboat characters who hadn't slowed down very much in passing—to be fair, most of them had been quite considerate—but few had been as big as *Gulf Streamer* and none had been traveling as fast. I never got the shot away. I saw the tidal wave coming at us broadside and managed to get an arm around the mizzenmast; then *Lorelei III* was thrown over to starboard until I was sure the mast was going to hit the water—and as she struggled upright, she fell into the ditch the big sportfisherman had plowed in the water and rolled clear over the other way.

She came up again bravely, but out in the darkness the dim white shape of *Gulf Streamer* was coming around in a hard right turn. Deliberately using his wake as a weapon, Caselius obviously intended to return and give us another dose while we were still making like a mad pendulum and unable to do any accurate shooting. Okay, Ronnie, I told him silently, just make it nice and close again, *amigo*; I have something for you…

I'd managed to hang on to the rifle. I slammed it into its bracket and found my secret weapon, which had slid across the boat. I braced myself against the deckhouse while I pulled out the cork a bit and let gasoline leak onto the strip of khaki cloth. I rammed the cork home again and stood there waiting, not wanting to show a warning flame prematurely; besides, I wasn't going to hold a burning gasoline-and-dynamite torch any longer than I had to. The big sportfisherman was charging us again, like an angry bull. I had my finger on the lighter trigger, when *Lorelei* III's transmission snapped into gear and she started to move and swing…

"No!" I shouted. Hell, I'd had him coming in just right! I raced down the side deck and yelled into the deckhouse, "Damn it, Terry, *no*! Engine neutral! Rudder amidships!"

Turning, I saw that *Gulf Streamer* was almost on top of us. Apparently our slight movement hadn't been detected. There was no time to reach the aft deck; I braced myself between the rail and the deckhouse and snapped the trigger. The cloth exploded into fire instantly—and so did my hand, which had apparently received some gas spillage. The man on *Gulf Streamer*'s foredeck was gone; his body had apparently been jolted overboard. The one in the cockpit, leaning out to shoot past the cabin, seemed to be firing right into my face, but the motion was too much for him: a bullet hit the hull just below my feet, another thwacked through the safety glass of the deckhouse window at my shoulder, but nothing hit me. Then the cockpit was right there, and I tossed my bundle into it—and tucked my hand under my armpit to put out the fire.

I had a glimpse of the dark-faced man turning to stare at the flaming object. Apparently he'd been negatively conditioned to Molotov cocktails; after a stunned moment, he simply dropped his machine pistol and dove overboard to join his dead colleague.

The man-made tsunami hit us again and rolled us damn near ninety degrees to starboard and then only a little less to port. I hung on, watching the big sportfisherman rush away from us. There was a flickering light in the cockpit: the burning fuse. The white water under the stern diminished a bit as Caselius hauled back his throttles; then, presumably leaving the boat on autopilot, he was dropping down the ladder from the flying bridge. He made a dim target, receding rapidly. I grabbed the big Browning and tried to put the red spot on him, got him for an instant, and fired, but there was too much motion at both ends and the bullet went wild.

I was still bracing myself for an explosion over there, but nothing happened—except that the wavering light in the cockpit was dying. Then it was replaced by a definite pinpoint of flame as Caselius lifted my bomb into view; it made a delicate arc of light when he threw it overboard, that seemed to persist for several seconds after the flame was extinguished by the water. Okay, so I wasn't an explosives genius after all.

At the distance, in the dark, I could barely make out Caselius clambering back up the ladder to the big sportfisherman's flying-bridge controls; but I thought I saw him pause to give me a friendly salute in appreciation of my failed homicidal effort, as one good sportsman to another.

I grimaced and moved to the deckhouse door and started to speak to the woman at the wheel.

"Sorry I had to yell at you, Terry…" I stopped.

"Surprise, surprise," said little Lori Fancher.

29

Gulf Streamer had disappeared into the darkness. A glance at the radar showed her to be making a big sweep to windward for some reason; but there was nothing I could do about that. With the faster boat by far, Caselius had the initiative. My secret weapon having failed, I'd just have to tailor my defense to whatever attack he decided to make next. Meanwhile, since he was giving me a little time, I could spend it finding out what the hell was going on on board my own ship.

The girl at the wheel had no business being there, and she certainly had no business wearing one of my few white dress shirts. The garment covered her like a tent, which was a good thing, since she didn't seem to be wearing much else.

"I hope you don't mind," she said, rolling up a long sleeve that was getting in the way.

"The shirt? Be my guest."

"What do I do when that overgrown marlin chaser comes back?"

I said, "We'll keep on playing dead—well, dead in the water—until we see a good reason to let him know we've got power. Just stand ready to give it everything; I'll let you know when."

"I'm sorry I almost loused you up," she said. "I was trying to be helpful. I didn't realize... What did you throw at them?"

I told her. "But apparently the damn bottle didn't break, hitting that nice soft teak. Or maybe the dynamite cushioned it."

"Some cushion," she said dryly. "I thought that stuff was fairly sensitive. At least you aren't supposed to toss it around unnecessarily, are you, or smack it with a hammer?"

I frowned. "I wonder where our friend has got to? He's fresh out of crew, but I doubt that he's quit on that account, or gone back ashore for more men. Apparently, he's got none of his DAMAG goons handy; he's using Dorothy's Arab creeps." I stepped up on the side deck and looked all around, seeing nothing in the darkness but an occasional whitecap. I dropped back down into the deckhouse. "Okay, so how the hell did you get aboard?"

She said, "Not just me, skipper. You have another passenger up forward you didn't know about, but he's dead. It couldn't have happened to a nicer sex maniac."

I remembered hearing some activity on board while Teresa and I were waiting for Caselius to fasten the cabin door shut; apparently it had been decided to bury all available bodies in the same thirty-eight-foot coffin.

"Tell me," I said.

She said, "Well, they had me tied hand and foot on the other boat, and then they let Curly Bill Barstow at me. He thought it was just great, having me so humiliatingly helpless, after the way I'd slapped him down earlier. Do you want to know something, Matt? I don't think bondage is ever going to be a big thing in my life. The creep had lots of preliminary fun, deliberately destroying my clothes so he could get them off me, rag by rag, without untying me. When he had me deliciously naked and still helplessly bound, there was something he… he wanted me to do to him, you can guess what. He hit me a couple of times by way of persuasion, and then that woman stepped quietly into the stateroom behind him—he never even knew she was there—and put a pistol to the back of his head and blew him away, ugh! Not that I was complaining at the moment. They hauled the bodies, living and dead, over to this boat and dumped them into the forward cabin and closed the door. I kept trying to attract somebody's attention, but nobody heard me, way up there in the bow. Finally the boat took a real knockdown and threw me across the stateroom so hard it almost scrambled my brains… Shouldn't you be out on deck, doing something constructive?"

"Like what?" I asked. "The guns are ready. When he comes back, I'll just shoot him. Simple. I should have thought of it sooner."

She shrugged. "Well, all right… That masthead anchor light shining down through the clear plastic hatch gave me a little light up there, and when I came out of my daze; I saw that a strip of teak sheathing had got knocked loose where I hit, and there was a tricky little knife hidden behind it, just as if somebody'd known I'd need one."

I said, "Well, it wasn't exactly meant for you, but you're welcome."

She went oh. "I cut myself free and went looking for something to wear... What's the matter with your lady friend in the aft cabin? She seems to be either drugged or in kind of a coma."

I said, "She had a very rough time."

"Yes, I saw the bandage... Matt, there's a searchlight!"

The beam was working about a hundred yards to windward. After studying it briefly, I said, "Caselius must have come around to look for the guy who jumped overboard. If he locked his loran when it happened... Okay, he's got the man, dammit."

More lights had come on over there, enough to show us the shape of the big white sportfisherman as it maneuvered to make the pickup. It had to be a tricky job for one man handling sixty feet of powerboat; and just locating the man in the water had been a neat piece of seamanship. I wished to God we were playing our lethal games out in the kind of Western country I knew something about. This nautical nonsense gave me a terrible inferiority complex. The fact that I was pitting one eighty-horsepower power plant against two nine-hundreds didn't help.

I said, "Well, let's hope the Diving Desperado over there picked up a bad case of hypothermia and is shivering too hard to hold a gun."

Lori looked at me with instinctive disapproval; a man overboard was supposed to become, automatically, an object of sympathy. I yearned for the other Lori, the one who'd once warned me that just because certain people had got all wet didn't mean they'd become nice people, but that was the girl she didn't want to be.

She started to speak, but checked herself. She just said, "Well, here he comes; you'd better get out there and shoot him like you said... Matt."

"Yes?"

There was an odd little glint in her eyes, almost a look of anticipation. Maybe the Lori I wanted—needed here—wasn't so far away, after all.

She licked her lips. "It's... well, kind of déjà vu, isn't it? We've been here before."

I said, "Keep the faith, tigress."

The big sportfisherman was coming at us again, from astern, clearly planning to sweep down the port side; and something had changed. The plastic curtains of the flying bridge had been removed. Back at the topside station, I grabbed the .338. I managed to find the oncoming white hull with the laser sight and swung the unsteady weapon upward. I saw the red dot, wide and weak at such long range, waver across first one face up there and then another; I tried to hold on the left-hand one, slightly closer, and pressed the trigger. The fireworks were again impressive, as was the recoil, but I knew I'd missed.

So Caselius had his gunner with him up on the flying bridge this time—perhaps he didn't trust the man out of reach. I slammed the rifle back into its bracket and grabbed the shotgun. Now a machine pistol was firing up there. I swung the dim barrel of the twelve-gauge upward. Something rapped my hip lightly; Caselius's boy had got lucky. I pumped all six shotgun shells through the action as *Gulf Streamer* swept past—there's a lot of loose talk about wicked dangerous terrible semiautomatics, but the simple fact is that a good man with a slide-action shotgun can pump it faster than any corresponding self-loader can shuck its own shells through its deliberate, automatic action.

Then we were knocked onto our beam ends again, and Caselius was in a hard left turn ahead, coming back to take advantage of his own mountainous wake. I could feel blood running down my hip, and my right hand smarted a bit where it had been burned earlier, but I didn't think the bullet had done more than graze me, and the gasoline hadn't flamed long enough to do any serious skin damage. I didn't try the rifle on this pass; time was short, and I was busy refilling the magazine of the shotgun.

I stepped forward. "Lori! Hit him with the searchlight!"

The little girl was on the ball; the powerful beam lanced out almost immediately. I crouched in the shelter of the deckhouse, waiting for the range to close. There was only one head up on the flying bridge now, and it had to be Caselius; his diving-type crewman would have fled if I'd got his boss. Caselius, alone, was steering with his knees, or maybe he'd set the autopilot; somehow he'd managed to free his hands for shooting. Muzzle flame lanced out, and I heard bullets striking *Lorelei III* although the range was still long. I rose, preparing to shoot, and something hit my left side a heavy blow. It knocked the wind out of me, like being struck by a baseball bat.

Gasping, I saw our searchlight waver downward for a moment. I hoped it didn't mean that Lori had also been hit; friend Roland seemed to be a lot better marksman than his borrowed gofers. Then I glimpsed something that drove the thought, and the pain, from my mind: incredibly the searchlight had picked out, tumbling in the sportfisherman's curling bow wave, a bundle of yellow sticks and a green bottle—apparently we'd drifted into the area where Caselius had jettisoned my present, and there had been enough air in the bottle to keep the thing afloat.

There was no time to think. I just took the snapshot at forty yards, as if I'd seen a grouse flashing through an opening in the woods. It couldn't work, of course. It was a small mark, and at that range a charge of 00 buck, designed for deer-sized targets, formed a very loose pattern, and I wasn't even sure that the impact of a single buckshot…

The Atlantic Ocean turned itself inside out over there. For a moment there was nothing but a wall of white water in the glare of the searchlight. Then *Gulf Streamer* came blasting through it like a picture I'd once seen of the great old-fashioned battleships charging through the artillery waterspouts at the Battle of Jutland. I'll never know if the explosion damage had turned her, or if Caselius had spun the wheel deliberately; at any rate she was heading straight for us.

I shouted. "Lori! Full ahead! Hard right rudder!"

But the kid had already reacted to the threat. I had to steady myself as the old motor sailer lurched into motion. It was too late, of course. I had one final glimpse of *Gulf Streamer* with a large hole in her port bow and most of the glass blown out of her cabin and her tuna tower listing drunkenly; then the two boats came together with a violent crash. In the kickback from our searchlight, I saw a human body slingshotted out of the sportfisherman's damaged flying bridge by the impact; it struck the top of our deckhouse and bounced off into the sea.

I'd been thrown into the mizzen shrouds. The wrench brought alive the dormant pain of my wound. It took a moment to blaze through my body like wildfire; I kept waiting for it to peak and subside…

"Matt, wake up!"

"Who's asleep?" I mumbled. The flames of agony were actually dying a little. I seemed to be flat on the deck. I tried to rise. It wasn't easy. "Give me a hand, Lori…"

Then I opened my eyes and saw Teresa Bell kneeling beside me. I just couldn't seem to keep my boating dames straight.

"We're sinking," Teresa said. "The Fancher kid woke me up; sorry I passed out like that. She's getting the life raft overboard. She sent me to help you…"

A heavy splash aft interrupted her. We both looked that way.

"What the hell was that?" I asked.

"I'd better take a look." Teresa left me and came back.

Her face was expressionless. "It's your Mr. Caselius, hanging onto the stern ladder. He seems to be in bad shape. I guess he tried to climb up and fell back in. What do I do?"

"Help me up… Oh, Jesus!"

Remembering her stoicism, I was embarrassed by the noise I was making about a lousy little bullet wound. With her help, I made it to my knees, but at first the standing position seemed unattainable; then I made that, too. I stumbled aft and looked over the rail. The white face of Roland Caselius looked up at me. There was, of course, no plea for mercy; we both knew what had to come next. I took out the little .38 Special, but I was having a hard time just staying on my feet, and the weapon wouldn't steady on the target. Somebody nudged my arm. I looked at Teresa Bell. She was holding out her hand for the gun.

"If you want me to."

I passed it to her. She took deliberate aim and fired. Caselius seemed to hang there for a moment longer; then he slid down into the surging water astern. One of his hands gave an odd little flip as he disappeared, like the jaunty salutes he'd given me from time to time.

Mrs. Teresa Bell tucked my pistol back into its wet holster and helped me turn around. Lori was standing there, clinging to the mizzen rigging, staring at us as if we were both perfectly horrible people. Which of course we were.

30

I'm not going to apologize to the U.S. Coast Guard for my previous attitude, but I will say that the boys and girls seem to be good at what they do, even if some of what they do isn't worth doing. If they'd concentrate on being a great rescue service and forget about being web-footed drug hunters I might even get to like them.

Anyway, they found us in our floating doughnut and picked us up expertly and got us ashore expeditiously, after which the medical profession took over my case. Well, I'd been there before. The Beaufort hospital didn't seem very different from others I'd inhabited, except for the pleasant, but sometimes incomprehensible, southern accents.

Lori Fancher came to see me after my situation had been stabilized—at least I heard somebody telling somebody I was stable. I suppose it was good news. Lori was in one of her long-john costumes; this time the snug tights and big sweater were kelly green. She brought an armload of flowers.

She got them taken care of first; then she came to the bed and looked down at me for a long time without speaking, and said at last, "They tell me the bullet smashed a rib, a splinter of which punctured a lung, but you're going to live anyway. Of course, after what I saw on the boat, I can't help wondering if that's really such a good idea, Matt." Then she said quickly, "I'm sorry. I shouldn't have said that. I don't wish anybody dead."

I said, "You're a good man, Fancher. Too good for me."

"Yes," she said. "I am, aren't I? Maybe… maybe sometimes I wish I weren't, but…"

She gave an ugly little shrug, and fled. That afternoon Mac called me up. He also told me I was going to live.

"Do you remember Elmer Weiss?" he asked.

I had to think for a minute, lying there in the hospital bed. "One of the DAMAG specialists. Called Snipey. A long-range boy likes a .25-06, I suppose because he's kind of small and can't stand the kick of the seven emm-emms or the big thirties. Of course, a .25-caliber bullet will take a deer or a human being very adequately at quite long ranges. As Snipey Weiss has proved more than once."

"Yes, it was the gun that led the Washington authorities to him. He was having a special one made up, heavy barrel, laminated stock, four- to twelve-power telescope. We'd alerted them to the possibility that he might be involved—we'd also suggested a check on the lady poisoner, Espenshade, and some others on DAMAG's roster—but they might not have caught up with Weiss except for the fact that he did not have money enough to pay for the rifle when the time came to pick it up, so he tried to take it by force. When he brandished a pistol, the gunsmith shot him dead."

I couldn't help laughing. "Stealing a gun from one of those boys is like stealing a fresh-caught salmon from a hungry grizzly. I presume the reason Weiss was short of change is that his paymaster is polluting the ocean off the Carolina coast. Is Weiss's intended target known?"

"To somebody, but not to us."

I said, "Some things never change."

"In any case, it would seem that DAMAG is no longer a threat. Get well, Eric."

A day later, Mrs. Teresa Bell paid me a visit. She was back in her bureaucratic black costume—well, on closer inspection I saw that this expensive suit was actually a dark navy blue with a fine pinstripe, but the snug skirt and close-fitting jacket were familiar, as were the excellent legs in sheer navy stockings. She was wearing funny little spike-heeled boots, probably to conceal the fact that one foot was bandaged. Even so, it was hard for me to remember the bedraggled dame in soggy jeans and jersey who'd stoically endured a toasting session in *Lorelei III*'s aft cabin. She didn't move as if she hurt, but then she never had.

She said, "They tell me you're going to live."

"A few more reports like that and I'll begin to believe it."

"You'll be happy to know that Norfolk didn't blow up."

I said, "Why should I care? I don't know anybody in Norfolk."

She laughed. "The tough guy. Shoots a drowning man—well, with a little help—and then weeps for a sinking boat."

I said, "Who was weeping? That was just my allergy."

"Allergy?"

"To mouthy dames." I grinned at her and stopped grinning. "She was a great old boat, and I'd worked hard to help her make a comeback; why shouldn't I feel bad at seeing her go down?"

"Well, at least it shows you can feel. In this business, a lot of people can't." After a moment, she went on. "We found the bomb. As you suggested, it was strapped to one of the pilings at a certain slip in the Tidewater Marina, well below the lowest low-tide level. It was covered with barnacles and just looked like more pilings; but it had been well sealed and there was no corrosion inside all the lead and waterproofing. We got it defused; only a few hours later somebody hit the remote that would have fired it. We had, of course, arranged to trace the signal when it came, and they were considerate enough to try several times, enough that we could triangulate on the transmission. We were led to a large old farmhouse well outside town. Mrs. Dorothy Fancher opened the door. When she saw the officers, and me, she slammed it again before one of the men could get his foot into the crack. It was a heavy door, and we heard some massive bolts being shoved into place. The officers wanted to attack it, but I knew what would happen, and I managed to pull them back before the place blew up and burned. Mrs. Fancher's society-type dentist identified the body, what was left of it, after the ashes had cooled a bit. He was deeply shocked to find his wealthy lady patient dead under such circumstances."

I said, "Great, but what the hell was it all about?"

She said, "It turns out that the *Bonhomme Richard,* you remember, the carrier docked in Norfolk, had been the major carrier supporting Operation Desert Storm in the Persian Gulf. She is being mothballed. The U.S. Army apparently decided—or its public relations department did—to donate a plaque at the decommissioning ceremony to demonstrate its gratitude to the old ship and the U.S. Navy—with General Norman Schwarzkopf doing the honors."

After a moment, I said, "Well, I'm not really sold on any character in uniform; but I'm glad Stormin' Norman didn't get radiated. Irradiated? What's your situation in Washington now?"

She said, "Oh, great. They love me like a sister."

"Never had one, but most sisters I've met tell me their brothers give them hell."

She smiled thinly. "That's exactly what I mean. But don't worry about me. I'll make it." She looked at the flowers, still fresh and pretty on the dresser. "From the little girl?"

"A duty call. She's a conscientious kid, but she won't be back."

Mrs. Teresa Bell spoke deliberately. "Well, would you like for me to come again? I'm not much on flowers, but I could bring a box of candy."

I looked at her, and remembered that I'd thought her fairly unattractive when I first met her. Now I saw a handsome, well-built, well-dressed lady whom I knew to be very bright and extremely brave. So she was no chicken; who was?

I said, "Before I answer that, may I ask what's with Mr. Bell?"

"He died in a car accident several years ago."

I said, "Then I'd very much like to see you again, Teresa. And you don't have to bother with the candy."

She looked at me without expression. "Oh, eating it will give us something to do—until you're feeling better."

It did.

ABOUT THE AUTHOR

Donald Hamilton was the creator of secret agent Matt Helm, star of 27 novels that have sold more than 20 million copies worldwide.

Born in Sweden, he emigrated to the United States and studied at the University of Chicago. During the Second World War he served in the United States Naval Reserve, and in 1941 he married Kathleen Stick, with whom he had four children.

The first Matt Helm book, *Death of a Citizen*, was published in 1960 to great acclaim, and four of the subsequent novels were made into motion pictures. Hamilton was also the author of several outstanding stand-alone thrillers and westerns, including two novels adapted for the big screen as *The Big Country* and *The Violent Men*.

Donald Hamilton died in 2006.